HARD TO HANDLE

Titles by Lori Foster

THE WINSTON BROTHERS
WILD
CAUSING HAVOC
SIMON SAYS
HARD TO HANDLE

Anthology
WILDLY WINSTON

Writing as L. L. Foster

SERVANT: THE AWAKENING

HARD TO HANDLE

Lori Foster

BERKLEY BOOKS, NEW YORK

THE BERKLEY PUBLISHING GROUP
Published by the Penguin Group
Penguin Group (USA) Inc.
375 Hudson Street, New York, New York 10014, USA
Penguin Group (Canada), 90 Eglinton Avenue East, Suite 700, Toronto, Ontario M4P 2Y3, Canada
(a division of Pearson Penguin Canada Inc.)
Penguin Books Ltd., 80 Strand, London WC2R 0RL, England
Penguin Group Ireland, 25 St. Stephen's Green, Dublin 2, Ireland (a division of Penguin Books Ltd.)
Penguin Group (Australia), 250 Camberwell Road, Camberwell, Victoria 3124, Australia
(a division of Pearson Australia Group Pty. Ltd.)
Penguin Books India Pvt. Ltd., 11 Community Centre, Panchsheel Park, New Delhi—110 017, India
Penguin Group (NZ), 67 Apollo Drive, Rosedale, North Shore 0632, New Zealand
(a division of Pearson New Zealand Ltd.)
Penguin Books (South Africa) (Pty.) Ltd., 24 Sturdee Avenue, Rosebank, Johannesburg 2196,
South Africa

Penguin Books Ltd., Registered Offices: 80 Strand, London WC2R 0RL, England

This is a work of fiction. Names, characters, places, and incidents either are the product of the author's imagination or are used fictitiously, and any resemblance to actual persons, living or dead, business establishments, events, or locales is entirely coincidental. The publisher does not have any control over and does not assume any responsibility for author or third-party websites or their content.

HARD TO HANDLE

A Berkley Book / published by arrangement with the author

ISBN: 978-0-7394-9275-8

BERKLEY®
Berkley Books are published by The Berkley Publishing Group,
a division of Penguin Group (USA) Inc.,
375 Hudson Street, New York, New York 10014.
BERKLEY® is a registered trademark of Penguin Group (USA) Inc.
The "B" design is a trademark belonging to Penguin Group (USA) Inc.

PRINTED IN THE UNITED STATES OF AMERICA

To Frank Trigg, www.taggradio.com

Thanks for the phone interview, the insights into a fighter's life, and the perspective on ultimate fighting. Your generosity is very much appreciated.

And special thanks to *Fight!* magazine, www.fightmagazine.com

I really enjoyed the fabulous pre-fight party, and I scored some incredible photos!

Chapter 1

A light sheen of sweat clung to his body. With each heavy, broken breath, the musky, appealing scent of sex filled his nostrils. On a groan, Harley Handleman rolled away from the woman lying facedown beneath him. Eyes burning and his heartbeat still thundering, he fell onto his back.

Lord have mercy. She had drained him, used him up; he definitely felt sated.

But still, curiously, he remained unfulfilled.

Several minutes passed before his pulse slowed to a normal pace and cool air dried the dampness on his chest. The woman never stirred.

He was glad of that. Any small talk after sex bored him. Anything more than small talk annoyed him.

He was a prick and he knew it, but he told women upfront what he wanted, and what he didn't. Gloria—he didn't know her last name—had crawled into bed with him with her eyes wide open, her illusions dashed . . . and an anticipatory smile on her face.

Staring at the ceiling, Harley put his right arm behind

his head and, by male instinct alone, reached his left hand over to palpate a lush derriere. Silky skin encouraged the light caress, but it was an uninvolved gesture.

Already his thoughts had gone from sex to other, more pertinent things.

Life.

Family.

The upcoming fight.

His brain ticked like a bomb.

Because of his MMA fighting success in the SBC organization, and his easy carnal triumphs with women, most men would envy him.

But they didn't know everything.

They didn't live with his constant, gnawing need to not only succeed in mixed martial arts, but win an SBC title belt.

Thinking about it demolished his relaxed state; every muscle went taut.

So many times he'd come close to proving himself a champion, working his way through the ranks, annihilating every fighter in his path. Three times he'd been scheduled for the title fight.

He hadn't made it to a single one.

Fate played some dirty tricks, constantly tossing obstacles into his path to be champion. How many more opportunities would the SBC give him?

The disquiet he suffered had haunted him for too long. Some things were out of his control; other things were not. It was past time to make some changes.

Where to start?

An icy wind threw sleet against the windows. The light of a full moon and streetlamps added illumination to the darkened bedroom, sending shadows to dance over the ceiling. Second by second, Harley grew edgier until he could no longer stay still.

He sat up in the bed and swung his legs over the side.

Time to go. *Past* time to go.

Over his shoulder, he glanced at the woman still

stretched out on the mattress, her breathing soft and even in heavy sleep.

He never slept with women.

He couldn't.

His gaze tracked her soft body—from the soles of her arched feet, over that tantalizing rump, up the length of her delicate spine, all the way to her manicured fingertips.

He felt nothing.

He definitely didn't feel the need to snuggle down and sleep.

Anxious to go, he reached for the silk scarf binding her slender wrists to the slatted headboard. Thanks to her enthusiasm, the knot had tightened, making it difficult to undo. As Harley worked it free, she remained utterly limp in the way of sound slumber.

He envied her that.

Brushing long, tangled blond hair away from the side of her face, he studied her serene expression, her parted lips. A few strands of long hair tangled with her thick lashes.

Wanting something, some small response, Harley trailed a fingertip down her nape, her back, all the way to her tailbone.

She squirmed a little, sighed, and smiled.

His eyes narrowed; the smile was enough.

He couldn't control much in his life right now, but he had controlled her. He'd controlled the pace, her pleasure, and his own. On impulse, and because he was a bona fide ass man through and through, Harley bent and pressed a soft kiss to one cheek.

The woman snuggled deeper into the covers and let out another sigh.

Being a gentleman, Harley made sure to bring the thick coverlet up and over her before he left. Even indoors, the bitter weather left a bone-trembling chill in the air.

After carrying his clothes and shoes into the living room, he dressed. Then, holding his keys in a closed fist so they wouldn't make a sound, he put on his coat and exited her house for the frigid outdoors. The woman would want him to call again, and maybe he would.

But probably not.

Leaving the warm bed only made the night wind that much worse. The moon played peekaboo with heavy clouds, leaving Harley's path alternately well lit, then dark as sin.

But the weather didn't matter. To keep his options open, Harley never stayed over at a woman's place, just as he never brought a woman home to his place—wherever home might be at the time.

Right now, home was three hours south of Harmony, Kentucky, in a small cabin in the hills near Echo Lake. After fucking up his elbow and losing out on another title bout, he'd needed the seclusion, the time to reflect.

The time to do as he damned well pleased without everyone scrutinizing his every move, worrying about him, making assumptions on his state of mind.

The Jeep hummed to life, kicking hot air over Harley's jean-covered legs. Hands cupped together, shoulders hunched against the cold, he looked out the windshield at the rapidly sinking moon. The long, winding road to his rented cabin would take him into daybreak.

But so what?

He didn't punch a time clock—never had. Here in the hills where he routinely came to prep for a fight, he could use any schedule he wanted. His time was his own, and he bent it any way he liked.

The isolation worked to his advantage.

While rehabbing his elbow, he'd spent weeks jogging alone, pushing himself when he wanted, relaxing when he felt like it, all in higher altitude. Without the lure of fast-food restaurants, he'd eaten only specially prepared meals that had him especially lean and muscular. Getting up at dawn—or sometimes, as now, being *still* up at dawn—made it convenient to work on cardio and stamina.

He was in the best physical condition of his life, and soon he could rejoin Dean's gym to start boning up on technique. Sublime had already defended his title belt once.

Next, if things worked out as they should, he'd have to defend it against Harley.

But even if the SBC set up the fight, who knew if he'd actually make it into the competition? Every damn time things seemed to be going his way, something bizarre happened to fuck up his plans.

He hated it.

He was fed up. He . . .

Ah hell.

Putting the Jeep in gear, Harley backed out of the driveway, past the tall pine trees until his tires hit the snow-covered gravel road. He would not sit around stewing on the unfairness of life.

Instead, he put his mind to thinking about all he planned to do that day.

This was his third year staying in the same cabin. Like the lovely lady he'd just left, tourists were the norm right now. They came and went, a new crowd each year, and that suited Harley fine. So far, the only familiar female face in town was that of Anastasia Bradley, the woman who rented him the cabin.

Anastasia knew to hold the place for him during certain months. They had an unspoken but solid agreement that worked for them both.

She had guaranteed rental on her cabin.

He had a reliable place that suited him.

With his thoughts bounding this way and that, Harley drove through the dark night. Sure enough, gray dawn cut through the never-ending sleet by the time he started past Anastasia's cabin, which sat half a mile down the hill from the one he rented.

To his surprise, she was out front already, bundled up head to toe and chopping—or attempting to chop—wood.

What the hell?

It was all of about twenty-five degrees and blustery to boot. Even the roosters weren't awake yet. The ax she swung probably weighed more than she did.

Frowning, Harley pulled into her drive. She had an

ancient CD player blaring hard rock music and didn't hear his approach.

Dangerous.

They were far from the minuscule town, hidden in heavy woods, with no neighbors to speak of.

The ebb and flow of female tourists meant Harley didn't have to worry about any one woman becoming too clingy. But there were just as many men traveling through the area, strangers who could be nice—or not.

Living in seclusion was unsafe for any woman, but especially a woman who didn't take necessary precautions.

After turning off his Jeep and getting out, Harley watched Anastasia. On many levels, she fascinated him.

She never came on to him, didn't try to impress him, and spoke as up front as any man, but with less colorful language.

He appreciated those qualities every time he did business with her.

As a man, he wondered at her apparent indifference to him. Not that he was conceited. But . . . yeah, he'd come to expect it from women.

Right now, Anastasia wore a navy stocking cap pulled down low over her shoulder-length dark hair, a hooded sweatshirt over that, and a lumberjack-type coat over that. Quilted knee boots protected her feet.

She swung the ax with verve, and inaccuracy. If he didn't intercede, she'd maim herself.

Out of self-preservation, Harley kept his distance. "Anastasia!"

The wind sucked away his words, making them indecipherable from the music. Damn it.

Looking around, Harley spotted a long stick and a rock. He chose the rock.

Tossing it just beyond her, so that it landed in the meager pile of splintered wood, he waited.

Anastasia paused, stared toward the rock, and without haste or worry, looked over her shoulder. Above her red nose, her dark brown eyes warmed. "Harley."

She set aside the ax and strode toward the porch to turn down the music. Mitten-covered hands coming up so she could blow warm breath on them, she approached. "What are you doing up so early?"

It was more a matter of being up late, but Harley kept his business to himself. He nodded toward the woodpile. "Planning a fire?"

"Hopefully not, but with this weather, electricity is never guaranteed. There's plenty up at your cabin, don't worry. I made sure of that over the summer. But my supply was low."

Had she personally chopped the wood on his front porch? He had serious doubts.

Though he'd just wrapped up an all-night sexual marathon, no man with a conscience could walk away from her predicament. "Go on inside." He headed for the ax. "I'll finish up."

"No way!" At five-five, Anastasia was damn near a foot shorter than him. That didn't stop her from making a stand, though. She rushed around in front of him and planted her boot-covered feet. "You are a guest renter, Harley Handleman, not a hired hand. There's absolutely no way that I can allow you to—"

Small talk was not his forte. Harley walked around her, away from her objections. After situating a log on the chopping stump and hefting the ax, he spared one glance for Anastasia. "Stay back so you don't get hurt."

Her brows pinched down. "I mean it, Harley. Don't you dare—"

He split the log with one blow.

Nonplussed, Anastasia loosened her rigid posture. "Oh. Well." She let out a breath. "You made that look easy."

Harley shrugged.

She started to pick up the split pieces, but he had it done before she could. She crossed her arms. "You're good at this. Much better than me."

No kidding. Because he'd only seen Anastasia in the colder months, he hadn't had much opportunity to examine her physique without thick sweaters, sweatshirts, and bulky layers. But no amount of clothing could disguise her small bone structure and slight weight. He saw it in the delicate lines of her throat, her slender wrists and tapered fingers.

"I'm a man," he said, and figured that was explanation enough.

"A male chauvinist," Anastasia clarified with amusement, "but granted, a fit one. I suppose it wouldn't hurt if you only did a few pieces . . ." She trailed off, undecided and arguing more with herself than him, since Harley paid her no mind and just kept working.

"I'll go inside and make some coffee."

Harley didn't reply. He didn't know if he wanted coffee or not, but by the time he finished, he might, so he let her do as she pleased.

At least she'd be inside, out of the weather.

In his peripheral vision, he saw Anastasia pause on the porch to remove her messy boots, then go through her front door.

With her out of the way, he got down to the business of chopping wood. To his surprise, it felt good to swing the ax and watch the tumble of fat logs turn into a tidy woodpile.

Before long, he'd worked up a sweat, so he removed his coat. By the time he finished, close to an hour and a half later, his undershirt and flannel shirt were both damp from a mixture of sweat and sleet. He swiped a sleeve across his brow, and it dawned on him: he hadn't given the SBC much thought while working.

Huh.

Perhaps chopping wood was just the cure he needed.

Or maybe he'd been too busy thinking about Anastasia to ponder anything else.

The sleet had softened to a damp snowfall. Most of the area now glistened in a layer of ice.

Anastasia stuck her head out the door and caught him standing there, doing nothing more than appreciating the sight of ice on tree limbs, rocks, and the woodpile.

"Harley?" she called out. And when he turned to her, she said, "Come on in for some hot coffee. It'll warm you up."

"I'm warm enough." But because he wasn't all that tired, and he didn't feel a need to rush back to his cabin to sleep, he picked up his coat and went to the door she'd left standing open for him.

In a quick glance, he scanned the interior where a warm fire flickered in a wood-burning stove, sending waves of welcome heat everywhere. Her place looked different from the one she rented out. Less rustic. Prettier.

Her wood furniture was sun-washed oak, almost white, in some European-inspired design. The upholstered pieces had soft fabrics with lots of decorative pillows. Throw rugs almost completely covered the hardwood floors. Silk flowers sat on one table, but other than that, she didn't indulge a need for bric-a-brac.

From what Harley knew of her, the clean, feminine style suited her personality.

"My boots are wet." He didn't want to soil her rugs.

"Take them off."

He looked toward her—and was caught. She'd shed the thick layers and now wore only body-hugging white leggings that showed off slim, shapely legs. A huge, pale pink sweatshirt hung to just below her behind. White-and-pink-striped socks covered her small feet.

As he stared, she bent at the waist to remove something from the oven. Dark hair, disheveled from the outdoors, swung down to hide the side of her face from his view.

Not that he was looking at her face anyway. Nope. The sight of her heart-shaped ass held all his attention.

For a slim, fine-boned woman, Anastasia had a few generous curves.

Still contemplating that sweet behind, Harley said, "The bottoms of my jeans are wet, too." All the way to his knees in fact.

Using an oven mitt, Anastasia set a batch of fresh-baked cookies on the range top. She looked at him then, caught him staring, and said without a single twinge, "Take your jeans off too if you want. I'll toss everything in the dryer."

Did she think he wouldn't?

Harley gave her a brief study, saw she didn't look the least bit teasing or ill at ease, and mentally shrugged. Why not?

Removing his wallet, keys, and cell phone, he tucked them into his coat pocket and hung the coat on a wall rack by the door. The wet laces on his boots proved difficult, but he finally got them untied and set them on the front porch, next to hers.

After closing the door, he stripped off his flannel shirt, unsnapped his jeans, pulled down the zipper . . . and stepped free.

Without so much as a curious glance at his snug boxers, Anastasia came and took the clothes. "I really do appreciate all the chopped wood. You went above and beyond, Harley. I should be set for a while now."

Like his cabin, only bigger, hers was one main room with living, dining, and kitchen areas flowing together. Only her bathroom and two bedrooms were separate. But the doors stood open, probably to benefit from the heat of the woodstove. Harley saw her neatly made bed, an office of sorts in the spare bedroom, and a very tidy, all-white bathroom.

Going to a stack washer and dryer tucked into the corner of the kitchen, Anastasia tossed his damp clothes inside. As she set the dial, she said, "Take a seat, Harley. Make yourself comfortable. I'll get you some coffee."

"Thanks." If she could pretend it was normal to have morning coffee with a man in his underwear—a man she hadn't slept with—then he sure as hell wouldn't let it bother him.

In a snowy white undershirt, black boxers, and thick white crew socks, he seated himself in a fancy padded chair at her round dining table. Wind continued to whistle outside; inside, the fragrance of burning wood and warm cookies created a coziness unfamiliar to him.

"Do you have heat other than the woodstove?"

"Same as you," she said. "I have electric space heaters. But I like the scent of a wood fire better. Problem is, the heat from the woodstove doesn't warm my bedroom enough, so sometimes, when it's really cold, I crash on the couch."

Harley glanced at the couch, pictured her curled up there in something soft and warm, and said, "I'd never fit."

Her laugh drew his attention back to her.

"You weren't invited," she said, "but no, I don't suppose a man of your size would have room to stretch out on the couch."

Rather than put a filled mug on the table in front of him, Anastasia went to the trouble to fill a decorative tray with a carafe, cups, saucers, cream and sugar, cookies, spoons, and cloth napkins. The formality of it surprised Harley, yet he sensed it was routine for her.

"Cream and sugar?"

"I take mine black." He waited while she served him like a proper little host, then he sipped the coffee. "Perfect. Strong, the way I like it."

"Me, too." She lifted the plate of cookies, but hesitated. "I'm sorry. I wasn't thinking. Can you have cookies while training?"

"You know I'm in training?"

She tipped her head. "Was it a secret?"

"No."

"Everyone around here knows it, Harley. You're a celebrity."

"I doubt that."

"Now, come on. There's no need for modesty. You know you have a recognizable name."

"Maybe to some sports fans, but it's a limited audience."

"If you say so." She let it go with a shrug. "So tell me, will a cookie blow any special diets?"

Harley was fanatical about staying in shape, even when not training, but he wasn't stupid. "I'm not about to turn down warm fresh cookies."

She smiled so big, her deep brown eyes twinkled with golden lights. "Good. Then I'll give you three."

For several minutes, they ate and sipped coffee in

comfortable silence. That in itself was odd, because other than relatives, or his friends' significant others, Harley didn't indulge platonic relationships.

And that meant other than during sex, which was seldom quiet, he didn't indulge comfortable silences with women. But with Anastasia, it felt . . . okay.

Probably because she acted just as his female relatives did: disinterested in him as a man.

The sun broke free of the clouds, glaring through the windows extra bright as it reflected off the ice.

"Speaking of your training . . ."

"Were we?" He ate another cookie. Heaven.

"As often as you've stayed here, I never realized you got up so early to train."

"I keep irregular hours." Harley caught her in his gaze, and lowered his voice. "But this morning, I wasn't training."

"Oh, I just assumed . . ." Realization hit her, and she ducked her face to hide her smile. "Never mind, then."

Harley watched her. She looked very sweet and enticing in the pink sweatshirt. He never prompted an intrusion on his privacy, but now, he couldn't help himself. "Why does that amuse you?"

"It's just that I should have known."

She acted coy, not quite blushing, but close. It intrigued him. "Known what, exactly?"

Propping her chin on a fist, Anastasia grinned at him. "The town is small, hardly a town even, and not much goes unnoticed. Someone like you *definitely* wouldn't be overlooked, which means everyone pays attention to you, and . . . well, you've gained a . . . certain reputation around here."

Harley liked the way she teased—though he'd be willing to bet she had no solid information on him. "A reputation, huh? For what?"

"Being a ladies' man, of course."

As he thought: no real idea at all. Harley lifted his coffee cup to sip. "Have you been listening to gossip, Anastasia?"

"Gossip? No, more like bragging." She chuckled. "In the grocery store."

Curiosity got the better of him. Harley set his coffee cup aside and crossed his arms on the tabletop. Giving Anastasia all the intensity of his stare, he said, "Tell me."

"Oh, no." This time, she couldn't hold back the blush. "Not verbatim I won't. It was a little explicit for that."

"How explicit?"

She shook her head. "One woman wanted to know if anyone knew where you lived."

"Who?"

"They weren't women I recognized, so I assume they must be vacationers here for snow skiing."

He slowly straightened. "Did you tell her?"

"Of course not. I respect your privacy." When he relaxed again, she said, "None of the women seemed to know much about you, Harley, so you have nothing to worry about."

What the hell had she heard, and which woman was looking for him? He always made his intent clear up front; he'd never made any false promises.

"Forget about it, Harley. Other than that one question, I can promise you that all the chitchat was flattering."

Because Anastasia watched him, he said, "That's a relief."

She laughed out loud. "Come off it, Harley. You couldn't care less what others are saying about you."

Harley noticed that even in harsh sunlight, her skin looked soft and smooth, and free of makeup. After her efforts outside, her hair was a little messy, and somehow sexier because of it. She had very white teeth, full lips, and a habit of wrinkling her nose when she laughed.

Odd that he'd never noticed any of those things before.

But more than that, more than his sudden attention to her physical attributes, her insight surprised him. "You think so, huh?"

"Absolutely." And with confidence: "I'm a very good judge of character."

"Yeah?" Harley settled back in his seat, prepared to enjoy himself. "Says who?"

Anastasia sent him a smug look. "Many satisfied clients, that's who."

His left brow lifted an inch in disbelief. "Clients?"

Wrinkling her nose again, Anastasia nodded. "You didn't think I only rented out a single cabin as a living, did you? I would never be such a slug." She curled one leg up under her. "The rental brings in a respectable income, but it's not enough for me to live the way I want to."

"No?"

"No." Coy again, she said, "When you're not here, I seldom am either."

Both brows went up over that disclosure. Confessions? Suggestions? Harley just didn't know. But he considered hitting the road—in his boxers—right now.

Anastasia took in his expression and laughed. "Relax. I didn't mean it like that."

"Like what?"

"I'm not hitting on you, Harley."

No, she never had. He sighed. Questions popped into his mind, one right after the other, but he'd found that silence brought answers quicker than queries.

Sure enough, after a thirty-second pause, Anastasia continued. "I don't make a habit of being here for you specifically. We just happen to share a similar appreciation of the seclusion of the place. So while I'm here, I rent out the other cabin, and you always have it on hold for this time of year, so you get it."

"What happens the rest of the year?"

"I have a real-estate manager who rents it out for me. As a life coach, it's worth my while to travel for the job, so I do. Often."

How had he known her three years, and never heard of this? "A life coach, huh? That's . . . different."

"I guess." She leaned closer. "Are you familiar with the concept?"

"Not really."

Appearing anxious, she asked, "Shall I educate you, then?"

Harley could tell she wanted to, so he shrugged. "I'm all ears."

Her smile broke into a grin. "You're all something, Harley Handleman, but it's not ears."

From any other woman, that might've sounded like flirting. But Harley noted that Anastasia's teasing didn't hold a single ounce of flirtatiousness. It was more like a good-natured insult. He both appreciated her attitude, and felt nettled by it.

"Basically," Anastasia continued, oblivious to his emotional quandary, "what a life coach does is help someone to gain confidence in his abilities, discover his true path in life, and accomplish more goals with less stress involved. Not to brag, but I'm in pretty high demand, and I get requests from all over the country. When the price is right, I go to the client to work with him in his atmosphere, at his job and in his life."

Harley studied her. "So it's mostly guys you work for, huh?" When she looked confused, he explained, "You're referring to a guy. *His* goals, *his* confidence . . ."

"Oh. That was just as an example. I've worked for some women, too." Then she thought about it. "But you know, yeah, I have mostly worked with men. I always have a choice of clients, male and female, so I guess I just gravitate more to male clients."

Harley settled back in his seat and crossed his arms. He forgot that he was still in his underwear. "Do tell."

She compressed her lips, her thoughts hidden, then, as Harley watched, she shook off some unpleasant memory. "It doesn't matter."

"No?"

"The thing is, most people, men and woman alike, can get in a rut and then it's nearly impossible for them to be objective about what they want or need, and how to get it.

With agreed-upon time frames, I work with them to stay focused on positive creativity, balance their lives, and achieve their goals."

"By telling them what they should and shouldn't do?"

"I guess you could say that, but I do it in nonjudgmental, unbiased ways, and with their ultimate goals always in the forefront of my mind. It's always about what the client wants and needs, not what I think is right or wrong."

Incredible. "And your morals and ethics don't factor in?"

"I'm a professional, Harley. I keep my own personal preferences out of the equation."

He'd never heard of anything so bizarre. And he doubted anyone could be professional enough to keep personality out of it. "People pay you for that?"

"Absolutely. I get a good salary, plus all my expenses. But I have a high success rate, so I'm worth every penny."

For only a flicker of time, Harley wondered what advice she'd give him. But he snuffed that bizarre idea real quick. He kept his own counsel and he didn't want a busybody woman, even if he suddenly realized she was pretty hot, to go dicking around with his head. "When do you have to travel again?"

"Usually, as soon as spring arrives, I get back to work." She pleated her napkin and shrugged. "But I recently hit a glitch, so this year, I'm probably going to take an extended hiatus."

Harley waited, but Anastasia didn't expound on the "glitch."

She dusted off her hands and looked up at him. "What about you?"

"What about me?"

"Do you have a goal? One particular thing that you're focused on?"

Harley didn't hesitate. He was a highly motivated man who had plenty of goals. Most of them shifted in importance from day to day, sometimes hour to hour, depending on what was happening in his life.

But his number-one goal never altered. "I'm going to win an SBC title belt."

"Wow." Showing no signs of doubt, Anastasia said, "I've watched a few competitions. Winning the belt seems like a tall order. The fighters are pretty impressive, and title fights are hard to come by."

"They have to be earned."

"I take it you have a solid plan on how to reach that goal?"

"Damn right." Had she seen any of his competitions? Did Anastasia know of his missed opportunities?

"Great. You seem really positive, Harley, and you're obviously more than capable." Leaning closer, she said, "But let's assume you'd had several disappointments in that regard. That's where I'd step in and give you some direction."

Before he could laugh, she added, "And no, I'm not talking about your training. That's not my expertise at all. But so much can influence us—family, friends, work."

He'd learned that the hard way. "You aren't kidding."

"Those outside influences can easily throw us off track and cause us to make mistakes, if we let them."

Harley heard himself say, "Some things are out of our control," and then he could have strangled himself.

He did *not* share maudlin thoughts.

He did not complain aloud.

And he never, ever admitted to a loss of control.

Tilting her head, Anastasia measured his words. "I agree. But in those cases, how we react to the circumstances can make all the difference between success and failure. Sometimes it takes an objective outsider to see what you can't."

"Maybe." Disgusted with himself, Harley finished off his coffee in one long drink, and stood. He should never have accepted Anastasia's invitation. He knew better than to get chatty with women. It was his number-one rule.

Abrupt and not caring, Harley said, "It's getting late, Anastasia. My pants done yet?"

CHAPTER 2

A NASTASIA stared up at him, and Harley had the awful suspicion that she took him apart, analyzed all the pieces, and made conclusions on him in record time.

"What?" he asked with a little more heat than he intended.

A crooked smile appeared. "Nothing."

"What?" he asked again.

She shook her head. "I just got caught in your eyes for a second there. You have . . . really intense eyes."

As his temper racked up another notch, he crossed his arms over his chest and frowned at her. "My *eyes*?"

"*Pfft.*" She waved a hand at him. "Don't act like you haven't heard it before, Harley. With eyes like yours, I'm sure you've had plenty of comments."

"Maybe." Refusing to let her rile him, Harley calmed his breathing and wrestled for the upper hand. "But usually those type comments come from women who are in my bed."

A surprised laugh burst out of her. "I can imagine!" In rapid order, her expression changed from humor to appalled embarrassment and she held up both hands. "No, wait, I don't want to imagine."

Harley caught her wrists and, very gently, tugged her a little closer. She was very fine boned. And warm to the touch.

Now this was more like it. Seeing Anastasia wide-eyed, like a deer caught in the headlights, put him at ease. He asked in a low murmur, "Why not?"

She looked at his mouth and swayed toward him. "Why not what?"

Harley smiled. Why had he thought Anastasia would be different? She melted as easily as every other woman.

He was both relieved—and disappointed. "Why don't you want to imagine me in bed with a woman?"

Her gaze jerked up to his. She snorted and pulled away. "I'm too young for those type images, that's why."

Quickly turning away, she headed for the dryer, and the moment of hot sexual tension evaporated as if it had never been. "You know, Harley, not many people consider daybreak late, but your clothes should be dry by now. I'll get them for you."

So he had her on the run. Nice. But she'd recaptured her relaxed air and that annoying obliviousness to his state of undress. Not that he wanted her chasing after him.

Or did he?

While Anastasia went to retrieve his clothes from the dryer, Harley followed after her, automatically watching the sway of her hips, her loose-limbed gait.

Odd that he'd never before noticed the sexy way she had of moving. Of course, her lack of layers made it more obvious now.

"Dry and warm. Perfect." She turned and almost bumped into him. With a startled expression, she said, "Good grief, Harley. You're like a Ninja. I didn't hear you move."

Feeling provoked for reasons he couldn't name, Harley looked down at her, but said nothing.

And he didn't retreat.

With a laugh and a roll of her eyes, Anastasia moved back, and then handed over the clothes. "You're dangerous, Harley, but I still want to thank you for chopping all that wood. It would have taken me all day."

It would have taken her all week, but he didn't point that out. He stepped into his pants. "Dangerous?"

"And you know it, so don't pretend otherwise."

"Funny thing, Anastasia, you don't seem threatened."

She shrugged. "Yeah, well, I'm more immune than most, I guess."

"How so?"

"If I told you, it'd irritate you."

That irritated him. "If you told me what?"

Sighing, and appearing very put-upon, she said, "You really want to do this?"

Yeah, he definitely . . . No wait. Harley yanked up his zipper. "Explain *this*."

She waved a hand. "Banter back and forth. Get into the reasons why neither of us wants to get involved with the other." She wrinkled her nose. "Hash out our innermost feelings."

"God, no." Given half a chance, Anastasia Hedrick could do what lethal light heavyweight fighters couldn't.

She could scare him.

Her hand touched his shoulder, caressed, and finally patted—much like she might have touched an angry mutt. "That's what I thought."

In some indefinable way, Anastasia grew more infuriating, and sexy, with every passing second.

Harley pulled on his shirt and did a rapid change in topic. "Thanks for the cookies."

"It's the least I could do."

With his shirt on but unbuttoned, Harley headed for the door.

Anastasia stayed close. "Let's just hope the storms blow through and the electricity stays on."

"Yeah." He put his wallet and cell phone back in his jeans pocket.

Hands laced together in front of her, Anastasia fidgeted. "Well, if I don't see you again, good luck in your fight."

He gave her a quick look. "I'm scheduled here till the end of the month."

"Another two weeks, I know. But out here, I don't see anyone that often."

"By choice?"

"Pretty much." She smiled up at him. "You're only half a mile away, and I seldom see you. After today, I figure the odds of running into you just deteriorated to slim and none, and Slim's out of town. So I wanted to wish you luck before you go."

She'd used a lot of words to say something simple. "You think I'll avoid you."

She didn't have to confirm it for him; her expression said it all.

"Come on, Harley, stop thinking of me as a dummy. I'm a little more intuitive than you'd like, so yes, I know you'll avoid me."

And he would have. But now . . . "Will you miss me when I'm gone?"

The blunt question seemed to throw her, and she paused for a heartbeat. "I'll watch you on pay-per-view."

So she *did* watch. For unknown reasons, that gave Harley a lot of satisfaction. Perhaps because it meant she wasn't so disinterested after all. "And wish I was closer?"

That got her laughing. "You're incorrigible."

True. Maybe he wasn't the draw for her at all. Maybe she was just a fan of the sport. To find out, Harley asked, "You follow MMA competitions?"

"Not really. I've never gotten into any sport too much, but especially not the brutal stuff. I've only watched on the nights you're fighting, and truthfully, I still don't understand all the rules."

He leaned against the wall. "But you still watch. When I fight."

Her shoulders lifted. "I guess knowing someone makes it more interesting."

Harley started to tell her just how interesting he could make things, and his cell phone rang. "Sorry. Excuse me a second."

"Oh, sure." Anastasia moved back to the dining table and began clearing it.

"Hello?"

"Hey, bro, how the hell are you?"

"Barber." Harley glanced at his watch. "What are you doing up so early? Or haven't you been to bed yet?"

"I'll have you know I just left a warm bed. *Not* my own."

"Braggart." Harley grinned. "So you get laid, and then decide to call and pester me, huh?" Barber—who was *not* his brother—had the attitude and ability of a fighter, and the talent and career of a born musician. He was also funny as hell. From the start, they'd hit it off.

"Sure. Why not?"

"Dumbass. What if *I'd* been in bed?"

"You mean you aren't? Damn, man, I'm disappointed. You've just sunk drastically in my esteem."

Harley glanced toward Anastasia, saw she had her back to him, and murmured, "Actually, like you, I left a warm bed not that long ago. Then I saw my landlord chopping wood and stopped to help."

"Landlord, huh? Well ain't you a regular Boy Scout? I'm sure the guy appreciates it."

Harley sent another quick look toward Anastasia. Glossy and thick, her dark hair lay over her shoulders. Humming, she pretended to be busy. With every movement, her sweatshirt pulled against tempting curves. "I'm sure she does."

"She?" A lot of innuendo hung in that single word. "Now it's getting interesting."

"Sorry, but it's not." Not really. "So how about you? What's been happening? You wallowing in your new fame?" Barber's band had recently landed a deal with the SBC fighting organization to provide music tracks to the biggest events.

"I've been known to wallow," Barber admitted. "Things have been crazy busy, but right now I'm chillin' and getting back to my roots. For the next month or so, the band and I are hanging out in Harmony, doing a gig for Roger's Rodeo. So I'm here—and you aren't. Dean said you were off licking your wounds. Sounds kinky and self-gratifying to me, but Dean wouldn't elaborate."

"Dean's full of shit and you can tell him I said so." They both respected Dean, so Barber took the comment as the good-natured gibe Harley meant it to be. "I was rehabbing my friggin' elbow, and you know it."

"Still? Man, it seems like eons ago that you dislocated that bitch."

"Six weeks." Six long, agonizing weeks—and another missed opportunity at the title belt.

"So where are you? I'll come to you and you can share your stash of hot babes."

Again, Harley's gaze went to Anastasia. In the small space, how could she not hear every word? "Sorry, no harems here, only a limited selection of snow bunnies." He saw Anastasia smile, and it annoyed him.

Why wasn't she insulted?

Or more interested?

"Bullshit," Barber said. "If that was the case, you wouldn't be there."

"Maybe." Harley relaxed back against the wall—and continued to watch Anastasia.

With nothing left to do, she tried to give him privacy by staring out a window. He couldn't stop himself from visually tracing the shape of her body.

The spark of deep interest ignited into a flame. That wouldn't do.

Making up his mind, Harley said, "You know what? I'm anxious to get into some real training. I could probably head out of here in under a week."

"Don't cut your downtime short on my account. I'll be around for a while."

Anastasia turned to look at him. He'd never before left the cabin early, so his sudden announcement had to have thrown her.

Not that she showed it.

She just analyzed him . . . and came to her own conclusions.

While keeping his attention on Anastasia, Harley assured Barber, "It's not a problem."

The sooner he got away from her, the better off he'd be. He did not get involved with women like Anastasia.

He did not let women dissect him.

"I have a few things to take care of in town, but I should be done by the end of the week. Your lazy ass better be raring to go when I get there."

Harley disconnected the call, and then said to Anastasia, "Sorry about that."

"No problem." She left the window and approached him.

"Something's come up."

"I heard."

Harley waited for the inquisition.

She said nothing, just smiled up at him.

Well hell. He gave in first. "I know I was scheduled until—"

"No biggie. I'll prorate your time here and mail you a reimbursement for the unused week."

Like hell she would. He was the one breaking the contract, not her. "Keep it."

She shrugged. "Fine."

Damned, annoying woman. Then he caught the teasing glint in her eyes. Jesus, when was the last time he let a woman get his goat? Especially a woman who only agreed with him?

He crossed his arms. "You like being unpredictable, don't you, Anastasia?"

"Absolutely."

That she admitted it only made it worse. "You're not going to ask me a single question, are you? Even though every other woman would."

"We've already concluded that I'm not every other woman, haven't we? At least, not where you're concerned." She patted Harley's chest, surprising him. "If I'm unpredictable, then you're inscrutable."

She made it sound like an insult. "I call it private."

"Call it whatever you want, but you wear it like a coat of armor." After stepping around him, Anastasia opened the door to peer out. "It's frigid, but the sleet has stopped for now." She faced him again. "You better get going before the roads get too icy. Getting uphill to your cabin might not be too easy, even in a Jeep."

Harley shrugged into his coat. "Worrying about me?"

"Now why would I do that? You're a big boy."

Anticipating her reaction, he said low, "And here I thought you hadn't looked."

Of course her gaze went straight to his lap. Harley almost laughed, especially when heat rushed into her cheeks, but he held it back.

Anastasia caught herself real quick and gave him a wry smile. "You're incorrigible."

"Just honest." Still watching her, he added, "Or did you really not notice?"

Refusing to acknowledge the question, she held out her hand for a platonic farewell. "Until next year, Harley."

Harley looked at that impersonal, outstretched hand, and made up his mind.

Screw it.

On impulse, because he couldn't quite stop himself, he bent down, intending to kiss her good-bye.

Anastasia turned her face so that his mouth touched her cheek instead of her lips.

They both went still . . . for about three seconds.

In that blink of time, Harley registered the silky texture of her skin, the softness of her hair, the enticing scent of delicate warmth, unique to every woman.

He leaned away and studied her.

Bemused, Anastasia shook her head. "Sorry, Harley, but that's just nasty."

Masculine ego rebelled. "Nasty?" What the hell type of insult was that?

"You've been with another woman," she said without accusation. "I have no idea where your mouth has been, but I know I don't want it on my mouth afterward."

Well hell. Harley felt like a kid who'd just been chastised. He was still trying to come up with a reply when she spoke again.

"Next time you think you want to kiss me, make me first on the list, and I might surprise you by being more agreeable."

Next time? Not likely. He wasn't entirely certain why he'd made the attempt this time. "Sure thing, Anastasia. I'll try to remember that."

Anastasia easily read him, and laughed. "No, you won't. As soon as you leave here, you'll forget we ever had this conversation. And truthfully, Harley, so will I. Now go before this becomes memorable."

First insulted, and now ordered out.

Again, Harley told himself that he should never have stopped in the first place. But . . . he had to grin at her *cajones*. He saluted her and left.

In no way did Anastasia Bradley act like any other woman he'd known. But her uniqueness only made her more off-limits, because she'd be more complex. And he didn't need any complications in his life.

This time, he'd have no distractions from his goal.

No. Definitely not.

Walking against the hard wind, Harley went to his Jeep, and he was still grinning when he got inside.

Too bad she was right, that he'd have to avoid her.

And even if he didn't, he was leaving very soon. As she'd said, it was doubtful he'd see her again anyway.

He'd drop the key in her post office box in town, and then he'd drive away.

But . . . having a woman so quick-witted and independent tied to his bed for a few hours would be a special treat.

If Anastasia would agree—which he doubted.

But he could think about it. And Harley knew he would.
For hours.
Maybe even days.

As Harley jogged past her house on the return to his
cabin, Stasia stood back from the window. At this time of
year, night came early up in the hills, and with lights on inside, she'd be easily visible.

If he looked her way.

But he didn't.

He jogged twice a day, once in the morning and then
again at early evening. No matter how dreadful the weather
got, as long as the road crews cleared a path, he was out,
pushing himself, proving his stamina.

In between the jogging, he worked out at his cabin with
a modest supply of weights and portable equipment.

And around that, he visited the town and did . . . God
knew what.

But he'd be leaving soon, very soon, and so Stasia
watched through the windows for him, always anxious for
a glimpse.

They hadn't spoken since that early morning three days
ago.

She'd been mentally kicking her own butt ever since.

What in the world had she been thinking? It didn't matter that the intelligent side of her insisted she'd done the
right thing. It didn't matter that her pride applauded her decision *not* to be another notch on his proverbial bedpost.

Harley Handleman had wanted to kiss her.

Probably the *only* time he'd ever want to kiss her.

Likely because she'd been flirting, leading him on, acting very out of character.

And she'd turned him down.

Not just saying no, but calling him *nasty*.

Acid burned her stomach with the appalling memory.

She hadn't meant to flirt. But there was something about
Harley that brought out her teasing nature.

Maybe it was his eyes. They were so vivid a blue, so piercing, that when he looked at her, she felt naked and had to fight the urge to conceal herself.

Or maybe it was his impressive physique. The man had strutted around in his underwear as if he did so every day, in front of presidents and popes alike. *Not* looking had been a sheer act of desperation.

He had the blond hair of a surfer, the body of an athlete, the eyes of an angel, and a charisma that could warm cold stone.

But most likely it was Harley's wounded soul that drew her. When she looked at him, when she peered beyond the rugged exterior, she knew that he'd had some ugly things in his past, hurts that hadn't gone away, memories that would haunt him forever.

He was the most capable man she'd ever met, and though he tried to hide it, also the most vulnerable. On many levels, she both liked and admired him. He was strong and self-sufficient, handsome and very fit. Relaxed and friendly.

Likable.

Okay, so he was an obvious womanizer—in a charming, quiet, understated way. The analytical part of Anastasia insisted that was a defense mechanism. Given enough time and an opportunity to delve into his personality—which would require knowing him better—she'd learn why he felt so defensive.

As a life coach, she could probably even help him.

But Harley kept his thoughts on most things to himself. He was a big, bold, gorgeous enigma.

What she knew of his sexual exploits, she'd heard from women, not him. She also heard that he never treated women poorly, didn't address them as objects, and he never deceived his way into their bedrooms.

He was a gentleman. Controlled, but kind.

And considerate.

Hadn't he stopped on her birthday and spent more than an hour chopping wood? Okay, so he hadn't known it was her birthday; that just made the gesture more generous.

Maybe she could blame her birthday for the bizarre way she'd teased him. She *had* been melancholy, waking midway through the night to ruminate on mistakes that a twenty-seven-year-old woman shouldn't make.

With Harley no longer in sight, Stasia went to her couch and flopped down. She put her head back and closed her eyes. Her favorite music played from her stereo, but she barely heard it.

Had she given Harley the wrong impression? Had she led him on? Memories wrestled in her mind, making her uneasy.

Her last male client had called her awful names, the least of which was "tease."

He blamed her for a ruined marriage, a crumbling life.

His wife, whom Stasia had never met face-to-face, blamed her, too. The poor woman had even threatened suicide.

Stasia squeezed her eyes tighter, deliberately blocking that awful remembrance.

What did Harley think of her now?

Or did he think of her at all?

Determined to stop torturing herself, Stasia got up and went through the routine of making dinner, even though she wasn't hungry. Cooking for one never took long. By the time she finished preparing and eating a chop and vegetables, the temperature had dropped even more and another storm blasted the area. Giant, wet snowflakes covered the ice, making the road invisible.

She looked at her meager pile of wood in a brass holder by the wood-burning fireplace, and resigned herself to going out. Better now, she told herself, than after her shower, when she'd only be wearing her pajamas.

Bundling up head to toe, Stasia braved the weather for the woodpile. With her arms laden, snow clinging to her nose and eyelashes, she was on her way back in when headlights cut through the dark, stormy night.

Since no one else lived on the road above her, she knew
who it would be. She looked up, and seconds later, Harley's
Jeep came into view.

She paused in the middle of her barren yard.

The Jeep slowed, and then stopped in front of her.
Harley rolled down his window.

Stasia took one look at his frown, and issued a warning.
"Don't even *think* about getting out of that Jeep, Harley. I
mean it." She adjusted her load. "I'm managing just fine on
my own."

"You look like a walking igloo."

"Actually, it's refreshing," she lied—and fought back an
icy shiver.

He smiled, and Stasia marveled that such a handsome
man could be an ultimate fighter. Sure, he had a few small
scars and a definite kink in his nose. But somehow, that
only added to his charm.

His blond hair, always disheveled, curled up over the
rolled edges of his dark knit hat. Even in the slight illumination of her porch light, Harley's electric blue eyes shone
brightly, framed by long, dark brown eyelashes. Many
women would kill for eyes like that, but on Harley, they
didn't look feminine so much as imposing.

"I'm leaving tonight," he suddenly announced. "Right
after a few hands of cards with the guys."

Her heart sank to the pit of her stomach, which made no
sense at all. They had nothing but a business arrangement.
What he did and when he did it shouldn't matter to her at
all.

But damn it, some small kernel of secret desire remained.

Covering her reaction, Stasia glanced up at the sky in
doubt. "Good luck with that. I have a feeling if you hang
around for long, you won't make it out of here."

"The roads are probably clearer in town and the Jeep is
good in bad weather. But it doesn't matter. I promised to
give a few of the guys a chance to win back the money I've
been taking from them since I got here." He flashed a ras-
cal's grin. "I usually go home with the pot every night."

"So you're a card shark, huh?" His grin was enough to warm her a few degrees. "Is there anything you're not good at?"

"Yeah." The humor faded from his expression. "A lot of things, actually."

Stasia caught the sincerity in his lowered voice, the look in his eyes. "Like what?"

He shook his head. "We'll save that for another time."

"I guess I'll have to take your word on it then." With nothing left to do, Stasia nodded. "Well . . . until next year, Harley."

He hesitated, staring at her, holding her captive in that awesome gaze of his until she felt the load of logs slipping. Then he straightened in his seat. "Next year, Anastasia."

Why did that sound like a promise?

Grinning again, he said, "Now get inside before your feet freeze to the spot." He put his window back up and pulled away.

Resisting the urge to watch his taillights fade away, Stasia headed for her porch. With Harley now gone, the entire area seemed too quiet and still—a frozen, somehow eerie wasteland.

Unsettled, she looked around, noting the moon shadows, the few hushed animal sounds. And something else.

The snap of a twig.

The crunch of steps on ice.

Her eyes widened, trying to see beyond the glow of her porch light. Tall evergreens swayed from a bitter wind, and the cold settled into her bones, making her shiver.

Probably a deer, she decided. Or a fox. Dismissing any thoughts of danger, Stasia rushed inside, dropped the wood in the bin near the stove, and secured her door.

At least her cabin was nice and toasty, and well lit.

To fight off her strange mood, she turned up her rock music and delved into researching possible clients for her next job. These days, she always did extensive research on anyone asking to hire her. No way did she ever again want to find herself in an explosive situation like her last.

A few hours later Stasia had just finished a long shower and was about to put on her pajamas when the phone rang.

Jarred from introspective thoughts, she jumped, then stuck her head out of the bathroom to grab a quick glance at the clock. She couldn't imagine who might be calling her so late. With a towel wrapped tightly around herself, she darted out and grabbed up the portable phone off her dining table.

"Hello?"

"Anastasia Bradley?"

The brisk but scratchy voice wasn't familiar to her, and her unease resurfaced. She perched on the edge of a chair. After the warmth of the steamy bathroom, a chill chased over her, and she curled her toes. "Who's calling, please?"

"Satch Handleman," the voice said with impatience. "I'm Harley's uncle."

Harley's uncle! Why would he be calling her? "Oh, hello, Mr. Handleman."

"I've been trying to reach Harley with no luck. I know he rented a cabin from Anastasia Bradley, so if that's you, I could use your help."

"I'm sorry. Yes." Sitting up a little straighter, she said, "This is Anastasia, and yes, Harley rented his cabin from me."

"He's not answering the phone there."

"He's not there, that's why."

"Yeah, I figured that one out on my own." More impatience. "I tried his cell too, but he's not answering that either."

"Here in the hills, the cell phones rarely work. Add to that a snow and ice storm, and reception is iffy."

"Damn."

Cautious now, Stasia said, "I hope nothing is wrong."

"No one's dead, if that's what you mean."

Relieved, Stasia rested back in her seat. "I wish I could help you, Mr. Handleman, but I'm afraid Harley already left."

"Left *where?*"

The demand stiffened her back. "It's not for me to say, sir, but a few days ago he got a call from a friend and re-arranged his schedule."

"To come home?"

Unwilling to intrude on Harley's privacy, Stasia said, "I'm not really sure. I overheard the phone call, but not the particulars."

"When did he leave the cabin?"

"A few hours ago. Maybe seven or eight o'clock. But he was going to play cards in town for a while before he headed out."

"And just how do you know all that?"

Harley's uncle sounded very suspicious. "He stopped by my cabin to say good-bye and told me so." A heavy silence made Stasia uncomfortable. "Mr. Handleman? Are you still there?"

"Interesting," he finally muttered.

"That Harley would play cards?"

"No, that he'd bother to tell you good-bye."

"Oh." Now why was that of interest? Should she mention that she was already outside, or Harley probably wouldn't have bothered?

"You two involved?"

"No!" She hadn't meant to sound so appalled by the absurd question. Good grief, she'd almost shouted her denial. After a quick deep breath, Stasia said in a calmer tone, "Of course not. That is, Harley just rents property from me. I was out gathering wood when he passed by, so he stopped—only briefly—and said good-bye. There wasn't anything more to it."

"Hmmm."

Stasia found Harley's uncle to be as enigmatic as Harley himself. "Not to be nosy, sir, but . . ."

"Call me Uncle Satch."

She blinked. He wasn't *her* uncle. "I, uh . . . Thank you." She cleared her throat. "I suppose if it's really important, I could try going to town to see if Harley is still at the club playing cards."

Uncle Satch hesitated only a moment, and then asked with concern, "You mentioned a storm. Is it safe for you to be out in the weather?"

Just like Harley. "Yes. I have a four-wheel drive, and I'll go slowly."

"If you're sure, then yes, it's important. Thanks. When you find him, have him call me ASAP."

"Yes . . . Uncle Satch." Stasia felt like an idiot. She went back to the couch where she'd left a pen and her scattered papers. "I'll leave here in under five minutes, and it takes me about fifteen minutes to get to town. If Harley isn't there, is there a number where you'd like me to call you so that you know he hasn't gotten your message?"

"You can call my cell."

Anastasia wrote down the phone number and tucked the slip of paper into her purse. The second she hung up, she ran into the bathroom and, feeling even more ridiculous, brushed her hair and cleaned her teeth before changing into warm clothes.

She was a nice person, she assured herself, even as she pulled on her boots and a thick, hooded sweatshirt.

Making a run into town in the middle of the night during a near blizzard wasn't a big deal. She'd have offered to do the same for anyone. It had nothing to do with a desire to see Harley one last time.

Definitely not.

Okay, maybe just a little.

But she *was* nice, and would have done the same for anyone.

In no time at all, Stasia was bundled toes to nose. The second she stepped outside, she felt that edgy uneasiness again. It had to be the awful weather, she told herself. A heavy layer of snow blanketed the area, causing tree limbs to bend, ice to crackle.

As she neared her truck beneath the carport, Stasia noticed that the newly accumulated snowfall almost disguised recent tracks around her property. She bent to study the markings, but the light from the cabin wasn't adequate

to see much other than indentations. And with so many animals in the area, it could have been anything—most likely
the deer she'd heard earlier. They seemed larger than deer
prints, but the harsh winds could distort anything.

As proof of that, the carport hadn't adequately protected her truck from blown snow and ice. Almost frozen
over, she had to use her gloved hands to brush over her
door until she found the handle. Careful to keep the snow
from falling into her seat, she climbed in and started the
engine, turned on the defroster and heat full blast, and then
used precious minutes to clear the outsides of all the windows.

By the time she finished, her nose was bright red and
despite her thick socks and gloves, her fingers and toes felt
frozen.

Was any man worth this much hassle?

She doubted it.

If she hadn't already promised Uncle Satch . . .

But she had, so she might as well get it over with. She
got in the truck and carefully steered away from her cabin.
Her tires crunched through icy snow and after some guess-
ing, she found the nearly hidden road.

CHAPTER 3

THE darkness of the night and the frigid temperatures forced Stasia to use extra caution on the winding, hilly roads. To her surprise, she wasn't that far from her cabin when headlights showed up behind her. The trailing vehicle closed in, and then rode her bumper, crowding her. The reflection in her rearview mirror nearly blinded her. She couldn't see the vehicle clearly, but given the height of the headlights, she assumed it to be a large truck.

Uncertainty curdled in her stomach. Beyond her cabin and Harley's, there wasn't much on the road. It led off for a few miles, then finally hooked up with the main drag. Anyone going anywhere—other than to her cabin or the rental cabin—would be better served to use the main roads. Why anyone would be on this road now, especially in a snowstorm, she couldn't fathom.

But maybe those tracks around her car hadn't been caused by an animal after all.

Telling herself to keep her imagination in check, Stasia tried to encourage the other driver to back off by slowing even more, barely rolling along the frozen roadway. She'd just passed a closed service station, nearly invisible with the outside lights off, when the vehicle behind her revved its engine.

Seconds later a large muscle truck sped past her.

It cut so close that Stasia swerved to avoid contact and almost slid off the road. Hands clamped tight on the steering wheel, she reminded herself not to slam on the brakes. If she did, she'd definitely go into a spin and probably wreck.

She fishtailed, gliding over the icy road, all but stealing the breath in her lungs. Finally, with her careful maneuvering, her wheels again caught the road and the truck righted.

If she hadn't been going so slow, if she wasn't familiar with the awful road conditions, if her truck wasn't heavy and her tires weren't good . . .

So many ifs. And the other vehicle hadn't even bothered to slow down.

With relief, Stasia watched its lights disappear far ahead. It took a few minutes more before her heart stopped thumping and she began to relax. She even laughed at her fanciful imagination. Most likely, the people in the truck were no more than drunken vacationers who'd lost their way.

That made a lot more sense than assuming any evil intent against her.

Maintaining her snail's pace, Stasia headed down the steepest road and finally the center of town came into view. Relief stole over her. She'd deliver her message, say goodbye to Harley—assuming he hadn't left town yet—and return to her warm cabin in no time at all.

To keep from picking up speed on the steep incline, she touched her brakes.

Nothing happened.

The truck slipped, tires spinning, and she pressed down harder on the brake.

If anything, the truck went faster.

"Oh, shit. This can't be happening." Hunched over the steering wheel, her every muscle clenched for control, she tried to think. Her wheels hit a hidden pothole in the road, and the truck bounced hard.

Horrified, Stasia tried again, pumping the brake pedal, but it felt spongy and didn't catch. Panicked anew, she stiffened her leg, pressing the pedal all the way to the floorboard.

Nothing.

"No, no, no." Her heart lodged in her throat. Oh, God. This couldn't be happening.

The town, or what most in the area called a town, consisted of no more than a cluster of establishments: grocery, bank, post office, small department store, restaurant, movie theater, and a bar with illusions of being a club.

Farther out, folks could find a lumberyard, furniture stores, and other assorted necessaries, but that involved travel that only the locals indulged in.

Without brakes, her truck roared and bounced at a dangerous rate. Stasia saw cars parked along the cross street at the base of the hill, and a few late-night partiers just heading home.

She had to do something, and she had to do it quickly.

Teeth gritted, she steered the truck to the right, easing it toward the side of the road, hoping to hit the rough gully where friction would help slow her.

Instead, the truck hit a patch of ice and began skidding. Her passenger door ground against the snow-covered hill, careened the truck back out into the street, and, to her horror, sent her into a mind-numbing spin.

She screamed, and seconds later landed against a solid obstacle.

The truck slammed to a stop with jarring impact.

Her seat belt grabbed her with brute force, forcing a grunt of pain. Her head snapped forward, and then back again.

Seconds ticked by before she gathered her wits enough to open her eyes. Disoriented, it took her a minute to realize that she now faced the opposite direction, and was on the wrong side of the road. A mountain of snow piled high by the street crew when clearing the roadway earlier in the day smashed against the driver's side of the truck.

There'd be no driving out of this mess.

Fingers shaking, she turned off the engine and then just sat there, catching her breath, taking quick inventory of herself and her truck.

Her heart thumped hard enough to cause pain.

Her breath rushed, causing a sick echo in the quiet interior of the truck.

Other than being rattled, *very* rattled, she felt . . . uninjured.

Because the impact was all on the side of her truck and not the front, her airbags hadn't opened. With a hand to her forehead, she closed her eyes in relief. Her seat belt had kept her secure. Somehow, she had survived intact.

Knowing she couldn't just sit there, Stasia took a few deep breaths, then, hands shaking, she unhooked her seat belt. Crawling over to the passenger door, she got out to investigate her situation. It was so dark she could barely see outside the beam of the headlights, but it was clear that both front tires and one back tire were deep in a snow-filled ditch. It'd take roadside assistance to get her truck free.

Not that it mattered. Without brakes, she wasn't driving anywhere.

Now what?

A gust of wind almost took her off her feet. She pulled her hat lower, covered her nose and mouth with her gloved hands, and looked down the hill, maybe a quarter of a mile away. A few people stared in her direction, but without streetlamps, Stasia doubted they could see her. More likely, they'd just heard the noise and wondered at it.

At least the truck was off the main road, so she wouldn't cause any other wrecks.

Still trembling at the close call, she crawled back inside and turned off her headlights, but turned on her emergency blinkers. She grabbed the contents of her purse from where they had dumped onto the floor and shoved them back inside her purse.

She locked the truck, slung her purse strap securely around her neck, wrapped her arms around herself, and started trekking down the steep hill. Her feet sank so deeply into the crunchy snow that it fell into the tops of her boots and hindered her every step.

Stasia didn't let herself think about the wreck, or why her brakes hadn't worked, or the noises she'd heard long before leaving her cabin.

She concentrated on reaching Harley, and Lord help her, he had better be there. If he'd left already, she didn't know what she would do.

KEEPING all his attention on his cards, Harley shrugged off the female hand on his shoulder. Oddly enough, he wasn't in the mood for a woman, hadn't been in the mood since that strange visit with Anastasia.

Somehow she'd bewitched him, thrown him off his game, at least his game with women. Poker was something altogether different. He'd stayed over to play cards to give the locals a chance to regain their losses, but he kept winning. He couldn't leave with all their money. He had to stay for one more hand.

That was what he told himself anyway. He refused to acknowledge any other possibilities for his reluctance to get on the road.

The small hand touched his shoulder again, and again, he brushed it off. After the first woman had approached him, he'd been distant, almost rude to all interested females. He'd already slept with one of the ladies bothering him, and he wasn't interested in a repeat performance. This was her third attempt of the night, and he was starting to feel surly about it. She'd been pushy to the point of annoyance.

Ignoring how closely she stood behind him, Harley placed his bet. Nothing happened. No one stirred.

Disgruntled, he glanced up at Ned, who sat across the table from him. Ned, as well as everyone else at the table, stared just beyond Harley.

And that prompted Harley to look, too. He glanced over his shoulder, and started in surprise.

Damn! So it wasn't the blonde who'd been bugging him, but an altogether unexpected female visitor.

"Anastasia?" Pushing back his chair in a rush, Harley reached for her. With ice clinging to her eyelashes and her fair skin chafed bright red from the cold wind, she looked more miserable than any woman ever should. "What the hell happened? Are you all right?"

Teeth chattering, she whispered, "Yes."

And then, to Harley's surprise, she slammed up against him and stuck her nose against his throat.

It felt like an ice cube, and he jumped.

She held on to him like a lifeline, trembling uncontrollably. It was late, the storm had worsened, but here she was.

As he put his arms around Anastasia, three of the women he'd ignored glared at him, but to hell with it. He obviously had a few things to attend to other than a card game or a few bruised egos. "I'm out, guys."

Ned crowed, "That means you lose!"

"Fine."

"No." Still shaking like an earthquake, Anastasia pushed back and sputtered, "Finish your hand, Harley. I'll wait."

Like hell! Her stoicism nearly made him hit the roof. For days he'd been thinking of her, *wanting her*, to the point that he'd turned down other women more suited to his special tastes.

Now Anastasia was here, frozen but in one piece.

It was clear that she'd come looking for him.

No way in hell was he waiting. "Take the pot, Ned."

When Anastasia started to speak, Harley gave her a stern look and she went quiet again. After quickly collecting his personal belongings, Harley led her toward the bar.

"Coffee, Sheila. Lots of sugar and a little cream."

Seeing Anastasia's state, the owner, working tonight as a barmaid, brought the order in a hurry.

"Harley?"

"Yeah?"

"Like the pied piper, you have a following."

He glanced back and saw that all three women had clustered up closer, and were now watching him with mixed expressions of annoyance, yearning, and jealousy. He shook his head. "Don't worry about them."

"If you say so."

A million questions clamored in his mind, but Harley worked in order of priorities. He peeled off Anastasia's coat and sodden hat, then her gloves. They were good quaility, sturdy, but not enough to fend off the weather tonight.

"You're soaked. What the hell were you doing? Playing outside?" He hung everything on a wall peg without much hope of them drying anytime soon.

Anastasia ignored the question to wrap her fingers around the mug of hot coffee that Sheila offered. She didn't sip it. Not yet. She just held it under her nose and absorbed the warmth, the steam.

"I'm waiting, Anastasia."

Sighing shakily, she closed her eyes and took one small sip of the coffee. "Your uncle called."

"Uncle Satch?"

Her eyes opened, and she sipped again. "You have other uncles?"

He would not start this game with her again. "What did Satch want?"

"For you to call him."

"Why?"

"I don't know." Shaking so badly that she almost spilled the coffee, Anastasia said, "It's important, but he said no one's dead or dying."

Harley marveled at her. So she hadn't pried, but she had found out enough to keep him from panicking. "You walked here to tell me that?"

Steam from the coffee lifted around her face. "I'm not stupid."

The hat had flattened her hair, her nose was cherry red, her cheeks wind-chapped. She looked frosty and uncomfortable and . . . adorable.

Harley narrowed his eyes. "So you didn't walk?"

She shook her head. "Did you know that your cell phone isn't working?"

"No reception."

"Your uncle couldn't reach you."

Harley studied her. "You could have given the number of the bar."

For a single heartbeat, Anastasia looked like a trapped doe. "I didn't think of that."

Or maybe she'd wanted an excuse to see him again. Insane as it seemed, that thought brightened his mood. "If you drove here, then it must've been with your windows down, and that doesn't make any sense."

She swallowed hard, shook her head, and finally looked up at him with big dark eyes. "I don't mean to be forward, Harley, but would it be too much to ask if I could burrow up and steal some body heat while you use the phone to call your uncle? I can explain everything after that, but I swear, I've never in my life been this cold."

For inexplicable reasons, her request nearly made Harley hard. "Come on."

Putting one arm around Anastasia, he led her through the crowd toward the back hallway near the bathrooms and the pay phone. Ignoring the hot stares of women and the knowing smiles of men, he used his free hand to unbutton his flannel shirt along the way.

When their positioning in the bar guaranteed a modicum of privacy, he took the coffee from Anastasia and sat it on the floor, then turned her to the wall, opened his shirt, and pulled her against his chest. He put his arms around her under her shirt and rested his chin on the top of her head.

As much as possible, he surrounded her.

With a soft moan, Anastasia crawled into him, as close as she could get.

His thick thermal shirt and her sweatshirt still separated them, but it didn't matter. Feeling Anastasia curl in tight, her breath on his throat, her hands knotted near his abdomen, was more intimate than anything he'd experienced in years. Her back was silky smooth, but chilled, and trembles continued to course through her.

"Call your uncle, please," she muttered against his skin.

He didn't want anything to disturb the moment. "In a minute." A gruffness sounded in his voice, but he hoped that Anastasia didn't detect it.

"Harley," she warned around her shivers. "I nearly froze to death just to relay that message to you. Now call him."

Bossy. But cute. "Fine." Digging change out of his pocket without dislodging Anastasia's position against him, Harley reached out for the phone.

She turned her face so that her cheek rested flat against him.

He opened his other hand on her back, fingers spread wide to keep her pressed close.

Uncle Satch answered on the first ring. "Where the hell are you?"

Well used to his uncle's surly manner, Harley replied in a calmer tone, "In town. Why?"

"I've been trying to reach you for hours."

"So I heard. What's up?"

"That woman with you?"

Rather than make assumptions, Harley asked, "Woman?"

"Anastasia Bradley."

Harley's fingers contracted on her smooth skin, then he began stroking up and down her spine. "Yeah. She's right here." *As close as a fully clothed woman could be to a man.*

"I like her."

"You don't know her, Uncle Satch."

"I know more than you think."

Harley let out an aggrieved sigh. "Did you call me just to talk about women?"

"We weren't talking about women. We were talking about one woman."

"Satch . . ."

"But that's not why I called."

"Then why?" His uncle wouldn't hunt him down without reason. "What's happening?"

Tension sizzled through the phone line. "Just about everything."

"Meaning?"

"Magazine interviews, promo shots, a new sponsor, and get this—a friggin' commercial."

Harley went still. "You're shitting me."

Anastasia stirred against him, and Harley tightened his hold. He wanted to keep her right where she was—at least until she warmed up.

Uncle Satch said, "I told you I was getting the word out. Well, my boy, it's out. The SBC has caught on to your background, all the shit that's kept you out of the title fights—"

Alarm slammed into Harley. No. Hell no. He didn't want his private life thrown out there for public consumption. "Wait a damn minute, Uncle Satch. You know how I feel about that. I don't—"

"You're a real human-interest story, my boy, the poster child for overcoming adversity. You represent the spirit of a true MMA fighter, a winner against all odds, private and public. And now the SBC is convinced you're the next best thing to sliced bread."

Through gritted teeth, Harley said, "I don't want to be a poster child."

"After all you did for Candace—"

On a surge of anger, Harley gripped the phone tighter, so tight that he felt capable of breaking it. "Listen to me, Uncle Satch. You will leave my mother out of this."

"Your mother was my sister. I can speak of her whenever I want."

Fuck. "Satch . . ."

"And that selfish twit, Sandy."

Harley's voice lowered to a furious growl. "Sandy is nothing to you, and I will *not* have her mentioned. Period. Ever."

Anastasia pushed back to look at him, curiosity and sympathy in her eyes. Damn it, the invasion on his privacy was starting already, and Harley felt his careful control slip a notch.

No. He wouldn't let that happen.

Uncle Satch was like a freakin' freight train once he got started. He didn't hear anything other than his own intentions.

But Harley would make him listen. "Uncle Satch—"

"What really got to the powers-that-be is this last time, with you getting taken out of the fight because you helped Sublime's woman. If that isn't newsworthy—"

"It's *not.*"

"—then I don't know what is. You're a hero without even trying, and now that it's getting out there, your upcoming fight is causing a huge stir. You and I know that you're invincible, but because of outside forces, you're being seen as the underdog."

"I don't give a shit what anyone else thinks."

"Well, I do. And right now, everyone wants you to win."

Not his opponent, Harley thought, whoever it might turn out to be. Trying a different tack, he asked, "Do I even know who I'm fighting yet? Is Sublime going to give me another shot?"

"Now, Harley, be patient. You'll get the title shot. But given the turn of events, the SBC wants to build you up a little more, really capitalize on your growing popularity to bring in the crowds. Everyone's suddenly interested in you, and we need to feed off that before we give them the big prize."

Harley groaned. He didn't want to feed anyone. He wanted the belt.

And he wanted it now.

"The websites are going nuts—you're all the buzz in the chat rooms, and fan sites are popping up left and right. I've got an official site in the works, but in the meantime, the fans are doing a great job of showcasing your talents."

Satch finished all that by saying, "With so much going on, I need you back here."

God. Harley could only pray that his uncle didn't turn things into a circus. Rubbing his chin on the top of Anastasia's head, he said, "I was heading out tonight anyway."

"Good. We've got to tailor this thing around your training."

"Thing?"

"The headlines, the wave of interest."

Trying again, Harley said, "Listen to me, Uncle Satch. I was never out for the attention. You know that. I just want to fight and win."

"Yeah, well, nobility doesn't pay the bills."

"Stow the sarcasm. We're not hurting for cash and you know it."

"Damn it, Harley, the truth is, you're too damn good-looking. Couple that with an endearing background—"

"*Endearing?*"

"—and now the SBC wants you as the new face of the sport."

Worse and worse. "What the hell happened with Sublime? I thought he was the damn face."

"That's just it. Sublime has drawn in this huge female audience. The demographics went from fifteen percent women to twenty-five. The organization wants to capitalize on that growth and according to them, you're the next hottest guy fighting."

Hottest? Harley frowned in distaste. "Let Sublime keep that rep. I don't want it."

"Look, forget Sublime. This is about you now."

Fresh alarm sent his adrenaline surging. *Forget Sublime?* Like hell.

Harley liked Sublime well enough, but that had nothing to do with the sport, or with winning a belt. Sublime was the guy standing in his way to the title, period. "What's going on, Uncle Satch?" His muscles clenched. "Is Sublime pulling out?"

"Now, Harley—"

"Answer me, damn it!"

"He's beat two contenders in rapid succession."

"Two?" Well hell, Harley thought. He'd missed one somewhere, when he never missed a single fight. Of course, he'd been so wrapped up in the rehab on his elbow, isolated from the rest of the fight world . . .

"Yeah, two. He fought O'Brian in your place, then four weeks after that, he knocked out Houston in the first round. He's in high demand everywhere, from product endorsements to speaking engagements on every damn sport show or segment in the country. And Harley . . . the man loves his wife. What can I say? Simon Evans is not a man content to be without challenges."

"What the fuck does that mean?" Did Sublime no longer consider him a challenge? Did he just assume he'd win without accepting the possibility of a loss to his golden record?

Satch let out a long sigh. "He's thinking of moving into a different arena. He's been offered a real lucrative deal to announce fights instead of participate in them. He's in negotiations right now. If things work out . . . he's retiring again."

Holding the phone away from his ear, Harley struggled to keep his disappointment in check. He needed to vent. A fight would do.

Or a good fuck.

He glanced down at Anastasia.

She shivered against him, small and tender and . . . in need of his warmth.

Shit. He didn't just want sex. He could have that now, tomorrow, and the next day, no problem.

He wanted Anastasia.

One calming breath didn't help, so Harley drew another. Then another.

When Anastasia tried to look up at him, he crushed her close, leaving her no choice but to relax against him.

Finally he brought the phone back to his ear. "So fighting Sublime is a long shot now?"

"Afraid so, but this is even better."

Trying to put his foot down, Harley snarled, "I am not doing anything stupid."

"I wouldn't ask you to. All you've got to do is what you've always done."

"And that is?"

"Seduce the ladies and charm the men—but you have to do it at key times, like when the right people are paying attention."

"I hope you're kidding." His uncle suggested a complete farce. Harley wasn't an actor, and he wasn't going to start putting on fronts for the press.

"The bad attitude won't change anything, Harley, so knock it off. Look at it for what it is—just one more step toward the big prize."

"I don't see how."

"It's all tied together. The favorites get all the breaks."

"That's bullshit and you know it. Sure, the fans like some fighters more than others. But everyone earns their position; no one gets it for free."

His uncle let out a long sigh. "After missing several opportunities—"

"*Satch,*" Harley warned, feeling his muscles twitch again. "Don't go there."

"—you need the damned opportunity offered to you before you can take advantage of it. Don't fool yourself: the SBC is out to make money, and fan favorites bring in the cash, so if the audience demands it, it'll happen that much sooner."

He might have a point. Not that Harley would admit it.

"We need you in a title bout, and we need you to win in a big way. No judges' decision. We need a knockout or a submission. Then we'll really capitalize on all the attention and before you know it, you'll be in Sublime's position, with a dozen opportunities knocking on your door and time enough to choose what you really want."

"Not to put pressure on me or anything, right?" Without really thinking about it, Harley withdrew his hand from under Anastasia's shirt and stroked his fingers through her hair.

It had a further calming effect on him.

"You're a damn boulder, Harley. You can take some pressure."

Harley rolled his eyes. "Yeah, I suppose I can." Arguing with his uncle was pointless. In the end, Harley would do what he wanted, and not a single thing more. Besides, although Anastasia no longer shivered so badly, she was still clinging to him, trying to get warm through and through. She needed his attention—and he'd prefer talking with her than his uncle. "Soon as I see Anastasia back to her cabin, I'll head home and we can figure all this out."

"Tonight?"

"I'll get home tonight, but it'll be late. We can talk in the morning."

"First thing, then. Breakfast at eight—no later. We've got plans to make."

"Fine. But, Uncle Satch, do *not* agree to a single damn thing until I get a chance to see what it is, and think about it. I mean it."

"Let me know when you get in, Harley. Drive careful. We can't afford for anything to happen this time."

Didn't he know it? "Just try to relax. Things will be okay. I feel it."

"From your mouth to His ears."

Harley hung up the phone and looped his hands at the small of Anastasia's back. It was easier to focus on her than the upcoming issues with the SBC. "Better?"

"Yes. Thank you."

She didn't pull away, and Harley didn't urge her to. He liked their current position, even if it equaled a sweet torture.

"Who's Simon Evans?"

So she had been listening? "A fighter, better known as Sublime. Real good-looking, or so the women say."

"He shaves his head?"

"Yeah."

"I've seen him." She nuzzled her face against him. "He really is gorgeous." Then she tilted her head back. "But no more so than you."

Given the recent news from the SBC, Harley didn't take her comment as a compliment. It was all bullshit. He'd win favor with fans and the SBC brass because he was the best, not because women found him attractive.

Changing the subject, he touched her still-cold nose and said, "Time's up, Anastasia. You obviously didn't get this frozen from driving here, so start at the beginning and tell me exactly what happened."

CHAPTER 4

"I'M not really sure."

She sounded sleepy, and that worried Harley. He put his palm to her forehead, but her skin no longer felt like ice. "Okay. So what do you *think* happened?"

With her forehead again on his sternum, she said, "I lost my brakes."

"Lost your brakes?"

"Coming down the hill to town." Another shiver, this one likely from nerves, ran through her. "It was so icy, and the wind was enough to toss a semi off the road. I was going slow, real slow. Then I went to touch my brakes—and nothing happened."

Harley went rigid. "You sure you didn't just slide a little?" The look she gave him had him verbally backing up. "I'm not insulting your intelligence, Anastasia. It's just that the roads are shit tonight and even the best driver could lose control."

"Tell me something I don't know. After I deliberately steered into the gulley to try to slow the truck, I did a few spins and ended up facing the opposite way on the wrong side of the road. Luckily, I slammed into a snowbank."

Harley got an awful visual of her inside the truck. "You call that luck?"

"It's better than crashing through a building, or God forbid, running over someone." She snuggled tighter to him. "I had the brake to the floor, Harley, and it didn't matter. The truck just picked up speed. I didn't know what else to do."

He returned her embrace. "Given you didn't kill yourself or anyone else, I'd say you did great."

"Thanks. But then I had to walk about a quarter of a mile to get here. That doesn't sound that far, except that it's so damn cold outside. The wind is brutal, and the snow's coming down so fast that half the time I couldn't see where I was stepping. It was up to my knees—and even higher than that whenever I accidentally went off the road."

Good God. Harley pictured her struggling through the storm and it made him furious. He doubted she weighed more than a hundred and ten pounds, and most of that was soft curves, not sturdy muscle.

Only a quarter of a mile away—but she could have died out there and because she lived alone, who would have noticed?

And he'd kept her waiting while he talked with his uncle on the phone. "You should have said something, damn it."

She shrugged.

"Were you hurt at all?"

"Amazingly enough, not even a scratch."

"You're sure? Sometimes with car wrecks, you don't realize how badly you're hurt until after the shock wears off."

"I'm cold, Harley, maybe angry, and a little scared. But I'm not in shock."

Harley wasn't entirely convinced of that. Most women might become clingy after the fright of a near wreck.

Anastasia wasn't one of them.

In all his dealings with her, he'd gotten the impression of staunch independence and incredible strength. The drama of a crash might make her edgier, but it'd take more than that for her to show so much vulnerability.

Something more had happened. If it wasn't shock that had her crushing so close, then what? "I understand scared. You could have been killed. But why be angry?"

With emotion simmering in her dark eyes—the kind of emotion that could be fury—Anastasia looked up at him. "Right before I wrecked, someone was following me, right on my bumper." She drew a shuddering breath. "Almost like the driver wanted to force me off the road."

Harley held her arms just above her elbows. With his thumbs, he caressed her. "So who was it?"

She shook her head. "It was too dark for me to tell. But on a night like this, why would anyone, even an idiot, drive so recklessly?"

"A drunk, maybe?"

"It's possible." Her eyes narrowed. "But you know what I think?"

Harley braced himself. "What?"

"I think whoever was trailing behind me is also the person who cut my brake lines."

HARLEY was big and safe, and best of all, warm. It felt very nice to have his arms around her. But Stasia knew she had to stop hanging on him. Whatever had just happened to her, it wasn't his problem. He needed to head home, tonight, right now. He had other, very important priorities and she was a big girl who could attend to her own issues.

Putting her palms to his chest, Stasia tried to ease him back. "I'm okay now."

He didn't budge. "No, you're not."

Stasia felt the tension vibrating through him. And here she'd only been focusing on her own upset! She stopped pressing away to look up at him.

While he'd spoken to his uncle, she'd been unable to tune out Harley's end of the conversation. It didn't take great insight to know that he butted heads with good old Uncle Satch on a regular basis. "Harley?"

He took one hard step back, picked up her coffee, and

handed it to her. "It's cooled enough now. Drink it, and then we'll go look at your truck."

"You need to head home."

"I will. Afterward."

Trying to decide how to handle him, she sipped at the coffee. "Harley, listen. I'm sorry. I shouldn't have dumped all that on you. I just . . . I had to say it out loud, that's all. I don't expect you to—"

As if in deep thought, he spoke without looking at her. "Shush and drink the coffee."

"I will not shush!"

He glanced at her in a dismissive way. "Fine. Talk if it makes you feel better."

But she could tell he wouldn't be listening. He was clearly making plans—plans that included her—and he didn't intend to discuss it with her.

"You can't be serious."

His brow went up. "About?"

"Any of this." Did she look like a child in need of his help? "For one thing, it's too dark to see anything on my truck."

"I can see fine."

Deterring him wouldn't be easy. "The snow will already be covering the truck, so trying to look at it would be pointless. Besides, I'd rather go to the police."

That got his attention. "Yeah? Do you have police here?"

"Well . . . I guess. I mean, surely we do, right?" Stasia had never had need of law enforcement, so she couldn't be sure. Spending only one season in an area, sometimes less, supplied her with the basics, but not all the ins and outs. "Doesn't every town have at least a sheriff or something?"

"I don't know." Hands on his hips, Harley paced away, then back again. "Something about this doesn't sound right."

Stasia didn't need his help, but she wanted his trust. "You don't believe me?"

His frown worse, Harley turned and planted one fist on

the wall beside her head. He leaned in until his nose nearly touched hers. "Of course I believe you. Why wouldn't I? You're not the hysterical type to make up crazy stories."

She felt caged in, but his words reassured her, and did more to warm her than the coffee had. "That's nice of you to say, but you don't really know me."

"Yeah, I do." His gaze went to her mouth, but shot right back to her eyes. "Even before you told me about the other vehicle, I knew something else was going on."

"You did?"

He slowly nodded. "You've been plastered on me like a wet shirt, when usually you go out of your way to keep an emotional distance."

Stasia cleared her throat. "Being *plastered* to you would be a physical closeness. Not emotional."

The corners of his mouth lifted in the slightest of smiles. "Maybe, but tonight it was both." His hand cupped the side of her head. "And just so you know, I wasn't complaining. Not even close."

Because he was dead-on, Stasia didn't debate it with him. "Okay, then . . . thank you."

Changing his stance, Harley situated himself so he could chafe her arms when she wasn't sipping coffee, smooth her hair when she was. He pampered her, which she hadn't expected and wasn't sure she wanted, but enjoyed all the same.

When she'd finished all the coffee, Harley stepped back and looked her over. His gaze lingered in key places, not that he could see much through her bulky layers. But the heat of his gaze made her wish he wasn't leaving so soon.

In only a few hours, he'd be gone—until next year.

"You know what, Harley?" she whispered. "I'm going to miss you when you're gone."

Eyes so light a blue should have looked icy. On Harley, they radiated the same warmth as the center of a flame. No wonder others, even sports commentators, had made note of the unsettling intensity of his gaze.

"I have a million questions. But your clothes are wet in more places than they're dry." His voice was low and gruff and, in some way, seductive. "We need to get you out of them."

Anastasia froze, then forced a careless laugh. "And to think people told me you were smooth."

A smile shown in his eyes. "You know what I mean, honey."

Endearments? Now? She couldn't fathom why a bright red nose and shivering limbs would encourage him to intimacy. "Honey?"

With an arm around her, Harley started walking her toward the front of the bar. "Anastasia is too many syllables to keep spewing."

"Spewing?"

He glanced down at her with sympathy and understanding. "There's no reason to be nervous with me. I know you've had a rough time tonight; I have no intention of coercing you into bed."

Like he'd even need to, Stasia thought with disgust. At the moment, nothing sounded more appealing to her than crawling up close to Harley and staying there, for any and all reasons.

At the back of her mind, she knew someone had tried to hurt her tonight. Not knowing why only made it worse. Being close to someone so big and strong would be only one of many enticements to snuggle with Harley. "Right, sorry," she muttered. "My brain is still a little frozen."

Without interrupting his pace, Harley cupped her jaw, tipped her head toward him, and kissed her forehead as if it meant nothing, when it felt like so much.

"Tell me what your family calls you."

A simple, avuncular kiss on the head shouldn't have tripped her up, but it took her a second to unglue her tongue. "Why?"

"Because you have to have a nickname, and while I think 'Anastasia' is pretty, it's too damn long."

She agreed. "I've always thought that parents shouldn't name their children anything with more than two syllables."

Harley grinned.

"They call me Stasia."

His hot hand pressed against the small of her back. "I guess that'll work since you have a problem with endearments."

He hadn't given her a chance to decide if she had a problem with endearments or not. So much had happened, not the least of which was his rapid about-face concerning her. He'd gone from keeping her at arm's length, to treating her like a little sister, to touching her like a lover.

After leading her back through the crowd to the front of the bar, he stopped by her coat, hat, and scarf hanging on the wall. He bunched the material of her coat in one fist— and was displeased.

Not understanding him, Stasia said, "You're going to give yourself wrinkles frowning like that."

He turned to face her. "Your coat is still wet, so it's not going to be much good to you in this weather."

His words rang with accusation. "Don't look at me like that. It's a good coat, a *warm* coat, and it has weatherproofness built in."

To make his point, Harley lifted a saturated lapel. "That's a joke, right?"

Seeing it reminded her of how it felt to wear it, and she shuddered. "No." She yanked the coat out of his hands. "It *is* a good coat and it's usually more than adequate. The problem is that I never expected to wear it in weather this bad for so long. But then I never expected to lose my brakes either, or to have to walk into town, or . . ."

Her voice trailed off; he wasn't really listening to her anyway.

As he took his own coat off the hooks, he said, "You can wear mine."

"No."

Very slowly, he turned to face her. "It's not up for debate, Stasia."

"I agree. I'm not wearing it, and that's that. And before you get all huffy about it—"

"I don't get huffy."

"—you should remember that I don't take orders from you."

He looked at the ceiling for a double beat before pinning her again with his gaze. "Think of it as a gentlemanly offer, not an order."

"Doesn't matter. Either way, I don't want you to sacrifice for me."

"Sacrifice?" Harley took a beleaguered stance. "Maybe you failed to notice, but I'm not already chilled to the bone, and I have on a couple of layers. I'll be fine."

Like a layer of flannel and thermal would be enough to protect him from the cold? She shook her head. "No. Thank you."

"You're going to wear it, Stasia." He softened that statement by adding, "I don't want you to freeze."

Hearing him say her shortened name did funny things to her. Only family and a few past boyfriends called her that. "I don't want you to freeze either."

"You've seen me in my underwear."

At that, a few people glanced up, making Stasia feel conspicuous. "Yeah, so?"

"So you had to notice that I have a fair amount of meat on my bones, especially compared to you."

She shrugged. "I noticed."

"Good, then you'll trust me when I say I'll be warm enough."

God knew she had bigger concerns than who wore what coat, but still she heard herself say, "This is ridiculous. I really don't think—"

Suddenly the entire area died.

All lights. All sounds. Gone.

Inside and out.

Even the people stopped talking, stopped in their tracks.

Harley hauled Stasia behind him, and she could feel the abrupt fighting tension in him. He moved again, and her back bumped into the wall.

How had he known the wall was there? The darkness

was so encompassing, she couldn't see her own hand in front of her face!

Without so much as a second thought, he'd protected her back with the wall, and her front with himself.

Obviously, Harley believed her about her brakes.

"Sheila," he called out, "don't you have a flashlight or something?"

"I'm on it." A glass broke, Sheila cursed, and after a few seconds more of rustling, a bright utility light flashed on. After scanning the crowd of blank faces, she announced, "Must be another power outage."

Everyone looked toward the windows but could see nothing in the black abyss.

Stasia felt like weeping. Damn it, she'd wanted nothing more than to return to her cabin, take another hot shower, and then curl up beneath her warm blankets in bed. Unless she got back home quickly, her woodstove would die out, leaving the cabin cold. And without electricity, her meager water supply would provide only enough warm water for a flash shower.

Thinking about a *cold* shower made her groan.

"What's wrong?" Harley asked her.

"Nothing."

"You made a sound."

"Of disappointment, Harley, that's all. My cabin is going to get cold quick."

"Yeah."

He kept her behind him, but she could practically feel him thinking. Probably trying to figure out a way to help her.

Not in this lifetime.

"Harley, stop. It's not your problem. I'm a big girl, and I can take care of myself. And don't forget, you promised your uncle you'd get on the road."

"After I took you home."

"I would appreciate the ride. But that's all."

He turned to face her. In the darkness, Stasia could only see the glimmer of his eyes.

"Do you have any enemies?"

She laughed—but Harley didn't. "Enemies who would cut the power to an entire town? No, Harley, I can't think of anyone resourceful enough to do that. It's just an outage, that's all."

Still he didn't relax. "Forget the outage and think about your truck. It's possible that something just went wrong with your truck, right? A maintenance problem maybe? Have your brakes been scrubbing at all?"

"No. I would have had them checked if they did." She put a hand to her forehead. "I maintain my truck, Harley. I have the oil changed every three thousand miles, and everything is checked over then. Any little dings, any lights that come on, I get the truck serviced."

Harley put a fist beneath her chin and tipped up her face. "That's what I figured. You strike me as the type who takes care of her belongings." His thumb brushed her bottom lip. "So, Stasia, who tampered with your truck? A *friend*?"

It made her brain cramp to think about it. "I don't know. I guess there are people who don't like me." One particular couple came to mind right away. Then she shook her head. "But I can't think of anyone who'd want me dead. And taking out my brakes is the kind of thing that could kill someone."

"Exactly." His hand went from her chin to the side of her face. "Someone tried to hurt you, you don't have a phone, and now you don't have electricity."

She winced and hoped he couldn't see her.

"Do you really think I'm just going to leave you alone with all that?"

Oh God. She didn't want to be responsible for keeping him away from his uncle. "Look around, Harley. I'm not alone." And if he'd give her a few seconds to think, she could probably figure out what to do. Because he was right; in the off chance that someone came looking for her, she didn't want to be alone in her cabin.

Harley continued to stand there, saying nothing, but she felt his disapproval.

Damn him.

"I have an idea."

Sighing, he dropped his hands. "Let's hear it."

"If you wouldn't mind too much, I could grab a few things from my cabin, then ride with you to the nearest motel. You'll be taking the expressway home, so I'm sure there'll be a lot of choices along the way. You can just drop me off and then be on your way."

In answer, Harley ran a hand through his hair.

"It probably won't add but another hour to your trip."

"It's not that. I have time to spare."

"If you're feeling gallant, don't. I'm a big girl. I know how to deal with my own problems. I'll wait until tomorrow when the roads are clearer and the electricity is back on, then I'll catch a ride home and get everything straightened out."

The crowd stirred uneasily. A few candles and a flashlight weren't sufficient to keep card games going. Then a fight suddenly erupted—someone must've caught someone else trying to make off with the pot.

Curses filled the air. Crashes sounded around them. Several people headed outside, a few others came in. From one heartbeat to the next, chaos reigned.

"Time for us to go," Harley said to her, and two seconds later, he began stuffing her into his coat.

This time she didn't argue. "Fine. Thank you. But I can dress myself."

He pulled the collar together under her chin. "I don't know what it is, Stasia, but something's not right tonight. I feel it. The sooner we're away from here, the better I'll like it." He took her hand and turned them to go; Ned stood there, blocking them.

A lighter in Ned's hand gave off scant illumination. The play of light and shadows turned his craggy face into an eerie visage. "I need a favor, Harley."

Again, Stasia found herself shoved behind Harley, but he kept one hand on her as if to reassure himself that she wouldn't get taken away.

"I'm in a rush, Ned."

"Yeah, and you're with Anastasia, I know." That clearly puzzled him; but then, she had never dated while staying at the cabin, so she could understand Ned's confusion. "I'm sorry to intrude."

"What is it?"

Ned's lighter went out. He muttered to himself, clicked it several times, and it came on again. "Sorry. The thing is, my ride just passed out drunk."

"Your ride?"

"Yeah, me and Gene were hanging out all day and just ended up here. He drove."

Harley rubbed his face. "So what do you want from me?"

"I don't live far from here, but it's too damn cold for me to walk."

"And too dark," Stasia added, thinking of the people who'd run her off the road. On a night like this, it'd be far too easy for someone to get seriously hurt.

"Can you give me a lift?" Ned asked.

Harley didn't immediately answer.

Stasia nudged him for his rudeness.

"I'm just a few miles down the road," Ned promised him. "It won't take you long."

"Couldn't you ask someone else? I'm anxious to get Stasia back to her place."

To Stasia, that sounded far too sexually suggestive, so she hurriedly explained, "I got stuck out in the weather when my truck went off the road."

"You weren't hurt?"

"No, I'm fine, just anxious to get back to my nice warm cabin."

"Yeah, me, too." Ned cleared his throat again. "But that's just it, Harley. You're the only one I know with a vehicle who can make it there."

Stasia said, "Like me, Ned lives up the hill."

Harley turned to her. "And you know this how?"

Positive that Harley glared at her, but unable to see him,

she reached out—and her hand bumped into his rock-solid abdomen.

She snatched it back. He was closer than she realized. "It's a small town, Harley." Damn, her voice sounded strained. "Everyone here knows everyone else."

Harley said nothing, but Stasia knew he watched her, and because it unnerved her more, she stepped to the side of him.

Sheila lit more lanterns and when she placed one closer to them, Ned put away the lighter. He now stood in shadows, but didn't look quite so creepy.

"Of course we'll give you a ride, Ned."

Putting his arm around her shoulders, Harley asked her near her ear, "I agreed to that?"

"You're a reasonable man. You were going to."

Ned looked back and forth between them. "I appreciate it."

Harley gave up with ill grace. "I'd leave you in here until I had my Jeep going, but I'm not sure that's a good idea."

Stasia agreed. "I go where you go."

He smoothed a hand over her hair, dragged the hat down over her head to cover her ears, and said, "Then let's get to it."

The second they stepped outside, a gust of strong wind nearly toppled Stasia. Harley kept her tucked in to his side, shielding her with his body while they located his Jeep. It took another half a minute for him to get the near-frozen door open.

He started the engine and turned on the heat. While Stasia huddled in her seat, trying to stay warm, Harley and Ned cleared the windows. Even freezing, she would have offered to help with that, especially since she wore Harley's coat, but she already knew it'd be useless.

When Harley finally got behind the wheel, Stasia stared at him. He didn't shiver. Hell, his nose hadn't even turned red. But he did hold his hands out to the heater and let them warm.

"How are you?" he asked Stasia. "Warm enough?"

That should have been her question to him. "I'm fine. I think your Jeep is warmer than the bar."

"Probably." He looked over his shoulder to the backseat. "Buckle up, Ned."

"Oh, right." Ned, who'd been busy hugging himself and shivering uncontrollably, struggled with the restraint before finally getting it latched into place. "Got it."

Harley put the Jeep in drive and rolled out of the parking space.

Stasia marveled at that. She'd expected him to be stuck at least a little. "I like your car."

"Jeep. They're a vehicle all their own, and yeah, I like it, too." He drove with proper caution, almost as slowly as Stasia had, and they made it to Ned's place without encountering another car on the road.

When Harley pulled up to the driveway, Ned released his seat belt and sat forward. "I really appreciate it, Harley."

"No problem," Harley said, but added, "Stasia insisted."

"Want me to leave my coat with you?"

"I'm all right, thanks."

"You're sure?"

Stasia saw Harley's impatience, but Ned seemed oblivious. "Positive. Go on in. We'll wait here until you're in the door."

Ned thanked them again, said his good byes, and reluc tantly left the warmth of the vehicle. Taking very high steps—almost hops—he dashed through the thick snow across his lawn to the front stoop. If he had a walkway, snow had long since buried it. After a few seconds of fumbling, he got the front door open, flipped on the porch light, and waved them off.

"You should have taken his coat," Stasia told Harley. "Or I could have taken it and given you back yours."

"The man smells of day-old sweat. No thanks."

"That's just Ned. He's clean, but I think the smell of his garage clings to him."

"Ned owns his own business?"

"You pass it on the way to the cabin, but it sort of sits off the road behind some trees. I'll show you." They rode in silence until Stasia saw Ned's garage. "There it is. He does routine maintenance and repairs. Ned might seem a little goofy, but he does a good job, so he stays busy."

Harley didn't answer, and Stasia looked at him. He kept glancing in the rearview mirror.

"What are you doing?"

"I thought I saw headlights."

She jerked around and stared, but they'd gone around a bend and she couldn't see anything. Voice low, she asked, "Do you think it's the same truck?"

"Don't be afraid, Anastasia. I'm not going to let anyone hurt you."

His arrogance chased off her unease. "Listen up, Tarzan, I wasn't asking for your protection."

"You've got it anyway." His shoulders flexed. "And good thing for you, because here he comes."

"Oh, God." She twisted around again. Far behind them, headlamps shone against the darkness of the night. "Do you really think it's the same truck that tried to run me off the road?"

"I guess we'll find out." Harley shifted, settling into his seat and getting a firm grip on the steering wheel.

The lights closed in.

"Whoever it is, he's driving faster than us."

Harley agreed. "He's catching up."

Stasia squeezed her eyes shut. "I can't believe this."

"Believe it." He glanced at her briefly, then returned his attention to the road and rearview mirror. "Wanna tell me about any enemies while there's still time?"

Her stomach knotted. "It's far-fetched."

"Then this is the night for it."

Stasia had to agree. She looked over her shoulder again. The truck gained on them. Because of the storm, it'd take at least another ten minutes to make it to her cabin.

Not enough time.

"It's a long story that, by necessity, I'm going to shorten."

"Go."

"One client misunderstood my interest in him. He thought it was more personal and . . . and he told his wife that he wanted a divorce so he could marry . . . me."

Harley whistled.

Keeping an eye on the approaching truck, Stasia explained, "We had never done anything intimate, I swear. I only encouraged him about his business and talked to him about family problems as I do all my clients, but—"

"You don't need to justify yourself to me."

Good thing, because she had no justification.

The lights drew closer.

Heart hammering, Stasia rushed through the rest of her tale. "When he told me his intent, I set him straight. I told him I had *no* interest in him personally."

Harley snorted. "Bet he took that well."

She shook her head. "He refused to believe me. He hounded me for months, first trying to court me and then railing at me and calling me names. It got so ugly. Finally he tried to go back to his wife, but she couldn't forgive him." The memories burned, and she lowered her voice to a whisper. "She now suffers severe depression."

Lacking her emotion, Harley said, "Guess he blames you for that too, huh?"

Stasia blamed herself. She should have seen his infatuation, should have been clearer, should have . . . "I haven't heard from him for a month or so."

"This is why you're taking time off work?"

"Yes." The headlights reflected off the mirrors. "Harley, he's going to hit us."

"Not if I hit him first."

CHAPTER 5

S TASIA couldn't believe her ears. *"What did you say?"*
"Hold on." Harley slammed on the brakes, and the truck, taken by surprise, swerved hard in an attempt to miss rear-ending them.

It wasn't entirely successful.

The front bumper of the truck clipped the back bumper of the Jeep. Harley kept control of the vehicle with some cursing, and ended up on the side of the road.

The truck didn't fare as well. It swerved wildly before hitting a patch of ice and doing a three-sixty. The driver struggled, got the truck aligned, and came to an abrupt stop in the middle of the road, facing away from them.

He didn't drive away.

Stasia stared at Harley in utter horror. *"Are you out of your mind?"*

"They would have rear-ended us, babe. At least this way, I kept control of the situation."

Control? He called this control?

Harley carefully backed up and steered the Jeep around

until his headlights shone into the cab of the other vehicle. "There're only two of them."

"*Only* two?"

He put the Jeep in park. "Listen to me, Anastasia. Soon as I get out, slide over here behind the wheel. Lock the doors, keep the engine running, and stay inside. If you need to, drive around us and go back to town."

Drive around us . . . Her mouth opened, but no words came out.

When she said nothing, Harley moved away from her and opened his seat belt.

"Oh, no you don't!" Stasia launched herself at him. Her stupid seat belt hindered her, so all she could do was grasp at him.

"I'll be right back."

Hands clenched in his shirt, Stasia tried to hold on to Harley. Something in his expression scared her. He looked distant and enraged and . . . she didn't know what to do. "You're not going out there, Harley Handleman, so forget it!"

"I don't have time for you to go hysterical on me now." He pried her fingers loose, held them in his warm hands, and gave her a squeeze. "They're sitting there, Anastasia, just waiting. They aren't going away. If we try to leave, they'll just turn around and follow us, maybe to your cabin. At least here I can see them and know where they are."

Panic had her talking fast and too loud. "Let's just go back to town, then. Someone there can help us."

In contrast, his tone was icy with rage and in complete control. "I don't think they'll let us past them—unless I make them."

"Harley, they could have guns."

His eyes narrowed. "Anyone pulls on a gun on me, I'll make him eat it."

Incredulous, she slumped back in her seat. "You're a lunatic. You really are. Oh dear God, I've aligned myself with a certifiable lunatic."

Stony-faced and eerily calm, Harley opened his door. "Do exactly as I said and you'll be fine." He got out.

"Yeah, fine." Immediately, Stasia scampered over and got behind the wheel. She left the door open, though, so Harley could hear her. "Fine enough to drive past your body after they trample you into the snow."

Harley didn't acknowledge her, but he hadn't taken two steps when she remembered that she wore his coat. If the bullies didn't kill him, he'd freeze to death!

Except . . . he didn't look cold.

Or afraid.

He looked like six feet of walking rage.

Idiot. Fool. The Jeep's headlights lit the scene. Knowing she wouldn't miss anything, Stasia shut the door and locked it.

No need for them both to die.

Her eyes were so wide, it felt like they might fall out of her head. With her heart threatening to explode, a cold sweat sticking to the back of her neck, and her muscles tensed to the point of pain, she waited.

Before Harley reached the truck, two people got out.

Only two, as he'd said.

But they were big brutes, bundled from head to toe in warm layers.

One of them carried a tire iron.

Stasia put the Jeep in gear. If she had to, she'd run over someone to help Harley. She'd—

Everything seemed to happen at once, so fast and smooth that she barely comprehended what her eyes saw.

The unarmed man swung a fist at Harley, and got kicked in the face for the trouble. Obviously the cold hadn't stiffened Harley's muscles. He was fluid and loose and remarkably fast.

The attacker's head snapped back. As if in slow motion, his limbs went limp and blood splattered out, staining the white snow and ice. The man hit the frozen ground hard, lay still for a moment, then curled to his side in evident pain.

He didn't get up.

Roaring, the other man rushed forward, every awkward footstep kicking up clumps of snow and ice. He wielded the tire iron like a bat, drawing it beyond his shoulder and then swinging hard.

Unmoving, Harley waited for him; at the last second he ducked. Momentum would have carried the bully face-first into the snow except that Harley came up with a beefy punch against his chin, then another to his gut, and another to his crotch.

Stasia winced.

Each punch drove the man back another step. The rod fell from his loose fingers and sank into the snow, disappearing.

Harley landed another bomb to his face, and the man flailed backward. With one last punch to the temple, the man toppled backward, arms and legs out like a beached starfish, unmoving.

Slack-jawed, Stasia couldn't believe what she'd just seen. Harley had walked right through two assailants as if they were nothing.

She'd seen Harley fight in the SBC, but those bouts were more methodical. They lasted longer, too. Of course, these men weren't other trained fighters. But they were obviously thugs, practiced in attacking innocents, and Harley had made it look *so* easy to fend them off.

Fascinating.

While she sat there in amazement, Harley half-lifted one man and went through his pockets. Stasia didn't know what he was hunting for, but he must have found it, because he straightened and turned to look at her.

Even from that distance, she saw the electric blue of his eyes reflected in the glaring headlights. Anger vibrated off him. He remained coiled, ready.

And in her peripheral vision, she saw the other man coming toward Harley.

The man held a compact black item, barely visible in the night—until he stepped into the light.

A gun.

Screaming would do her no good, not that she could get a sound past the constriction in her throat anyway.

Without any plan or much forethought, Stasia barreled toward the gunman. The Jeep bounded over snow piles and icy patches at Mach speed. Leaping out of her path, the man half-climbed atop his truck and clung to the side door. She narrowly missed hitting him.

Foot on the brake, Stasia jammed the Jeep into reverse and looked over her shoulder.

Harley gaped at her.

Both men scrambled to get in their truck, hopefully to leave. But Stasia remembered the gun, which meant the men were willing to shoot.

Where better to do that than within the safety of their vehicle, while Harley stood out in the open?

She wouldn't take any chances.

Again, she put the pedal to the floor. The Jeep's wheels spun on the ice, making her fishtail before the deeply treaded tires gained traction.

She aimed for the truck.

If they collided, it'd surely rattle both attackers, giving Harley time to disarm them.

Disappointment smothered her as the truck throttled out of her path. The back end skated sideways before gaining purchase on the road and racing away at breakneck speed.

Frantic with nerves, Stasia watched the taillights grow dim before remembering to hit her brakes. The Jeep freewheeled for a heart-stopping moment, then slid in sideways, and came to a neck-wrenching halt only a foot from Harley.

He hadn't moved.

Stasia threw her door open and explained in a one-word shout: *"Gun."*

Calm personified, Harley put his hands on his hips and closed his eyes. He appeared to be silently counting.

When he opened his eyes and spoke, his voice was low and even. "You want to tell me what the hell you were doing?"

Stasia stared at him in confusion. Adrenaline had her teeth chattering. Anxiety left her breathless. She gulped down a breath and tried again. "He had a *gun*."

Harley just waited.

She reached out and grabbed a fistful of his flannel. "I didn't want him to shoot you!"

Head dropping forward, Harley inhaled deeply. Then again. His breath left a foggy plume between them. "I wish you hadn't interfered, babe."

"*What?*" Stasia considered smacking him. "I *saved* you." She gestured at the truck. "They're leaving."

"Are they? Or are they just retreating so they can return, better prepared?" He lifted a black-and-silver gun to show her. "I appreciate your concern and your effort. But I'd already disarmed one guy, and the other dropped his weapon when you almost ran him over."

"He did?" How had Harley noticed that?

Harley nodded. "With them both being unarmed, I had a good chance to find out who they are and what they want."

Dismay prickled inside her. She had goofed in a big way. She wrapped her arms around herself. "I suppose you planned to beat it out of them?"

"If necessary. At the very least, I would have restrained them so we could get them back to town, and to the authorities—whatever authority there might be in this county."

"I see." Damn, she felt like a dolt.

Harley touched her hair. "There was really no need for you to drive my Jeep off the road."

Uh-oh. Dread burned her throat like acid. "Off the road?"

Releasing her to lean on the roof, Harley said, "The Jeep does great in nasty conditions"—he nodded at the back tires—"but I don't think we'll be driving anywhere tonight."

Stasia stuck her head out the door and looked.

Oh hell. The rear tire had dropped over a sharp ledge in the frozen ground at the side of the road. They were good and stuck.

Numb, she whispered, "What are we going to do?"

"I'll think of something. Sit tight." With that statement, Harley strode away from her.

Like she had any choice?

Stasia watched him plod through the snow to the middle of the road. He searched around for a bit, kicked aside the disturbed snowdrifts, then bent and came up with another gun.

He lifted it to show to her.

They now had both guns, which she supposed was good in case the truck came back. Did their attackers know they were stuck? Would they see them as sitting ducks? Would they gather more weapons and return?

Sick at heart, choking on anxiety, she waited for Harley's return.

With the fighting over, she noticed him starting to shiver. Fluffy snowflakes covered his blond hair and his shoulders. His face was ruddy with the cold. Snow clung to his jeans all the way up to his knees.

And she'd stranded them.

Damn it, she didn't want to cry in front of him, but her day kept going from bad to worse.

"Scoot over," he told her when he got back to the Jeep.

She climbed over the center console. "Harley, I am so sorry."

"Don't worry about it."

He was so cavalier, but how could she *not* worry? Removing a glove, she brushed at the snow clinging to him, put a hand to his jaw. He had beard shadow coming in, and his skin was cold. "Are you okay?"

"Yeah." Distracted, he brought her palm to his mouth and kissed it, then released her as if the intimate touch hadn't happened at all.

Stasia sat in stupefied silence while he checked both guns, set them in the cup holders, and reached past her to the glove department. "I need you to carry a few things. Can you do that?"

Before she could reply, he dropped a slim flashlight, a vehicle registration, and a proof of insurance card into her lap.

"Okay, sure." She tried to be as calm as him. "Why do you need your proof of insurance card?"

"I don't want to leave any ID behind in case the Jeep gets ransacked."

That made sense. Good thing one of them was still able to think straight. "Where do you want me to carry this stuff?"

"We're not close enough to your cabin to make it there, and I don't trust those guys not to return. If they want to find you, the first place they'll look is where you live."

She agreed. "So where do we go? We can't walk all the way back to town." Then she held up a hand. "Or I should say, I can't. You seem impervious to the weather, so I have no idea what you can do."

Ignoring most of what she said, Harley moved and spoke quickly, turning off the Jeep and stowing the guns in his waistband beneath his shirts. "We passed that station a little ways back. It's dark there, so they might not have noticed it. I wouldn't have if you hadn't pointed it out as Ned's." He pocketed the keys and opened his door. "Stow that stuff in your pockets and get ready to roll."

"You don't have a coat."

"I know."

When Harley got out of the Jeep, Stasia pulled her glove back on and followed. The Jeep had a generous cargo area. It was packed with luggage and various pieces of athletic equipment. He dug out two hooded sweatshirts, pulled one over his head and handed the other to her. "Hang on to that. You might want it later."

After retrieving one small satchel, he moved the rest of the luggage aside and pulled a storage crate forward.

It amazed her to see him retrieve duct tape, a first-aid kit, flares, a multiheaded screwdriver, and a space blanket out of the crate.

"You travel prepared."

"Always." Loaded down, he locked the Jeep and then hauled her close to his side. He draped the blanket around them both. "We'll share body heat. Try to move quickly. I want to be inside the station before the goons get brave and make another pass at us."

"Ned keeps it locked up."

"Don't worry. It's not a problem."

Of course not. Nothing was a problem for Harley Handleman, hero at large. While she was badly shaken, he took it all in stride. With her pockets filled and the sweatshirt hugged against her chest, she trudged along with him.

She didn't ask him how he expected to get inside; she simply trusted that he would.

WHEN the shadowy exterior of the garage came into view, Harley hugged Anastasia a little closer. "Almost there."

She didn't reply. He knew the cold had taken its toll on her, but he didn't know what to do about it. The wind cut like a knife and if he didn't get them indoors soon, she might get too depleted to make it on her own.

For one brief moment, he considered carrying her, but one look at her staunch, determined expression, and he knew Anastasia wouldn't allow it. She doggedly put one foot in front of the other, keeping pace with him even though her legs were much shorter, and not nearly as thick with muscle.

He admired her, damn it.

Remembering how she'd gone on automatic pilot, reacting despite her fear to come to his rescue against a loaded gun, would have made Harley smile if his lips didn't feel stiff from the freezing temps. It didn't matter that her help was unnecessary, or that she'd botched the attempt by running the Jeep off the road.

She'd cared enough to try.

After they crossed the lot, Anastasia tried to make a beeline for the front door. "No." Harley led her toward a

small copse of trees that helped block the wind. He tucked
the blanket around her. "Wait right here while I check it
out."

She groaned.

"I know, I'm sorry. But I want to make sure no one beat
us here."

"I should go with you. Just in case."

"Just in case what? Trust me, I'll be more able to handle
an ambush without worrying about you." He withdrew one
of the guns and pressed it into her gloved hand. "Know
how to use this?"

She shook her head.

"Release the safety." He showed her how. "Then just
aim and shoot. Usually that's enough whether you hit anyone or not. Just make sure it's not me before you pull the
trigger, okay?"

She groaned again and dropped her head against his
chest. "I'm miserable, Harley."

"I know. Me, too. It won't be much longer now, I promise." He tipped up her face. "I know you're tired, honey, but
stay alert for me, okay?"

When she nodded agreement, Harley kissed her forehead . . . then the bridge of her nose . . . and because he
couldn't stop himself, her mouth.

The touch was brief, and given the numbness from the
cold, almost imperceptible. But her eyes opened a little
wider, reassuring him.

He forced himself to walk away.

He couldn't remember ever being so cold, but for now
he couldn't let it matter.

Maneuvering through the dark, he went around to the
back of the building. He couldn't see any footprints, but
with very little light and the constantly falling snow, that
wasn't surprising.

The door felt secure, as did two high windows and a lift
garage door. Harley put his ear to a window and listened,
but heard nothing. The windows were frosted over, so he
couldn't see inside.

He went back around front and checked those doors, too. Far as he could tell, everything remained secure. Using the screwdriver he'd brought with him, he jimmied the lock and got the door open. The narrow beam of his flashlight bounced off a cracked vinyl seating area, a desk, two ancient vending machines, an interior door, and another lift garage door.

He held the gun in his hand and as quickly as possible did a quick surveillance inside.

Clear.

The furnace had died with the electricity, but the station would shelter them from the howling wind.

CIRCLING around to the side, Harley found Anastasia hunkered down on her haunches, her knees up to her chin, her arms around her legs. She stared straight ahead and she had the gun at the ready.

Softly, so he wouldn't startle her, he said, "Anastasia?"

She jumped to her feet—thank God she didn't shoot him. In fact, she handed the gun back to him with alacrity. "We can go in now?"

Poor thing. He pulled her close. "Yeah, we can go in."

She moved ahead of him, rushing into the garage. Harley followed. He was tired and cold, and the thought of removing frozen layers tempted him. But first things first. He closed the door and as a precaution stacked some heavy tires against it.

Close behind him, Stasia asked, "What are you doing?"

"I'm blocking the entrances so if anyone tries to get in, we'll be forewarned."

"How can I help?"

Surprised, Harley glanced at her. Her voice shivered as badly as her body; she'd been through too much. But she looked determined to lend a hand.

His admiration grew. Damn it, he couldn't remember the last time he'd admired a woman for her courage.

"The garage doors are bolted from the inside, so they're

secure. You could put something—a can or anything that'll clatter—up by the windows and the door around back."

"Okay."

"Here." He handed her the flashlight. "Take this with you. I'll check the front desk for another one."

The beam of light hit him in the face, making him wince before she lowered it. "How can you see to search the desk if I have the flashlight?"

"My eyes will adjust. I have good night vision."

Her long sigh echoed in the quiet garage. "I'm convinced you have good everything. It's almost disgusting, how good you are at everything." With that remark, she turned to do as he asked, and Harley tracked her progress by the movement of the light.

It didn't take him long to locate a heavy-duty security light on a shelf behind the desk. He also found matches, but no candles.

Because he preferred to be prepared rather than taken off guard, he went on the assumption that the men *would* be back, and if they returned, he needed a plan.

He didn't want to alarm Stasia, so while she was off barring the entrances, he searched out a good place for them to rest, away from the windows and anyone who might peek in.

Ned had a small employee break room with a coffeepot set up on a rectangular table, and another round table with four plastic chairs around it. Against one wall was an aged leather recliner. It was a little on the grimy side, but it'd hold them both.

That is, if Anastasia could be convinced to bed down with him.

The room offered the convenience of a john and no windows for prying eyes.

It'd be safe enough.

On the round table, Harley set out the supplies he'd brought along and all the change he had. In his tote, he had the basic necessities: toothbrush, razor, soap, clean socks and boxers. The vending machines would supply snack-type food.

Peeling off his hooded sweatshirt, he laid it over a plastic chair to dry. He stowed the toiletries in the bathroom, readjusted both guns in his waistband, and went to check on Stasia. He found her still bundled head to toes in her outerwear, stacking empty oil cans on the windowsills. The flashlight that she held in her teeth trembled.

"Good job."

She glanced at him, then took the flashlight out of her mouth. "Thanks. I put a chair against the door, but also sat some cans there."

Physically, she looked on the ragged edge. Other than a bright red nose and cheeks, her skin was pale, her lips chapped. Exhaustion darkened the skin beneath her usually bright eyes.

But emotionally, she had the same strength he'd noted in her before.

He held out a hand. "Come here."

Using the flashlight, she checked her security measures one last time, then joined him. "It's warmer in here, but I'm not ready to lose your coat. Sorry."

He didn't yet tell her that more than the coat was going to have to come off before she'd get warm. Wet layers wouldn't warm her; shared body heat would.

"I found a place for us to settle in for the night. There's a coffee machine, so if the electricity comes back on, we'll be in business."

"It won't." Because he held a flashlight, she turned hers off and dropped it in the pocket of his coat. "It's usually out for a day or longer."

With an arm around her, Harley led her toward the break room. "At least the vending machines are loaded with candy and chips, and they're so old, they don't run on electricity."

"The cola machine does."

He glanced down at her. "If you want a Coke, I can get it for you."

"The same way you got the door open?"

She didn't sound accusing so much as curious. "I learned some useful talents when I was younger."

"I can imagine."

He grinned. "I was never a thief, but I had rowdy friends who enjoyed teaching me things. My mom used to have fits about it."

"I can imagine that, too."

"There's a bathroom you can use. The water is cold, but as long as we leave it trickling through the night, the pipes shouldn't freeze."

"Through the night?"

"I don't think we're going anywhere anytime soon, do you?"

"I suppose not." She looked around the break room with dismay. "Ned will have to thank us for saving his pipes."

"I don't think he'll mind that we're here."

"No."

"Stasia." Harley turned her to face him. He plucked the hat away and ruffled her hair. "You need to take all these wet clothes off."

She bit her lip, ducked her face, and nodded. "I know."

"You do?"

"The clothes are soaked and freezing, which means I'll continue to freeze." She turned to survey the room. "I don't suppose you found clean clothes anywhere? Or a few blankets?"

"At a garage? No. But I have clean socks and that hooded sweatshirt. With the solar blanket, you'll warm up." He tipped up her face. "I'm going to help you undress, okay?"

"No, I don't think it is. I'm sorry, but I feel . . . seduced or something."

Harley frowned at her. "I'm not going to—"

"Yeah, I know. You wouldn't take advantage of a half-frozen woman traumatized by the attack of armed thugs."

"I hadn't realized you were traumatized."

"A little, but it doesn't matter."

He frowned in incomprehension.

"It's you, Harley. The way you look at me and how you sound when you talk to me. I know you just want to make me comfortable, but when I look at you, I almost feel . . . naked."

He tried not to laugh. Holding out his hands to his sides, he said, "Sorry, Stasia. I didn't realize. I wasn't deliberately—"

"Being seductive. I know. It's just the way you present yourself. It's . . . who you are."

"Anastasia." He dropped his arms. "Do you think you could let me finish a sentence on my own? For the sake of accuracy, maybe?"

She waved for him to go on.

"I was going to say that I'm not deliberately showing you how I feel. Because yeah, I'm not immune to being alone with a sexy woman while I get to play the big capable guy. But I thought I had it under wraps."

That got her attention. "You get excited over the caveman role?"

His smile went crooked. "You have no idea. If you cried a little, I'd probably have a boner already." He touched her cheek. "All guys like to play protector. It's a basic instinct thing."

"Hmmm." Her eyes narrowed. "The thing is, with you, I get the feeling you aren't playing."

He shrugged. True enough, he'd always filled the role. "Anyway, we're not stripping down for pleasure, but for survival. So off with the duds."

"That was better, but only by a little." She glanced at the bathroom. "I opt for privacy, thank you."

"If you insist." Harley handed her the thick socks and the sweatshirt that she'd mostly kept dry inside her coat. He opened the bathroom door. "I'll be out here, rounding up some food."

"Aren't you getting undressed, too?"

"Down to my boxers, yeah." He nudged her into the smaller room. "Make use of the toiletries if you want. They're mine, so no garage grease."

"Thanks."

Harley shut the door for her and walked several paces away. The room was small enough that he could hear her rustling movements, the flush of the toilet, the running of water.

He pulled a table over by the lounge chair and set both guns there. He retrieved a variety of food from the vending machines and, with a modicum of effort, managed to finagle two Cokes, too.

With everything arranged, he looked around the room. As he'd thought: they'd be comfortable enough.

If Anastasia would just stop hiding in the bathroom.

CHAPTER 6

SHE should never have insisted on sitting alone in a different chair. She knew Harley was annoyed with her, and damn it, she couldn't blame him. It was too cold for modesty, and too scary for independence. Except for the howling wind and the occasional "settling" noise typical of all buildings, silence filled the station.

But two people had chased her down, run her off the road with harmful intent. They'd carried guns.

To shoot her?

She couldn't stop thinking about it, and every small squeak had her fearful of their return.

Sitting safely in Harley's embrace had been almost too tempting to resist. But the sweatshirt she wore only hung to her knees, and the socks covered her feet and ankles. Not much leg showed between the two, but she was without pants, and worse, so was Harley.

When she'd stepped out of the tiny, grease-smudged bathroom, she'd found him in his boxers again. He wore thick socks that matched hers and his thermal shirt, which was barely damp.

All in all, he looked like a macho ad for men's underclothes.

The one flashlight left everything in deep shadows.

Intimate. Seductive—despite the circumstances.

Or maybe because of them.

With her sitting at the table, wrapped in the blanket, and him on the lounge chair, oblivious to his state of undress, they'd eaten the pilfered snacks in near silence.

All the while, Stasia felt him looking at her in that quiet, introspective way of his. She was morbidly aware of the two guns, one on the table near her, the other right next to Harley's hand.

When they finished with the food, Harley suggested they get some sleep. And because of her insistence, they'd bedded down for the night in separate chairs.

Nearly an hour had passed, or so she guessed. She didn't have a watch and couldn't see the clock in the room. Harley hadn't said much after failing to talk her into the lounge chair with him. She sat in the straight-backed chair, wrapped in the blanket, her head resting on her folded arms on the hard table.

She was such an idiot.

"Did you recognize either of those two men?" he suddenly asked.

The sound of his voice, after nothing but muted breathing, further jangled her nerves. "No."

"Me either."

Outside, the wind whistled. Ice crackled. Tree branches groaned.

"I don't suppose you caught their license plate number?"

She shook her head, knew he couldn't see her, and asked, "Did you?"

"No. But it was an older model Ford with extended cab."

"It was?"

"Yeah. Had a roll bar and off-road lights. I'd say maroon, or maybe black. Hard to tell in the night."

Stasia marveled at his attention to detail. "I can't believe you noticed all that."

"I can't believe I didn't get the damn plate number. That's what we really needed." He fell silent again.

She would have preferred that he talk. At least then she didn't dwell on her own grim fears. "It's really eerie in here, isn't it?"

"It's dry and safe."

"Yeah, but . . . eerie too, with the howling wind and the stillness in the air. And I swear, I hear bugs crawling around."

"Stasia."

Something in the way he said her name gave her pause. "What?"

"Enough already. I can hear your teeth chattering." His tone gentled. "Come here."

She didn't know what to say to that. She was so cold, there wasn't anything she could do about her chattering teeth.

"Look." He half sat up and turned toward her. "If it'll reassure you, you're not even my type."

"Is that so?" Now why did that insult her?

"And if you were," he continued, "there isn't time enough and the conditions aren't right enough for what I'd want to do. With you. *To* you."

Now Stasia sat up. Eyes wide, she stared toward Harley's voice. His body was a bulky shadow without details. "And that would be . . . what?"

He was silent a moment, then finally said, "Come over here and I'll tell you."

He'd given her an easy way out of her stubbornness. She wanted to be near him, warm and safe. She wanted comfort from her awful memories.

"Fine." Creeping carefully, Stasia felt around until she reached him, then stood beside the fully reclined padded leather chair.

Harley pushed away the shirts he'd used as a covering, unwrapped the blanket from around her, and said, "Crawl on in and get comfortable."

"God." Stasia did just that, sprawling out over him, her head on his big hard shoulder, her arm around his muscled abdomen. Heat, scented with Harley's unique smell, radiated off him in comforting waves. It felt so good that she moaned.

Harley shifted a bit, making more room for her, tucking the blanket around them both. His mouth touched her ear. "Better?"

"You feel like heaven." As the warmth sank into her, sleepiness followed. She gave a huge yawn. "I'm sorry, Harley, but I'm exhausted."

"I know. Go on to sleep."

"Oh, no you don't." He'd roused her nosiness and she wouldn't be able to get a sound sleep without an explanation. "Not until you tell me what it is you'd want to do."

His fingers sifted through her hair. "You sure you want to have this conversation?"

"By the second, my curiosity grows."

Tender and lulling, his hand continued to move over her head, smoothing her hair, massaging her scalp. "All right then." He put a kiss to her forehead. "If I had you the way I want you, you'd be stretched out naked on a bed, wrists tied and thighs open, so I could have you at my leisure."

Tied? Stasia went rigid—with mixed emotions.

She wasn't afraid.

Harley might be a mixed martial arts fighter, used to bloody battles, but he didn't brutalize women.

So he had a bondage fetish? Interesting.

The visual wasn't actually displeasing. In fact, something inside Stasia heated and curled in scandalous delight.

But her independent nature rebelled at the idea of any form of helplessness. She shook her head, refusing him— and herself. "Forget it, Harley. That's not going to happen."

His fingers continued the magic in her hair. "A challenge? Not a good idea, babe."

She bit her lip. "I know you wouldn't . . ."

"Force you?" He shook his head. "No, never."

"I was going to say coerce."

"Not even that. As you already claimed, I don't take advantage of women in bad situations. And I suppose you could call this situation bad."

She jerked her head up to see him. "You wouldn't?"

His shoulder lifted in a shrug. "I hate it that you're spooked, and with good reason. You're out of your element, and I know you're worried. But I'm not going to let anything happen to you."

"So much confidence."

He shrugged again. "The thing is, the idea of having you has been tempting me for a while now. I've been fighting it, but it's not easy. And accepting a dare could hardly be called coercion, now, could it?"

Suspicious, titillated, Stasia frowned and asked, "You've done this before, then?"

"This?"

"The whole bondage thing?"

"I've done it before."

Unbelievable. And strangely exciting.

She heard the smile in his tone when he asked, "I've shocked you?"

"A little maybe. You're so blatant about it."

"Well, don't start trying to analyze me. It's all simple enough."

Only Harley would make such a ridiculous claim. "How so?"

"There's a lot in my life that I can't control." He paused, then said matter-of-factly, "Missed opportunities for the title belt most of all. And no, I'm not going into that right now."

"Everyone has things that happen unexpectedly, things that go against their plans."

"Maybe. I don't like it." He kissed her earlobe. "So when it comes to sex, I enjoy taking complete control. Not only over myself, but over a woman, too."

"Are you trying to convince me?"

"Circumventing questions, if I can."

"Well, that's not working."

She heard his grin when he said, "If a woman makes her interest known, I explain up front what I want."

Very blatant! "The way you're doing with me?"

"Yes."

"And women *agree*?"

He leaned close to her ear again, teasing her. "They beg for more."

No way. She started to sit up, but Harley levered just enough of his weight against her to hold her still. "Don't rush off again." His voice was low, seductive, and vaguely amused. "You've just stopped shivering."

"But you're saying women—"

"Love a little helplessness." His fingers teased over her cheek, her shoulder. "Especially when I make it worth their while."

"I'm . . . speechless." And shamefully, she admitted to herself, a little turned on. She thought of gossip she'd overheard from vacationers in the grocery store, how they'd complimented Harley, called him controlling . . . But she hadn't realized, and now that she did . . . Good grief.

Did he really do it to balance his life, to take charge of what he could? Or did he just plain enjoy a little dominance over women? He didn't strike her as the type. In fact, she'd always thought Harley would appreciate shared pleasure.

Fracturing her thoughts, he whispered, "You have no idea what I could do for you, Anastasia." And then his voice went rougher still as he added, "Or how much you'd enjoy it."

Oh, she believed him. Even now, just from the teasing of his breath, tingles ran up and down her arms and over her nape.

Temptation beckoned . . .

But some things couldn't be changed overnight.

She drew a breath. "You're right, Harley. I'm not your type."

"Somehow, that's not mattering so much anymore. Maybe because I think you don't know yourself well enough to make that judgment. Or maybe because, at this moment, I just don't care."

She turned her face up, trying to see him in the dark. "So if I was interested in you, but not in . . . the whole domination thing, you wouldn't turn me down?"

His arms went around her. His nose touched hers. "Hard to say, honey. The thing is, I don't believe in half measures."

"Is that a yes or a no?"

His smiling mouth touched hers, turned for the brief touch of a kiss, and eased away again—but not far. "Want to make me an offer and we'll find out?"

She considered it. It was incredible, but . . . this one night would never happen again. In the morning, help would come and Harley would leave town.

Tonight, stranded alone together with the excuse of fear and cold . . . she *could* say yes.

Who would know, or fault her?

Before she could make up her mind, Harley put a hand to her jaw and held her face still beneath his. "Understand, Anastasia. I'm talking about one night. This night."

"I know." She had no illusions about a future with him. He was not a man ready to settle into a relationship. And why should he, when women chased him?

"Tomorrow I leave and that's that."

"I know." He had a fighting career and intended to be champion in his weight class. His priorities didn't include a significant other.

"I have no intention of getting overly involved with any woman."

"So you've said." Her brain churned over the possibilities. It was dark, cold, silent. The proverbial "morning after" would be rife with rescue attempts and explanations about the attack, keeping awkwardness at a minimum.

"Anastasia?"

"I'm thinking about it."

He made a rough sound, part frustration, part growling need. "That's your answer, then." Turning to face her in the chair, he pinned her down with one heavy thigh.

The position was far more comfortable than she'd imagined while sitting alone at the table. "I said I was thinking about it."

"Yeah. And that's more encouragement than I needed. So I suppose, yes, I'd be interested, even without restraints. But just for one night. *This* night."

"Don't beat it into the ground, Harley. I get it." Her mind made up, Stasia slowly wrapped her arms around his neck. She could feel his erection, already full against her.

Distracted, she said without thinking, "You really are big."

"Yeah? I hadn't noticed."

That made her laugh, and eased some of her anxiety. "Fibber."

"Just teasing you so you'll relax a little. You're coiled so tight, I'm afraid you're going to go off screaming any minute."

"No screaming, I promise." Although she couldn't make any promises about moaning.

"Before you say yes or no, think about it. I don't want this to be a spur-of-the-moment decision that you'll regret later."

"No regrets." With the last of her chill chased away, she said, "Honestly, Harley, that tonight-only stipulation is part of the lure for me. If I'm out of character right now, doing spontaneous stuff I wouldn't normally do, who cares? I won't be seeing you again anyway."

He held her face, his thumbs stroking her cheekbones. "Then who will know if you give in to a fantasy, too?" And with that warning, he slid his hand to her shoulder and gently pressed her flat to her back.

Her heart raced; she bit her lip but didn't offer any resistance.

Fingers spread, he felt over her in the dark until he cupped his big hand over her thigh and urged her legs wide apart. His fingers lingered, teasing over her inner thigh, down to her knee, back up again—but not quite high enough.

A shiver rippled through her, and he whispered, "Very nice, Anastasia."

She started to say, "Thank you," but couldn't get the words out.

"Let me make you more comfortable."

Oh God. She had to close her eyes. But the second she did, she felt Harley raising her arms up high above her head.

"No ties to restrain you," he murmured, "but I want you to keep your arms there anyway. Pretend for me. Do you understand?"

"Yes."

"Now," he said, "we only have one small problem."

She opened her eyes and tried to see him. "What is it?"

He kissed her lightly. "I don't have a condom with me."

HARLEY hated lying to her, but he wasn't about to give in to the overwhelming urge to have her. Not completely. If he did, he wasn't sure he'd be able to resist the craving to come back for more.

As he kept insisting, this could be no more than a one-time thing.

What he *could* do, and would do, was see to her pleasure. It'd be torture for him, but a sweet kind, worth the discomfort sure to burn him through the rest of the night.

Stasia started to lower her arms, and he caught both wrists in his right fist, then transferred them to his left so he'd have a hand free to touch her.

For now, he held her loosely. "No moving, honey, remember?"

"But you said—"

"That I don't have a rubber. I know." Bending, he nuzzled her lips. She had such a soft mouth; he could taste her mouth for an hour and not be tired of it. "Don't worry about it."

"Harley . . . I'm sorry, but I don't take those types of risks."

"Me either." She smelled really nice, too. Better than any woman he remembered. Sort of sweet and warm, very sexy.

His cock throbbed, but he wouldn't relent. He wanted her too damn much, so much that it threatened the rigid leash on his control. "Just hush and let me show you all the safe things that we can still enjoy."

"But—"

Her protest turned into a gasp as he used his free hand to cup a breast. She wasn't overly endowed, but she was a handful, firm and soft. "I wish I had more light to see you."

A breathless sound left her. "I might not do this in more light."

If she thought he'd let her hide in the dark . . . *Damn*. Since they wouldn't be doing this again, and he couldn't very well expect her to welcome a flashlight shone over her, he had no choice but to allow her the inhibitions.

Harley drew a breath, and said, "Then I'm glad it's dark."

But in his mind, he thought: bright sunlight. If he had his way, he'd have her naked under an afternoon sky with the hot sun on her skin. He'd be able to see all of her—and she'd have no way to hide from him.

The image in his mind stirred him further, and he cuddled her breast.

Under the layer of clothes, her nipple stiffened. Feeling urgent, Harley leaned down and nipped carefully with his teeth.

By reflex, she tugged at her arms, but he didn't let her go, and she relaxed again, then moaned.

"You're wearing too many clothes." He half–sat up beside her. "Keep still."

He could hear her fast, urgent breaths, but she didn't move. Smiling in satisfaction and need, Harley pushed the sweatshirt up above her breasts. He took a moment to cup both breasts, gently holding, caressing . . .

If he waited much longer, his control would slip.

"I need your panties off." Hooking his fingers in the waistband, he said, "Lift your hips, honey."

She hesitated only a heartbeat.

He slid the silky scrap of material down her legs and off her feet. He dropped it onto the floor. "Part your legs again." As soon as she did, he pressed his palm firmly against her, covering the neat triangle of curls, heat, and dampness.

They both stilled.

His heart pounded.

Collecting himself, hoping to savor the sensations—for her—Harley slowly leaned down and took her mouth in a full-blown, tongue twining, wet kiss.

He meant to get her closer to the edge, to ease her into readiness.

But Stasia blew his good intentions to hell and back. The way she returned his kiss, how she pressed her pelvis up against him, squirming and hungry, destroyed his resolve.

Before he knew it, his hands were all over her, and soon after that, his mouth was on her everywhere, too. Her nipples drew tight as he licked over them, then sucked hard. Her belly hollowed out when he pressed several damp kisses down her rib cage.

Reacting totally on instinct, he simply wanted to devour her—and that was so unlike him. He liked playing with women. He relished the foreplay, building the pleasure, making women taut with need.

This time, he was the one on the ragged edge.

Hell, maybe the circumstances of the day had affected him more than he'd realized. So Stasia wasn't into being tied; she *was* dependent on him, needing him, and maybe that was enough.

Whatever drove him, he was more turned on than he could ever recall. He should just take her and be damned for the rest. He really was leaving in the morning and that'd take care of any impulse to see her again—something he wouldn't, couldn't allow.

After learning his lesson on relationships, he wasn't dumb enough to jump into another, especially not right before a grueling training schedule.

He opened his mouth on her skin just below her navel, gave her a tender love bite, left a hickey, and trailed his tongue to her hipbone. "Jesus, you taste good."

Her soft moan was the only reply.

To his surprise, Stasia kept her arms raised as instructed. Harley felt the straining of her body as she locked her hands around the top of the chair, helping to constrain herself.

Breathing hard, he lifted up a little, barely able to see her in the darkness. He trailed his fingertips down one taut arm, to her armpit, and then to her breast.

He was so hard, he hurt with need.

Bending down, he drew her nipple deep into his mouth, and at the same time, wedged his hand back between her slim thighs. He could feel the wetness of her desire, her distended clitoris, and more than anything he wanted to go down on her.

But not just yet.

Still sucking on her nipple, he searched his fingers over her. With each pass over her clit, she flinched, tightened, breathed harder and faster.

Slipping his fingers lower, he moved over slick lips swollen with need. So perfect.

Gently, he parted her and, without warning, worked two fingers deep into her.

Her thighs clenched, her body bowed.

She cried out, but immediately muffled the sound, turning her face to the side and trying to still the rhythmic roll of her hips against his hand.

Unwilling to let her hold back, Harley brought his thumb up and over her clitoris, urging her on. Breath held, his own excitement churning, he worked her, timing his movements to hers.

And to his surprise, she started coming.

Damn. She was incredible, hot. Keeping his hand between her legs, letting her ride out the pleasure at her own pace, he lifted up alongside her so he could feel her frantic breaths against his mouth.

"Very nice, Anastasia," he whispered.

She pressed her face against his throat, doing her best to bite back her raw groans. She didn't entirely succeed, which pleased Harley a lot.

When she gradually settled back against him, he kissed her forehead, but left his fingers deep inside her. The contracting of her inner muscles ceased, and now he just enjoyed the warmth and wetness of her.

Smiling to himself, Harley told her, "You can lower your arms now."

She gave another soft moan. "I don't know if I can or not." But she did, loosely draping them around him and snuggling into his side.

After a few seconds, she asked, "Maybe you could move your hand now?"

"Not just yet. I like how you feel." Slowly, he stroked his fingers out and back into her, and she sucked in her breath. Relishing her reaction, Harley asked, "Too much?"

"Yes." Again, she ducked her face. "All of it is too much. I've never . . . That is . . . you make it seem pretty easy. I'm surprised."

After easing his fingers away from her, he rested his hand on her bare hip and hugged her closer to his chest. "I'm glad you enjoyed yourself."

"I did. Thank you." She toyed with his chest hair. "I'm sorry that we can't—"

"I'm fine." And he was. Horny as hell, rigid with lust, but still feeling pretty satisfied with how things had progressed.

"Maybe I could . . ."

Harley caught her wandering hand, lifted it and kissed her fingers. "You don't need to do anything except kiss me good night, and then get some sleep." He tucked the blanket up around them. "We're both exhausted."

Seconds ticked by before she asked, "Are you sure, Harley?"

"Very sure." It was better that he *not* have the memory of coming with her. It'd make it easier—he hoped—to put her out of his mind once he left Echo Lake. "Now go to sleep."

Surprising him again, she did just that, fading into a deep sleep within minutes. For his part, Harley stared into the darkness, listened for intruders, and wondered why it felt so right being here, now, with Anastasia.

BARBER heard the ringing of the phone and stretched out onto his back. Immediately, a small, warm body curled into his side and a slender thigh went over his abdomen.

Hello.

He lifted his head and surveyed the naked body wrapped around him. Nice.

He already had morning wood, but now he had appetite to match it.

The phone rang again.

Reaching out, he snagged his cell phone with his right hand, and used his left to cuddle a lush tush. "Hello?"

"It's Satch."

Barber looked over at the woman. She opened sleepy eyes and smiled at him. "Morning, Satch. What's up?" *Other than me.* He grinned at his own humor and dropped his gaze to the voluptuous breast cushioned against his ribs.

Very nice.

"Harley there with you?" Satch asked.

"I'd kick his ass if he was. Why?"

Harley's uncle, who took life far too seriously by Barber's way of thinking, didn't appreciate the joke. "He's missing, damn it."

"Missing? I just spoke with him a few days ago." The little female let her fingers do some walking, and Barber closed his eyes in appreciation.

"I spoke with him yesterday and he was supposedly heading home. He swore to me he'd be here for breakfast bright and early."

Barber glanced at a clock. It was only eight. "So maybe he's sleeping in." He'd certainly planned to.

"I'm at his place and he's not here. Hasn't been here." Then with suspicion, he asked, "Have you listened to the news at all in the past twenty-four hours?"

Barber recalled going to Roger's Rodeo late the previous afternoon. He'd spent a few hours eating, shooting pool, and relaxing. After that, he and Roger had discussed band business. Barber wanted to hire a female singer, and Roger had been real helpful with advertisement. He'd also provided a room at the bar for Barber to use for auditions.

So far, they hadn't gone well. Getting another female singer anywhere near as good as Dakota would be tough. But Dakota now did her own thing, and more often than not, it meant sticking close to her husband's side.

He missed her. More than he'd ever expected. If only he'd realized sooner how he felt about her, that she was much more than a friend. If he'd made a play, she might not have slipped away to another man.

Damn Simon Evans, the likable jerk.

In the early evening, with no good prospects in sight, Barber had taken solace with the little lady currently in his bed. He'd barely survived a night of carnal overindulgence. "Can't say as I have."

Satch's impatience was obvious. "Echo Lake, where Harley was at, got clobbered by a blizzard. The governor just claimed a state of emergency. Power's out everywhere."

"So Harley must've holed up somewhere, right?" Barber caught the woman's wrist and tried to pry her fingers loose so he could give Satch the attention required.

She tightened her grip, making him wince—and relent. Getting stroked made it tough to listen, much less talk, but what the hell, he'd manage.

"He would have found a way to call me. Something's wrong. I feel it."

Well hell. Harley had told him that Satch's uncanny intuition had proved right on more than one occasion. "So what d'you want to do, Satch?"

"I'm going to drive down there and check on him, but I could use some company just in case."

Stiffened nipples moved against him. The woman gave a low moan and pressed herself closer to his thigh.

Barber cleared his throat. "How far away is it? Hours I mean, not miles." In bad weather, mileage seldom mattered.

"Three hours, give or take. Most of the area north of Echo Lake is clear, so the roads won't be shitty till we're practically there." Already assuming Barber would accompany him, Satch said, "We'll keep our cell phones on and if he can call us, he will. In the meantime, I got the feeling he needs some help."

The woman's mouth latched on to Barber's chest. She nipped him with her teeth, laughed softly when he jumped, and started kissing a path down his rib cage.

"I'm in."

"Good. You're at Roger's motel? I can pick you up in ten minutes."

"Ten minutes?" A warm tongue moved over him, and a second later, a warmer mouth enclosed him. "Make it twenty."

Barber disconnected the call, tossed the phone onto the floor, and laced his fingers through soft blond hair. "Damn, darlin'."

She released him with a smile and a lick of her lips. "You like that?"

"I'm alive, ain't I?"

"Do I get the job with the band?"

Barber barely held back a laugh. "Hell no. Sorry, honey, but the second I took you to bed, it was a foregone conclusion you wouldn't suit, because I never mix business with pleasure."

Her face colored. Her bottom lip stuck out. "You didn't like my voice?"

Barber pulled her down to his chest, then rolled atop her. Voice husky, he said, "I like your mouth a whole lot more." He kissed her while palming a soft breast, and felt her tension ebb away.

Against her throat, he asked, "So what's it to be, sugar?

Stay or go? And remember, I only have twenty minutes, and we're counting down fast."

Her nails sank into his shoulders and her thighs parted. "I'm definitely staying."

Barber stroked a thumb over her nipple. "Then I'm definitely glad." He sat up long enough to find a rubber, and got his day off to a good start.

CHAPTER 7

HARLEY woke with Anastasia's back to him, her rump up against his crotch, and a definite chill in the air.

No electricity yet.

Nothing more had happened during the night. While she'd faded into a deep sleep, he'd dozed only lightly, waiting, listening—and enjoying the feel of Anastasia, her scent, remembering the soft sounds she'd made, the way she'd tried to muffle the moans of her climax.

His hand was on her stomach, and Harley spread his fingers wider, touching her hip bones with his thumb and pinky.

Such a delicate woman, but with so much strength.

So sexy, but so inexperienced.

Damn, the things he could do to her, teach her, the fantasies he could bring alive . . .

But as he'd told her, he kept things brief and avoided involvement. It still amazed him that she wanted him enough to agree to those terms.

It wasn't easy, but he levered himself out of the chair without waking her, then tucked the blanket up around her shoulders. Wearing only a shirt and thick socks, Harley stretched the kinks out of his muscles before looking around for his boxers and jeans. He pulled them on, put one of the guns into his waistband, and crept out of the room.

His every footstep echoed on the linoleum floor. Careful not to bump into anything, he went to the front of the station and looked out through a window.

Bright morning sunlight cut through a cloudless sky and reflected off layers of ice and snow in blinding display. So much snow blanketed the area, Harley wondered if they'd be able to get out, or if help would be able to get in.

Not that he'd mind spending another day stranded with Anastasia. As long as those men didn't come back with reinforcements, he could handle everything. They had enough food, shelter, and water to last them.

Thinking of water made him wonder about the pipes, and he checked the different sinks in the work area, and the break room. Luckily, it all still worked.

Unwilling to awaken Anastasia, he crept back to the front of the garage and opened the door. Two feet of snow blocked the entrance. Harley found a shovel, cleared a small path, and communed with nature.

He was just zipping up his jeans when he heard the approaching vehicle from a distance. Stepping back inside and securing the door, he watched and waited.

An enormous yellow truck bearing a wide snowplow dug through, forming a high ridge at the side of the road. To Harley, it looked like a county truck, especially with the flashing yellow light atop the roof. Behind the truck, he spotted his uncle's black SUV.

Relief warred with disappointment. He shoved the disappointment to a dark corner of his mind. It was better this way.

Stepping out to the small area he'd cleared, he waved his arms.

Both trucks stopped.

Uncle Satch got out and walked to the driver's side of the plow. Money was exchanged.

Huh. So his uncle had arranged the rescue? That didn't

really surprise Harley. He was well used to his uncle's inge-
nuity. He'd been witness to it ever since his father's death.

Knowing he'd been spotted, Harley went back inside
and headed for the break room.

Curled on her side, her dark hair half-hiding her face,
Anastasia slept on. He hated to wake her, but he didn't want
her embarrassed when his bossy uncle descended on them.

Sitting down beside her, he stroked her hair back,
tucked it behind her ear.

She stirred, stretched a little, and finally her eyes opened.
She blinked at him.

Something very tender, very intimate stirred inside
Harley. He didn't smile, but pleasure spread through him.
"Hey, sleepyhead."

"Harley?"

Now he smiled. "Forgotten me already, huh? I'm
crushed." Just to see her reaction, he slid a hand beneath
the blanket and over her rounded hip.

She scrambled into a semi-sitting position. "What time
is it?"

"I don't know. I hadn't thought about it." He picked up
his watch from where he'd left it on the table. "Almost
eleven thirty. Why?"

Somewhat disoriented, she pushed back her hair and
looked around their shelter. Comprehension dawned. She
focused on Harley, and blushed. "Still no electricity?"

"Afraid not."

She sat up the rest of the way, keeping the blanket tight
around her. Eyes puffy and voice scratchy, she said, "I'd
kill for coffee."

Harley patted her thigh. "That can be arranged shortly."

"It can?" She squirmed, then scooted half off the chair.
"Excuse me."

"Sure thing." Harley stood and picked up her other
clothes. "Here. Take your panties and jeans into the bathroom with you. We're about to be rescued, and I assume
you'll want to be dressed."

She froze. "Rescued?"

"Yeah, my uncle is here with a snowplow."

"*Here?*" After squeaking out that single horrified word, she looked to the door, and her eyes widened in shock and embarrassment.

Harley followed her gaze, and there stood not only Satch, but Barber, too. Together, the two men more than filled the doorway. They were both ruddy-faced from the cold, and covered in snow. Satch stood at an even six feet, and Barber topped him by two inches. In their heavy coats, they looked imposing.

Satch frowned, but Barber, grinning like a fool, said, "Hope we're not interrupting."

Satch stepped in front of Barber. "What the hell happened here? Are you all right?"

"We're fine." Taking pity on Anastasia, Harley picked up the second gun and headed toward the men. They both glanced at the weapon with curiosity. To head off their questions, he said, "We can talk out front while Anastasia wakes up." He added, "I don't suppose either of you has coffee?"

Keeping a speculative eye on Anastasia, Satch nodded. "There's some left in the thermos in the car."

"Perfect." When he reached the doorway, Harley looked back over his shoulder. Anastasia hadn't moved. "While you get ready to join us, I'll get the coffee for you."

"Thank you."

He winked at her. "You're very welcome." Then he put a hand each on Satch's and Barber's shoulders to push them out of the room. "Let's go."

Barber said, "I don't suppose—"

"Not a word, Barber. Now walk."

They'd barely cleared the room when Barber burst out laughing. "You sly dog. Your uncle was fretting like an old woman, and you're here holed up with a babe."

"First things first," Harley said. "Was the snowplow heading back to town?"

"I don't think so," Satch replied. "He said something about clearing the path up to a couple of cabins."

"Anastasia's place." Harley nodded in satisfaction. "Good. That means he'll free up Ned."

"Ned?"

"He owns this station, but I imagine he's snowed in, too. I'd like to see him before I leave."

"If he doesn't come to us, we can go to him." Barber studied Harley. "You look like you need that coffee, too. I'll be right back."

"Hey, if you see the snowplow still, tell the guy I'm going to need a tow truck to get my Jeep back on the road. Ask him if he can send someone our way."

"I hear him coming by now." Barber hurried out the door.

While he was gone, Harley stared toward the break room and wondered what was keeping Anastasia. Shyness? Modesty? Was she trying to pretty herself up, even under such extreme circumstances?

No. Anastasia wasn't that superficial.

"The town is immobilized," Satch told him as he wandered around the station, examining all the protective measures taken against intruders. "I had a hell of a time just getting a plow up here. What equipment they've got, they have running everywhere. But for enough money, we should be able to get what we need."

"Does your phone work?" Harley asked.

"Hasn't since I got in Echo. Too many mountains, I guess. The phones in town are all out, too. Must be some lines down somewhere."

Barber returned and handed the half-empty thermos to Harley, then stripped off his coat. "It's colder than a dead witch's tit in a brass bra out there."

"Did you catch the driver?"

"Yeah. He has a tow truck. He said for a Franklin, he'll come back with his hitch and get you right and tight."

"Hell."

Satch rejoined them. "Consider it cheap, under the conditions." He didn't smile. "You've got this place set up like a fortress. What the hell went on?"

Indicating they should both sit in the waiting chairs,

Harley said, "We were attacked last night. I took the guns off two men—strangers to me and Anastasia—who first tried to run her off the road, making her wreck her truck, then they came back and tried to do the same to me."

"Holy shit." Barber sat down hard. "The idiots were armed?"

"One pulled a gun, but dropped it in the snow when Anastasia nearly ran over him. I took the other gun off his friend, after I'd pounded on him a bit."

When Satch held out a hand, Harley gave him a gun to examine.

"Smith and Wesson nine millimeter." Satch turned the gun at every angle, hefted it in his hand. "Pretty common, but looks like whoever had it kept it in good shape."

"I don't know if they intended to really use them or not." Harley crossed his arms over his chest. The chill in the air was enough to make his bones ache. "But I wasn't about to take any chances."

Satch nodded. "That's why you broke into the station, and set up booby traps for anyone who tried to sneak in."

"Yeah."

Anastasia tapped on the wall, announcing herself.

All three men turned to stare at her.

Harley fought off a smile. She'd straightened her hair and splashed her face. She wore her now-dry jeans, the sweat-shirt he'd given her, and the thick socks. "Good morning."

Her smile wavered. "I don't want to be too hopeful, but I recall you mentioned a possibility of coffee?"

He held up the thermos. "Barber braved the weather again to bring it in for you. If I recall, there's powdered creamer, sugar, and cups in the break room."

"Barber? The man you spoke with on the phone?"

"None other." Harley reached out a hand to her and she came to stand beside him. "The other man I spoke on the phone with was my uncle, and that's him scowling at you. Anastasia, meet Barber and Uncle Satch. Guys, this is my landlord and cohort against crime, Anastasia Bradley."

She strode to Barber and held out a hand. "Thank you for the coffee."

Barber accepted her hand with old-fashioned gallantry. "My pleasure."

Next she reached out to his uncle. "Uncle Satch," she said, making Harley raise a brow. "I did deliver your message, but everything went downhill after that. I'm sorry for the trouble."

"Not your fault." Satch patted the seat he'd just vacated. "Sit yourself down and I'll get the coffee for you."

"Oh, no, I'm fine."

"Nonsense," Barber said, and he took her arm. "Grab a seat. Are you warm enough?"

And so it went, much to Harley's consternation. They treated Anastasia with kid gloves and a kind of familiarity they reserved for significant others.

Maybe they'd misunderstood the situation, but he couldn't very well correct their impressions in front of Anastasia.

Not that he had much of a chance anyway. Once the tow truck driver returned, Harley got right to the business of getting his Jeep operational again. And there was no reason for Anastasia to wait around in the cold while he did so.

At his insistence, and Anastasia's lack of objection, Barber agreed to take her to town so she could get more comfortable.

"Harley?"

Telling the tow truck driver that he'd meet him by the road, Harley turned to face Anastasia. Wearing his coat again, her hat hanging loosely in her hand, she stood in the garage doorway and waited for him to come to her.

As he approached, she watched him with big brown eyes and an unsettled shifting of her feet.

Nervousness from her now? Harley paused in front of her and lifted a brow.

She hesitated, glanced back at Satch and Barber, who stood a few feet behind her, and cleared her throat. "I need one private moment, please."

"I was just about to get my Jeep pulled free."

"I know. I promise it won't take long."

Dreading the inevitable—sort of—Harley took her arm and walked with her around the corner. He could feel the rapt gazes of his friend and his uncle, but he avoided looking at them.

He already knew what they were thinking.

Once he and Anastasia were out of sight of everyone, she smiled up at him.

"Everything okay?" Harley asked, and then waited to hear her ask about seeing him again, if he'd call, if he'd visit her . . .

"Everything's fine. But I know this is my last chance to say good-bye to you."

Did she think he planned to sneak away without another word? Not a flattering thought. "I'll see you in town before I head out."

She nodded. "I suppose. But there's no place there for me to speak privately with you. I wanted to . . . well . . ." She ducked her face, but quickly met his gaze again. "I'd have preferred looking a little better for this, but it can't be helped. So . . ."

Confused, Harley studied her, but said nothing.

A smile slipped over her mouth and she shrugged, then went on tiptoe, wrapped her arms around him, and plastered her mouth to his.

Hell yeah.

Harley didn't mean to, but his arms went around her waist and he crushed her close.

He hadn't realized how badly he wanted to taste her again until her mouth touched his. Then he knew he was starving for her.

What a kiss it turned out to be—hot, deep, a prelude to what could follow, if only they had time and privacy enough to go where that kiss naturally led.

But they weren't alone. His uncle and Barber waited in the other room. The tow truck driver waited on him, likely with plenty more work to do today.

Lingering would only encourage her—and him.

But Harley didn't stop the kiss. He meant to. He kept telling himself that it was enough, to pull away, to get going on all he had planned for the day—but he couldn't.

Anastasia's small, cool hands went to his face; she nipped his bottom lip, kissed his chin, then *she* ended the kiss and hugged him fiercely. "Good-bye, Harley."

Damn. Why did she have to make it sound as final as he'd meant it to be?

He put his chin to the top of her head. "You're sure you're okay?"

"I'm terrific."

Now why did *that* annoy him? Maybe because he was the one with the parting pangs this time. Damn it, he knew he'd miss her, and selfish as it seemed, he wanted her to miss him, too.

"Good."

She leaned back, smoothed her hands down his shirt, and smiled. "You are truly a remarkable man, Harley Handleman. I mean that."

"Spoken like a woman satisfied."

"True." She laughed, but quickly sobered. Her gaze searched his. "I'll be watching all your future fights and cheering you on, but I already know you're going to excel. You have enough drive and dedication for ten men."

"We'll see."

She patted his chest, then dropped her hands. "I've held you up enough. You need to get going. It just didn't seem right to simply say good-bye."

"No." In fact, saying good-bye at all didn't feel right.

"Thank you for everything."

Harley frowned. "I didn't do anything."

She laughed. "Thank you for being modest, too." Hooking her arm through his, she said, "All right, then, let's go."

Barber and Satch had moved closer to the wall separating them, and they didn't even try to deny eavesdropping, the dumbasses.

The moment Anastasia saw them, she went to Barber. "Thanks for waiting. I'm ready now if you are."

With a glint in his eyes, Barber opened his mouth—and Harley said, "He'll be right with you."

Satch, who never missed a thing, told her, "Come on with me, Anastasia. We can chat while Harley reads Barber the rules."

"Rules?"

Satch winked. "There're always rules."

Ready to strangle his uncle, Harley waited impatiently while he led Anastasia away, and then he turned on Barber.

Barber said quickly, "There are rules?"

"Yeah, 'fraid so." Keeping all humor from his tone, Harley said, "Watch her closely, but keep your hands to yourself."

Grinning, Barber tugged on his earring. "So it's like that, huh?"

"No, it's not. But it's not open territory either. Not for you."

Trying not to laugh, Barber asked, "What's wrong with me?"

"I know where to find you."

"Ah. Good point." The laugh won out, and Barber, never knowing when to shut up, said, "I'll pretend the two of you are hitched. How's that?"

Far as Harley knew, the danger wasn't over yet, and until he knew the local authorities were on it, he didn't want her out of Barber's sight. He needed to make sure that Anastasia was all right before he left. "Pretend any damn thing you want if it means you'll keep her safe without getting too familiar."

"I think I can manage that."

"She might want you to take her by her cabin so she can grab some stuff."

"I'll make the offer."

Harley nodded. "Don't let her linger, and be on your guard. Those idiots might still be hanging around. It'll be safer in town."

"I'll keep an eye out."

"After I get my Jeep back on the road, I'll see to her truck, then I have a quick errand to run. I won't be long, though."

"I'll feed her breakfast while we wait for you." Barber grinned again. "Wanna kiss her good-bye one more time before I leave with her?"

"No." And with that, Harley walked through the garage, out the door, and up the snowy yard to the road where the tow truck driver waited.

He didn't look back.

It didn't take too long to get his Jeep on the road. Once that was accomplished, he made sure it would run, and then spent a few more minutes seeing that Anastasia's truck got safely towed to the garage where Ned could work on it. He tried to look at her brake lines, but so much snow and ice stuck to the undercarriage, he couldn't see shit.

He wouldn't be satisfied until he had all the facts, but for now, there was nothing he could do.

Maybe that explained his reluctance to leave her.

Sitting beside him in the front seat of the Jeep, Satch asked, "You're convinced someone damaged the lady's truck on purpose?"

"Yes."

"That and the attack later were related?"

"Absolutely."

"Hmmm." Satch mulled things over in his mind. "I'm glad your Jeep wasn't damaged, but if her brakes are gone, then she's out of commission, unless you take the time to get it fixed before we head out."

It was tempting, but Harley didn't want to mislead her about his intentions. "That could take a while, and Anastasia isn't the sort who'd want someone else in her business anyway."

"Independent, huh?"

Harley shrugged. She was, but no more so than most women. Being an old-fashioned guy, Satch didn't realize that women today were well equipped to handle their business on their own. "The driver needed payment up front, and

I wanted to make sure her truck made it to the garage before he went off to a dozen other calls, thanks to the weather."

"So you paid him?"

"It wasn't that much." He glanced at his uncle. "But that's going to piss her off enough without me overstepping myself further."

Satch grinned. "But by the time she finds out, there won't be anything she can do about it."

Unless she tracked down his address somehow, she wouldn't know where to send repayment. Harley wondered if she'd go so far as to search him out.

Did he want her to?

No. It was better that they just made a clean break of it.

Of course, that wasn't entirely in his hands. As an SBC fighter, he wasn't all that anonymous. Any number of trainers, fighters, sponsors, or friends could give her information on him that'd lead her right to his front door. It had happened with groupies, and with the media.

"I'll talk to Ned before we leave," Harley added. "He's the guy who owns the garage." He wanted to explain to Ned why they'd broken in, and he wanted to have a contact who could keep him apprised of any other trouble Anastasia might have.

"That's it?"

Again, Harley shrugged. "Without knowing who attacked us last night, there's not much else I can do."

"I don't like to think of that little lady here all by herself with that kind of trouble around."

"Me either. But because her cabin is pretty secluded, Anastasia had already planned to ride with me to a motel along the interstate. She'll spend the night while she gets things in order. Until then, Barber will see that no one bothers her."

Satch snorted over that. "He might see to that and more."

"Not with Anastasia, he won't." As the interior of the Jeep warmed, Harley felt his muscles relaxing. "Even if Barber gave it his best shot, Anastasia's not that kind of woman."

"You know her that well?"

A chunk of frozen snow slid from the roof, down the windshield, and off the hood. "I know her well enough."

"You warned Barber away from her?"

"Not that it was necessary, but yeah, I did." This was one of those times when Harley wished his uncle would show a little more respect for his privacy. "I didn't want her hassled, that's all. She's been through enough."

Satch sized him up in one long look. "Got it."

Annoyed now, Harley said, "Before you ask me, no, I'm not involved with her." Not much anyway. But that last kiss . . .

"You're sure?"

"Anastasia Bradley isn't my type." Not that it seemed to matter when he got too close to her. He looked his uncle in the eyes and said, "You've got nothing to worry about."

"Who's worrying? I just asked." Satch reached over to clap Harley on the shoulder. "I know your head's in the sport, where it needs to be. Right?"

"Yeah."

"Good." Satch looked out the window at the bright morning sunshine. "Soon as we get you home, I'll set up some stuff. The SBC is real interested in getting some candid shots of you with ladies."

Harley made a sound of disgust.

"Don't act like it'll be a hardship. You're always with one woman or another. For once it's going to benefit your career."

"That's bullshit. Who cares about my social life?"

"Fans do, that's who. I told you, the SBC is jacking up their female demographics with personal stuff on the fighters. Google it, and you'll see what I mean."

"I don't believe this."

"Start believing. The powers that be want the world to know what a ladies' man you are."

"No." *Hell* no.

"It'll be a great exposé. And Harley, they only do that for the guys they think will be champion. This is their way of ensuring you get more viewers when you're on the fight card."

"More like they want to ensure their bottom line."

"Which is good for you, too. Just think about it. Women'll be drawn to your charisma and men will envy you. It's a win-win deal."

"I said no, Uncle Satch." Firm, Harley again gave his uncle a direct look. "My personal life is going to remain personal. I'll gladly do publicity shots and pose with whoever you want. But I'll be damned if I want some camera freak following me around all the damn time."

"Simon Evans did it, and so did Havoc."

Hard to imagine, but that didn't change things for him. "No."

"You've got nothing to hide. So you have a healthy appetite and the ladies enjoy it. So what?" Grinning, Satch slugged Harley in the shoulder. "When we throw in some background on you, you're going to be a modern-day hero."

Harley's head started to throb. "No is no, Satch. It's not up for discussion."

"But—"

"Actually," Harley interrupted, ready to put an end to the discussion in the most expedient way possible, "now that I'll be training, I don't plan to be with any women."

"You're insane."

Harley almost laughed. Satch, like most men, couldn't fathom the idea of life without sex. Before today, Harley couldn't have either, not for long, anyway. But at the moment, he couldn't think of a woman who appealed to him except Anastasia, and she was out of the question.

Abstaining for a short time wouldn't be a hardship.

"Like I keep telling you, Uncle Satch, I'm dedicated."

His uncle looked so shocked, Harley had to look away.

In a quick turnaround typical of Satch's gambits when things didn't go his way, he asked, "So what does Anastasia do? How's she going to get back and forth to work with her truck out of commission?"

"She's not working right now."

"Huh. I didn't figure her for the type to be unemployed."

"She's not." Because Harley didn't want his uncle to get the wrong idea about her work ethic, he explained, "She's a life coach."

"Seriously?"

Doing a double take, Harley said, "You know what that is?"

"Sure." And then, "You didn't?"

Harley should have known. There seemed to be very little that his uncle wasn't familiar with. He ignored the question. "I take it she's real successful at it, but she said she's taking some time off for a few months."

Satch nodded. "I saw right away that she wasn't an ordinary, run-of-the-mill person. Coaching others isn't easy, you know. You need a boatload of patience and understanding, a keen intellect, and the ability to be unbiased in all things."

Did Satch think that because he coached Harley?

Probably.

"Yeah, she's all that," Harley said, cutting off the string of accolades. "Gutsy, too."

"How so?"

Remembering, Harley grinned. "She's the one who ran my Jeep off the road. But she did it trying to rescue me."

Satch listened intently as Harley related the story, and then declared, "I like her."

"Yeah, well, don't like her too much." He put the Jeep in gear. "We'll be out of Echo shortly, and that'll be the last I see of her."

"And from what you said, that's just fine by you, huh?"

"It's the only way I'd let it be." Harley steered the Jeep around and, rather than drive directly to town, headed to Ned's. He wanted to talk to him about Anastasia's truck, and although he didn't plan to let anyone know, he wanted Ned to call him when he found out if Anastasia's brake lines had been cut and notify him if anything else happened.

After today, he wouldn't see Anastasia again, but that didn't mean he wouldn't worry about her.

CHAPTER 8

WITH most of the town shut down, people had gathered at the bar. Sheila kept it well lit, the crowd gave off body heat, and it seemed a good central location for folks to buzz about the weather. Locals mingled with vacationers, while a couple of deputies circulated among them, organizing cleanups and repairs, and taking reports. They'd already spoken with Anastasia, and now they talked with Harley.

Barber lounged back in a seat and amused himself through observation. People fascinated him, especially women—and men when they got hooked on women.

Harley might not realize it yet, but he was good and hooked. It showed in the way he kept glancing at Anastasia, and in the way he had to force his attention back to the deputy each time. A stacked blonde kept trying to get his attention, but Harley never even noticed. He was too busy trying not to stare at Anastasia.

Should he tell Harley that it was all over for him?

Barber grinned and decided against it. After being told that there wasn't much that could be done to track down the men who'd attacked them last night, Harley looked ready to beat someone to a pulp with very little provocation. It was clear that he didn't like the idea of leaving Anastasia alone and unprotected—especially when Harley himself wanted to protect her.

Better not deliberately annoy him further just yet.

He could save it for later.

For her part, Anastasia did her utmost not to look at Harley, even when he turned over the guns and gained the attention of most everyone else in the bar. Oh, she was aware of Harley, had been aware of him from the moment he'd stepped into the bar with his uncle.

But bless her heart, she had pride and gumption galore.

Barber also noticed that, even a little bedraggled from a rough night and lack of finer facilities to pretty herself up, she looked cute as could be.

He understood Harley's interest. He also knew Harley didn't plan to cultivate that interest, not for any woman for any length of time.

Poor sap. He really thought he could call the shots on romance.

Leaning forward in the booth, Barber crossed his arms on the tabletop and said to Anastasia, sotto voce, "You know, sugar, it's okay to look at him. He won't notice, and I promise not to tell anyone."

To his surprise, Anastasia shook her head but didn't deny the obvious. "Thanks, but I'd rather not. I don't want him to misunderstand and think that I plan to chase after him or anything."

Her bluntness threw him. "Because you don't?"

"Plan to chase him? No way." Her big brown eyes met his without reserve. "My personal pride aside, Harley was very clear about his intentions and I respect that. Besides, he's got enough on his plate."

"How so?"

"He has to prepare for his upcoming fights while dealing with his uncle." She half-laughed. "That can't be easy."

Blunt *and* observant. "You picked up on that, did you?"

"The tension between his uncle and him?" She snorted. "I have eyes. Any fool can see that Harley loves Satch, but Satch does like to cross the boundaries, doesn't he?"

Barber sat back. "Not for me to say."

"Ah, prudent, are you? That's a good quality for a friend to have."

When she smiled at him, Barber noticed that she had a nice mouth.

Very nice.

A fist slugged him in the shoulder, not hard enough to be an outright challenge, but definitely hard enough to get his attention real quick.

"Quit daydreaming, you ass."

Barber glanced up to find that Harley had joined them, and he looked more than a little disgruntled. Barber grinned. "Leash that dog, Harley. I was just making silent observations, that's all."

"Well, stop making them." Harley seated himself beside Anastasia, crowding in close to her and making her scoot real fast to give him room. He took her coffee cup and helped himself to a drink in the familiar way of lovers. "The way things stand, there's not much hope of catching those bastards from last night."

"So I was told," she said. "Unless they screw up again."

Looking testy and primed for battle, Harley said, "You mean unless they come after you again."

"I suppose." Unconcerned, she peered at her coffee cup in bemusement. "I won't be returning for a few days, so it doesn't matter. In the meantime, everyone will be on the lookout."

Her reassurance did little to appease Harley. "And when you do return, you'll be back at that damn cabin, isolated and an easy target."

Her smile stiffened. "Why do you insist on calling me an idiot?"

Harley bunched up. "I didn't. I called you small and female."

Pausing, she thought about it, and then shrugged. "I

can't deny being female, and I suppose compared to you, I'm small."

Harley's eyes narrowed. It fascinated Barber to see how easily she got to him.

"Actually," Anastasia said, "I'm thinking I might go ahead and take another job. It'll keep me out of town for a while, at least until things around here get back in order."

"A job with another man?"

Barber barely contained his hilarity. He had to purse his mouth like he'd just swallowed a lemon. But damn, Harley had it bad.

Putting a hand on her file of papers, Anastasia said, "I haven't decided on the job yet. There're a lot of prospects." Taunting him, she asked, "Does it really matter?"

"No." Harley finished off her coffee. "Should I get you another cup?"

"Thank you, no. I was done with it."

He nodded. "Your truck's at the garage. After Ned got my Jeep free, I had him tow it there."

She went still. "I could have seen to that myself."

"I know, but it's already done." He set down her empty mug. "I also went by to see Ned before coming here, and he said he'll work on it first thing. He has to dig his way out of the snow first, but he plans to get to the garage by early afternoon. I don't know how long the phone lines will be down, but I told him you'd keep trying to reach him until you could get through."

Smile stiff, Anastasia said, "Gee, you've taken care of everything, haven't you?"

"Harley's a real mother hen on occasion," Barber said, enjoying their banter.

Opening her purse, she got out a checkbook. "How much do I owe you for the tow?"

"Forget it."

"I'd rather not."

Satch strode up to the booth, an intense expression on his face. "The weather report says sunny skies and no more precipitation. With any luck they'll get this mess cleaned up pretty quickly."

Anastasia smiled at him. "Satch, could you tell me how much I owe Harley?"

Crossing his arms over his chest, Satch asked, "For what exactly?"

Barber choked, looked at all three of them, and choked some more. Damn, but knowing Anastasia and Harley spent the night getting cozy, so many good lines came to him he had a hard time restraining himself. Of course, he couldn't say what he wanted to say, not with a lady present.

Understanding him, Anastasia shook her head. "You're a terrible tease, Barber."

Harley stood, took her checkbook from her, and stuffed it back in her purse. "He's a shitty driver, too."

"Is he?"

"The worst." Catching Anastasia's arm, he urged her from her seat. "That's why I want you to ride with my uncle instead, and Barber and I will ride together—with me driving."

"Now wait a minute," Satch protested. "You and I have stuff to talk about, remember?"

"If it's about photographers, no, we don't. Everything else can wait until we get back to Harmony." He stepped out of the booth, tugging Anastasia along with him.

"You're being stubborn, damn it."

Stiff-necked, Harley said, "I made up my mind, Uncle Satch, and you're not changing it."

Satch turned to Anastasia with a scowl.

She lifted her shoulders. "Sorry, Satch. If you'd rather I get a ride with someone else, I'm sure I could get a lift—"

Quickly retrenching, Satch said, "No, no, I didn't mean that at all." With another glare at Harley, he gave up and said, "I'll go warm up the SUV."

"It really wouldn't be a problem—"

Red-faced, Satch said, "You're riding with me, and that's that." He stormed away.

"Thank you," Anastasia called after him. "I'll be right out."

Hands on his hips, Harley watched his uncle go.

Barber waited to see what Harley would do, and when he just stood there, looking undecided and reluctant, Barber ribbed him. "Now you can unleash the dog, Harley."

Harley's pale-eyed gaze swung to him. "I'll settle up with you later."

Well-trained opponents quailed under that vicious look, but Barber just laughed. "Damn, man, I'm going to have nightmares for a week now."

"Shut up, Barber."

"Regrets are a son-of-a-bitch, bud, and we both know if you keep holding back like that, you'll regret it."

Challenged, Harley looked back at Anastasia. She obviously had no idea what they were talking about. Her brows went up in question—and Harley gave in.

He cupped a hand behind her neck. "Barber's a pain in the ass, but he's dead-on this time."

"About . . . ?"

"This." He put a very public claim on her by way of a scorching kiss.

Watching Harley lose the fight, Barber thanked the heavens that he wasn't strung out on a woman right now. Thanks to Simon Evans's endorsement to the SBC, his music was taking off bigger than he'd ever expected, and he had his hands full with a thriving career.

There was a time when he'd felt broken over losing Dakota to Simon, but now . . . well hell, he had too many blessings to hold a grudge, and he got to keep Dakota as a friend, so all in all, he had the world by the ass, and he liked it that way.

Harley came up for air, ran a thumb over Anastasia's bottom lip. His mouth firmed, his gaze went cold; he dropped his hand and, without another word, turned and walked away.

Barber watched him go with a chuckle. "Pathetic." He turned to say something more to Anastasia, and found her still standing there, her mouth slightly open, her eyes dazed.

At least the feelings were mutual, Barber thought. For his friend's sake, he was glad of that.

He shook his head, chucked her under the chin, and whispered, "Regroup, honey. The whole bar is looking."

As if jolted by electricity, she snapped to attention. She didn't bother with their audience, and instead stared at Barber. "I'd already told him good-bye."

"Yeah, I know, at the garage. Apparently he thought another farewell was in order." Just as he'd thought keeping Barber away from her had merit.

Barber lifted the coat she'd been wearing and held it out to her. "You ready to go?"

"That's Harley's coat. You can return it to him for me."

"He didn't ask for it."

"I know. But mine is still hanging where he left it last night, and now it's dry, so I don't need his anymore."

Barber read through the reasonable explanation to the core of her meaning. "You don't want any reminders?"

She slanted him a look. "I don't want to be tempted to contact him for any reason."

"Like returning a coat?"

"Exactly." Ignoring the avid stares of the people milling throughout the bar, she retrieved her coat and put it on.

Carrying her overnight bag, laptop, and file folder, Barber followed her.

She took the laptop from him. "I guess this is it."

On impulse, he said, "Hang on a sec." Setting the overnight bag beside her, he went to the bar and requested a pen and paper from Sheila. After he wrote down his number, Barber tried to hand it to Anastasia.

She held up a hand, refusing the paper. "I won't be calling him, Barber."

"It's my number, not Harley's."

"I assumed as much."

"You did, huh?"

"You wouldn't give out Harley's number without knowing me better. But you're giving me your number in case I want to get in contact with Harley."

Once again taken aback at her shrewd perception, Barber stared down at her. "Did it occur to you that I might be hitting on you?"

"No. You and Harley are friends."

He put the paper in her hand and curled her fingers over it. "Keep it anyway, just in case you change your mind. Okay?"

Parked out front, watching them through the big glass window, Harley beeped his horn.

Anastasia rolled her eyes.

Barber laughed again. "We better go before he comes in here and demolishes me."

"He wouldn't."

"Yeah, I think he would. It's actually pretty interesting—and that's why I gave you my number. The fact he has you riding with his uncle instead of me is amusing. Harley's not acting like himself. I think that might be a good thing."

After a long thoughtful moment, she shrugged and shoved the slip of paper into her jeans pocket. "All right."

Smart girl.

He lifted her luggage and together they exited the bar. Harley never left his Jeep, but he did stare—hard—as Barber got her and her belongings settled into Satch's vehicle.

Barber figured on a few weeks, a month at the most, and Anastasia and Harley would be together again.

If not, he'd finesse a reunion himself. That was the least he could do for a good guy like Harley.

ANASTASIA felt very conspicuous sitting beside Satch in the SUV. He'd made it clear that he didn't want to be separated from Harley, and though he didn't act too disgruntled about the arrangement, she still felt uncomfortable knowing that she'd put a kink in his plans.

"You want me to hit a drive-thru and get you something to eat?"

"No, thank you." She wasn't about to inconvenience him further. "I can get something at the hotel."

"You sure you got enough belongings?"

She glanced back at her one suitcase filled with necessities, her laptop, and the important files she'd retrieved in a quick trip to the cabin. "I have everything I need for now."

"Too bad those deputies couldn't do anything more than take a report and confiscate the guns. With any luck, they can use the weapons as evidence if they can ever catch anyone."

She turned her head to look out the window. "I doubt they will. Whoever hassled us last night has probably already taken off. They don't want to get caught and strangers are easy to pick out from the locals."

"You're not thinking about heading right back there, are you?"

"Not just yet, no."

As they drove north, a thick layer of white blanketed everything, but without so much ice, and without the bulk that buried Echo Lake.

"Harley spoke highly of you."

Unsure what Satch meant, Stasia gave up her perusal of the scenery. "He's a very nice man."

Satch gave her an incredulous look. "He thinks you're brave."

The absurdity of that made her laugh. "I was so afraid last night, I couldn't stop shaking."

"That's just intelligence. Anyone with a brain would have been afraid of two hoodlums with guns."

"Harley wasn't."

Satch rolled a shoulder. "That boy is more action than talk, always has been. He needs to learn better control."

Hoping to gain more insight into Harley's psyche, Stasia gave Satch her complete attention. "He seems overly contained to me."

"He's working on it. Used to be, he'd dive into every situation like a free-for-all. It wasn't until after he got burned a few times that he learned to think things through before reacting."

Or to not react at all? "Last night, when those men came

back, he seemed on automatic pilot to me. He was pretty darned impressive, too."

"Harley can handle himself, no question about that. But he's just plain lucky that he didn't get you or himself shot. Someone with better control would have analyzed the situation more closely, and chosen to duck the trouble, rather than face it head-on."

Insulted on Harley's behalf, she said, "I'm not sure I agree. When they first came on us, there really wasn't anyplace to hide, especially in the freezing cold. The circumstances called for quick thinking and fast action. Harley supplied both."

Satch shook his head. "He took a big risk, and he has to stop doing that. He wants a title belt, and that means he has to stick to a game plan, not go off half-cocked." Satch glanced at her. "Did he tell you what took him out of the last fight?"

"I overheard something about an injury to his elbow."

"It's a long story, but Dakota—Simon Evans's wife, though they weren't married at the time—had an ex who liked to cause her trouble." As if the memories annoyed him, Satch worked his jaw. "Harley likes to stop trouble."

"He got injured defending her?"

"Against three thugs. He put an end to the bastards, and got his elbow dislocated for his trouble."

Picturing it in her mind, how fast and fluid Harley was in action, Stasia sighed. "Sounds heroic."

"Yeah, sure. That's Harley. The SBC agrees, by the way. They like him. But they'll like him even more when he fights for the belt and wins. But he *has* to fight this time."

"I don't understand. You think he won't fight?"

"Hell, he's been offered title shots three times now. Every damn time, something gets in the way. If it happens again, who knows when the SBC will make another offer?"

"I didn't realize." And she felt sick about it. What if Harley had lost his big chance because of her?

Again Satch glanced at her, this time with speculation shining in his eyes. "He can win, no problem there. He's one of the most talented fighters I've ever seen. But he has to make sure he's in the fight, not on the sidelines with an injury."

Stasia wanted to know more, but she didn't want to pry. Once she got her affairs in order, she'd study the sport a bit on her own before watching on pay-per-view again.

"Harley tells me you're a life coach."

Now what was Satch up to? "That's right."

"Like it?"

"Yes. Very much." At least, most of the time she did. Other times . . . she didn't want to think about the drawbacks she'd only recently discovered.

"You any good at it?"

"I have an excellent success record and I come highly recommended." To tweak him, she asked, "Why do you ask? Do you need some guidance, Satch?"

"Me? No, no. I'm fine."

To hide her grin, Stasia looked out the side window again.

Satch drove on in silence for a bit until they came to a more congested area. "How about that place?" he asked, indicating a sign for a hotel off the next exit. The building was just visible from the highway. "The lights are all on, so they're not without power."

"I think the outage was limited to our small town."

"It's not a chain," Satch pointed out, "but sometimes the small places are better. More personal attention, you know. And it's not too far from Echo Lake."

"Yes." Stasia studied the billboard for the hotel. There were several restaurants nearby, and a convenience store. The area looked clean and well organized. "It'll do. Thank you."

Satch took the exit and drove up to the hotel. "I'll help you inside."

"That's okay, Satch. You've done enough. Really. If you'd just pull up to the door—"

While she spoke, he parked the SUV. "I insist. Besides, I wanted to talk to you about something."

Stasia felt dread crawl up her spine, but she pasted on a polite smile. "Okay then."

He turned off the engine and hustled around to her door. After she got out, he retrieved her luggage and laptop, and she took the thick file folder.

On the way in, he commented, "Harley said you were taking a little time off work."

"I was, but I'm rethinking that now. All things considered, it might be a good time to be away from Echo Lake for a while."

"Good, good." Satch's brows came down. "Harley's going to be in full-time training again."

Cautious, uncertain of Satch's motives but sensing a trap, Stasia said, "He told me he had an important fight coming up. Is it a title fight?"

"It will be, after the SBC builds him up."

The parking lot had already been cleared and only a dusting of snow blown by an earlier wind covered the ground. It felt good to be out of the knee-deep stuff.

Satch managed both her laptop and her luggage in one arm and held the door open for her. "I'd like to discuss hiring you."

She'd just stepped into the hotel lobby when he spoke, and she halted her step. "Hire me? But you just said you weren't interested."

"Not for me. For Harley."

He had to be kidding. Stasia blinked at him in disbelief.

Satch urged her farther inside. "He thinks he's focused, but after the stunt he just pulled—disarming two unknown nutcases—the truth is easy enough to see."

"And the truth is?"

"His brain is everywhere except where it should be. He needs to keep the upcoming fights in the forefront of his mind, and temper his reactions to everything around that. Otherwise he's just going to repeat past mistakes and unfortunate interruptions."

"Like a dislocated elbow?"

"Exactly."

Flabbergasted, Stasia asked, "Would you have had him stand by while his friend's wife was hurt?"

"No. That's not what I'm saying."

In analytical mode, Stasia crossed her arms and studied Harley's uncle. "Should he have left me to fend for myself, to maybe freeze to death or get shot?"

"Of course not." He held her gaze. "But if his priority was the fight, he'd have hidden, not challenged the bastards."

"I see." But she didn't, not really. Was Satch insinuating that she'd somehow swayed Harley toward irresponsible behavior? And if so, why in the world would he want to hire her?

"I don't think you do, not yet. But that's why I wanted to talk to you. You could help Harley block out the negative influences."

Feeling her way, Stasia said, "Maybe you're unaware of Harley's preferences, but he was pretty up-front that once he said good-bye, he didn't expect to ever lay eyes on me again."

Satch waved that off. "I know. He made it clear that you weren't his type and things were over, otherwise I couldn't ask you to coach him."

Every muscle in her body stiffened. "Harley discussed me with you?"

"Only to reassure me. He seemed different with you, and that had me concerned."

Despite herself, Stasia's interest was piqued. "Different?"

Satch either didn't hear her curiosity or he overlooked it as unimportant. "When he told me he wasn't involved with you, I didn't know if that was the bona fide truth or not. But I watched you at the bar. You understand his priorities."

"And based on whatever you think you saw at the bar, you think Harley would welcome me as a life coach?"

"Hell no. He'd have a conniption if he knew I was hiring you."

Of course he would. "Then that's a problem for me, Satch."

"I don't see why, if it's for his own good—and it is. I always act in Harley's best interests."

Staring up at Satch, Stasia accepted the similarities between the two men. Satch was a tall, well-built, powerful man with blond hair only a shade or two darker than Harley's and eyes a similar hue of blue, but lacking the burning intensity.

She imagined that the two of them butted heads often. Tempting as the idea of more time with Harley might be, she knew the truth: she wasn't as indifferent as Satch wanted to believe. She didn't want to be an annoyance to Harley, and she most certainly did not want in the middle of their private problems.

Even if she thought she could help smooth those problems by acting as Harley's life coach.

"You'd be perfect," Satch said, pushing the point. "He's drawn to you, I could tell, so he'd trust you to give good advice—advice that'll help him in his career. And I can trust you not to start pushing for a romantic relationship."

"I can't see anything being perfect if I begin by misleading him. That goes against the bond of a client and a life coach." She held up a hand when Satch started to protest. "Let's back up a second. Exactly how do you expect me to help Harley when I don't know anything about the sport or the training process beyond what I've seen on television?"

"You can encourage him to follow through with things that'll gain him more recognition."

"Like?"

"The SBC wants to feature Harley in an exposé on his life. His background, his daily habits and routines. His social life."

"Whoa." Distrusting her own ears, Stasia laughed. "I haven't been close to Harley—much—but I can't see him welcoming something like that."

"He doesn't. In fact, he refused to do it." Hands on his

hips, Satch leveled a stern look on her. "And that's where you come in."

"Oh, no," Stasia protested. "That's where I butt out."

Satch eased in closer to her. "Look at it this way. Harley's not going to become a monk. We both know that. So how will it hurt? All the SBC wants is to get a few shots of him with the ladies. Nothing too intimate or anything. Totally PG-rated, I swear. Hell, most of the photos could happen at Roger's Rodeo."

"Roger's what?"

He waved a hand. "It's a local bar near the gym. Sort of a honky-tonk, but nicer I guess. Roger sponsors a lot of the fighters and in return they frequent his place, have a lot of the parties there and stuff. Roger's wife is sister to one of the fighters."

"All in the family, huh?"

"I suppose you could say so. Fighters hang out there just about every night and all through the weekend, which brings in fight fans and single women. It's a good deal for all involved." Satch took her hand. "You could get Harley to see the benefit of sharing himself a little, especially if it gets him what he wants in the end."

"The title belt."

"Exactly." Still holding her hand in his, Satch studied her. "You're considering it, aren't you?"

"No, not really." She couldn't—could she?

"I think you are," Satch said.

Freeing her hand from his with a fast smile, Stasia explained, "It's always been an automatic thing for me to analyze all the pros and cons in a job. But Satch, this job would be all cons." Except for seeing Harley again. But since he didn't want to see her, even that wouldn't be a benefit.

"You like my nephew, don't you?"

For sure, she lusted after him. But if she had to be honest with herself . . . "What's not to like? He's a terrific person."

Pleased, Satch nodded his head. "There, you see? You

and I know it, and the SBC wants the rest of the world to know it, too."

"I don't think I can help."

"You can, because he likes you, too. More than any other girl I've seen him with since Sandy put him in pieces."

"Sandy?" Then when the rest of what he'd said sank in, Stasia held up her hands. "Never mind. I can't envision Harley in pieces over any woman."

"Until Sandy, I couldn't have either." Shaking his head, Satch said low, "Harley didn't fall apart and snivel around or any of that melodramatic crap. But he withdrew in so many ways. He doesn't avoid the ladies—"

"There's an understatement."

"But he keeps himself far too private. One-night stands, that's all he has now. And because the shit that happened with Sandy went public, he wants everything as private as it can be."

Public humiliation would be rough on anyone. But for someone like Harley . . . Stasia had a hundred questions, but she refused to allow herself to pry. "Then don't you think he has a right to keep his private life separate from his sport?"

"Damn it, most of the guys would love this kind of publicity."

"Harley isn't most guys."

"No, he's not." Imploring her, Satch said, "Think about it, Anastasia. You could get him to do it. All he has to do is play nice with the ladies while the cameras are around. Some dancing, a few kisses or whatever, some implied intent—"

It was the "or whatever" that made Stasia's stomach cramp. "Sounds like you want me to be Harley's pimp."

Brows crunching down, Satch took a quick step back. "It's not like that at all! The SBC only wants to capitalize on his appeal to women."

And he was appealing, Stasia thought. In a big way.

Did Satch have any idea of his nephew's fetishes? No.

Harley was too private for that. "I'm sure if you have someone waiting around with a camera, there'll be opportunities galore."

"I don't think so. Harley told me he was cutting out female companionship during his training."

Her eyes almost crossed—until she thought more about it. "Isn't that typical? I mean, I've always heard that sex before competition was a no-no."

Satch snorted.

"So it's not?"

"For most men, hell no. For Harley . . ." Satch scratched at his throat. "Let's just say it's downright alarming for him to want to fly solo. Especially right now. He has a lot of promo coming up—pre-fight parties and events, stuff he wouldn't attend stag, and if he did, he wouldn't be alone for long."

Stasia imagined hordes of women vying for Harley's attention, testing his resolve.

It wasn't a pleasant picture for her.

"Gee, Satch. With Harley so irresistible, maybe you wouldn't even need me. Maybe the female populace will handle the problem for you."

He regarded her with censure. "Now, don't get snippy."

"Snippy?" When Satch grinned, he looked so much like Harley that Stasia almost relented.

"Come on, Anastasia." He held out his arms. "Take the job, and help Harley to reach his goals."

"You just told me he'd have a conniption."

"If he knew I'd *hired* you. But we could keep that part to ourselves. If you just show up and offer some friendly advice, how would he know?"

"No." There were several reasons that wouldn't work, her pride being first on the list. "Harley will assume I'm chasing him, and as you've pointed out, he has enough women dogging his heels already. One more would only annoy him."

"Usually I'd agree. This time . . ." Satch shrugged. "I think you're different."

She didn't dare hope that was true. It'd be all too easy to fall hard for Harley Handleman. "Doesn't matter. I can't work in an underhanded way. It goes against my philosophy of helping the client. There has to be trust and honesty."

"Maybe I misread things," Satch said. "I thought you'd probably want to help him."

"I'm not convinced he needs any help." Harley was a very capable man. Too capable. And contrary to what Satch thought, probably too controlled. "Besides, he made it clear that good-bye was good-bye, final and forever."

"He could change his mind, with a little help."

It was Stasia's turn to pace. She did want to help Harley, if in no other way than to assist him in getting his uncle to butt out of his personal affairs.

Not what Satch had in mind, but it would be in Harley's best interests—and Satch claimed to want that.

She turned to face him. "I refuse to force myself on him."

Satch was blank for two seconds, then he fought a big grin.

Men! In some ways, they were all alike. "I didn't mean *that*." Stasia could feel her face heating.

"I know." He chewed away the signs of humor and cleared his throat. "What if Harley contacts you first?"

"Why would he?"

Shrugging, Satch said, "Any number of reasons, but most likely to make certain you've got everything settled and that you're okay after the attack."

"It wasn't that much of an attack, and it didn't faze Harley. Besides, he doesn't have my number."

"I could give it to him."

She paced again—and finally came to a conclusion. "I tell you what. I'll need a little time to get my own business in order and to get my truck repaired. Let's say two weeks."

"Two weeks for what?"

"If Harley contacts me at all in those two weeks, then I'll make a point of dropping in on him to *offer* my services as a life coach. If he sends me packing, then that's that."

"But . . ."

Stasia paid no mind to his objection. "I won't be too pushy, but maybe I can convince him to let me help out." She opened her purse, dug out a business card, and handed it to Satch. "My cell phone number is on there. That's the best I can do. Take it or leave it."

Satch hesitated, but in the end he accepted the card. "All right, then. I'll make it easy on Harley and leave this someplace where he'll run into it."

"I doubt it'll make a difference."

"I think it will. But promise me that you won't tell Harley I hired you."

That wouldn't be a problem, since she had no intention of allowing Satch to pay her a dime. "As long as I'm comfortable doing so under the circumstances, I'll keep our conversation to myself."

Relieved, Satch suddenly pulled her in for a big bear hug. When he set her back from him, his hands on her shoulders, he looked stern. "You use caution now, you hear? If you go to your cabin, take someone with you. Don't take any chances on your safety."

Like uncle, like nephew. "I'm smart enough to ensure my own safety, Satch, I promise."

"I'm counting on it." He tapped her card against his thigh. "I better get going."

"Thank you for the ride."

He started away. "Remember what I said. Caution."

She stood there until he'd left the hotel. As she walked to the front desk, she wondered what she'd gotten herself into.

But then again, Harley probably wouldn't call, which would mean she hadn't gotten herself into anything.

It'd just be good-bye, as Harley had said.

CHAPTER 9

HARLEY gripped the phone a little tighter. "You're sure?"

Sitting at the table across from him, listening to his phone conversation without compunction, Barber lifted a brow.

"Shit." He never should have waited so long to call. He'd fought with himself, and ended up losing anyway. "All right, Ned, where's she at now? What do you mean you don't know? She's not still at the hotel? How long ago did she leave?"

Frustrated at the lack of answers, Harley paced away from Barber. This early in the day, Roger's Rodeo was nearly empty except for a few of Barber's groupies hanging around, hoping to get his attention. "All right, fine, but if you hear anything else, let me know. Yeah, call me on this number. Thanks."

He closed his cell and then just stood there, undecided on what to do, or if he should do anything at all.

Barber cleared his throat. "Trouble?"

"I don't know."

"I take it the little lady's gone missing?"

Harley shook his head. "I don't know that either." He rejoined Barber at the table, but pushed away his half-eaten breakfast. "Her brake lines were cut clean."

"No fraying? That had to be deliberate."

"Yeah. And since she lives up a damn hill, and the weather at the time was as bad as I've seen, it has to mean someone wanted to see her hurt. But why?"

"She has enemies?"

"Not that I know of, but then I don't know that much about her background. Ned said she also found footprints around her property."

"I figured the snow would've buried any tracks."

"Not on her front porch, or around back where the house blocked most of the downfall."

"You think someone was trying to break in a window?"

Harley shook his head. "Doesn't sound like, since no one entered. But maybe they were trying to look in the windows."

"To see if she was home alone?"

"Shit." Harley pressed the heels of his palms against his eye sockets, but it didn't help relieve his tension. "After getting some things from her cabin, she had been keeping in touch with Ned from the hotel where Satch dropped her off."

"At least she's staying safe."

"I don't know." Harley concentrated on relaxing. "She told Ned she was checking out yesterday, and he hasn't heard from her yet today."

"A whole day, huh?" Being a wiseass, Barber whistled. "Maybe we should call in the National Guard."

Pinning Barber in his gaze, Harley suggested, "Maybe we should go five rounds sparring."

Laughing, Barber said, "You need to get laid, dude. You're way too high-strung."

When Harley snarled, Barber held up both hands. "Okay, okay. You're on the no-sex rule. I get it. Just ease your finger off the trigger. That's better." Grinning ear to ear, he said, "I didn't mean to rile you."

"Yes, you did."

"Well, now you're riled, so I'll stop." Being more serious, Barber leaned forward on the table. "She's probably just off checking out a new job or something."

"Without her truck?"

"Like I heard her tell you, Harley, she's a smart lady. Odds are she has a rental through her insurance."

"I suppose."

"Seriously, Harley, there's no reason to get on the worry wagon so soon."

Harley wanted to explode. Not worry? He wished someone could tell him how. Since leaving Anastasia nearly two weeks ago, he'd done nothing but worry. And think about her. And remember . . . too much.

Jumping into a grueling routine hadn't helped.

Driving himself to exhaustion hadn't eased him one bit.

Hell, he should have had her when the opportunity presented itself. If he'd made the most of the situation, she'd probably be out of his system already. He wasn't a man meant for sacrifice. Not when it came to sex.

But hearing her come, feeling her tighten and squirm . . . Damn, it had been sweet.

Barber tossed back two aspirin with a tall glass of orange juice.

Feeling mean, Harley asked, "What's wrong with you? Hungover?"

"Lack of sleep, actually." He rubbed his temples. "I was up late auditioning singers, then up early to have breakfast with you."

"No luck finding a songbird, huh?"

Barber snorted. "None of them are Dakota."

Harley shook his head in pity. "You're still hung up on her, aren't you?"

"Hell no. I value my face too much, and Simon would ruin it if he thought I had a thing for her still. But on the stage, she's a tough act to follow."

"Maybe you're just too picky."

"And maybe you should have told me you'd be lousy

company, and I could have gone home to bed." His gaze went to the gaggle of young, enthusiastic, and willing women eyeing him from a short distance away. "Preferably with a sweet young thing."

"Or two?"

"Now you're talking." Barber looked away from the women, his dismissal of them obvious. "You know, I could probably convince one of them to take pity on you, if you'd give up this idiotic idea of celibacy."

For whatever reason, Harley couldn't work up any enthusiasm for the chase. "You have an odd obsession with my sexual prowess."

Barber snorted—and rubbed at his temples again.

In his own negative mood, Harley enjoyed Barber's misery. "Know what I think? You're too damn old to be burning the candle at both ends the way you do."

"I'm twenty-nine, you ass. A year younger than you!"

So sensitive about his age? Harley wondered at it—and ribbed him a little more. "Huh. Really? Must be the bags under your eyes that age you."

Barber narrowed his bloodshot eyes. "Now seems like a good time to tell you that I gave her my phone number."

"Who? Dakota?" He looked beyond him at the women huddled at a small table. "Or one of those moony-eyed groupies trying so hard to get your attention?"

His smile tight, Barber shook his head and enunciated clearly, *"Anastasia."*

Harley froze.

Satisfied with that telling reaction, Barber lounged back in his chair. "Yeah, so see, you can relax, bro. If something was wrong, she'd probably call me."

At a loss, Harley just stared at him.

"Now don't go figuring ways to take me apart. She said she knew I was giving it to her in case she wanted to get in touch with you. And as we've both already noted, I'm not up for a skirmish today."

Harley still stared. *Barber had given Anastasia his number?*

"What?" Barber slumped further. "Don't lie to yourself, man. You know damn good and well you want her to call you."

Harley didn't know any such thing. In the time away from Anastasia, he'd had a dozen different urges, all of them conflicting.

Through stiff lips, he said, "If I had wanted her to have my number, I would have given it to her myself."

Holding up his arms, Barber said, "That's why I gave her my number instead. At first glance, she seemed likable enough, but with chicks you never can tell. They can go wacko"—he snapped his fingers—"in an instant. We've both seen it happen. If Anastasia turns into a stalker, why then, I've sacrificed myself, right?"

Harley pushed back his chair and started to say something, but nothing came to mind.

Barber grinned at him. "I think my head is starting to feel better."

"If you'd get a damn haircut, your head wouldn't hurt so often." Barber's hair now hung long enough that he had to tie it back most days. When he performed onstage, he left it loose and looked like a cross between a hippie and a trained assassin.

"Dude, you know the ladies dig my ponytail. Turns 'em on. And it goes with the earring." He took in Harley's rigid stance and for once, he wore an honest smile. "Come on, Harley. Why don't you stop torturing yourself and admit the inevitable?"

Leave it to Barber to go straight to the crux of things. "Go fuck yourself." And with that, Harley walked off.

"Don't worry, bro," Barber called after him, "I can see you're stressed. I'll pick up the tab on this one, but you'll owe me a meal."

Without looking back, Harley gave him a one-finger salute. He wasn't *stressed*, for God's sake, and he hadn't eaten the damn breakfast, so why should he pay for it?

Harley fumed all the way to the house his uncle had chosen for him to buy. He fumed on his way in the double front doors, as he kicked off his boots in the foyer and shed his thick coat in the formal living room.

He fumed as he walked through the kitchen, past his uncle who looked at him over the top of his newspaper. He went to the granite counter and rummaged through the stacks of bills, sponsor proposals, and advertisements spread out there.

"Looking for something in particular?" Uncle Satch asked.

Harley turned on him. Satch wore rumpled boxers and nothing else. His hair stood on end and reading glasses rested at the end of his nose. At fifty-seven, he was still fit, still toned, but he looked tired.

He also looked a little wary as he took in Harley's mood.

Damn it. Satch was the closest relative Harley had left. Subduing his temper with an effort, Harley asked, "Where's her number?"

"Her who?"

It wasn't easy for him to hide the signs of resurging annoyance. "Anastasia Bradley. You left her card here where I'd see it. And I did. Now what'd you do with it?"

Satch snapped his paper and went back to reading. Or back to pretending to read. "It should be there somewhere." Feigning disinterest, he asked, "Why do you need it?"

"I'm calling her. Why else?"

The paper came back down. "For what?"

"To see if she's okay."

Satch nodded. "Good idea. I've thought about her several times, worried about her a little. Look on the fridge. I might've put the card there."

Harley looked and sure enough, the card was smack-dab in the middle of the refrigerator door, held in place by a magnet advertising Roger's Rodeo, the bar where he'd just left Barber, and where local SBC fighter events happened on a weekly basis.

Snatching off the card, Harley headed for the den. He

didn't want his uncle listening in and making more of the call than existed. He didn't know what he'd say to Anastasia, and in case he sounded like an idiot, he wanted privacy.

Dropping into a comfortably padded desk chair, Harley propped his feet on the desk and picked up the cordless phone.

Not only had his uncle chosen the house, which wasn't far from Dean's gym where Harley routinely worked out and sparred, but he'd also had it furnished.

He'd done a good job, never mind that Harley hadn't wanted the responsibility and commitment of a house, much less one with four bedrooms and three bathrooms, a game room, and an indoor pool.

But Satch had worked too hard on it all for Harley to complain to him.

After his father's death from a stroke, Uncle Satch, his mother's brother, had stepped in to help in a million different ways. Harley remembered him filling in as a father figure, there whenever his mother needed him, kind and generous—all in all, being a damn good big brother to his mother, and a considerate uncle to him.

When his mother died a few years ago from cancer, Satch became Harley's only family—and his manager. Sometimes he was a real pain in the ass, but he always meant well, and Harley wasn't cold-hearted enough to ever say or do anything to hurt him.

Deep down, he knew he owed Satch, probably more than he could ever repay him. And if he had to be honest, the pool was a kick.

Harley dialed the phone and waited.

Breathless, Anastasia answered on the fourth ring. "Hello?"

Just hearing her voice had a calming effect on Harley. Not that he sounded all that calm when he growled, "It's Harley."

Silence stretched out, then: "Harley! It's nice to hear from you." Honest pleasure sounded in her tone. "How've you been? Is everything okay?"

He felt like an ass.

He'd made such a big production in limiting their time together, driving it into the ground that once they parted ways he didn't expect to hear from her again.

And he hadn't.

Moderating his tone, Harley asked, "You're okay? You sound winded."

"I'm great. Just got in the door from shopping, in fact. You?"

Of course she was fine. Hadn't he told Satch how resourceful, gutsy, and smart she was? "Ned told me you were right about the brake lines. They were cut."

"Crazy, isn't it? I could have been killed, or killed someone else. The deputies are assuming it was a random act of violence—like a prank gone wrong. You know, two yahoos with too much to drink and not enough sense to behave in a civilized way. Nothing else has happened."

If it had been boys involved, instead of grown men carrying guns, that story might have been more plausible. "You haven't seen the truck again?"

"I haven't been back to Echo that much, but no one else has seen them."

He segued right in to his next statement. "Really? Because Ned mentioned that you'd left the hotel. I just assumed you'd gone back to Echo."

She went quiet, a precursor to her temper. "You and Ned have been chatty."

Harley didn't have a good answer for that. "He was concerned."

"Really? *Ned* was? Funny, he didn't say anything to me."

Pinching the bridge of his nose, Harley managed two deep breaths. "Are you moving back to your cabin?"

"Actually, no. Not permanently and not right away. I've already packed up some of my belongings and I hired an older retired couple to keep an eye on both cabins."

Harley hated the thought of her there by herself alone, vulnerable. "Going somewhere?"

"To see my folks for a while. I'm not sure how long.

After that . . . well, I have a job in mind." She cleared her throat. "If it works out, I don't think I'll be back at the cabin for a while. But if not, then when I go back, I'll get some extra security lights installed."

At least she planned to leave the cabin for now. "What's the job?"

She went silent for a stretch, then said, "I keep all my jobs strictly confidential."

Harley's hand tightened on the phone, and he heard himself saying, "While you're at the cabin, if anyone bothers you, call me."

Laughter rang in his ear. "And you're what, Harley? Only a few *hours* away."

Eyes closed, he said through his teeth, "Three."

She laughed again. "I'll be fine. The deputies promised to make a few trips past my cabin, just to keep an eye on things. They also gave me their cell phone numbers, and they're a whole lot closer than you are."

That made sense, except he didn't like their added familiarity. "Sounds to me like they're hitting on you."

Another laugh. "No, it wasn't like that. They're just doing their duty."

"If you say so." New tension cramped his muscles. "Where do your folks live?" Hopefully, well away from Echo Lake.

"Not far from you, actually. Southern Kentucky. Why?"

"Idle curiosity, that's all." *Liar.* For some idiotic reason, knowing she'd be nearby made his pulse leap.

Was she thinking about a visit with him, too? Harley shook his head. "You getting your truck back soon?"

"Ned's working on it, but he got slammed with rush jobs on things, even some of the vehicles for the county. Since I had a rental, I told him he could prioritize. I should have it tomorrow, and then I'll return the rental and head to my parents' place."

"I guess you're glad to be out of the hotel."

"It wasn't too bad. I pampered myself with room service."

Harley smiled, almost said that he would have joined her, and caught himself. "I better get going."

"You've started training?"

"Nothing but." Because that sounded like a complaint, he tacked on, "I'm fortunate that some of the best fighters around frequent Dean's gym. He and Sublime are both phenomenal, Mallet's getting there, and Barber, when he's in the right mood, is good for sparring."

"When's your next fight?"

"I don't know yet. I need to get back in fighting shape first."

"You looked in excellent shape to me."

A grin slipped up on him. He'd heard plenty of compliments, but coming from Anastasia made it special. "Thanks. There's fit, and then there's ready to fight. It'll be a few weeks before I can even think about competing. If it works out, I'd like six or eight weeks to prepare."

She went quiet for a moment, then whispered, "You sound good, Harley. You sound happy. I'm glad."

Damn, how did she turn him inside out so easily? "You, too."

"I'll let you go. Take care and . . ." She hesitated.

"What?"

With a shrug in her tone, she said, "I don't want you to worry. I'm not going to misconstrue this call."

There she went again, saying the unexpected, confusing him and pricking his temper. "Misconstrue it how?"

"It doesn't take a genius to see that you're a protective person. It probably didn't seem right to you to leave after everything that had happened. But I'm an adult, I really am fine, and the trouble is over, so there's no reason for you to think about it again."

In other words, she wanted him to forget her?

Frowning, Harley closed his eyes, struggled with himself, and just when he thought he might have figured out a reply, she whispered, "Good-bye, Harley," and hung up on him.

Disgusted, confused, and strangely discontented with the entire situation, he dropped the phone onto the desk.

Damn, damn, damn. That hadn't gone as he'd wanted, but since he wasn't sure what he'd wanted, there wasn't much he could do about it.

Satch stuck his head in the door. "Everything okay with Anastasia?"

Eyes narrowed, Harley wondered if his uncle had been listening in the entire time. His timing seemed awfully convenient. "She's fine."

"Good." He stepped into the den. "You have a phone interview this afternoon." Handing a printout of the information to Harley, he said, "Make sure you wrap up your workout in time. Oh, and we're getting some new photos after dinner."

Idly glancing at the magazine's logo and demographic percentages, Harley said, "Didn't we just do that?"

"Months ago. You need something new. Something *now*. The photographer is donating his shots as long as he can use them in his portfolio."

He glanced at Satch. "If you say so."

"I've got you some new gear, too."

"Let me guess: from sponsors?"

"Yeah. Don't forget, you need to be seen wearing the stuff—"

"And drinking the stuff, and eating the stuff—"

Satch held up some keys. "And *driving* the stuff."

No fucking way. Curious despite his contempt for his uncle's over-the-top promotional efforts, Harley sat forward in his seat. "A car?"

"Leased free to you for three months. Longer if you get up to the title shot, yours to keep if you win."

In disbelief, he came out from behind the desk. "What is it?"

"Dodge Charger with a hemi. Black. Five speed. Top-of-the-line stereo and DVD system. It's a pimped-out fifty-thousand-dollar car—yours just because you're you."

Like most men, Harley liked cars . . . but unlike some guys, he preferred to keep it real. "I have a Jeep."

Satch waved that off. "The Jeep is fine, but Dodge wants

to see you in their Charger." He lifted his shoulders and grinned. "It's good promo for them."

Still skeptical, Harley crossed his arms. "Do I have to have their name tattooed on my ass or something?"

"Nope, just drive the car to the next few interviews and live appearances. And wear one of their shirts occasionally."

Harley shook his head. This newfound fame was getting out of hand. "All right. Thanks Satch."

Taking advantage of Harley's softened mood, Satch pressed other issues. "About some photographs with the ladies—"

"I'm not seeing anyone."

"A situation easily changed!"

Harley put a hand on Satch's shoulder. "Let's go see the car before I head out for the gym. I'm seeing a Thai boxing coach first today, then working on takedowns and take-down defenses after that, so I don't want to be late."

Satch went along, but he didn't relent. "What about some ringside girls? I talked to two of the new ones and they'd be thrilled for the chance to be photographed with you. No one would have to know you weren't actually dating them . . ."

"No." The SBC hired sexy young things to flaunt themselves between rounds. But every fighter around hit on them, and that made them uninteresting.

"You're being unreasonable, Harley."

They stepped into the garage and Harley saw the car. Sweet. And insane. "For now, why don't you just let me enjoy the new ride without hassling me on other stuff, okay?"

"Suit yourself." He launched into a sales pitch of sorts as Harley opened the driver's door.

But the car wasn't exciting enough to keep Harley's thoughts off of Anastasia.

Given how he felt after talking to her, he was starting to wonder if anything could.

CHAPTER 10

T HE new routine left Harley wiped out, so he was in no mood for the reporter or the photographer working on the damned exposé. Sunday was the only day he didn't train in some way, which meant Saturday night was his only night to blow off steam.

And despite his wishes, Satch had scheduled him for an interview.

Unlike other fighters, Harley didn't believe in cutting out everything he enjoyed. If he wanted a beer—as he did now—he had a beer. Same with a fat, juicy burger or a slice of sweet cake, though those cravings hadn't hit him lately.

He limited the indulgences to a brief binge on Saturday night. The rest of the week he stuck with a strict and clean nutritional plan with plenty of water, lean meats, and fibrous carbohydrates. Most mornings, his breakfast was a protein shake.

A gangly guy in glasses leaned in closer to Harley. "Can you give me a rundown of a typical week of training for you?"

Trying to block out Barber's smirking face in the seat

across from him, Harley shrugged. "On average, I spend about thirty hours a week training."

A recorder got shoved under his chin. "We'll do some taping of that later, but until then, why don't you tell us exactly what you do in training. Give us some details."

Trying for subtlety, Harley eased the recorder away from his face. "My routine varies. I alternate weight-lifting and strength training with conditioning and nontraditional pacing."

"Such as?"

He shrugged. "Swinging a sledge hammer, throwing tires, stuff like that. I also work in cardio exercises each week. Sprints, jogging, running hills and stairs, and laps in my pool. Three times a week I strengthen my wrestling skills, and twice a week I focus exclusively on my takedowns and takedown defense. Then there's the days when I work on submissions, practice my kicks, knees, and elbows."

"How many coaches do you have?"

"Depends. Dean Conor, the owner of the gym and currently my trainer, augments the workouts by bringing in specialists with wrestling, boxing, Brazilian jujitsu—that sort of thing. One day a week is dedicated to mixed martial arts."

"You enjoy that?"

Harley looked at the guy and wondered at such a stupid question. "Without the MMA, I wouldn't be much competition for anyone." He took another swig of his beer.

"I talked with Dean Conor earlier. He said he has to pull you back sometimes, you work so hard."

"After my elbow injury, I have a lot of catching up to do. Besides, I've never shied away from hard work."

With renewed enthusiasm, the reporter jammed the recorder close again. "You mentioned your pool. I heard you recently moved into more permanent digs here in Harmony."

Harley nodded. "My uncle picked out the place. Satch Handleman. He's also my manager, and he does a great job." Harley knew Satch would enjoy the plug.

"Now that you're settled here in Harmony, are you seeing anyone special?"

"No."

The reporter looked blank, but quickly rallied. "I understand you're a renowned ladies' man. How do you feel about being credited with building the female audience for the sport?"

Shit. Harley hated questions like this. "You need to field that one on Sublime. I think I saw him around here somewhere earlier. If the ladies are hanging around, it's likely due to him."

Pleased, the reporter grinned at him. "I'm told he got things started."

Harley winked. "They don't call him Sublime without reason."

"Rumor has it that Sublime is retiring. How do you feel about that?"

"I hadn't heard." But he had, and it infuriated him.

The reporter pursued the topic. "After dislocating your elbow, you were counting on Sublime to give you another chance at the title belt. Isn't that right?"

"I had hoped for another shot, yeah."

"So if he's bailing now—"

Idiot. "Look, Simon Evans is an honorable guy. He's newly married, he's been here, done this, and now he's done it again. If he says he's going back into retirement, then he has a good reason that has nothing to do with me."

Voice conspiratorial, the reporter asked, "You think he's dodging you?"

Harley laughed. When the reporter just looked at him, he shook his head. "You don't know too many SBC fighters do you?"

"Uh . . . not personally, no. But I've been following the sport for a while now."

Leaning forward, crowding the guy, Harley said, "Then you should know that SBC fighters, especially those of Sublime's caliber, wouldn't dodge Satan himself. Simon would come in and take him apart. Gladly. I have too much respect for the guy to say otherwise."

"Would you have beaten him?"

"Who the hell knows?" Harley dropped back in his chair. "I'm no slouch either, as I'm sure Sublime would tell you. When you get to a certain level, it's anyone's fight. Sometimes it comes down to conditioning or speed. One thing is certain: it would have been a battle." With that, Harley made a winding gesture with his finger, telling the reporter to wrap it up.

"So what's next for you? If Sublime retires, who will you fight?"

"Whoever the SBC puts before me. I'm not picky. Bottom line, I'm here to compete and win. Period."

The photographer closed in to capture his frown, his determination—and nearly blinded Harley in the process.

Shutting off the recorder, the reporter said, "Great job. Interesting stuff, man. Hope I didn't offend?"

"Not too much."

Pulling back, the reporter looked around as if seeking help.

Harley laughed. "Thanks for your time. I appreciate it."

"Oh yeah, sure. My pleasure." He gathered his equipment. "We're nowhere near done, but this is enough from you for now. We're going to hang around here, though, talk to a few of your colleagues, get some candid shots and stuff. So just ignore us and be yourself."

As the reporter hurried away, Barber asked, "How much will you pay me *not* to talk to him?"

"Not a single cent. Say whatever you want. I've decided not to give a shit."

"A real change of heart, huh? So does that mean you're done being celibate for now?"

"No." Tipping up his longneck for a generous swig, Harley ignored **Barber**'s laughter, even though he knew it wouldn't do him any good.

The second the reporter and photographer had showed up, Barber started grinning. He was enjoying himself too much to back off.

He liked Harley's predicament.

But Harley didn't.

Ever since he'd walked into the bar, the women had been on him. Nothing unusual in that. A lot of females hung out at Roger's place, hoping to hook up with a fighter. Some of them were fans, some groupies, some just out to have a good time in the most expedient way.

Knowing what his uncle had contrived, Harley had repeatedly sent them packing.

Much to the photographer's annoyance.

The problem, as far as Harley was concerned, was his honest lack of interest. He wasn't just thwarting his uncle's plans to showcase his personal life for the masses.

He flat-out wasn't tempted.

Maybe it was the grueling training schedule combined with nonstop promotion that left him too tired to be intrigued by the thought of carnal activity.

Maybe it was the lack of variety in women. They were all attractive enough, and more than willing. Too willing, in fact. A little reserve might've sparked things.

And maybe he should stop lying to himself.

He knew damn good and well why he wasn't interested, but that didn't mean he had to share his burden with Barber.

"You know, Harley, I can understand restricting yourself to one beer, considering your training schedule and all. Getting wasted wouldn't be good. But you aren't even allowing one woman. You're at . . . what? Zilch? Zero? It ain't natural."

Not looking at Barber, and avoiding eye contact with anyone female, left Harley with nowhere to look but at the tabletop. He idly drew a finger through the round watermark left behind by his beer—and hoped the photographer didn't take a shot of him doing it.

Leaning forward in a pretense of confidentiality, Barber cleared his throat. "I'm asking 'cuz, you know, if you're not into ladies anymore, I might need to pick up the slack—"

"Give it a rest, Barber."

"Talk to Barber, buddy. Tell me what ails you. Maybe I can help."

Stretching his arms high above his head, Harley yawned and said, "I think I'll call it a night."

"It's barely ten and this is your only night out! Besides, that poor photographer is stuck hanging around, trying to get the money shot for you."

"He can wait all night for all I care."

"Relent, dude. Make your uncle happy. Thrill the photographer."

Harley rolled his eyes.

"You're caving, I can tell. And you know the only way we'll get rid of the press peeps is to give 'em what they want." Barber grinned. "And speaking of that, opportunity is heading this way right now."

"What?" Harley looked around and saw two women headed toward them with blatant intent. "Well hell."

"I get the redhead," Barber told him. "You know I'm partial to redheads."

"I thought it was blondes."

"The blonde is taken. And if Simon hears you talking about Dakota, he'll maul both of us. You can have the brunette. No, Harley, don't turn tail and run on me or I'll be forced to call you names."

"So?"

"I'll tell the ladies you're impotent. I'll tell them you cry yourself to sleep. I'll say you wet the bed—"

"Shut up, will you?" Closing his eyes, Harley waited, and a second later the two women were there. Because the small table only had two chairs, the redhead plopped herself right into Barber's lap.

He didn't mind in the least.

The brunette propped a shapely ass on the table right in front of Harley, barely missing the wet ring on the table.

"Easy, darling," Barber warned. "Harley's in a bad mood."

"Ahhh, poor Harley," she said, leaning down and sticking her manicured fingers into his hair. "Maybe I can make you feel better."

"Am I interrupting?"

Harley looked up and encountered a familiar face—one he'd never thought to see again.

The timing sucked. He hated scenes, and any time a woman from the past showed up, a scene was sure to follow. "Gloria, right?"

"You remember!"

"We met at Echo Lake."

"That's right. We did." Her smile said they'd more than met, but Harley pretended not to notice.

The woman sitting on his table didn't cut corners. She said, "Scram, Gloria. He's already been claimed for the night."

Gloria blushed bright red. "I just wanted to say hi. I didn't realize you were from this area, Harley."

It was such an obvious lie that Harley felt bad for her. "Do you live around here, too?"

"No. I'm just passing through the area and stopped in for some entertainment."

Before Harley could reply to that, the woman on the table said, "He's entertaining me."

Gloria's smile stiffened. "So I see."

The photographer had a field day shooting fast shots, one right after the other.

Before things got any worse, Harley held out a hand to Gloria. "I hope you enjoy the town while you're here." The comment lacked intimacy, and rang of a polite dismissal.

She took his hand and nodded. "Thank you." When the woman on the table made a rude sound, Gloria released Harley and stepped back. "Okay then, have fun." And with that she sauntered off.

The woman on the table said, "Real smooth. Does that happen to you a lot?"

Harley looked into big blue eyes, heavily lashed. "Do I know you?"

"Not yet, but Barber does, and he's told me all about you."

He'd kill Barber later.

"Look, honey, unlike your miffed cupcake, I'm not here

to ruin your night. But the photographer said they're doing a big exposé on you, and that means coverage for me—if I can convince you to let me stick close for a few minutes. So what do you say we lend each other a hand?"

Harley looked her over. Not too bad. "At least you're honest."

"And I'm no pressure. So let's dance." She popped off the table and took both his hands. "Come on, big boy. It'll cheer you up, I promise. Dancing makes everyone feel better."

"I don't need to cheer up."

Being insistent, she tugged on him until Harley felt compelled to either stand or be unspeakably rude.

"One dance," Barber told him. "It'll do you some good, appease the damn photographer, and save me from your moping."

"I don't mope, damn it." He started for Barber.

The woman moved in front of him, smiled widely, and Harley had to admit she was appealing.

"I'm Crystal." She planted both hands on his chest and started backing him out to the dance floor. A discreet amount of cleavage showed beneath a clinging V-necked sweater. "I've watched you fight. You're really good."

Taking his gaze off her boobs, Harley asked, "You're a fan of the SBC?"

"*Love* it." Without invitation, she draped her arms around his neck. "If it makes you more comfortable, we can talk about the competition and nothing more. Like most fans, I have my favorite fighters."

"'S that right?" Harley looped his arms loosely around her waist. His hands rested on generous hips currently swaying to the music. "Like who?"

"Simon Evans is hot."

He smirked. "Yeah, that's what I hear."

"And Havoc is awesome."

Amused by her, Harley said, "He has deadly elbows."

"But they've got nothing on you. I'm giving you a year, tops, and then I think you'll overshadow them both." She pushed up against Harley, letting him feel her curves, and her interest.

Unfortunately, it didn't stir him at all.

Well hell.

Picking up on his lack of interest, she said, "It's okay, honey. I won't insist. Dancing is more than enough for me."

Might as well, Harley decided. It beat going home to sit in front of the television with his uncle, or being harassed by Barber and his unending wit. And it would put an end to the press for the night.

A bonus, that.

Barber and his band were off for the rest of the night, but recorded music blared from speakers, loud and heavy on the beat. The woman was soft and she smelled nice enough, like rich perfume. She stood about five-ten, tall enough that he didn't have stoop to hold her. She didn't wear an overabundance of makeup and she hadn't yet played grab-ass with him.

As the photographer closed in, Harley asked, "Why do you want to be in the pictures?"

"I do some local modeling, and this would be great exposure for my portfolio. Might even get me some national recognition." She spared him a coy smile. "It never hurts to be in the proximity of a studly fighter."

"Studly, huh?" Maybe her company would prove enjoyable, and if he gave it a chance, he might even find a stir of lust somewhere.

Though he doubted it. Even with the pep talk he'd just given himself, he felt more annoyance than anything else.

While in training, Harley took only one day off and tomorrow was it. If he didn't let off some steam tonight, he wouldn't get another chance for a week.

Making the effort, he asked Crystal, "You live around here?"

"No. My friends and I are taking a short break from college. One of them has family near here. We heard all about Havoc's gym and how so many of the fighters train here.

Since we're all fans of the sport, we decided to tag along with her."

To be safe, Harley asked, "You're how old?"

Her smile teased him. "Old enough for anything you might have in mind."

"Since I only have a dance in mind, I suppose I can agree."

Laughing, she said, "I'm twenty-two. No worries."

When she hugged herself closer to him, swaying to the music, Harley lifted his wrist to check the time—and his gaze snagged on a small female body making its way through the crowd.

He stiffened. All over.

In places that Crystal misunderstood.

Just what the hell was Anastasia Bradley doing here, in town, in Roger's Rodeo? Harley tracked her every step.

She hadn't yet spotted him.

Then he saw her focus on Roger, and head in his direction.

His arms automatically tightened on Crystal, who took the gesture as encouragement.

The photographer had a field day.

Well hell. He really would have to kick Barber's ass for putting him in this predicament.

WHEN Stasia first walked into Roger's Rodeo, she wondered how she'd ever find Harley with so many people crammed inside. That is, if he was even at the bar. Sure, Satch had said that the fighters hung out there, but that didn't mean Harley was here, now, on this particular night.

Determination took her through the very busy, two-story bar. Under her feet, the floor shook with loud music and laughter. Muscular men who she assumed to be fighters mingled with a mostly female group. Occasionally one of them would give her an encouraging gesture, but she was here to see Harley, no one else.

The barest amount of research had shored up her decision

to offer him assistance with his current goals. As she'd seen many times in her line of work, Harley was a man taken off the right path by the person closest to him. Even while well-meaning, family could be very destructive.

She needed more insight, more input, and a better knowledge of the sport. But she felt she already knew Harley. Much as he tried to conceal himself and his true nature, it shone through. During their ordeal in the storm, it had been doubly apparent.

Harley needed a nudge, and she was the woman to give it to him.

In the crowded bar, one man appeared to be overseeing things. Stasia headed for him, but when she got close, a taller woman with light brown hair stepped into her path with a deliberately careful smile. "Hello. May I help you?"

Drawing back, Stasia said, "I'm not sure. I'm looking for Harley Handleman. His uncle told me that he frequents this place a lot."

The man leaned around the woman. "Harley is expecting you?"

"Well . . . no. He'll be shocked and probably displeased, but I don't plan to molest him or anything."

Smiling, the man politely nudged the woman aside and then held out a hand. "I'm Roger Sims. I own the bar." After shaking her hand, he put his arm around the woman. "This is my wife, Camille."

"Nice to meet you," Stasia said, a little confused by the introduction when she'd only wanted to find Harley.

"We sponsor the fighters," Camille explained, "because my brother is Dean Conor, better known as Havoc."

Small world, Stasia thought. "I've heard Harley and Barber mention him."

"You know Barber too, then?"

In brief, Stasia said, "We met when he and Satch came to Echo Lake, more or less to rescue Harley after he got snowed in with me."

"Sounds like you're friends, then." Camille smiled. "I hope you don't mind that my husband and I feel protective of their privacy. They sometimes meet very pushy fans who refuse to back off."

"I understand completely. And I promise not to be too much of a bother to him."

Roger spoke again. "I can find Harley for you if you want."

"No, that's okay." If Harley was forewarned, he very well might dodge her. "If you could just point me in the right direction, that'd be great."

"He's with Barber," Camille said, "and they were sitting on the far side of the room."

"Harley just finished filming an interview," Roger told her, "and I think the photographer is still hanging around."

Ah. If that was the case, then maybe Uncle Satch was wrong, and Harley didn't require coercion to go along with Satch's plan. Not that she'd had any intention of trying to convince him anyway.

In fact, if Satch knew her intent, he'd probably do his best to send her packing. "Thanks. I appreciate the help."

Roger stopped her. "Would you like me to take your coat? I can check it for you."

"That's okay. I don't really expect to be here too long." She waved and headed off, but not before seeing Roger and Camille put their heads together for some private conversation.

About her? It seemed probable.

Getting through the crowd proved tricky because Stasia had to cross the dance floor and the gyrating bodies kept bumping into her. She hefted her purse strap higher on her shoulder, held her coat closed over her jeans and turtleneck, and with her head down, forged a path through the human congestion.

When she reached the other side, she found a vacant wall and stationed herself against it. From that vantage point she'd be able to look for Harley without being trampled.

After scanning the crowd multiple times, she finally spotted Barber. He sat at a small table in a recessed corner, entertaining a woman on his lap.

For the longest time, Stasia just watched him, even when he started making out with the woman. It fascinated her to see such a public display, never mind that no one else appeared to be paying them any mind.

Even at a distance, she could see that Barber seduced the woman with much success. Given half a chance, Stasia thought the woman might ravish Barber right on the spot.

Not that he was resisting all that much.

Was Harley off somewhere doing the same? Or did his training keep him from it? She hoped—

Suddenly, in mid-kiss, Barber looked up and caught her staring. The redhead tried to kiss him again, but he dodged her to stare blank-faced at Stasia.

Oops. With her cheeks going hot, Stasia lifted a hand and gave a lame wave of greeting.

Barber appeared dumbfounded to see her, and then he quickly twisted around and searched the room until his gaze landed on someone specific.

Following his line of vision led Stasia to the sight of Harley on the dance floor, all cozy with a very lushly built young lady. Harley had the woman's wrists held in one of his at the small of her back, his other hand on her nape while she played vampire on his neck.

Stasia's stomach dropped, but she managed a cavalier smile as she looked back at Barber. Shoring up her daring, she headed for his table.

Barber was in such a hurry to get to his feet, he nearly dumped his date. "Anastasia. I didn't know you were here."

The redhead glared at her.

"No reason you should." Anxious to get the hell out of there with her composure intact, Stasia cleared her throat. "I'm so sorry to interrupt, Barber. I was looking for Harley, but I see he's otherwise occupied. If you could just give him a message for me—"

"You can give it to me yourself."

Oh hell. Stasia winced at the tone of Harley's voice. The second he spoke, dread overtook every other expression on Barber's face, which didn't exactly reassure her either.

CHAPTER 11

PASTING on another firm smile, Stasia looked up at Harley. "Hi, Harley."

Scorching heat shone in his blue eyes.

His blond hair was mussed, his nostrils slightly flared. He looked turned on, which made her feel about two feet tall because she'd walked in on something so blatantly sexual.

On the dance floor.

Good old Uncle Satch could just find himself another life coach. Harley was more than she could handle.

"Stasia." The corners of his mouth tightened. "What are you doing here?"

The woman glued to his side watched her with territorial purpose. Somewhere beside them, a flash went off, and Harley turned to a photographer with a glare so hot, the poor guy retreated behind the crowd.

Barber and his redhead waited in silence.

Stasia felt . . . naked. Conspicuous. In front of the firing squad.

She straightened her shoulders. "Is it a restricted bar? I didn't realize."

"I didn't mean that." Harley took a step toward her. "I didn't expect to see you again."

"Yes, you were real clear on that, and why. But I'm not here for that."

"No?"

"Listen, why don't you get back to your . . ." She gestured toward his date. ". . . entertainment. Then if it's convenient, we can speak in the morning. I believe you have my phone number?"

She'd taken only half a step when Harley's fingers wound around her upper arm, not hard enough to hurt, but definitely firm enough to restrain.

So close that she could smell the other woman's perfume that clung to his clothes, Harley whispered, "Let's talk now."

Awkward.

Very, very awkward.

Leaning back, Stasia looked around him and saw the disappointed young lady, arms crossed, waiting to see what her role would be.

Stasia's smile was starting to hurt, damn it. "That'd be rude, Harley. You already have company, and I don't mind waiting."

"I mind." Still holding on to her, he turned and faced the two women and Barber. "I need a few minutes." Those words no sooner left his mouth than he shook his head. "Or an hour or two, actually."

The girl puckered up. "Maybe I can get a rain check then?"

"No point. Enough pictures were taken."

"Not by my measure."

All but vibrating with some strange emotion, Harley said to Stasia, "Wait right here."

"Sure, why not?"

Her comment must have given him second thoughts, because he said to Barber, "Keep her here, okay?"

"With chains if necessary," Barber promised.

Harley strode off with the young lady, going only far enough to speak privately.

"Buck up, sweetheart," Barber said to Stasia. "He wasn't interested in her anyway."

"Odd. He looked very interested on the dance floor."

"That was for the photographer."

"If you say so."

The girl was not happy. She put her hands on her hips and rattled off a long appeal. When Harley just shook his head, she tried plastering herself to him again.

"Tenacious, ain't she?" Barber asked.

"Very."

"I sort of like that in a girl."

Stasia rolled her eyes at the same time Harley pried the girl loose. He cupped her chin, said something that must've cajoled her, and came back to Stasia.

He opened his mouth, but she spoke first. "You're a snake charmer, aren't you?"

Barber laughed.

The redhead didn't. With a vicious glare at Stasia, she jerked herself away from Barber.

"Hey," he called after her. "What'd I do?"

She went off in a huff to her friend. Together the two women exited the dance floor.

"Well hell," Barber said, directing his comment at Stasia. "I didn't know it was an all or nothing sort of deal."

"I'm sorry."

"I have a weakness for redheads."

"And blondes," Harley said. "And brunettes in a pinch."

"I was already primed, damn it!"

Hearing Barber speak so blatantly about his sexuality made Stasia uncomfortable. "This is ridiculous. I really am sorry, Barber. I didn't mean to run her off. Maybe if I leave—"

"You're not going anywhere," Harley said. "Barber will survive."

"Yeah, I will." Barber winked at her. "Besides, she'll

probably be back, and in the meantime, I have a few more women I need to talk to."

"Spreading it around?" Harley asked.

"Interviewing, actually. I can line up ladies tonight to audition in the morning. Do me a favor, and don't let her run off anyone else." He saluted them and left the floor.

Stasia watched him go—until Harley caught her chin and brought her face around to his. "I don't think I like you staring after Barber."

"I wasn't. That is . . ." She sighed. "He's very sexual, isn't he?"

Mouth grim, Harley said, "You don't need to worry about Barber's sexuality."

"He's throwing it around the room so that no one can miss it!"

For what felt like an eternity, Harley just stood there, spine straight, eyes narrowed as he looked at her.

Stasia squirmed under the impact of that laser gaze. "Forget Barber," she finally said.

"Good idea."

She gave him a quelling look. "Listen up, Harley, I'm not going to stand here while you try to intimidate me."

"Intimidation had nothing to do with it. I'm just trying to decide."

"Decide what?"

"If we should go someplace private or if it'd be safer to stay here on the floor with you."

Safer? Her chin went up. "For your information, I have no interest in molesting you as your brunette did. You can relax about that."

"You're here." He took a step closer. "There's no way in hell I'm going to relax."

He looked almost pained, which made Stasia soften. "Am I really such a threat?"

"Threat? No." He looked at her mouth, then down her body. "Lose the coat."

Instead, she pulled the lapels together. "I don't think so."

"Yeah, maybe it's better that you don't." He inhaled deeply, and put both hands on her shoulders. "I'm already fighting to keep my hands off you."

Talk about throwing around the sexuality! "Harley." She glanced at his big hands on her shoulders. "You're touching me."

"Not even close, honey."

Those gravelly words drew her gaze up to his face again, and Stasia was stunned to see him looking so fierce. Trying to be cavalier, she said, "You're not making any sense. Not even close to what?"

His thumbs caressed. "To how and where I want to touch you. But right here in the middle of the floor probably isn't the best place."

"We can agree on that much."

He glanced around the room, scowled at the photographer who again stood nearby, his camera at the ready, and said, "Come on."

"Where are we going?"

His jaw flexed. "Someplace more private."

Stasia stood her ground. "Whoa. I'm not budging, not if you plan to . . ."

Looking down at her, he whispered, "Have my hands on you?"

"Yeah." Heat rolled over her, almost weakening her resolve. "Not if you plan to do that."

"Not just yet. But there's a magazine doing a piece on me and the photographer is just hoping to get another shot, since you ran off the first model."

"That girl?" So she hadn't been a date? "You weren't really with her?"

"Did it look like I was?"

"Most definitely."

"Good." The corners of his mouth tilted. "I met her about five minutes before you walked up. I danced with her so another woman would leave me alone, and so the photographer could take enough shots to be satisfied."

Stasia wasn't sure if that made Harley's behavior better or worse. "Poor Harley, under so much pressure."

"You have no idea." He touched her jaw. "Crystal claimed to understand, but she still wasn't happy to have the evening end so soon."

Lifting her brows, Stasia said, "She left a hickey on your neck."

"Yeah?" He put fingertips to his throat, then dropped his hand. "But she never touched my mouth, so you can't use that argument again."

"What argument?"

"That I should kiss you first—if I want to kiss you."

"Oh."

"And I do, Stasia." He stared down at her mouth. "I will. But not here."

Again, Stasia resisted his effort to lead her away. "I already told you, Harley, I didn't come here for that."

With his eyes up on the ceiling and his mood disgruntled, he turned to her again. He put his hands on his hips and appeared to be counting.

Finally he muttered, "Well hell."

"What?"

His shoulders lifted. "Photographer or not, your purpose or not, seems I just don't care." He moved closer. "I'm still going to kiss you."

"Now wait a minute." Stasia started to back up, but on the crowded floor, there wasn't much room to maneuver.

Locking his gaze on hers, Harley stalked her, moving forward as she scrambled back. "Afraid of me?"

"No, but I know my own limits."

"Meaning you want to kiss me, too?"

"I'm taking the Fifth on that one, Harley." When she bumped into the wall and couldn't retreat any farther, she straightened and said, *"Harley,"* as a warning.

He gave a faint smile and, mimicking her, said, "Stasia."

He stood so close, she had to tip her head way back to see him. "I really don't think—"

"We had an agreement," he interrupted.

"Yes, I know." She tried not to think of how badly she wanted that kiss. "We agreed that we wouldn't see each other again. Believe me, I remember."

He braced his hands on the wall beside her head. "But here you are."

"If you'd stop deliberately flustering me, I could explain why."

His attention moved to her mouth. "Not just yet." And then he bent toward her. Just before his mouth touched hers, he said, "I told you good-bye. That should have been it. Since it wasn't, don't ask me to hold back." His breath teased her lips. "Not again. Not this time."

THE kiss was . . . everything Harley remembered it to be. And damn, but it felt right, as right as breathing or sleeping—but a hell of a lot more energizing.

Holding her face in his hands, Harley adjusted to give himself better access. Her lips opened and he deepened the kiss, tasting her with his tongue, not slow and seductive as he'd first intended, but frenzied and fast, practically devouring her. Against his chest, even through her thick coat, he could feel the frantic pounding of her heart.

He'd more or less told her to stay away.

At the moment, he was damn glad she hadn't.

Wishing she were naked, Harley tangled his fingers in her thick hair and kissed her until they were both breathless.

Her fingers twisted in the front of his shirt, trying to draw him closer when he was already smashed up against her. Thinking of her stretched out on a bed, his for the taking, he eased back and whispered, "Stasia, baby, do you have a room?"

Her mouth followed his. "Not yet."

Had she come straight to him then, as soon as she got into town? The thought excited him.

Or did she not need a room because she planned to leave as quickly as she'd arrived?

Disliking that idea, Harley said between kisses, "We'll get you a room. Right now."

"Now?"

He heard her confusion, and though he felt like a cad, he wanted to play off of it. "Yes, Stasia. Now. Tonight." He looked into her heavy eyes. "Unless you want me to take you right here in the bar?"

"Take me?" Frowning, she pulled back, licked her lips. "Don't be absurd."

Absurd? "You know you want it, too."

Always brutally honest, she said, "I want you. Yes." After a second, she looked up at him. "But have you forgotten your preferences?"

"No." Hell no. The thought of her stretched out, straining, accepting . . . damn, Harley got a boner. He touched her cheek. "I swear, you'll love it."

And just that easily, she retreated. Hands pressed to his chest, she gave a shaky laugh. "Sorry, Harley, but it ain't happening."

He'd see about that. Given the way she'd responded to a simple kiss, the fact that she admitted to wanting him, it was only a matter of time.

When he just watched her, waiting, she gave a crooked smile. "I keep telling you that I didn't come here for that."

"I'm not sure I believe you." He didn't want to believe her. What else could she possible want?

She folded her hands behind her and struck a more relaxed pose against the wall. "Actually, I was looking for a job."

Something akin to disappointment stabbed into Harley. "A job?"

Nodding, she confirmed, "Here in Harmony."

"In Harmony?" He felt like a deranged parrot, repeating her every word.

"That's right."

Anger straightened his spine. "With who?"

"Actually, Harley . . ." A wide smile put dimples in her cheeks, giving Harley warning. "With you."

Harley drew back—and a camera flash went off in his peripheral vision. The photographer was still lurking around, and the bastard had just caught Harley in a state of shock.

For a man who kept his emotions underwraps, being exposed, caught off guard, was unacceptable.

He'd have to do something about it, and that meant doing something about Stasia.

Like having her.

Enough times to get her out of his system, but on his terms.

He smiled at her. "I see."

BARBER sauntered up to the bar and ordered a beer. Because it'd be his third of the night, he made a mental note to find himself a ride back to his motel—either with a woman, which would be his preference, but if fate dealt a losing hand, then with one of the fighters who abstained from alcohol.

He'd made friends with many of the fighters, and sparred with a lot of them, too. The contrast of full-go physical activity to late nights performing kept him in good shape.

But damn Harley, he was right. He was getting old, at least too old to keep up the grueling schedule of late. Hell, five years ago, pulling two all-nighters in a row wouldn't have fazed him.

Especially when Dakota kept him company.

But Dakota was now married to a good guy, and whenever he put in extra hours, he spent the following day with a headache and a churning gut.

"Shit."

"Ah . . . excuse me?"

At the intrusion of that squeaky little voice, Barber pivoted on the bar stool. He found himself looking down at a very short gal sporting a red button nose and chapped lips, bundled head to toe in bulky outerwear. On her head sat the most ridiculous hat he'd ever seen.

He stared at it in awe. Black velour felt with an asymmetrical fit, a pleated brim, and finished off with a silk band and of all things, a turkey feather, it was worthy of a little staring.

When the girl cleared her throat, Barber brought his gaze to her face. Clearly, she'd just come in from the outdoors. As he looked her over, her bottom lip trembled—from cold or something more, he couldn't say.

She looked to be a little chunky—maybe. Hard to tell under the boxy coat that hung well past her knees. Bright green eyes stayed glued to his face. Round cheeks and a rounder chin lent her an impish appearance.

Though she appeared a little bedraggled, she still screamed style, from her perfect makeup to her manicured nails, now clenched in tight hands, trying to find warmth.

Normally, she wasn't at all a woman to catch his attention . . . except that she also had beautiful long red hair. It spilled out from under the hideous hat, falling down her back, over her shoulders, wavy and thick.

Intriguing.

Interest sparked. Barber relished the familiar feel of fresh, instantaneous chemistry.

He locked gazes with her. "Hello there."

She swallowed audibly. "You cursed."

He hooked his boots on the bottom rung of the stool and leaned back against the bar. "Not at you, sweetheart. I didn't even know you were lurking there behind me."

"Oh." She licked her lips nervously.

He made a tsking sound. "Shouldn't do that."

Startled eyes met his again. "What?"

"Lick your lips that way." Just saying it tightened his abdomen. Damn. Maybe it was the combined thoughts of Dakota and missed opportunities with the reality of aging, but he was in a bad way, in desperate need of a little relief. "They're already chapped. Licking will only make 'em worse."

"Oh." She licked them again.

Barber narrowed his eyes, and resisted further comment

on licking and mouths and any other thoughts guaranteed to give him a boner. "Is there something I can do for you?"

Her shoulders went back—which thrust her breasts forward. "I'm here to audition."

When Barber started to speak, she stuck up a palm. "I know, I'm horribly late and I apologize for that. Public transit isn't entirely reliable and I don't have a vehicle of my own at hand. It took me several minutes to get the coat clerk to hold my luggage for me. And then finding you in this crush wasn't easy."

She spoke fast in inane chatter. Barber despised inane chatter. Except that now, it was sort of . . . cute. "Been rough, huh?"

"Frustrating for sure. And it did put me behind schedule. But I want to audition nonetheless, and you should hear me. It's an imposition, I know, and for that I'm sorry. But I'm here and you're here, so—"

Barber leaned in close, stealing her thunder, her breath and her nerve. Near enough to kiss her, he whispered, "Okay."

"Okay?"

He shrugged, and to keep her from fainting or fleeing, he settled back again with a smile. "On the merit of that hat alone, I'll hear you."

"Oh." Her hands went to her hat. "Yes. Thank you."

Picking up his beer, he took another deep drink, then gestured at her. "Go ahead."

Eyes widening, she dropped her hands and looked around at the crowded bar. *"Here?"*

Demure women rarely—like maybe never—turned him on. Today, the personality trait pushed all his buttons. Measuring her reactions, Barber gave another shrug. "Why not?"

"But . . . I assumed . . . that is . . ." Her bottom lip started quivering again. In a near-desperate plea, she leaned in to say, "I'd truly prefer someplace more private."

Now that deserved another drink. Barber finished off his glass and set it down for the bartender to refill. "All right, doll. I'll bite." Relaxing on the stool, he put his elbows back on the bar and let his knees angle out.

Her gaze went straight to his crotch, but shot away with the speed of light. Bright color stained her fair cheeks.

Enjoying her, Barber asked, "I'm all willing, but just how private do you think we need to be?"

Just when he thought she'd either faint or run away, she pursed her pucker and stared him straight in the eyes. "Private enough that you can actually hear me, and that I won't be distracted with all the noise."

"Maybe you're confused, honey—"

"No disrespect intended, but I am not your honey and it's very unprofessional to refer to me as such."

Barber slapped a hand over his heart. "I've been smote through and through."

"What?"

When he left the bar stool, she stumbled back several steps. "Listen up, sugar. I am who I am, and I speak how I speak. If you want in on the gig, you have to get used to it."

Her round chin firmed. "Fine."

"And we often perform in bars. If a little noise throws you off, that's a big problem, a real indication that you aren't cut out for what we do."

Her lips joined the chin in firming. The redness of her nose deepened. "I see."

"If crowds make you shy about your voice, for certain you can't—"

She inhaled a broken breath. "You've made your point, okay? I get it."

Ah hell. Barber saw the tears hanging on her lashes, willed them not to fall, but she blinked and that was that. They trickled down, over those smooth cheeks and to the corners of her sexy mouth.

Great. Just freaking great.

As she swiped away the wet tracks forming down her face, he accused, "You're crying."

"No, I'm not."

He gave her an incredulous look. "Yeah, you are."

She sniffled, started digging in her pockets, and said, "Ignore it, please. I'm tired and out of sorts, that's all."

Snatching up a paper napkin from the bar, Barber thrust it toward her. "Oh yeah, it's real easy to ignore a babe bawling."

She went rigid from head to toes. "I am *not* a babe!"

Barber eyed her. "Fine. You're not a babe. Just the opposite. A hag, even."

"Now listen here—"

Relieved to see anger replace the weeping, Barber fought a laugh. "Take it easy already." He watched as she mopped her face, and then loudly blew her red nose. "Better?"

"It's nothing. Don't concern yourself." She held the now messy napkin in a fist at her side. "Shall I sing for you now?"

She had to be kidding. Barber worked his jaw. "At this point, I think I need the privacy." He looked around, spotted Roger, and said, "Come on."

CHAPTER 12

TRUSTING her to follow him, Barber wove his way through hordes of customers across the crowded floor. When he stopped in front of Roger, the girl bumped into his back.

Eyes closed, Barber counted to five, then turned to face her. "I see you made it."

She hastened back a step and said in accusation, "You're taller, so you could see your way better. If I hadn't stuck close, I'd have lost you."

"Got it." He turned to Roger with a "help me" look. "Got someplace private I can use for a minute?"

Jumping the gun on the wrong assumption, Roger glanced at the girl, then at Barber. "Seriously?"

Barber rolled his eyes. "It's an audition, Rog. And if you make her cry again, I'll brain you."

"She was crying?" He looked at her more closely.

The girl gasped, which made Roger smile.

"Ignore Barber," he said. "He's sometimes surly like that." Roger held out his hand. "I apologize for any unintentional disrespect."

"Thank you." All prim and proper, she took his hand. "I assume you're the proprietor?"

"Roger Sims. Yes, ma'am."

"I'm Jasmine Petri. It's very nice to meet you, Mr. Sims."

"Call me Roger. Any friend of Barber's, and all that."

"Thank you, Roger. But Mr. Henry and I aren't truly acquainted. Yet."

Barber wanted to knock their heads together. "Can we wrap up these social niceties, or what?"

Jasmine said, "I see exactly what you mean, Roger." Then to Barber, "I'm sorry that common courtesy is so distressing to you."

Roger laughed.

After glaring at him, Barber asked Jasmine, "Do you want to audition or not?"

"I do."

Great. "So Roger, do you have a damn empty room or not?"

Mimicking the girl, Roger said, "I do." With a smile, he said, "Follow me."

Digging out a hefty key ring, Roger led them to a locked hallway, let them inside, and said, "Use any room you want. I'll relock the outside here, but it should open from the inside without a problem. Be sure the door shuts tight, though, if you would."

Jasmine again offered her hand. "Thank you very much, Roger. I appreciate the assistance."

"My pleasure, Jasmine. Good luck with your audition."

Before she could reply further, Barber caught her arm and hustled her away from the door. "If we're going to do this, let's get on with it, please."

SMILING, Roger shut the door and headed back to the main area of the bar. He saw sparks in Barber's future, and it amused him. Hell, everything in life amused him these days, probably because he was so damn happy.

In such a short time, both his hotel and his bar had quadrupled in business. Best of all, he'd married the woman of his dreams.

Life was so good that it sometimes scared him. In the past, he'd made mistakes, ugly mistakes, and now he wasn't sure he deserved anyone as lovely as Camille.

But by God, he had her, and he planned to do everything in his power to make her the happiest woman alive.

He found his lovely wife chatting with her brother, Dean, and Dean's wife, Eve, near an exit. Approaching her from the back, he admired the graceful lines of her tall body, the sexy but sophisticated twist in her light brown hair, and the way her long legs looked in high heels.

Seeing her made his heart flutter, as much now as it always had.

When Roger reached her, he hugged his arms around her and kissed the side of her neck. He loved her so much that it hurt—a good kind of hurt, the kind he couldn't live without.

Cam turned to him with a smile. "Roger." Laughing, blushing a little, she put her hand to her neck where his mouth had just been. "What's that all about?"

"I'm a lucky man and I know it."

Dean gave a small smile, and slipped an arm around his own wife. "If I had a drink, we could toast ourselves as lucky men."

Eve said, "Hear, hear!"

It pleased Roger that Camille had such good friends and such a solid family—family that now included him in their ranks.

"It's midnight," Roger told her. "Why don't you head home and get some sleep? I have another half hour of work to do, then I'll be on my way, too."

"You're not staying to close?"

He kissed the end of her nose. "That's why I hired managers, so they could handle those type things."

"I'm ready to go." Eve covered a yawn with her hand.

Dean said, "Yeah, me, too."

"Well, I'm not the least tired, so you two go on." Cam hooked her arm through Roger's. "I'll wait for my husband."

He felt that familiar thump in his heart. "If you're sure?"

"I can help you with your work."

Because he valued every second with her, Roger accepted. "Thanks." An arm around his wife, he said, "Dean, Eve, I'll see you both later." Together, he and Cam went to his office. Once inside, Roger smiled at her, then locked the door.

"What are you doing?"

"Putting off work." He stepped back up to her, and opened his hand on her hip. "Have I told you lately that you look more scrumptious every day?"

"Married life obviously agrees with me." Her light brown eyes softened in that special way of hers. "And Roger, you compliment me all the time."

"I tell you the truth." Overwhelmed with his feelings, Roger kissed her throat, behind her ear. "I will always tell you the truth. I swear."

"I know." She sighed, and accepted him. "I love you, Roger."

Thank God. He didn't reply. He couldn't. Instead he took her mouth in a scorching kiss. If they lived to be a hundred, he didn't think he'd ever be able to take her, or her affection, for granted.

She simply meant too much to him.

SEVERAL doors lined the hallway. Barber peeked into each one until he found a room mostly empty except for extra chairs. Flipping on a single light, he lifted a chair off a stack, dropped it to the floor, straddled it, and said to Jasmine, "This'll do."

She looked around at the high ceilings before finally forcing herself to face him. "Please keep in mind that acoustics can affect a performance."

"Noted." Barber folded his arms on the back of the chair and let his curiosity take over. "Tell you what, Jasmine. How about you lose the coat and hat so I can see you?" His pulse sped in anticipation. Voice going gruff, he added, "For the sake of stage presence, you know."

For the briefest moment, she clutched the coat tighter. Then she caught herself, nodded, and carefully removed the hat. With her free hand, she stroked her fingers over her scalp, shook out her hair, and let it tumble down her back.

Her hair was incredible. The single fluorescent lamp lent amazing highlights to the long curls, showing shades of gold, auburn, copper, and russet. Being that Barber's carnal plans had only just been thwarted for the night, his brain made the leap to how that silky hair would feel trailing over his body—if they were both naked.

He shook himself.

Best to see the rest of her before he mired himself in fantasy. Breath bated, he waited while she slowly, like a damn striptease, opened the many buttons down the front of her long coat.

It seemed to take her forever, and he was about to explode with expectation when she finished and shrugged the heavy covering off her shoulders. She immediately turned, giving him the back view of a generously rounded body in a long dark skirt, boots, and thick sweater.

Putting the coat beside the hat on a stack of chairs, she hesitated, hesitated some more, and finally turned to face him.

Ridiculous as it seemed, Barber thought he might bust his jeans. Large breasts made the conservative sweater sexy, and rounded hips added oomph to the otherwise plain skirt.

While he sat mesmerized, she prepared herself by shaking back her hair, folding her hands together in front of her, and smiling at him.

Without warning, she burst into song.

Barber started.

Damn, talk about jarring a guy back to the here and

now. But when he got his attention off her bod and onto her voice, he had to admit she sounded great.

Better than great.

Son-of-a-bitch. It figured that she'd be perfect.

He knew all too well that it wasn't an easy thing to sing without music, on cue, in a cramped room, without a microphone.

For such a short girl, Jasmine had a big voice.

For a woman quick to tears, her presentation was striking and bold.

Barber relaxed and enjoyed her.

And accepted the quandary.

He wouldn't sleep with a female member of the band . . . and Jasmine would be a perfect addition. As a singer, she was everything he'd been looking for since Dakota left the band. Unique, talented, capable . . .

Now what should he do?

WHEN she finished the song, Jasmine felt her self-consciousness return. It was always that way. While performing, she lost herself. But now, with Barberosa Henry staring at her, she wanted to wilt.

Or hide away.

Salty tears stung her eyes. For most of her life, she'd fought the propensity to weep over every little thing. Happiness, sadness, anger, anxiety . . . it seemed all emotions made her well up.

Humiliating.

Especially in front of her idol.

She nearly jumped out of her skin when he said, "Nice."

Relief almost took out her knees. "Thank you."

At the sound of her wavering voice, his dark brows came down. "What's wrong now?"

Jasmine quickly shook her head. "Nothing." Oh God, she sounded like a squeaky frog.

Barberosa pushed to his feet. "You're not going to cry again, are you?"

"No." She wouldn't, she wouldn't . . . Thank God, the emotional upheaval subsided. "I'm just tired." Her smile quivered. "That's all."

Suspicion filled his gaze. His voice went gruff. "Well, if you think you can compose yourself, we have some things to discuss."

Please let him hire her. Jasmine locked her knees, gripped her hands together, and squared her shoulders. "Shoot. I'm ready."

Instead of saying what he had on his mind, Barberosa walked a slow circle around her. Knowing he looked her over sent her heart into her throat.

When she couldn't take it anymore, she asked, "What?"

"The band has an image."

She nodded with enthusiasm. "I know. I've been following your music for some time now. I first saw you in a bar, about five years ago."

"You don't say?" He lounged back against the wall and crossed his arms over his chest. "Was probably a real dive, huh?"

"Not too bad," she assured him, although she couldn't really remember much about the setting. All she remembered was her complete and utter fascination with the lead singer.

"You enjoyed the show?"

Enjoyed was much too tame a word. "You and the others blew me away."

He turned his head, studying her. "Five years ago, you'd have been a kid."

"I was seventeen." Fond memories settled her smile. "I allowed myself to be talked into fudging an ID and I went to the bar with a group of college friends."

"Boyfriend?"

"Ex-boyfriend now, but yes, the bar was his idea."

Brown eyes took her measure. "Hoped to get you drunk and make a little whoopee, huh?"

Jasmine drew back. "I beg your pardon?"

"The boyfriend. That's why he chose a bar for a minor?"

It still stung, to think of how she'd been treated that night. Jasmine cleared her throat. "Not that I see how it concerns you, but I don't really know what his plans were. Soon after entering the bar, we parted ways."

"Ah. Difference of opinion?"

His nosiness surprised her, and threw her off guard. Jasmine hadn't expected it, and wasn't sure how to respond to it. "Actually, he wanted me to drink, I was more interested in listening to your band, he got smashed, and I called a cab home."

Barberosa put a hand to his chin. "But not before seeing the show."

Lifting a shoulder, Jasmine gave him the truth. "I was so enthralled in your music, I didn't really care what Barry did."

"Barry? What kind of pansy-ass name is that?"

"He's now a very successful banker."

Barberosa snorted.

Such an odd man. Jasmine took a breath, and continued. "Later I saw you perform with a woman, and I loved it even more, but she wasn't always with the show."

"You've seen us more than once?"

"Every chance I got. The woman you had was so good, I always thought that you needed a permanent female singer in the band."

"That'd be Dakota. She's the best."

Jasmine's hopefulness faded. Did Barberosa plan to settle for second-best then? She forged on. "It wasn't until just recently, after I read an interview about you in a mixed martial arts magazine, that I realized Drew Black had hired you to do music for the SBC."

"It's a great gig."

"But you still like live performance?"

He lifted one bulky shoulder. "I like staying real with my roots."

Then maybe he'd stay real enough to consider hiring her. "The interview also said that you were considering the addition of a female band member."

Rather than address her point, Barberosa rubbed his chin. "So let me see, you'd be about twenty-two now, huh?"

"Yes."

His gaze went over her again. "Still a kid."

"I'm legal."

One brow lifted. "Barely."

Fed up, she took two steps toward him and demanded, "What does that possibly have to do with whether or not I'd fit in the band?"

Slowly, as if he had all the time in the world, Barberosa pushed off of the wall and came toward her. "You feel the sexual chemistry between us?"

Sexual chemistry? "What are you talking about?"

"You don't feel it?" He gestured between them. "'Cuz it's kicking me in the guts big-time."

Putting a hand over her pounding heart, Jasmine said, "I had no idea."

"Now you do." He came closer—and she found it prudent to back up.

"But . . ." Heat rushed through her, making her gasp. "We haven't even been properly introduced!" Not that she didn't already know everything there was to know about Barberosa Henry; she'd been admiring him, been infatuated with him, for five long years.

But now she also knew how potent he was in person.

And how his dark-eyed gaze could entrap her when he stared at her in just that way.

It was unsettling—and very exciting.

Somehow, Barberosa caught her hand and stalled her retreat. With his mouth tipped in a crooked smile, he said, "You're Jasmine Petri—I heard that much when you and Roger were getting acquainted. You already know I'm Barber."

Though he did no more than hold on to her hand, nervousness made her babble. "Barber is short for Barberosa? It's unusual." *And charming,* she thought. "I discovered your name by asking the bartender that first time. He just said Barberosa, not Barber, so I didn't realize—"

"*If* I made you part of the band," Barberosa said, interrupting her and retaining his hold on her hand, "you'd have to do a wardrobe overhaul."

Jasmine looked down at her clothes. "You don't like my outfit?"

He chuckled. "You look like a well-rounded schoolmarm."

Well rounded. Of all the nerve! Like a slow boil, insult replaced her fascination.

Damn him, she would not take idle potshots at her weight, and she absolutely would not give him the pleasure of getting too upset over it. She brought her chin up and leveled her gaze on him. "Understand up front, I will not be put on a diet."

Further flustering her, he lifted her hand to his mouth and kissed her knuckles. "Enough with the assumptions, doll face." He carried her hand up to his shoulder. "I wouldn't ask you to change a single thing about the body, just the window dressing."

Her tongue stuck to the roof of her mouth. She couldn't even find the wit to chide him on his absurd and unprofessional endearments.

Okay, so while she'd fallen in love with Barber's music, she'd also become more than a little besotted with the man himself. It wasn't surprising, given that every woman in the audience had been ready to swoon at his feet.

Barberosa Henry had a way of singing all lyrics that felt very intimate. His voice was heavy and hard, like the man, but touched with an underlying sincerity that wormed into a woman's heart.

Seeing him in person had only amplified those twitchy feelings. He was tall and muscular, and he oozed testosterone as well as sensuality.

The way he moved, talked—the way he looked at her . . .

Jasmine had a difficult time getting oxygen into her starved lungs. She eased her hands away from him and took a step back. "Uh, Barberosa—"

Voice low and rough, he chided, "That's an awfully big mouthful, and it makes you sound like my mother."

"Oh." His *mother*? Good grief. Of course he had to have one, but somehow she couldn't picture it.

With his thumb, he gently brushed her cheek. "Call me Barber."

"I'll try to remember." She cleared her throat. "What type of wardrobe did you have in mind, then?"

Holding her hands out to her sides, he surveyed her body. "It'd be nice to show some skin. And cleavage." He stared at her chest. "Got a problem with that?"

"No." She'd simply think of it as a costume. All performers had them.

"Good." With his hold on her hand, Barber led her to the door. "Then let's call it a night before I make the wrong decision."

"Wrong decision?"

At her question, he stopped, but kept his back to her.

Jasmine waited, but he just stood there as if wrestling with himself. Finally he looked at her over his shoulder. "I've had three beers."

"Really?" If there was a point to that, Jasmine missed it.

"I'm far from drunk, but I never leave clear thinking to chance."

"Clear thinking?" She had no idea what he meant.

Abruptly he turned. "I've got a bad hankering, Jasmine Petri. For you."

"Oh!" She backed up again.

He remained still, as if glued to the spot. "Thing is, I don't mix business with pleasure. So before I do something dumb, like trying to seduce you—"

He hadn't been trying? Good grief.

"—which I'd probably regret tomorrow when I have to go back to auditions, I figured we'd make a quick exit. You know, remove temptation from my path and all that."

Incredulity clouded her vision. "You arrogant ass!"

His brows lifted. "Too much honesty?"

Shoving past him, Jasmine said, "You think you can just

snap your fingers, and I'd jump at the chance?" She stormed down the hall toward the door leading to the dance floor. "Ha!"

From somewhere close behind her, Barberosa asked, "Ha?"

She looked back at him and said louder, *"Ha!"*

"I take it you're not interested then?"

Insufferable egotist. She couldn't believe his nerve. Oh sure, she was interested, but . . . Best if she kept her feet moving, even as sarcasm won out over tact. "Given a choice between you or a job, I'll take the job, thank you very much."

Just as Jasmine reached the door, Barber's hand came past her and he opened it for her. That put him far too close, and she shot out into the busy bar.

He caught her shoulder. "Don't rush off mad."

"Mad?" She sucked in two quick breaths. "I'm insulted."

"Are you too insulted to still be interested in the job?"

She crossed her arms and, feeling mulish, grumbled, "No."

"Then can I expect to see you tomorrow, in something more appropriate for a rock band? Let's say here at the bar, around dinnertime. I'll be performing, but I'll make time to give you a listen."

Her mouth fell open. Never in her life had she encountered so much oddity in one meeting, over one job, from one human being. "Tomorrow? But . . . I don't even have a room yet. I traveled seven hours by bus just to get here."

"Is that a yes or a no?"

She hadn't come this far just to be rejected over her clothes. "I suppose I could find an appropriate clothing store."

"I'll call Eve. She's Havoc's wife, and she's got style. She can pick you up and take you out tomorrow morning."

Again Jasmine's mouth fell open, and she stared at him. "Barber! Don't be ridiculous. I can't ask a stranger to—"

"No, but I can because I'm not a stranger. Trust me, Eve'll be happy to do it."

Just then a gargantuan man covered in tattoos, dancing with a tall, willowy woman, bumped into them. Barberosa turned, did a double take, and interrupted them.

"Gregor, I need to steal your wife."

"The hell you will," the giant said, but he didn't look concerned. He drew his wife to his side and asked, "What can I do ya for?"

Jasmine gaped. She'd seldom seen anyone so big or so imposing. Between the bulging muscles, the tattoos, and some serious cauliflower ears, he looked vicious—but he smiled amicably enough.

The tall woman laughed at her. "I had the same reaction when I first met him." Then in a stage whisper, she added, "That's why I married him."

Regaining her wits, Jasmine snapped her mouth shut. "I'm so sorry. I didn't mean to stare."

The giant grinned. "S'okay, darlin'. Now that she legally owns me, Jacki doesn't mind so much when I'm ogled."

Jasmine's face went hot. "I wasn't ogling really, it's just that you're so . . ."

"Big," his wife supplied. "Awesome. Imposing."

The giant preened. "I understand."

His wife elbowed him and then held out her hand. "I'm Jacki, and the behemoth is Gregor, my husband. If we waited for either him or Barber to do a polite introduction, we'd both die of old age."

Jasmine took her hand. "Thank you, Jacki. I'm Jasmine Petri."

"Possibly," Barber interrupted, "a new member of the band."

"Yeah?" Gregor looked at her anew. "You thinkin' with the big head, partner, or the one below your belt?" He caught Jacki's elbow when she threw it this time.

She turned on him. "She's not deaf, you idiot."

Gregor said, "She also doesn't look like she fits Barber's band."

"Which is where you come in, doll face." He grinned at Jacki. "Any idea if Eve is still hanging around?"

"I think so. Why?"

"Well, Jasmine here has the pipes and the presentation. But as Gregor rudely noted, the clothes are lacking."

"Never said that," Gregor protested. "Just said they weren't in sync with your band."

"Exactamundo. So, I thought Eve could take Jasmine shopping for more appropriate rocker duds, then I'll take another listen to her tomorrow, so I can, ah, get the whole experience."

Gregor snickered.

Jasmine wasn't sure if she should slug Barber, laugh at the absurdity of it all, or leave while she still could. At the moment, she couldn't seem to decide.

"If I was the shopping type," Jacki told her, "I'd offer. But honestly, I suck at the whole girly thing."

"She does," Gregor confirmed with a grin. "Shoppin' is one of her least favorite things, thank the heavens."

"But now Eve . . . Barber has the right idea. She and Cam, my sister, are world-class shoppers and would love an opportunity to do a makeover."

"Um, I'm not sure I need an entire makeover—"

"Yeah, you do," Barber told her. "Leastways to perform with me, you do."

Gregor snickered again.

Why fight the insanity? Jasmine thought. She looked only at Jacki and said, "He has such a remarkable talent, it's a shame he's such an ass."

Jacki never missed a beat. "I know what you mean. Almost makes you feel sorry for him, huh?"

Barber grinned. "I've got a thick skin, ladies. If you want to wound me, you'll need to try harder."

"You have a very thick head, too," Jasmine told him. "Maybe that's why the insults didn't sink in."

"Possibly." Then he touched her hair. Just that. A single stroke with two fingers, along a curling tress. "Now, about a room for you . . ."

Jasmine froze.

Gregor lifted both brows.

Jacki rolled her eyes. "Roger's hotel is nice enough, and it's centrally located to just about everything in Harmony. He always has rooms available, too."

Grateful for the icebreaker, Jasmine nodded. "Thank you."

Leaning down, Barber told her, "He's the same Roger you already met."

Wow. "So he has this place *and* a hotel?"

"That's right. He's also a pretty good brother-in-law." Jacki pulled out her cell phone. "I'll call Eve."

Not long after Jacki explained the situation over her phone, a very stylish woman came bearing down on them with visible anticipation.

Jasmine saw her destiny being swept away.

CHAPTER 13

"I don't trust that smile, Harley. What are you up to?"

Harley looked around at the crowded bar and knew he was close to cracking. He needed some guaranteed privacy.

Right now.

He took Stasia's hand. "Come on."

"Here we go again." She frowned at him. "Where do you want to go?"

He had no idea. "Out of here."

"Harley, wait—"

He turned on her with barely leashed impatience. He wasn't angry at her, but he was determined to take control, so he did his best to moderate his mood.

Still, his voice sounded harsher than he wanted when he said, "I'm leaving, Stasia." His nose almost touched hers. "Right now. You can either come with me or not. Decide."

Reasonably, she said, "If we're going somewhere to talk, then I'll be happy to go with you."

Her composure in the face of his upheaval stymied Harley. Through his teeth, he said, "Great."

He concentrated on keeping his expression inscrutable as he led her back through the bar. The feel of her hand in his, warm, small, secure, did funny things to him.

How the hell could he miss holding a woman's hand? What was he, in grade school?

He went past Gloria, who tried to get his attention.

Past Crystal, who crossed her arms and pouted.

Near the middle of the floor, he spotted Gregor, Dean, their wives, and Barber clustered together with a red-haired woman he didn't recall meeting.

He paused by Barber. "Be a pal and keep that damn photographer off my heels."

Barber looked at Stasia with understanding. "Sure thing, bro. But you'll owe me."

"Whatever."

The unfamiliar woman stared after him. The others just moved to form a line and before Harley had gone five feet, he heard the photographer protesting. He glanced back, and saw Gregor barring his way while Barber and Dean chatted him up.

Perfect.

Trotting to keep up with him, Stasia said, "What's your problem with the photographer?"

"I don't like having my every thought caught for posterity." In most situations, he kept his thoughts well hidden. But around Stasia . . . she made everything sharper, especially his lust.

And his protectiveness.

Around her, he often felt raw, exposed, and so on edge that control seemed an unattainable attribute.

He wanted her, and he'd have her, but he didn't want her face advertised as his latest conquest in a damn MMA magazine.

"Aren't the photos to promote you?"

"Forget the photographer." After reclaiming his coat from a young lady near the front door, Harley drew Stasia outside. "Did you drive?"

"Yes."

"We'll worry about your truck later." He led her toward the Charger and unlocked the passenger door. "Here we are."

"Wow. New car?"

"It's a long story." He waited until she was seated and then shut the door and hurried around to the driver's side.

"This is really nice, Harley. I'm impressed."

"Don't be." He got the car started and turned the heater on. "Have you eaten?"

"Not recently."

Knuckles tight, he drove out of the parking space and onto the road. Every possible emotion churned. He wanted her, but he didn't want to want her. He was glad to see her when he knew that to be dangerous. Having her near was a comfort that he hadn't realized was missing.

"You want to go back to my place, or to a restaurant?"

Her small hand touched his upper arm. "Considering your mood and how easily I'm swayed, I think a restaurant might be better, don't you?"

No. Better would be getting inside her. Better would be holding her close and clearing his head with a mind-blowing come. "Whatever you want, Stasia."

"I want to talk to you."

"Yeah. In a little bit."

She sat back against the seat, and Harley could practically hear her thinking.

"Okay," she suddenly said, "I've changed my mind."

A quick glance at her face didn't clear things up at all. "About?"

"I need to rent a room for the night. Tomorrow I hope to find more permanent arrangements. A house to rent, an extended stay—"

She planned to stay? "Far as I know, Harmony doesn't have either. But Roger might be willing to work with you on it." Harley couldn't believe those words had come from his mouth. His brows pinched down. "How long are you talking?"

Honest to the end, Stasia said, "That depends largely on you, which is what I'd like to talk about."

"Me?"

"You." She drew a breath. "Why don't we go to a hotel so I can rent a room, and then we can clear the air a little?"

If he got her alone in a room, he'd lose it. "How do you figure we do that?"

She stared out the windshield. "I could start by spelling out my plans."

That almost scared him. But what the hell? He may as well hear it. "Go."

"I'd like to be your life coach."

Of all the things he'd imagined . . . "No."

"I wouldn't charge you."

"Hell no."

She rushed into explanations. "It'd be a sort of payback, for all your help in Echo Lake, and before you explode—"

"I don't explode," Harley ground out, feeling very close to doing just that. Damn it, where had his hard-won composure gone to?

"I know," she said. "But the thing is, I think occasionally you should."

He gave her a disbelieving stare. "That's a joke, right?"

"Harley, look, I've watched some of your fighting tapes, and I've talked to some people."

Talked to some people. Apprehension slammed into him. He steered to the side of the road and drew the car to a jarring halt, put it in park, and turned to face her.

Barely able to get the words out, he whispered, "You did what?"

"It's not what you're thinking."

Bullshit. "You talked about me with other people?"

Stasia knotted her hands together. "All in all, I've learned what I could about your sport. That's all."

Ah. Professional talk, not personal. He could handle that. Maybe.

"Idle curiosity?" he asked her, but he knew it wasn't.

"No. I've taken what I learned and applied it to you. To your style of fighting."

"Now you know my *style*?" What the hell was she

thinking? And here he'd thought Anastasia so grounded in reality, so reasonable and different from other screwy women.

So different to . . . him.

Unhooking her seat belt, Stasia twisted to face him. "In the beginning, when you fought your way up the ranks, you were like a maniac. Every move was automatic. Even when another fighter knocked you down, you were throwing punches and kicks. That's how you won, Harley, and that's who you are."

His brain throbbed. "I don't fucking believe this."

She frowned at his language, but it didn't shut her up. "Now you're so controlled that you've lost part of your edge."

Lost his edge? "I'm on a twelve-win streak."

"Yes, I know. You've only ever lost a few fights, and one of those was doctor stoppage from a cut above your eye. Otherwise you probably would have won." For emphasis, she leaned toward him. "But Harley, you aren't having as much fun anymore."

No, he wasn't. And so much insight from her—from any woman—didn't sit right. "It isn't about having fun. It's about a title belt."

"That's the ultimate goal, I know. And I understand why. But I think it'd be easier for you to get if you were a happier, more carefree man. If you turned loose your basic instincts."

Determined to get her mind off her harebrained idea of dissecting his fighting style when she didn't know jack about it, he whispered, "My basic instinct is to take you to bed." He looked at her mouth. "What do you think, Stasia? You ready to try a little submission?"

"Nope." She answered without hesitation. "Not today, and not tomorrow. Not ever."

"We'll see."

Her mouth twisted. "We're talking about your career, Harley."

"I'm talking about being inside you."

"Harley!" Her poise slipped. "There's a very natural inclination inside you to let it all out in the ring. I'm not talking about poor sportsmanship. No one would ever accuse you of that."

"I hope not." Giving up on sex for the moment, he put his head back and closed his eyes. Didn't it just figure that the first woman he wanted specifically—not just for sex, but for . . . well, *more*—would want to dick around with his career?

"When you fought those men who attacked us, you didn't plan out anything."

Without opening his eyes, he asked, "How would you know?"

"I *saw* it." Enthusiasm sounded in her voice. "You were so fast, so smooth. You reacted. Period. That's what's missing in your fights now."

"Nothing's missing in my fights. Just ask Uncle Satch. I'm the new sensation for the sport. That's why photographers are dogging my ass and interviewers are interrupting my workouts and every product supplier out there wants me endorsing their shit."

She retreated, softened. "None of that is bad, Harley."

"Maybe." He firmed his chin. "But it seems strange they'd be doing that if something was missing in my talent, huh?"

The seconds ticked by in silence. The car idled. Traffic went past.

Finally, her voice small and hurt, she said, "You think I'm way off base, don't you?"

He opened his eyes and turned his head toward her. "No offense, honey, but yeah. You are. But don't feel bad. The nuances of extreme fighting aren't something you learn overnight."

Stasia hesitated, giving him pause, then she firmed her resolve. "A fighter's basic nature isn't something that should be mutilated either. I think that's what your uncle is doing to you." Again, she touched his arm. "Just because you missed out on a few opportunities for the belt doesn't make icy control the answer."

His blood froze. "What do you know of that?"

Her tongue came out to slick over her lips. "Not a whole lot, actually." Cautiously, she measured her words. "I know that you were offered a shot at the belt early on, and you missed the opportunity because . . . of an illness in your family."

Her words prompted so much pain that Harley laughed. "An illness in my family, huh? Is that your idea of tact?"

She closed her arms around herself. "Harley, it's cold. Couldn't we go someplace—"

"No." He put the car back in gear and, after a quick glance in the side-view mirror, pulled back onto the street. "The conversation is over."

"You're being stubborn."

He made a U-turn and headed back to the bar. "I'll take you to your truck."

She gave a long, frustrated sigh and ended it with a curt, *"Fine."* Turning to look out her window, she added, "I won't beg you to listen to me."

"Good."

"Not tonight, anyway."

Meaning she hadn't given up at all?

Hell, Harley knew stubbornness when it got shoved down his throat, and for whatever reason, Stasia was going to be stubborn about this.

They made the return trip to the bar in uncomfortable silence. Harley drove into the parking lot and even before he had the car completely stopped, Stasia opened her door, jumped out, and slammed the door again.

He shoved the car into park and rushed to follow her. "Wait a damn minute."

"Conversation is over, Harley. Remember?"

He slipped in the snow, cursed, and caught up to her just as she reached her truck. She stopped abruptly. So did he.

Her front driver's side tire was slashed.

"Son-of-a-bitch," Harley said.

Stasia stared at it a moment, then she looked up and scanned the surrounding area. When she spotted no one, she circled her truck to ensure no other tires were damaged.

"The rest okay?"

She nodded. Under her breath, as if Harley wasn't standing there right beside her, she muttered, "Damn it," and then she headed toward the bar.

"Where are you going?"

"Inside to make a few calls. It's too cold out here." She looked over her shoulder at him. "And no, I don't need your manly assistance. I'm more than capable of calling roadside service all by myself. I can find my own hotel room, too. Go home with a clear conscience, Harley."

He pointed back at her truck. "Someone did that on purpose!"

"Duh, Sherlock. That was obvious." And then with more sarcasm, she added, "It seems to happen every time I'm around you. Heck of a coincidence, huh?"

Incredulous, Harley caught up again, and then stepped around in front of her, forcing her to wait. "Are you insinuating that I had something to do with it?"

She rolled her eyes. "No, of course not. I'm just saying . . ."

"What?"

She repeated, "Heck of a coincidence, huh?" Then she shoved her way around him. "But don't you worry about it, Harley. By tomorrow afternoon, I'll be gone."

The thought of her leaving made his stomach burn. "Gone, as in back to Echo Lake?" He stayed right on her heels.

"I'm currently without a job, so yes, back there. But as I told you, the local law enforcement is keeping an eye on things."

They got one step inside the bar and he caught her arm. "Damn it, Stasia, hold up just one second, will you?" When she didn't, he added, "Please."

Arms folded, Stasia faced him. "Fine. What is it?"

Harley released her and rubbed the back of his neck. "I don't want you to leave yet."

"And I don't want to be tied to your bed."

Damn it. He shot a quick glance around and noted that several people had heard her, and were now avidly listening. "Keep it down, will you?"

Eyes lighting with amusement, she said, "Sorry," and lowered her voice to a sugary whisper. "I thought your propensity for domination or control or whatever you call it was widely known."

Harley gave her a narrow-eyed scrutiny. How had he missed her inclination toward sarcasm? "What's wrong with you?"

Going on tiptoe, Stasia said, "I'm frustrated at your bullheaded inflexibility and disappointed that you won't let me at least try to help you and I'm not anxious to go back to Echo Lake, but now I don't have much choice."

Good God. He reared back. "All that, huh?"

"Did you want me to lie to you?"

"No." They stared at each other, both breathing hard. "While you're spilling your guts, will you admit that you want me as much as I want you?"

"I already did. I'm not ashamed of being attracted to you, Harley. I even fancy the idea of being tied up by you—but I'm not going to do it so you can get that look out of your eyes."

Pulse racing, he eased closer. "Why not?"

"First of all, my pride." She held up a hand. "And yes, Harley, it's about pride. I'm too independent to give up that much control. And even if you were willing to forego the kinky stuff—"

"Whisper, Stasia. Please."

"Oops." She obliged. "Even if you were, I don't want to be one more woman in a long line of conquests. That's definitely not what you need."

"I disagree."

"I'd rather help you with some life issues—"

"I don't have any life issues, damn it."

She struck a smug pose. "Spoken like a man who refuses to see the truth."

Harley turned his back on her in the hopes that not see-ing her would allow him to think more clearly. Unfortu-nately, she took it as a dismissal and walked away from him.

When he turned back around, she'd gone into a stairwell to use her phone.

Damned annoying woman!

To make matters worse, the sounds of a noisy group en-tered the alcove. Harley looked up, and there stood Dean and Eve, Gregor and Jacki, Barber and the redhead all close by, collecting their coats and hats.

Surprised to see him back at the bar, they looked toward Harley. He locked his jaw and silently prayed they'd leave without heckling him.

Stasia closed her phone and came back up alongside him. "Roadside is on their way."

"I'll wait with you."

She shook her head. "Not necessary, Harley. You must have other more important things to do."

Harley just knew Barber was smiling over his predica-ment. "I'm waiting with you, Stasia."

She shrugged. "Suit yourself."

"If I do that," he said lower, "we'll both be quickly naked."

"Here?" She shook her head in mock disapproval. "Very kinky, Harley."

Barber chose that inauspicious moment to make his presence known to her. Right behind her, he said, "I proba-bly shouldn't have heard that, huh?"

Stasia spun around, saw the group with Barber, and gave Harley a glare. "You could have told me."

"You were too busy trying to brush me off."

"I wasn't—"

"More truck trouble?" Barber interrupted.

"Someone slashed her front tire."

"Damn, woman. How many enemies do you have?"

Stasia looked at her audience and glared again. "Only one that I know of."

Harley's mouth went tight. She was way too casual about it. An enemy was news to him.

Barber asked, "Anyone I can dispose of for you?"

The others squeezed in closer, their curiosity ripe. Stasia shook her head. "I doubt any of this is related. Don't worry about it."

Harley didn't have to see his friends' faces to know what they thought of that.

Before any more could be said, Stasia put a hand on Barber's arm. "But could you do me a favor, Barber?"

Deliberately avoiding Harley's gaze, Barber smiled and said, "Name it."

"Introduce me to some fighters. I want to learn more about the sport."

Jacki laughed and dragged Gregor forward with her. "You'd do better to talk to Dakota. She's Simon's wife and she knows ultimate fighting inside and out."

"True enough," Barber said. "The woman is a phenom."

Eve stuck out her hand and introduced herself.

While everyone got acquainted, Harley stood aside and stewed. Anastasia knew of someone who might want to do her harm, and she hadn't mentioned it. Why?

He'd find that out, and more, before he let her out of his sight.

Though he was mostly lost in thought, Harley picked up enough on the conversations to know that Stasia had just been invited into the wives' inner circle. He wasn't sure how he felt about that.

Other than Dakota, who wasn't anyone's idea of a typical female and who really did have an unusual grasp of the sport, the wives shared a skewed take on the whole fighting scene. For the most part, their interest started and ended with blind support of their husbands.

But if talking with the wives would keep Stasia from trying to analyze him, then what the hell? He didn't mind that at all.

When Barber offered to see her safely to Roger's hotel, along with the redhead, Harley said, "I'll take her."

In a long-suffering voice, Stasia said, "I will see myself there, thank you very much."

"Excuse us." Harley put his arm around her and walked her several feet away. None of his friends even made a pretense of giving them privacy. Standing in front of Stasia so they couldn't see her, he gave them his back. "We need to talk, Stasia. About a lot of stuff."

"Now, come on, Harley. How can you want to talk to me *and* want me to leave? That doesn't make any sense."

He was losing the fight and he knew it. Without making an issue of it, he drew a deep, fortifying breath. "I'd like you to stay for a while."

Stasia tipped her head. "You're kidding, right?"

"No."

"You mean Mr. One-Night Stand is having a change of heart?"

He leveled a look on her, and gave her a taste of her own medicine. In a mere whisper, he said, "My heart has nothing to do with it, Anastasia. Just because I got *you* off that night doesn't mean I've lost interest. If you'll recall, I went to sleep with a hard-on."

Warmth entered her face and her eyes darkened. She looked around his shoulder at their audience, then back at his face. She licked her lips. "I did offer—"

"No good. Half-measures would never cover it. I need to be inside you, buried deep, with enough time to get my fill. And as you know, so far that hasn't happened."

Her eyes deepened to chocolate brown. "And as long as you have those control fetishes, it won't." Smiling, she clarified, "Happen, I mean."

"Are you a betting woman, Stasia?"

"Usually, no."

"Chicken?"

"I call it prudent."

"I call it chicken."

She put a hand to his chest. "Tell you what, Harley. We could get together for dinner tomorrow if you like."

"Tomorrow?"

"Sorry. Tonight, I'm going to get my tire changed, then I'm going to the hotel. I'm exhausted and in desperate need of sleep and quiet time to think and regroup. Tomorrow morning I'm meeting with the women for a shopping trip, and then we're doing lunch."

Harley narrowed his eyes. If she'd come to see him, she hid it well. "Fine." Tomorrow was his only day off, but he'd find plenty to do. "Works for me."

"Where and when should I meet you for dinner?"

"I'll pick you up. Six o'clock?"

"Sounds good." She glanced at his mouth, then rolled her lips in and looked away. "Oh good, roadside service is here."

Harley watched her walk out the door into the dark, cold parking lot.

Barber stepped up beside him. "Got ya in a pickle, doesn't she?"

"Yeah."

His admission surprised Barber, who laughed. "Since I've had a few beers, I'm going to turn over my keys to Jasmine."

Keeping his gaze on Anastasia as she directed the roadside serviceman toward her truck, Harley asked, "Who's Jasmine?"

"A redheaded hottie who I think is going to be in the band."

That got Harley's attention. He looked at Barber, then toward the plump redhead. Interesting choice. "You *think* she is?"

"Yeah. Haven't entirely made up my mind yet."

Harley laughed. "Got your own pickle, huh?"

He shrugged. "She'll be checking in to the hotel tonight, too."

"Roger's got to love all the traffic to his place."

"The band and I get our rooms for free, so it's the least I can do." He put a hand on Harley's shoulder. "Anyway, Jasmine and I will make sure that Stasia gets safely to the hotel. How's that?"

"Appreciate it." And with that confirmed, Harley walked out to Anastasia, bid her a fast good night, and then, with her gaze boring into his back, he got in the Charger and drove away.

If Anastasia wanted to play games, they'd play.

But it was his game, so in the end, he knew he'd win.

He always did.

As long as fate didn't screw him over again.

CHAPTER 14

THE house was quiet when Harley got in. He locked up, started to his room, and Satch appeared.

"Just getting in?"

Harley propped a shoulder on the wall. "Yeah."

Holding up a glass of milk, Satch said, "I'm having some cookies. Want some?"

"Thanks, but I'll pass."

"Probably a good idea. Might as well stay on weight."

Harley didn't point out that his weight had never been an issue for the sport. He stayed in year-round good health and never had to work off more than a few pounds to meet the weight-class requirements. "Everything okay, Satch?"

"Yeah, yeah. Things are fine."

Sometimes Harley worried, no doubt residual effects of losing both parents. "You're not overdoing it?"

"Course not." He took a drink of his milk. "I heard that little girl was in town."

"Little girl?"

"Anastasia Bradley."

His uncle's connections never ceased to amaze Harley. "Should I ask how you know that?"

"It's not a secret. I talked to a photographer, who described her. So it is her?"

"Yeah."

Studying his milk, Satch asked, "Did she say what she wants?"

"No, but don't sweat it, Uncle Satch. I've got it under control."

"Of course you do." He smiled up at Harley. "Well, good night then."

Wondering at his uncle's evasive attitude, Harley said, "Good night," and went on down the hall to his room. Because his and his uncle's bedrooms were located on opposite ends of the house, they each had their privacy, but the kitchen proved to be neutral ground.

Had Uncle Satch been waiting on him? Probably. He liked to try to steer every facet of Harley's life, including his personal relationships. Not that he'd succeed. Harley gave him leeway, but he drew the line whenever his uncle overstepped himself.

These days, it happened more often than not.

He had a feeling that with Anastasia around, it'd be a daily issue to be dealt with.

As Harley brushed his teeth and then stripped off his clothes to climb into bed naked, he thought of all the ways Uncle Satch and Anastasia were likely to butt heads.

Satch wanted him to keep ultimate control.

And Anastasia wanted him to loosen up.

His life was about to get more interesting.

"I think I'd sooner go to the dentist than do all that shopping."

Stasia looked up from her lunch to see a very striking blonde in casual clothes standing with Cam's sister, Jacki. Eve, Cam, Stasia, and Jasmine had gotten acquainted over the shopping expedition, now Jacki was ready to join them, and Stasia would be willing to bet that was Dakota with her.

Eve laughed. "We know your preferences well enough, Dakota. That's why we only invited you and Jacki to the lunch to talk about the SBC."

Dakota held out a hand to Stasia. "I'm Dakota, Simon's wife."

Stasia grinned ear to ear. Here was her opportunity to learn more about Harley's sport. "It's so nice to meet you." She gestured toward Jasmine. "This is Jasmine Petri. She'll be joining Barber's band."

"No kidding?" Dakota shook her hand too, and then dragged out a chair. "Barber already hired you?"

Jasmine nodded. Stasia had noticed that the woman was on the shy side. Eve had basically chosen her entire wardrobe without a whole lot of input from Jasmine. Luckily, Eve had excellent taste. Jasmine would look like a rocker, but without overly flaunting her assets.

Knowing Barber, that probably wasn't what he'd had in mind.

"Just last night," Jasmine told Dakota. "Well, maybe. He said he wanted to see me dressed differently before he made it official."

Dakota sat back in her seat. "Did you tell him to stuff that? You can dress any damn way you want to."

"Oh, I didn't mind. I really didn't have any rocker type clothes."

"So? Who's Barber to say how you should dress?" Dakota held up a hand to signal the waitress.

Eve lifted a large bag. "You should see everything we got her, Dakota. Corsets, mesh tunics, new jeans, lace-up boots . . . she's going to blow Barber's mind."

"Very cool stuff," Jasmine enthused.

"You look great in all of it." Stasia had picked up a few items of her own. "I really enjoyed all the shopping, and now I have a better idea of where everything's located."

"Planning to stay around?" Dakota asked.

"That's up to Harley." Stasia explained about being a life coach, and what she wanted to do for Harley. Dakota listened intently, pausing only long enough to put in an order for a burger and fries after the waitress had brought her a malt.

"You know what we should do?" Dakota swallowed down a crispy fry. "We should have a girls' night out. You all could come to my place to watch tapes of the guys fighting. I have most of Harley's because I watched them when I thought he and Simon would fight. Now that they aren't . . . We'll analyze things, see how his style has changed. Then Monday we can go to the gym and get a bird's-eye view of the workouts and sparring."

Jacki, Cam, and Eve all quickly gave their excuses.

Dakota laughed. "They're wusses when it comes to the actual flesh on flesh stuff."

"Blood," Jacki said with a wrinkled nose. "Can't stand it, especially when it's on Gregor."

"Like that gargantuan brute gets bloodied all that often." Dakota shook her head. "Usually his opponents are put out of the competition before Gregor has had a chance to get sweaty."

"There are also twisted limbs, grunts, and groans." Eve shivered. "It can be unsettling."

"Not to mention the less-than-appealing smell of sweat that permeates the walls of the gym," Cam added. "You pack twenty mostly naked sweaty guys into a room together, and the air gets thick."

"Mostly naked?" Jasmine looked up with wide eyes. "I think it sounds sexy." They all burst out laughing, which made Jasmine grin. "Well, it does."

Stasia smiled at her. "I have to admit, I'm anxious to witness it." And then to Dakota, "We're allowed in the gym?"

Dakota snorted. "They won't even try to keep us out."

"More likely," Eve said, "some of them will start showing off."

Sounded fascinating. "I'm in."

"Me, too," Jasmine said. Then she added, "That is, if I'm invited. I mean, I'm not boning up on the sport or anything—"

"By all means, you should come, too. Barber is a first-class fighter. He could compete if he only wanted to." Dakota lifted her shoulders. "But his music is his first love."

"How come you don't perform with him anymore?" Jasmine asked.

"I do on occasion," Dakota hedged. "But I can't tour with him."

Eve gave a laugh. "And the fact that Barber was sweet on her—"

"Is *still* sweet on her as far as most can tell," Jacki said.

"—means that big and bad Sublime gets real testy when the two of them are alone too long together."

"Oh, stop." Dakota laughed. "Simon knows neither Barber nor I would do anything inappropriate."

"Which has nothing to do with his possessiveness where Barber is concerned."

Dakota gave up. "Yeah, well, you've got me there." So that Jasmine wouldn't misunderstand, she said, "The guys get along great, but it was a little touchy there for a while. The fact that Barber is well over any infatuation he had—he *is*, Jacki, so don't say it—helps."

The others didn't notice, but Stasia saw how Jasmine sank a little in her chair.

So she harbored her own fondness? Poor girl. From what Stasia had seen, Barber wasn't a man due to settle down with one woman anytime soon.

When the talk turned to the SBC, Stasia got out her notebook to jot down thoughts and insights. Dakota went through the history, rules, techniques, and styles.

Eve and Jacki talked more about the personalities of the fighters. Most, according to them, were honorable men dedicated to their families. But, of course, there were always a few bad apples in the mix.

"That's why," Dakota said, "the SBC wants to feature select fighters, to showcase the more glowing examples."

Eve winked. "Meaning Harley."

"They've already featured my brother and Simon," Cam told Stasia. "And Harley, with his background, is an obvious choice for their next highlight."

Recalling the hints from Harley's uncle, a million questions popped into Stasia's mind. "I know he injured his elbow right before the last fight."

"Helping me," Dakota said. After half a minute, she shook her head and met Stasia's curious gaze. "My ex-husband was a real prick. He'd been hassling me for years. It's a long story, but when he showed up again—"

"With a knife," Jacki clarified.

"Harley was there." Dakota gave a solemn smile. "They don't call him 'Hard to Handle' for no reason. He took on three guys without too much trouble. All with a dislocated elbow."

"You're kidding?"

Jacki made a face. "Gregor said he didn't even know his arm was hurt until Simon pointed out to him that it was sort of hanging funny."

Stasia shuddered. "Omigod. That's awful."

"Yeah." Dakota rubbed her forehead. "I swear Gregor enjoyed himself. Some other guys showed up, too."

Eve let out a breath. "The SBC is a family. The guys stick together. Unfortunately, Harley's elbow was already dislocated. Not that he let that slow him down when he knew Dakota was in trouble."

"They knew how Simon felt about Dakota, so she became family, too." Jacki smiled. "Or it might have been that they'd feel that way regardless of how things worked out with Simon."

Dakota laughed. "Yeah, maybe. But I feel terrible that Harley was unable to fight because of me."

Eve slugged her in the arm. "Not because of you. Because of that jerk."

"Who's now doing time," Cam said. "No one blames Dakota."

"But I know Simon struggled with retiring again without giving Harley a shot at the title, all things considered."

With complete confidence, Stasia said, "Harley wouldn't want the shot as a favor, or out of guilt. He'll get there no matter what. Your husband has no reason to concern himself."

The waitress came back to see if anyone wanted dessert. Both Jasmine and Dakota put in orders. Stasia would have liked to, but because she was scheduled to have dinner with Harley in only a few hours, she didn't want to completely stuff herself.

Stasia looked at her watch. Luckily, she'd driven separately to the diner. "I should get going."

"So soon?" Eve asked.

Making new friends was always a special treat. Except for Jasmine, whom they'd just met, they were all so close, and yet so different. As a people person, Stasia appreciated the variety.

"I'm seeing Harley tonight. Gotta get home and prepare." She bobbed her eyebrows and laughed. "He keeps me on my toes, that's for sure."

"So." Dakota leaned back in her seat. "You two are romantic?"

"You know Harley, right?"

"Yes."

"What do you think?"

"I think he's probably trying to run the show."

Stasia grinned. "He is running the show, at least for now. But no, we're not romantic. He made it *real* clear how he felt about that. But I've known him for a while now, and I'm interested in his career, so here I am."

A little worried, Eve leaned forward. "I don't mean to be forward—"

Stasia waved that away. "Speak freely. I can take it."

"Well, you seem more than interested in his career. And let's face it, Harley's one of those guys."

Cam nodded. "The kind that are hard to resist."

"The kind the you don't want to resist," Jacki put in.

"He's a fighter," Dakota said. "A good one, with a solid personality to go with it."

"In other words, he's the whole package. I know." Stasia sighed. "But I think I can handle it."

"Handle 'Hard to Handle' Handleman?" Dakota gave a crooked smile. "You'll be way ahead of a lot of fighters, then. Harley has plowed right through most of them. And right now, he's doubly distracted with opponents, because it doesn't look like Simon is going back. I begged and pleaded, but he wants to retire."

"You want him to fight?" Stasia asked.

"I want him to be happy. I don't want him giving up anything for me." She shrugged. "He says he's not."

"He says," Eve confided, "that she's irresistible and he can't stay away from her. I know, because Dean was bitching about it."

They all laughed.

Stasia enjoyed the female camaraderie, and how easily the women shared the male perspectives. "So if Harley doesn't fight Simon, then who?"

Everyone looked at Dakota.

She propped her elbows on the table. "Well, scuttlebutt has it that Kevin Kinkaid, better known as Killer, is due for a big fight. The way I think it'll roll out is that they'll fight Harley and Kevin, and whoever wins that fight will get a title fight against Andrei Mann."

Stasia was amazed at her knowledge. "Killer Kinkaid?"

"Yeah, cute nickname, huh?" She rolled her eyes. "A few years back, he knocked three guys out in a row, and then broke the next guy's arm in two places."

Stasia's heart skipped a beat.

"Don't look like that. He didn't do anything illegal or overly brutal, although he now has the rep anyway. Sometimes, when a fighter's adrenaline is pumping, he doesn't realize how close to jeopardy he is. The guy Kinkaid fought didn't tap, even in a tight arm bar. He was still swinging at Kinkaid, so Kinkaid applied a little more pressure and . . . snap."

The women all winced.

"Even after the break, the guy didn't know he was injured. It was Kinkaid who clued in the ref. He stopped the fight, they called in the doc, and sure enough, she pronounced the arm broken. It wasn't until later that everyone found out just how badly broken it was."

"Does that happen often?"

"Luckily, no."

Stasia gulped. "So if Harley beats Kinkaid—"

"Don't let Harley hear you say *if*. And don't worry about it. I think he will."

A fraction of Stasia's tension eased. "Okay, so he'll beat Kinkaid, and then he'll have to fight Mann?"

"That's my prediction, but it hasn't been announced or anything yet. Harley should hear something soon. Since Simon is retiring again"—she paused to smile and show her pride—"then it only makes sense for them to go through the ranks and pit the best together."

"So you're saying that those with the best records are Harley, Kinkaid, and Mann."

"That's right."

"Gregor's in a different weight class," Jacki pointed out. "But he'll be going for a belt soon, too."

"Next time up," Dakota predicted. "He's due. But for the light heavyweights . . . those are the three guys that I've narrowed it down to. We'll see."

By the time Stasia left the lunch, she felt she had not only the "on paper" explanation of the sport, but an emotional take on it, too. Each of the wives had a different love/respect/acceptance for ultimate fighting, so their viewpoints differed. What stayed the same was their love of the fighters they'd married.

With fighters traveling so much, not just within the country now but all over the world, it wouldn't be an easy alliance. Training took major dedication, and while it seemed the men did a great job balancing it all, their career choice wouldn't be ideal for many women.

What Stasia wanted to know now, more than anything else, was the reason behind Harley's other missed title belt opportunities. She had a feeling Dakota knew, but Stasia hadn't asked, and Dakota hadn't offered.

They both accepted that it was Harley's private information to share, and they both respected that.

It was getting dark when Stasia pulled into the parking lot of the hotel. After a sunny, mostly mild day, night brought with it a definite chill. But after the horrid conditions at Echo Lake, she wouldn't complain.

Lifting her purchases out of her truck, she hurried across the lot and in the front doors. It surprised her to find Harley and Barber standing inside. Because Harley still wore his coat, she assumed he'd just arrived.

"You're early," she accused. Just once she'd like to be totally put together for him. So far he'd seen her chopping wood, half-frozen and shaken from fear, and frazzled from a long trip.

Harley gave her a quick once-over, and he didn't smile. "I'm here to see Simon."

His ice-cold iron control was back. Surely he and Simon weren't about to butt heads. She knew Harley would be disappointed at Simon's decision to retire, but she couldn't see him holding a grudge over it.

She looked around the hotel lobby. "Simon is here?"

"He's stopping by to see Barber."

Stasia looked at Harley's friend. "You're staying here, too?"

"Roger gives the band a suite of rooms whenever we perform at the bar. It's part of our pay package."

"Oh. That's nice."

"And convenient." Barber must've picked up on her concerns because he squeezed her shoulder. "They aren't going to maul each other, Anastasia. Meeting in my room guarantees no press."

"And no photos," Harley said.

"Oh, of course. An out-of-the-way place makes perfect sense." She smiled at them.

They stared back politely, but as if they had other things to do and she was holding them up.

"Well . . ." Stasia started sidling away. "I need to shower and stuff, so I guess I'll see you in a little while."

"I'll come to your room to get you at six."

"Right." Might as well use the opportunity to get more information on the upcoming evening. "You didn't say where we were going. How should I dress?"

Though he never looked away from her face, Harley's gaze grew heated. Almost as a challenge, he suggested softly, "Wear a skirt."

The way he said that, Stasia knew the skirt was more for him than the sake of proper attire. But she wouldn't let him continue to fluster her.

She smiled without a care. "No problem. I can do that." Luckily, she'd just bought the perfect outfit. She took two steps. "'Bye, Barber."

"Enjoy the shower, doll."

The last thing Stasia saw was Harley putting Barber in a headlock.

Barber's laughter followed her down the hall.

CHAPTER 15

L OUNGED out on one of the two full-size beds in Barber's room, Harley stared toward the television, but he
didn't really see or hear it. His thoughts centered on Stasia.

In the shower. Naked.

Would she wear a skirt as he instructed? Without realizing it, he smiled.

Stasia could be so unpredictable. She didn't pull her
punches verbally or emotionally. He could count on her to
give it to him straight—whatever it was she wanted to give
him.

If she offered more half-baked analysis on his fighting
style, he'd have to set her straight. Anything else . . . well,
it'd be worth it to see her again. Something about her relaxed him. Even when she talked nonsense on stuff she
didn't understand, he enjoyed her. Her face, her voice, the
scent of her—

"Damn, brother, you look like a man planning a full-
blown pillage."

Harley spared a glance for Barber, who put the safety

catch in the door so it wouldn't close all the way. "Just thinking."

"About women. Or should I say woman—Stasia." Barber left the partially opened door and went to prepare a fresh carafe of coffee. After turning down the sports station that neither of them was listening to, he dropped down to the other bed.

"She's up to something."

He looked at Harley. "Not that you're paranoid or anything, right?"

"Just cautious." Harley thought about what he said. He wasn't a man who shared a lot of himself, but now he found he wanted feedback. "She thinks I'm too controlling."

Barber flashed him a sideways look. "Well, duh, doofus. I coulda told you that Stasia wasn't the type who'd take to handcuffs."

Prickling alarm shot up his spine. Never, not once, had Harley told anyone, not even a best bud, about his sexual preferences. Beyond being respectful of the women he entertained, it was just plain private.

Only the women he'd been with, and Stasia, knew what he liked. But damn it, Stasia wouldn't have said anything. He trusted her sense of discretion.

Turning his head, Harley sent a menacing glare at Barber. "What the fuck are you talking about?"

He lifted his brows. "Sorry, man, but chicks talk. You should know that. And your blond bimbo—what was her name? Gloria? Anyway, she's spreading the word that you tied her up and did the nasty to her, and she loved it."

Gloria. "Shit."

Barber sympathized. "Yeah. Nothing is sacred, huh? Not even a little bondage between kink-loving partners."

"Shut the fuck up, Barber." Harley sat up. If Gloria was shooting off her mouth, there was a chance the press could get wind of it.

How would the SBC react? Not that it was any of their damn business. His private life was just that—private.

"Don't sweat it, dude. Far as I could tell, everyone she blabbed to was either impressed or intrigued."

Scrubbing both hands over his face, Harley contemplated how he'd handle the news if or when it came to slap him in the face.

"I say run with it," Barber suggested. "It'll give the gossipers something juicy to sink their teeth into."

"Can you be quiet one damn minute?"

Barber grinned. "I guess that means I can't beg details out of you?"

"No."

"Come on, Harley. It's not a big deal."

"I have too much on the line to let it get blown now over something so stupid." Feeling antsy, unable to relax, Harley got to his feet and paced. "After three failed attempts at the belt . . ."

"Look at it this way, bud. All the delays have built the anticipation. I for one can't wait to see you take the title. I know a boatload of fans feel the same. The more the fans get to know you, the more they love you. You're a rebel. Everyone digs that shit, so *seriously,* don't go off the deep end, okay?"

But Harley didn't want more anticipation. He just wanted the fight. Now.

To change the subject, Barber said, "I'm sick of hotel rooms."

Relieved to have something else to talk about, Harley said, "So get yourself a house."

"I travel so damn much, there's no point." Barber put an arm behind his head. "You like having a house?"

Harley thought about it. "Satch likes it."

"Do you?"

"The privacy is nice."

"Even with your uncle living with you?"

"I think he always will." It was just a fact of life that Satch considered them an inseparable team. "I like the pool and having a basement full of gym equipment. And ya know, I even look forward to cutting the grass in the summer."

"Yeah." Barber chewed that over, then grinned as he

came full circle. "Maybe if you let go of the ropes and chains, you could get Stasia to play house with you."

"Butt out, Barber." Harley wasn't about to discuss Stasia with anyone, not even a friend.

"So . . . *were* there ropes and chains involved?"

Too fast for Barber to duck, Harley snatched up a magazine and flung it at him. It whacked him in the head.

Laughing, Barber held up a hand of surrender. "You're so touchy these days." He tsked. "If I could find the perfect woman, I'd settle down in a heartbeat."

"Your idea of the perfect woman is already married, you ass."

That took Barber's mood on a sour turn, and he cursed as he sat up. "Why the hell does everyone insist on thinking I'm still in love with Dakota?"

"That's what I'd like to know." Simon pushed open the unlatched door. "It's damned annoying."

Barber grinned. "You're early, Sublime."

"Or you wouldn't have been discussing my wife?"

Harley watched Simon. Had he overheard Barber ribbing about bondage? If so, he didn't show it. As usual, Simon Evans was the epitome of control.

Only when it came to Dakota; then he always looked a little riled.

"Come on, Sublime! I have nothing but respect for her, I swear."

"Yeah, right." Simon came over to Harley and offered a hand. "Good to see you, Harley. How's the elbow?"

"Good as new." They shared a handshake and then moved to the small round table in the corner. "Thanks for meeting me here."

"Not a problem. I need to visit Barber occasionally anyway, just to deliver a kick to the pants so he remembers that Dakota is my wife."

Barber protested that with a laugh. "It's not something I'm likely to forget, now am I?" He turned a chair and straddled it. "I've moved on, Sublime. You know that. She knows that. In fact, I've got a new gal to sing with the band."

"Yeah?" Simon eyed him. "If she's a clone of my wife, I'm definitely kicking your ass."

That even made Harley laugh. "If she's the redhead I saw, she's not a thing like Dakota."

"Not even close," Barber agreed. "She's a girly girl. Manicure, superlong red hair. Prissy clothes. And she's got some extra padding."

Simon's mouth twisted. "You're right—that's nothing like Dakota."

"All that, and you're adding her to the band?" Harley asked, disbelieving the probability of it. She didn't sound like Barber's usual fare, or a woman who'd mesh with a hard rock, unruly group.

"She's got one hell of a voice." The coffee finished brewing and Barber stood up to fill three disposable cups. "If you two are free tonight, stop by the bar and you can not only meet her, but hear her sing. It'll be a sort of trial run now that she should have some new threads that'll help her fit in."

"What time?" Harley asked. He found he was equally curious about the redhead's performance and Simon's re-action to Barber finally moving on.

To Harley's way of thinking, Simon had been more than tolerant of Barber. If a flame from Stasia's past was still lingering around . . .

Whoa.

Harley quashed those thoughts real fast. What he had with Stasia sure as hell wasn't the lifetime commitment that Simon and Dakota shared. Not even close.

Right?

"Let's say nine or so. You in, Simon?"

"I'm sure Dakota wouldn't want to miss it."

"Great." A subtle tension eased from Barber's posture. "Get hold of Havoc and Gregor, will ya? We'll make a party of it to welcome the new songbird proper."

Simon looked at Barber for an exaggerated time, then turned to Harley. "Do you get the feeling that he doesn't want to be alone with her?"

"I'm getting that vibe, yeah." Harley scrutinized Barber, too. "She scare you, Barber?"

Barber sat the coffee cups in front of his friends. "Actually, my man, she shocks me."

"How so?" Simon took a sip of the too-strong coffee, made a face, then drank again.

Barber leveled a look on him. "My admiration of Dakota is no secret to anyone. Hell, half of Harmony feels free to comment on it twice a damn day."

Scowling, Simon plunked down his coffee.

"So being that Jasmine Petri isn't a damn thing like Dakota, I can't figure out why I'm considering breaking one of my cardinal rules."

Being facetious, Harley asked with feigned disbelief, "You have rules? Since when?"

"They've always been there." Barber held up a finger. "Number one rule—no sleeping with band members."

Harley choked on his coffee. "Well, that's a good thing. Other than Dakota, all the band members have been guys."

"Yeah, but it applied to Dakota."

Simon bunched up from his knees to his ears. Harley thought that if Simon didn't have a shaved head, his hair would stand on end.

"She wouldn't have had you, you dumbass."

"Yeah, I know that." Barber grinned. "But the point is, I never even tried. Didn't want to cross any lines, you know. The thing is, with Jasmine . . . She really is good, no disputing that. But I'm not sure having her in the band is worth *not* having her in my bed. Or maybe the rule doesn't seem so important now that it applies to Jasmine."

"And you've known her how long?" Harley asked.

"Long enough that I can't seem to stop picturing her buck-naked in my mind."

A tentative tap sounded at the door. Barber froze. Without looking, he said to Simon, "Don't suppose you closed it all the way?"

Simon took unparalleled delight in saying, "Nope. You had it open, so I left it open."

"Shit."

Fighting to keep his face straight, Harley leaned forward to see the door. A red-faced, redheaded girl stood there, fuming. "Ah. You must be Jasmine, right?"

"Yes, hi. I'm Jasmine Petri." Staring daggers at the back of Barber's head, she asked, "Am I interrupting?"

Barber closed his eyes a moment, then spun around with a welcoming and cocky grin. "Not at all, Jassy. Come on in."

She tripped over her first step. *"Jassy?"*

"Yeah. I think it suits you."

"It doesn't!" Reddish brows pinched down over a lightly freckled nose. "I prefer Jasmine, thank you very much."

Barber shrugged. To Harley and Simon, who were both now on their feet, he said, "Given the scathing reprimand I received yesterday for failing in my social duty, I suppose introductions are the thing."

Though Jasmine's face was hot, her voice sounded sweet. "Now, Barberosa, if it taxes your brain too much, we can forgo common courtesy. I wouldn't want you to hurt yourself."

"Barberosa?" Harley asked. "No kidding?"

"Damn," Simon said at almost the same time. "I like her."

Harley liked her, too. He elbowed Barber aside and held out a hand. "Harley Handleman. It's nice to meet you, Jasmine."

"Thank you, Mr. Handleman."

"Harley, please." Her hand was soft, gentle in his, and quickly withdrawn.

She nodded. "I've met Stasia. She's very interested in your profession."

That took Harley off guard. "You don't say."

"Several of us went shopping, and then we all had lunch together. Stasia kept the conversation very interesting."

Going cold inside, Harley wondered just what the hell they had talked about. Did Stasia now feel at liberty to discuss him in idle conversation?

There had been a point in his life where everyone gossiped about him, and he didn't like it worth a damn. He made a mental note to share his displeasure with Stasia first thing.

After delivering that zinger, Jasmine turned to Simon. "And you must be Mr. Evans. Dakota is so very proud of you."

"Call me Simon. Any friend of Dakota's and all that."

"Thank you. It was wonderful meeting her in person. I've been a fan ever since I first saw her perform. She's incredible."

"I agree."

"So do I." Barber, the only one still sitting, tipped his head back to see her. "You've got some big shoes to fill, Jassy."

Harley wanted to kick him.

Simon looked ready to throttle him.

Pasting on a very false smile, Jasmine said, "I only stopped by to ask you what time you wanted to see me tonight."

"I was just chewing on that." Barber rose out of his seat. "Why don't we sort out the details in the hall? That way if I have another verbal faux pas, I can spare myself the public flogging."

"If you don't watch yourself," Simon grumbled, "it's a very old-fashioned ass-kicking that you'll get."

"One well deserved, I'm sure," Jasmine said.

Barber took her arm and started her out of the room. Right before he went through the door, he glanced back at Harley with a wolfish expression and a bobbing of his eyebrows.

Harley shook his head. Instead of mellowing, Barber got more reprehensible with time.

Or maybe he really was still in love with Dakota, and this was his way of hiding it.

Simon strode to the door, removed the guard and let the door drop shut. "If deep down he wasn't such a good guy, I'd have to demolish him. But the truth is, he was a damn fine friend to Dakota when she needed one most. I sometimes wonder what would have happened to her without him around."

Reclaiming his seat, Harley said, "I know what you mean. She really had it rough."

"It made her the woman she is, and I love her, so I try not to dwell on it."

"You just ensure no one will ever hurt her again. I get it."

Not one to mince words, Simon nodded and then said, "I'm definitely retiring, Harley."

Ah hell. There it was—the thing Harley most didn't want to hear.

"I figured." While struggling with what he'd known would be inevitable, Harley dared another drink of the god-awful coffee. "I can't even say as I blame you."

"It wasn't an easy decision. Both Dakota and I feel indebted to you—"

"Don't." Harley couldn't say exactly why, but it insulted him to be thanked for doing what any honorable man would do. "The injury was my own damn fault, not yours, and not hers. I was caught off guard, and that's inexcusable on my part."

"Still—"

"Believe me when I say I'd do it again in a heartbeat."

Simon accepted that without another word. "I've been thinking about it, and since I won't be competing, I'd like to train you."

"Yeah?"

"I'd enjoy it. Retiring doesn't mean I want completely out of it. Investing in you will be almost as good."

"I appreciate that." Harley knew Satch would be thrilled. Between Dean and Simon, he couldn't ask for a better core camp to get him ready for the competition.

He was about to say more when his cell phone rang. Standing, Harley pulled the slim phone out of his jeans pocket, glanced at the caller ID, and said to Simon, "It's Drew Black."

The president of the SBC didn't make a lot of social calls. That he'd be calling Harley now could mean that some decisions had been made.

"About time." Simon sat forward.

Assuming he was about to get the details on his next fight, Harley answered with anticipation. But after he and Drew got through the cordial small talk, Harley got a shocker.

The fight was sooner than he expected. And it was a straight shot for the title.

BARBER had a difficult time listening to Jasmine's endless chatter about her shopping trip and girls' lunch out. But even in his distraction, wondering how much she'd heard before making her arrival known, he picked up on her enthusiasm and overall delight for her new wardrobe and new friends.

In the normal course of things, female chatter left his brain numb. But with Jasmine, it didn't matter what she said. Watching her lips move only made him want to kiss her more.

She was so animated in all she did, so . . . perky.

Comparisons came without his bidding.

Dakota had never been perky a day in her life.

Dakota filed her nails, but it took a very special occasion for her to suffer through a manicure.

Dakota was headstrong and iron-willed, and Barber couldn't recall ever seeing her cry.

He admired everything about her. He respected and adored her.

Until now, he'd really thought it'd take another woman just like Dakota to get him fired up. But damn . . .

When Jasmine spoke, she used her hands and changed her posture a lot. The movements were feminine and naturally flirtatious. Dakota never flirted. Barber wasn't sure she even knew how. When Jasmine shifted, her assets jiggled in a delicious way guaranteed to drag his already sidetracked brain into carnal supposition.

Everything about her was so unintentionally inviting that no way was Barber going to blame himself for his reactions.

Even the fact that Jasmine reveled in giving him hell, especially in front of his friends, turned him on. Why he liked that, Barber couldn't say. Maybe it was because most women were too accommodating, and after his recent taste of fame they were downright easy. That blind agreement suddenly seemed . . . boring.

"Anyway," Jasmine said, "Dakota shared some of the song lyrics with me. Wasn't that nice of her? She said they were favorites of yours. I recognized them, of course, and I'm pretty sure I know all the words, but just in case, I'll look them over."

"Good idea."

"She really is nice. I wasn't expecting that."

"She's great."

"We all had so much fun, we've agreed to get together again real soon."

"Yeah." Barber barely registered her comments. Today she had her long hair in an intricate and feminine French braid. Little curls had escaped and teased her cheeks and neck. Dainty earrings hung from her earlobes. Her flesh-toned sweater didn't show a speck of skin, but it did emphasize the generous weight of her breasts.

This skirt was even longer than the one from last night, and Barber found himself musing on her thighs. Would they be as soft and lush as her breasts and ass?

God, he hoped so.

She put a hand to her chest. "The food was so good, I ate way too much."

Barber looked at her glossy painted nails, the slim birthstone ring on her finger. He smelled the light fragrance of scented shampoo, and the subtler scent of warm female skin.

"I even got dessert," she said. "Peach pie."

"Peach, huh?" Man, he was sinking like a cement block.

Jasmine licked her lips. "It was heavenly. I could have eaten the whole pie."

"That does it." Unable to take it a second more, Barber caught her chin with his fingertips. "Sorry, sugar, but if you really want my attention, I have to alleviate the suspense."

"The what?"

He kissed her.

It was like kissing a warm board.

For about three seconds.

She melted with a lot of enthusiasm. Her arms went around his neck and she squirreled up close to him with a soft moan.

Barber lost it. In a clumsy rush, he backed her to the door and leaned into her, opening her mouth with his tongue, squeezing her hip with strong fingers. All in all, going off the deep end fast and hard.

The door opened behind them and Jasmine almost toppled into the room.

Barber grabbed for her and missed.

Simon, standing in her path, ended up with her filling his arms.

Unfortunately, in his surprised effort to catch her, his right hand went where it wasn't invited to go. Simon tried to readjust, which only pulled Jasmine's sweater into an awkward twist that exposed a narrow strip of pale flesh across her waist.

Simon tried to release her, but with all of Jasmine's frantic readjustment, she couldn't quite regain her feet.

Barber took her arms and yanked her upright.

"Omigod," Jasmine said, and humiliated heat poured off her.

"Now Jassy," Barber said, hoping to soothe her embarrassment. "Simon just copped a small feel and it was an accident, so it hardly counts." He straightened her sweater for her.

"Idiot!" Jasmine slapped his hands away and tried to do the straightening herself.

Both Harley and Simon stood there staring at Barber, their expressions a mix of hilarity, censure, and male understanding.

Finally, his expression fed up, Simon stepped around them. "For God's sake, Barber, you *have* a room."

Harley whistled.

And Jasmine cried, "*Barber*," and then, "damn it!"

She shoved him back and marched off down the hall, assumedly to her own room.

Still breathing hard, Barber watched her go. The back view was every bit as enticing as the front. Those perfectly padded hips swayed, more so with her anger. And she'd blasted him. Again.

Hell, she'd called him an idiot. Barber grinned. "God almighty, Harley. I think I'm losing it."

"You lost it years ago." Harley shook his head. "I have to go, too. Drew called."

"Drew?" Barber stowed the lust and gave his friend the attention needed. "No way."

"I have six weeks to prepare." Harley couldn't hold back his pleasure.

"No shit?" Barber grinned in expectation. "Title fight?"

"Nothing but. Drew is skipping the buildup. He says the time is right, and I'm not about to disagree."

Barber held out a fist. "Well hell, pound me up, dawg! This is cause for celebration, right?"

After rolling his eyes, Harley tapped the top of Barber's fist with his own. "Damn straight. And this time, I'm not going to let anything get in my way."

Anything . . . or any one? Poor Stasia would have her work cut out for her now. "You'll have the belt, dude. This is double cause for celebration. Don't even think of bailing on me tonight."

"I'll be there."

"With Stasia?"

"Probably." He punched Barber's shoulder. "After tonight, it's going to be all business."

"And very little pleasure. I know." As Harley left, Barber shook his head. Harley had been all business ever since he'd met him. The man had no real idea how to cut loose, which was why the idea of Harley and bondage had really thrown him. Kinky.

Barber grinned. The sly dawg. Maybe there was hope for Harley yet.

But with Satch always on guard, making sure that Harley kept it tight, he probably wouldn't have a chance to really sow wild oats.

Unless Stasia could help him with that.

Barber was betting on her, but in the meantime, he had his own business decisions to make.

Like whether or not to risk the peace in the band by hiring Jasmine Petri and having her, too.

CHAPTER 16

STASIA didn't want to blame Harley's distraction with her legs, but when the half-frozen mass hit his windshield, he was as shocked as her.

"Son-of-a-bitch."

Whatever it was, it had to weigh ten pounds or more. A fawn? She didn't think so. When it hit, it sounded like a chunk of cement crashing into the car.

Cold air blew in around the shattered windshield. Her nails dug into the leather seat of Harley's car.

Hands tight on the wheel, Harley struggled to see through the debris long enough to steer the car safely to the side of the road.

Numb with astonishment, Stasia didn't move. She was so stiff, she didn't think she could.

Harley unhooked his seat belt and reached for her. "Stasia? Are you all right?"

"Yes." Her gaze sought his. She swallowed down her fear. "What the hell was that, Harley?"

Grim, he touched her face, smoothed her hair. He

looked in the rearview mirror, out the side window. "I don't know. Stay in the car."

Two other vehicles stopped to see if they were all right. Other drivers rubbernecked as they passed, trying to see what had happened.

Stasia concentrated on breathing.

They were safe enough, just badly startled. This particular stretch of road wasn't secluded. Buildings lined the street. They couldn't be that far from the bar, although being new to the area, she didn't yet have her bearings on distances to different locations.

Along with another man, Harley walked over to the road to investigate what they'd hit. She could see it lying there, utterly still, stiff. Her stomach bottomed out.

Harley didn't look pleased. Stasia watched as he pulled out his cell phone and placed a call. Every couple of seconds, he looked at her.

It made her feel better.

Were they doomed? Why did things only happen when she was with Harley? Was it a warning of some kind?

He shook hands with the other man and returned to the Charger. He examined the windshield with obvious disgust.

When he got in the car, she saw the fury that he tried hard to conceal.

"What was it?"

"A dog."

Covering her mouth with a hand, Stasia fought tears. "Dead?"

"Don't get upset, honey. It's been dead for a while. Hell, it's frozen solid."

Her hand slid away. "But . . . what?"

"We didn't hit a live animal." He slowly inhaled, and let the breath out with ebbing rage. With approaching police lights reflected in his eyes, Harley locked his gaze on hers. "Someone threw a frozen chunk of roadkill at my car."

So many possibilities raced through Stasia's mind, she couldn't grab and hold a single one. One police car parked behind them, and another stopped near the dead, frozen animal.

That poor creature. She had such a special fondness for animals that it didn't matter if the dog had been killed in the street days or even weeks before. It was dead, and that was all that mattered to her heart.

But tears now wouldn't make the situation any easier for Harley, or help her in explaining a few things to the officers.

Harley reached for her hand. "We need to step out. You're sure you're okay?"

"I'm fine." She opened her seat belt and got out of the car just as the first officer reached Harley's side of the car. She circled the hood to join them, and waited while Harley explained what had happened.

The officer called it in, asked them to wait, and wandered off to do a cursory inspection of the area.

Harley put an arm around Stasia. "Warm enough?"

"I'm fine."

"You keep saying that."

"Because it's true."

"Are your legs cold?"

She flashed him a fleeting smile. "You're far too preoccupied with my legs, Harley. Most women have them, you know."

"Yours are very sexy."

Despite everything currently happening, it made Stasia feel good to get the compliment. While shopping with Jasmine, she'd bought the flattering denim pencil skirt. The hem hit just above her knees. She wore dark hose and ankle-strap shoes with it, and topped it off with a body-hugging white turtleneck. The outfit was stylish, warm, and flattered her figure.

Teasing Harley, she said, "You asked me to wear a skirt, so I did. I didn't realize it was just so you could see my legs."

"Actually . . ." He kissed her ear and whispered, "I was hoping to get my hands under your skirt when I made the suggestion." He leaned back. "But that thing fits you like a second skin. Looks great, but it sure wouldn't make it easy to cop a feel."

The pounding of her heart stole her breath.

Putting his forehead to hers, Harley said, "Had I known we'd be out in the cold again, I'd have told you to bundle up in jeans and boots."

She slipped her arms inside his coat, around his waist. "Harley, I have to tell you something."

The officer returned. "Sorry, folks. I looked around, but there's really not much to see. I spoke briefly with the other drivers who stopped, but they saw what you saw— something coming toward your car."

"A dead dog didn't run in front of us."

"I'd say not." The officer tapped a pad of paper to his thigh. "But whoever dumped it on your car is long gone. I'd say it was a prank." He looked at them. "Unless either of you has another suggestion?"

Harley started to say something, and Stasia stepped forward, away from his protective arm. "Actually, yes, I know someone who might dislike me enough to do such a thing."

Behind her, she could feel Harley's sudden tension.

The officer pushed back his hat. "Let's hear it."

Memories swamped in on her, compressing her lungs, burning her stomach.

Harley's hand enclosed hers, and that helped more than she wanted to admit. "I'm a life coach, which means I work closely with people to advise them on lifestyle decisions."

The officer was polite, but she could tell he didn't get it.

"My last male client misunderstood my intent. He . . . he thought I was emotionally involved, that I cared for him beyond a client." That sounded awful, even to her, so she rushed to her own defense. "I'm very careful to explain the boundaries up front, and I never, ever socialize with clients. I'm there when they need me, and I sometimes observe them in routine activities, but I don't partner with them."

The cop shifted his stance, hands on his hips, brow puckered.

Anxious to get it over with, Stasia said, "When he offered to leave his wife for me, I tried to set him straight. He . . . he didn't take it well. For a while he was a real nuisance, calling my business line all the time, trying to follow me home." She rubbed her forehead. "The last time I saw him, he called me awful names and blamed me for his ruined marriage."

"Do you know where this guy is now?"

Stasia shook her head. "Not really, but his wife was . . ." She couldn't get the words out. It hurt so much, just remembering.

Harley's hand squeezed hers again. "She was what?"

"Hospitalized. After everything that happened, she threatened to commit suicide. It was awful. And Larry made sure I got every little detail of the whole ordeal." Her stomach churned. "I don't know if they ever got back together, because I just stayed away. I was afraid any concern on my part would be misinterpreted by him again."

The cop became all business. "Okay, give me his name and the name of the hospital where his wife was at. I'll see what I can find out."

"Larry Grimes. His wife was Eloise." She shared the other details she could remember, and all the while, she prayed it wasn't Larry.

If that whole nightmare started again, she didn't know what she'd do.

It was another hour before Harley's car was towed away to get the windshield repaired and they'd retrieved his Jeep to drive instead. Stasia stayed silent, and Harley didn't press her.

"You still feel like dinner?"

She glanced at the Jeep's clock. "If we go out now, we'll miss Jasmine's performance."

"So do you want to just grab a bite at the bar? It won't be anything fancy, just a cold sandwich or maybe barbecue. But it's not bad."

"That suits me just fine."

Harley drove toward the bar. "I wish you'd told me sooner just how deranged that creep really is."

"There wasn't any point."

"No? What about your brakes? What about almost being run over?"

She shook her head. "I can't imagine Larry having any part of that. Until he flipped out on me, he seemed like such a nice guy. A laid-back, normal guy."

"Yeah, a real prince."

She chided him. "Don't be sarcastic, Harley. I'm not in the mood."

He fell silent again.

Stasia hated it. "I'm sorry. I guess I should have considered the possibility more seriously earlier. But it's not something I like to dwell on. I'd prefer to think what happened at Echo Lake was a prank gone wrong, as the officials suggested."

"And tonight?"

"I just don't know. If it isn't all related, it'd be one hell of a coincidence." And she couldn't convince herself of that.

Harley pulled into the bar parking lot and turned off the engine. When he faced her, he said, "It's not your fault, you know."

"That's the thing about blame, Harley. It's sometimes hard to pinpoint. Is it Larry's fault that he was so desperately unhappy, he misunderstood my intent? Was it his wife's fault for not making Larry happier? Her fault that she couldn't cope and would rather be dead than lose a man who didn't love her anymore, had maybe never really loved her?"

"Maybe," he said, "it wasn't anyone's fault. It just is."

She'd never get a better lead-in than that. "Like you missing the first three opportunities to fight for the belt?"

He withdrew in a heartbeat. "That was fate fucking me over, nothing more and nothing less."

She caught his arm when he reached for the door handle. "Harley? I hadn't told anyone else about Larry. Talking about it makes me ill, like I might throw up. It was so sad, and so scary, and I can't remember ever feeling so much like an idiot."

He relented and pulled her close. "I'm sorry, Stasia."

"I feel better, getting it out in the open. Talking about it."

"I'm glad."

She hugged him tighter. "I wish you'd trust me enough to share with me, too." Under her hands, his muscles went taut. Stasia held on to him. "I understand what happened with Dakota. And I think everyone is pretty damned grateful you were there with her."

"Gregor got there fast, too."

"But if you hadn't been there—"

"Not long after," he continued, "Simon and Mallet returned, too."

She hadn't met anyone named Mallet, but she assumed he was another fighter. "But *you* were there with her when she first got attacked by her crazy ex, and that's how you got hurt."

Nearly humming with anger, Harley sat back in his seat. After a few seconds, he relaxed enough to drop his head back and close his eyes. "I was taken off guard. I was thinking about other things, and they charged us. If I'd been as alert as I should have been, I'd have heard them, or seen them coming." He turned his head and opened his startling blue eyes on her face. "That's how I got hurt. It was my own damn fault. No one else's."

"And before that?"

He studied her, and must have decided it didn't matter if he shared. "Not long after I was offered my first title shot, my mom was diagnosed with breast cancer. Dad had died years earlier, and Uncle Satch was the only other relative we had. Mom was bad off, and it was too much for him to handle on his own."

Oh God. Stasia hadn't realized . . .

"After more tests, the doctors realized the cancer was pretty advanced. Even though the treatments were grueling, Mom tried everything. And still she got weaker by the day."

Her heart ached. "You took time off to care for her?"

Harley stared out the windshield. A lone streetlamp sent a slash of light into the car, lending a strange illumination to his features, gilding his blond hair, putting an unholy glow in his pale blue eyes.

"Don't make me sound noble. I didn't do it for her, as much as for myself." His voice went rough, breaking Stasia's heart. "I didn't want to let her go."

"She was your mother. I understand that."

His jaw flexed. His gaze became hard and cold. "She went through chemo and radiation, but the cancer had spread, and there wasn't much hope. She didn't last that long." He glanced at her. "We no sooner had the funeral than Uncle Satch wanted me back in training."

Though Stasia knew Harley's uncle meant well, his insensitivity had no real excuse. "Maybe he thought it'd help for you to have something else to focus on."

Harley shrugged. "I had to practically start over. I was still considered a new fighter and it wasn't easy to earn that first shot at the belt. I had to go through the ranks to get the same opportunity again."

"And you did?"

"Yeah. I put all my focus on that damn belt. I trained my ass off, and walked through guys with perfect records."

"And they offered you another shot." Stasia touched his arm. "What happened that time?"

Harley narrowed his eyes. "I fucked up. Even with all the time I spent training, I stupidly thought I'd fallen in love."

A terrible pang squeezed the air from Stasia's lungs. "Why is that stupid?"

"Satch didn't want me fooling around with girls. He wanted me to put all contact with females on the back burner." He gave her a long look. "Like that would ever happen."

She smiled.

Silence stretched out as Harley stared toward the parking lot. "It's a long, boring story, but the gist of it is that I thought I was in love with Sandy, so I was busy doing this balancing act."

"The sport and the girl?"

"Yeah. Satch was never happy, but I was making it work." He rubbed his thigh. "Or so I thought."

"What happened?"

"She got hit by a car."

"Oh my God."

"Yeah." He shook his head, stared out the window. "Really fucked her up. Cracked ribs, fractured leg, broken jaw. Sandy was miserable, more miserable than I've ever seen a woman. The guy who hit her . . . it was one of those freak accident kind of things. The sole on his shoe was loose and it got stuck on the pedal. He couldn't brake."

Suddenly Harley laughed, and it alarmed Stasia. "Harley?"

"He had insurance, and a shitload of guilt. So much guilt that he visited her at the hospital almost daily." The corners of his mouth curled. "And I guess that's when they fell in love."

Blindsided, Stasia just sat there staring at him. She hadn't seen that one coming. Not by a long shot.

"No, I'm not kidding," he said. "So don't ask. One day Sandy was claiming undying love for me, and then the next thing I knew she tearfully confessed to being in love with someone else. They told me together. Real brave of them. They held hands the whole time."

"Harley, I'm so sorry." She couldn't imagine such a thing.

"Far as I know, they're still married." He rubbed the bridge of his nose. "I got over her quick enough. That wasn't the big problem. The real bitch of it was the gossip. Everyone from neighbors to the SBC organization knew I'd been dumped after missing a damned title fight. Some pitied me, and some thought it was hilarious, a real kick in the ass. I figured it was a lesson to be learned."

Her mind made an immediate leap, and she spoke before she could censor her thoughts. "That's why you're so controlling now."

"You think?" Wearing a facetious grin, Harley pretended

to ponder that. "Maybe. It's for certain that I now know not to go off half-cocked, mixing up emotion with business. But it's not a whacko reaction, Stasia, so don't start with the amateur analysis again. How I live my life is a deliberate choice to avoid more chaos, not a reaction to a permanently damaged psyche."

As her brain churned, she barely heard him. "You couldn't control Sandy or how she affected your life, so you ensure that you control other women in the only safe way that you can: in bed."

Harley shook his head, and even went so far as to flick the end of her nose. "There's that analysis I told you to avoid."

"Something that obvious hardly has to be analyzed."

He leaned closer to her. "I like controlling women. It's a turn-on. That's all there is to it. If you'd let me show you—"

Before she could get seduced, Stasia pushed him back. "You can't manipulate life, Harley. It happens, whether you want it to or not."

"I can decide how it affects me."

She licked her lips, wishing for a way to convince him. All she could do was share her own truths. "When that woman threatened to kill herself, I realized that every day is a blessing, every breath is a gift."

"Yeah. I agree." He opened his Jeep door. "But my biggest gift will be the belt."

Stasia sat there while Harley came around and opened her door. Her thoughts moiled. She didn't move.

Bracing his hands on the roof of the Jeep, he leaned in. "Thinking about being spreadeagle on my bed?"

"No." She looked up at him. "I was thinking what an incredible, fascinating, and talented man you are."

Scowling as if insulted, he straightened and waited for her to get out.

At first, she thought he wouldn't say any more, but right before they entered the bar, he said, "All right, I'll bite. What part of my pathetic life confessions led you to label me as an incredible person?"

Smiling, Stasia leaned into him. "Harley. Some people are born blessed, with everything handed to them. They don't have to work hard, or overcome adversity. And if they're challenged, they fold up like a cheap deck of cards." She tilted her head back to see him. "But you're a self-made man. You know what you want, and you're going after it, regardless of how many obstacles get thrown in your way. You've lost both parents, gotten through heartbreak, and had some of the rottenest luck I've ever heard of. And still you're an honorable, hardworking man who's willing to help others in need."

"Jesus." He put both emotional and physical distance between them. Pulling her along by the hand, he led her forward. "Don't saint me yet, Anastasia. After I've blown your mind with sex, then you can consider it if you want. But not until then."

Drawing her into the crowded room where the band would play, Harley gave her no opportunity to reply. Seconds later, a roaming photographer started snapping shots.

Stasia didn't understand until Simon, Gregor, and Dean welcomed them to their table, and the talk turned to the title belt.

Harley would be fighting soon, and he hadn't even told her.

Maybe that fact said more than words could. He wasn't going to let her in, and she'd be fooling herself to think otherwise. She couldn't help him. He didn't want or need her help.

It was time to give up.

This time, he'd get the shot, and Stasia would rather never see him again than get in his way.

Tonight, she'd tell him good-bye.

For good.

THE knock on her hotel door nearly caused Jasmine to scream. She was so upset with herself, she wasn't sure what to do.

She'd made out with Barberosa. In the hallway. In front of his friends.

What was she thinking?

She hadn't been, that much was obvious. But it wasn't all her fault, and blast it, she should really give Barberosa a piece of her mind. Once she'd decided that, she forgot about her clothes and her anxiety over his reaction to them, marched across the floor, and threw the door open.

Barber said, "Hey there, ho . . ." His words trailed off. Mute, his mouth still open as he breathed a little hard and fast, he stepped into her room and kicked the door shut behind him.

His bold staring brought back all of Jasmine's uneasiness. She smoothed her hands over the cinched waist of her top. Eve had sworn that the tank-style corset with pink plaid off-the-shoulder sleeves and lace trim would be appropriate. Jasmine liked it because, although it covered most of her chest, the hook-and-eye closure down the front was edgy and sexy.

It went well with the short black pleated skirt with grommets for style. She wore black hose and ankle boots and some heavy silver jewelry that jangled when she put her hands on her hips. "What?"

"Shhh." Barber continued to stare. "Just let me soak this in a minute."

She went hot with . . . well, maybe not embarrassment. Maybe more like . . . interest. The way he looked at her, as if he might jump her bones at any second, made her want to jump him.

For too many years, she'd fantasized about Barberosa Henry. She adored everything about him: his music, his voice, his long hair, his incredible physique and bold manner. He was the manliest man she'd ever encountered, but with an edge and an innate sexiness that a blind woman couldn't miss.

Now she was within touching distance of him, and he was clear about wanting her, and he was even more potent up close.

For one brief second, Jasmine closed her eyes and re-lived that mind-numbing kiss in the hallway. Then she opened them and said, "No, Barberosa."

As he slowly circled her, he asked, "No?"

She jerked around to keep him from ogling her back-side. "*No*. You said it was you or the job, and I chose the job."

"Yeah, I remember that asinine ultimatum of mine." His gaze lifted to hers. "Damned stupid of me, huh?"

So much heat glimmered in his dark eyes, Jasmine was starting to feel exposed. Grabbing up her thick coat, she pulled it on and buttoned it up. "It wasn't stupid at all. I've thought about it, and I think it makes perfect sense."

"Yeah? Why's that?"

"You're not a man who's about to settle down. But I'm not a woman who plays the field."

"You'd like playing with me, Jasmine." He held her cap-tive in his gaze as he moved closer. "I promise."

Oh good grief. As her willpower tried to crumble, she threw up both hands. "No is no, damn it!"

He stopped, his expression enigmatic. "You weren't protesting when I kissed you."

"I know. I lost my head."

"In a nanosecond."

"Braggart!" Truth be known, she was dying to kiss him long before he took the initiative. "You caught me by sur-prise, that's all."

"I think I gave you what you wanted." He eased another step closer. "What you've been wanting. Admit it."

That did it. Angry tears sprouted, and that only annoyed her more.

"Ah, damn it." He rocked back on his heels in disgust. "Do *not* start crying."

She stopped trying to hold Barber back and instead closed the space between them so she could thrust her face near his. "Don't tell me what to do, Barberosa."

"Barber, damn it," he grumbled. "How many times do I have to tell you?"

"Fine. You want the truth, *Barber*? I've daydreamed about you since I first met you. That's right. You. Smoldering hot fantasies."

His brows rose so high, they disappeared under his long hair. "You don't say?"

She jabbed a finger in his chest. "Women have fantasies—and you're mine. But that's as far as it's going to go because this job is too important to me for me to blow it over a guy, any guy. So, *Barber*, you *will* back off, right now, or so help me—"

"Stow the redheaded temper, toots, I get it." Putting both hands to the back of his neck, Barber retreated.

In that particular position, his shoulders and biceps looked huge, his chest wide.

Damn, why did he have to be such an appealing man?

He dropped his hands and faced her. "It's not going to go away, you know."

Willing the moisture in her eyes to stay put, Jasmine said, "I will stomp it into submission."

The corners of his mouth curled. "Yeah?"

"Absolutely. I suggest you do the same."

He laughed. "You are almost too adorable, do you know that?"

"And you're almost too appealing." Her smile was mean. "Luckily, I have a lot of fortitude, so I'm sure I'll be able to resist you. And now that we have that settled, do you think we should get going? I don't want to be late my first night."

Barber went past her and opened the door with a flourish. He stepped back for her to precede him.

Wary of his sudden compliance, Jasmine sidled around him. As she passed, he leaned in and said, "I'll be interested to see how long the fortitude lasts, sweets."

She glared at him—and kept going.

With a hand to the small of her back, he started her down the hall. "Smashing duds, by the way. You look incredible."

Damn it. Her knees shivered. "Thanks."

"If you sing as good as you look tonight, everyone is going to love you as much as I do."

She stumbled on her own feet. Love her? Now why did he have to go and say things like that?

Jasmine's heart pounded, her tummy flip-flopped, and when they stepped outside, even the cold evening air couldn't ease the heat inside her.

Lord help her, when it came to Barber, she didn't know if her touted fortitude would be enough to save her after all.

CHAPTER 17

WITH boisterous encouragement from the customers, Barber and his band went straight into a third song. Filled with satisfaction, Roger relaxed back against the wall. Jasmine Petri was a fine addition to the band. Now if he could only find some way to sign up Barber long-term, even if only two or three times a year.

"What are you thinking?"

Cam had approached without him realizing it, and he smiled down at her. "Evil thoughts, actually. You wouldn't approve."

"Oh really?" Smiling impishly, she caught the knot in his tie and tugged him a few feet away to a more private alcove. "Let's hear it, Mr. Sims."

For a while now, Roger had noticed that Cam positively glowed. He prayed it was happiness that made her even more beautiful, because her happiness was what he wanted most of all. "Barber has become such a commodity, I was trying to think of how I might tie him to the bar. Even if we only got him here for special occasions, it'd be a huge coup."

"Why don't you just ask him?"

With a different approach already in mind, Roger smoothed back Cam's hair. Tonight she wore it loose and soft, and it turned him on. Of course, she could shave her head and it'd turn him on.

He laughed at himself. "Always the straightforward approach for you, huh?"

Cam nodded. "I've found it works best."

Not when you wanted to tie down a rising star, but Roger didn't say so. "If that's what you think I should do, I'll try it." First. And if it didn't work, then he'd resort to other ideas.

Pleased with him, Cam said, "Let's talk about it more before you make a move. I think we should figure out exactly what you want from Barber. Decide how often you can afford to have him here, and how seldom you'd be willing to settle for him. Come up with the price, the terms, everything. Then present it to him and see what he says."

"He doesn't have an agent yet," Roger pointed out, "and that amazes me, but it saves me from having to go through someone else."

"Barber is a very down-to-earth person. I can't see fame changing that."

"Me either." Roger tugged her into a hug and heard her very faint gasp, then felt the way she tried to ease away from him. He levered back with concern. "What's wrong?"

Putting her hands over her breasts, she said, "I'm a little tender, that's all."

Guilt crawled over him, mingling with desire. He asked low, "Was I too rough last night?" He recalled being insatiable, especially when she'd seemed more sensitive to his mouth, almost ready to come just from him sucking at her nipples.

That made her smile. "I loved it."

Damn. Roger cleared his throat, but it didn't help the sudden restriction in his pants. Remembering made him hot, and made him want to do it all over again. Right here, right now. "You're sure?"

Instead of answering, she grinned, leaned to look around

to assure their privacy, and then she said, "I was going to tell you tonight, but I don't think I can wait that long."

His heart beat slow and hard. "What?"

"I hope you'll be excited."

Imagining everything from awful to wonderful, blood rushed into his head. "Tell me."

She bit her lip, grinned, and said, "I'm pregnant."

The world closed in, Roger's vision dimmed—and then bright light exploded. "Pregnant?" He meant to shout, but it emerged as a very wimpy whisper.

Biting her bottom lip again and trying not to laugh, Cam nodded.

"Pregnant?" he said again, this time stronger, louder. "You're sure?"

"Yes."

Every ounce of strength left him, and he sank to his knees in front of her. She was so . . . slim. Her belly was flat, maybe even concave. He held her hips and kissed her through her dress.

"Roger," she whispered on a laugh. "Get up!"

He looked at her face, saw her blush; he loved her so damn much, he wanted to cry. "We're having a baby?" Damn it, he *was* crying. He pressed his face against her and held on.

Her hand in his hair, gently coaxing, Cam came down to her knees, too. "Yes, Roger. I'm not far along yet. I've only done a home test, but we can set an appointment with the doctor and he can give us a date."

He crushed her close. "God, I love you."

She cried, too. He heard it in her voice when she said, "I know."

As quickly as he'd gone weak, Roger felt superhuman. On a laugh, he surged back to his feet and scooped her up in his arms, turning her in a circle, kissing her.

Cam smiled at him, wiped his cheeks. "I love you too, you know."

"Thank you."

That made her laugh. "Oh, Roger. You are going to be such a terrific dad."

"I will," he promised. "I swear to you, I will."

Her smile trembled. "I don't have a doubt."

Someone rudely brushed against them, almost knocking them over.

Roger regained his balance, furious even as he turned to see who'd been so rude. He saw a massive man muscling a path to the edge of the dance floor. He paused at the outskirts of the crowd and started searching the audience.

Oh hell. Furious, Roger quickly set Cam back on her feet. "Stay here."

"Roger!"

Knowing how Cam felt about him getting involved in any physical altercations, he paused long enough to say, "I know, Cam. I promise I won't start anything. But this is my place and I—"

"Go." She smiled, showing her trust. "Take care of business, but avoid a conflict if you can."

"I will." He moved away from her and approached the jerk who'd rudely elbowed them. "Excuse me."

The guy glanced at him, then away. "Get lost."

Roger took in the buzzed head, the outrageous tattoos, the scars, and the attitude. "I'm the proprietor here. Can I help you with something?"

Without looking at him, the man said, "You can fucking well leave me alone."

More furious by the second, Roger narrowed his eyes. "I can have security here in two minutes."

"Yeah?" The guy stared down at Roger, which made him pretty damned tall given that Roger stood six-two. "By then I'll have found Handleman, so why bother?"

Not intimidated, but hoping to avoid a scene as Cam had requested, Roger said, "If you'd like to wait by the door, I can find him and send him to you."

"Don't bother."

Just then Barber bounded off the stage. He helped Jasmine down next. While the other band members headed for the bar to get a drink, Barber led Jasmine toward the tables where Harley and Stasia sat with Dean, Simon, Gregor, and their wives.

The big bruiser bunched his shoulders and smiled, showing several missing teeth. "I already found him."

HE came through the place like he owned it, elbowing people out of his way, a pissy look on his face.

Harley saw him right off. How could he miss him? While giving his attention to Stasia as she enthused on Jasmine's talent, he also kept track of the guy. He was built like a fighter, and he moved like a fighter, but Harley didn't recognize him.

Right behind the bully was Roger, and behind him, Cam. Wearing a furious frown, Roger spoke into a radio, no doubt calling security. Given the look on the man's face as he approached, Harley didn't blame Roger for anticipating trouble.

Harley figured it was about to come his way.

"Excuse me," he said to Stasia, cutting her off in midsentence. He pushed back his chair and moved around the table to stand in front of the women.

Naturally, the other guys caught on quick enough, and they too got to their feet. The man approaching grinned in evil delight, and pointed one massively muscled arm at Harley with intent.

So stupid. More than anything, Harley hated theatrics. Usually it was the guys without enough talent who resorted to such idiotic antics.

Stasia stepped up beside Harley. "What's going on?"

Hoping to insulate her from the ugliness, he said, "Move back against the wall and stay there."

"What?"

"Just do it."

Too late, the guy halted in front of him. "Hard to Handle. 'Bout time I found you."

Sizing him up, unimpressed with his ridiculous show, Harley asked, "And you are?"

"The guy who's going to break your fucking elbow this time."

Harley cocked a brow. "Be specific, will you? Do you mean now, later, or what?"

"In the ring, you jackass." His sneering gaze went to Simon. "Now that Sublime's run off, that leaves me and you."

Simon and Dean came up alongside Harley, and they both looked deadly. Wishing they'd back off and let him handle it, Harley relaxed his stance. "As you can see, Simon hasn't gone anywhere. He's right here."

"Yeah." The guy's lip curled. "Because he's worried about his little buddy." He laughed. "That's right. I heard that Sublime is training you."

Damn, news traveled fast. But then, if the idiot arrived in town today and first looked for Harley at the gym, he probably would have heard the latest developments.

"That's the plan so far," Harley said.

"It's not going to do you any damn good. I'm still going to destroy you."

Simon laughed. "You and a shitload of steroids?"

The guy lunged forward, but Dean stepped in front of him, stopping him with a hard shove to his chest. "This is my brother-in-law's place, Kinkaid. Do *not* start any shit here or I swear you'll regret it."

"Yeah, yeah. Can't be getting the place all messy spilling Handleman's blood, huh?" He retreated a step and glared at Harley with hatred.

Behind the men, the women clustered close in apprehension and dread—all but Dakota, who surveyed the scene with disdain.

Harley stepped forward, separating himself from the others. Kinkaid. So this was the man he would fight for the title. He was a big bastard, but also an idiot. "You say we're going to fight?" Harley shook his head, and told a provoking lie. "I've never even heard of you."

"Because you've been off licking your wounds, Handleman, that's why. But I'm unstoppable." Kinkaid thumped a boulder-size fist into his own chest. "I'm going to take you apart, and I'm going to enjoy doing it."

"Right. If you say so." Harley relaxed even more—to the point he knew he looked bored. "Now is there anything else you wanted before I get back to my company?"

So hot under the collar that his eyes bulged, Kinkaid screwed up his face. "What kind of chicken-shit talk is that?"

"I don't explain myself to morons. If we fight, I'll let my fists do the talking."

"Not if, when. It's been decided."

"You, my friend, have to pass a drug test first, and I've got my doubts on that score."

Kinkaid leaned closer. Through clenched teeth, he said, "Maybe you ought to stop talking right now, get a little taste of what I have in store for you."

Stasia said low, "Harley . . ."

And Kinkaid's gaze shot over to her. Malice lit his eyes and his mouth stretched into a mean smile.

Harley stepped in front of her. All signs of boredom were gone. "Don't even think about it, Kinkaid. You can't be that stupid."

Kinkaid laughed. "Why not? You wanted to fight Sublime, so you fucked his old lady to goad him into it. Almost worked for you, too." His eyes narrowed. "Maybe my luck will be better."

Pandemonium exploded.

Simon let out a roar, Dean tried to restrain him, and Dakota threw a sucker punch to Kinkaid's crotch.

As the poor sap went down wheezing, she said, "*I'm* Simon's old lady, buster, and Harley *never* slept with me."

Dakota hadn't pulled the punch at all, and Kinkaid hadn't seen it coming. She'd nailed him.

Eyes bulging and mouth slack in agony, the poor sap looked ready to puke, or pass out, or both.

Gasping, he said, "I meant before you."

In a wide-legged stance, her hands still in fists, Dakota tossed back her hair. "I don't want to hear about anyone before me."

Almost in slow motion, Simon pulled away from Dean. Vibrating with anger, he stepped in front of Dakota and pressed her back several feet. Looking like he wanted to say something, but was too furious to manage, he lifted her up, plunked her down in a chair, and leaned over her. He breathed hard.

"He had it coming, Simon," Dakota said.

Simon opened his mouth, started to speak, and couldn't. He was enraged. More than enraged. Everyone could see it.

Eve said, "Uh-oh."

"Don't," Simon whispered to his wife, "ever do anything like that again."

Dakota looked ready to spit. "Fine. But drag his sorry ass out of here."

"I planned to, damn it."

"Well good."

"Good!"

Harley laughed. They were the funniest married couple he'd ever encountered. If Simon had hair, he would have yanked it out in frustration. And if Dakota had once gone through life afraid, no one seeing her now would ever know it.

"If you two newlyweds could stop scrapping," Harley said, "maybe we could get the floor cleared of the debris and get back to applauding Jasmine's performance, which I think was pretty spectacular."

Dean looked over his shoulder and said, "Great. Roger's guards are here."

As three uniformed men dragged Kinkaid up to his feet, the idiot said, "You should leash that bitch, Sublime."

Incredulous, Simon roared and landed a nose-crunching blow on Kinkaid before Dean got him subdued again.

Roger threw up his hands. "Could we all please take a breather on the violence?"

Dean, struggling to hold on to Simon, glared at Harley. "You could help."

But Harley shook his head. "No, I'm not sure I can. I

don't want to risk an injury by grappling with Sublime, and if I take Kinkaid apart now, well, he and Dakota already tag teamed him to mush, so it'd hardly be fair. And I'll be damned if I'm going to help the idiot out of here."

With the support of the guards, Kinkaid wavered on his feet. "You're a fucking pussy, Handleman."

"Yeah, yeah," Barber said. "And it takes a real hero to pick a brawl in a public place, huh?"

Even with the blood dripping from his nose, Kinkaid managed a gruesome grin. "How many people are you hiding behind, Handleman? Men, women, fruity musician . . . got any kids to protect you, too?"

Harley sighed. "Do everyone a favor, Kinkaid, and concentrate on passing your drug tests so there'll actually be a fight, okay? I promise I'll show up, and then you can do your worst."

Kinkaid struggled against the hands holding him, but it was a half-baked effort at best. Harley figured if Kinkaid really wanted the fight, right here and right now, a dozen of the untrained guards wouldn't be able to hold him back.

But he apparently didn't. He'd only wanted to cause a scene.

Given that most of the bar was now watching in awed silence, Kinkaid had succeeded. The photographer was all over it, and a reporter had a tape recorder out, catching what he could.

No doubt the whole thing would be on the Internet within hours.

Pointing a finger with his right hand and holding his jewels with his left, Kinkaid said to Harley, "That belt is mine. Get used to the idea right now."

Harley watched as Kinkaid allowed himself to be dragged out. "Moron."

Barber said, "I don't think he likes you, Harley." And then he added with a frown, "Was he insinuating that I'm gay?"

"Sounded like."

Barber snorted.

The women were all aghast at the display of brutality,

except for Dakota, who stewed in mulish silence while Simon tried to find the words to tell her how she'd just displeased him.

Dean was pissed. "Can you ban him from the place?" he asked Roger.

"It's already done. If he tries to come in again, I'll have him arrested."

Harley saw that all the men were bristling, but then, bad sportsmanship did that to honorable fighters. Luckily, men of Kinkaid's ilk were few and far between within the SBC organization.

Suddenly Roger grinned. When everyone looked at him, he looped an arm around Cam and laughed.

"Something funny?" Dean asked. "This kind of brouhaha makes you happy?"

Roger's grin was so wide, his eyes watered. "Cam and I have news. It was almost overshadowed by that jerk, but now that he's gone . . ." He turned to his wife. "You want to do the honors?"

Dean said, "Do I need to sit down for this?"

"I'm pregnant," she said to everyone.

Dean grabbed for a chair. "Oh yeah, I definitely need to sit down."

Eve squealed and launched herself at her friend. While the two women danced in a circle, Roger said to his wife, "Ignore your brother. He's as thrilled as I am."

"Yeah," Dean confirmed, and he offered a hand to Roger. "Way to go, man."

Beaming with pride, Roger accepted hearty handshakes from everyone.

"Drinks are on me," Barber announced. "We've got a lot to celebrate." And without thinking about it, he pulled Jasmine up for a sound smooch that quickly got out of hand until Jasmine recalled herself and, blushing, ducked away from him.

Laughing, Barber hugged her close to his side and said, "We've got business with the band. Roger, way to go, you stud. Dakota, hell of a shot, hon. Simon, take some deep breaths. Harley . . . uh, you might want to attend to your date. She's looking a little green around the gills."

Pulled from the revelry, Harley turned to Stasia.

She just stood there, her mouth pinched shut, her gaze still and her posture frozen.

Damn. He recalled everything she'd just heard, and knew what ailed her.

The reporter butted in. "A few words, Handleman?"

"Not just yet."

"But you just dodged a fight. Care to give your side of it?"

Shit, shit, shit. Harley knew he had no choice. "I wasn't dodging a fight. Kinkaid was drunk, stupid, or both. I fight for the SBC. I do not brawl in my friend's establishment. If Kinkaid has a beef with me, he only has a few weeks to wait, and then we can settle it the right way. Period."

"You're taking this fight on short notice after rehabbing an injury. Do you think Kinkaid sees a weakness?"

"Six weeks is more than enough time for me to prepare and I'm currently injury free. If Kinkaid thinks otherwise, he'll have a rude awakening. Like I said, we'll settle this within the time frame the SBC set. That's soon enough for me."

"So you're not afraid of him?"

"If you think that, you're as dumb as Kinkaid." Taking Stasia's arm, he said, "Now if you'll excuse me, I have more important things to talk about than a fighter with a short fuse and a lack of class."

The reporter reluctantly pulled back.

Harley eased Stasia a few feet away from the group, out of range of prying ears. "You okay?"

She gave one brisk nod. Then, still all pinched up, she said, "Hate to tell you, but the reporter isn't done."

Harley twisted around, saw the reporter talking with spectators, and before he could blink, a camera flashed in his face. "Son-of-a-bitch. I hate the fanfare."

Turning her back to the camera, Stasia said, "Don't worry about it, Harley. You were . . . incredible. No one can say otherwise. That other guy came off as a jerk, but you held it together. You were so . . ."

Harley tipped his head and suggested, "Controlled?"

She hesitated before giving in with a shrug. "Yes." Her chagrined laugh showed her surprise. "More controlled than I thought any macho guy could be while being so provoked."

"It's what I keep trying to tell you, honey. Discipline is the name of the game, and all good fighters have it. Too much emotion just blows your game. You need cold deliberation to counter moves, not temper."

Brows scrunched, she considered what he said. "In a lot of the prefight interviews, I've heard the fighters say terrible things about each other."

Harley smirked. "Yeah, well, a lot of guys provoke each other with smack. It's entertaining to the fans and it adds to the buildup. But behind the scenes, most of us have trained together at one point or another. All the trash talk is just for show."

"What I saw tonight—"

"That was different. By coming to a public establishment and pulling family and friends into it, Kinkaid crossed the line."

"And you aren't upset about it?"

"Upset?" Harley wanted to beat him into the ground; his muscles clenched in involuntary anticipation. "When I get him in the ring, I'll make him eat those words. Bigmouthed bullies always piss me off. I enjoy teaching them a little humility."

"Oh." After letting that sink in, she looked off at the crowded floor. Barber and Jasmine again took the stage. Couples gyrated together and the music blared. "I think I should get back to my hotel room now."

Harley wasn't in the mood to explain himself, but he damned well hated having her think the worst of him. "Don't you want to grill me first?"

"About what?"

It wasn't like Stasia to be coy. That she'd do it now

bugged Harley. "You heard what Kinkaid said about me sleeping with Simon's woman. You have to have a million questions on that one."

She studied his face. "No, not really."

With a sound of disbelief, Harley crossed his arms over his chest. "Right. It's got you so disgusted that you're ready to cut the night short, but you don't have any questions?"

She shook her head. "No."

He came closer. "So it doesn't bother you that I slept with Simon's fiancé? That's real big of you, honey."

She rubbed her forehead, but quickly dropped her hands and gave him an antagonistic look. "Look, Harley, I know there's not a lot you wouldn't do with women. You revel in the whole bad boy rep and I understand why."

What the hell? What did she think she understood?

"But you're an honorable man, and poaching isn't honorable, so I know that, regardless of what Kinkaid said, you wouldn't have done that. You most certainly wouldn't infringe just to incite another fighter into accepting a challenge."

"I wouldn't, huh?"

"Of course not. It sounds cowardly—more like something Kinkaid would do."

Harley ran a hand over his head. Every time he thought he had Anastasia pegged, she pulled the rug out from under him. "Well . . . you're right."

"Of course I am."

Now, rather than feeling forced to explain, Harley found he wanted to. He needed Anastasia to understand. "Long before Dakota was ever in Simon's life, his fiancé at the time came on to me at a bar."

"Awkward."

"No kidding. I'd never seen her before, so I didn't know she was with Simon. I did sleep with her, but I did it thinking she was free and clear."

"Now there's a big oops, huh?"

"That's putting it mildly." Harley recalled how sick he'd

felt when he found out. "Explaining to Simon wasn't something I looked forward to."

"You approached him face-to-face, didn't you?"

Damn, but she did know him pretty well. "I had to. I wanted Simon to understand that she was the one trying to use me. She had some harebrained idea of making Simon jealous or something."

Stasia glanced at Dakota, who frowned as she listened to Simon grousing at her. "I can see how that worked out for her."

"Yeah." He smiled. "Luckily, Simon realized he wasn't in love with her anyway. Then he met Dakota, and the two of them have been duking it out ever since."

A look of envy came over Anastasia's face. "They're very much in love."

"Looks like." Harley studied her. "So you think you know me pretty well, huh?"

"Well enough to ignore outrageous accusations, especially when they come from someone like Kinkaid. Add to that Dakota's reaction, and I figured it was all hot air."

The timing wasn't right for Harley to investigate the feelings too much, but it meant a lot that Stasia trusted him, that she believed in his honor. "I appreciate that."

She met his gaze. "And well enough to know when to cut my losses."

A spark of alarm shot through him. "What does that mean?"

She inhaled slowly. "You've got your title fight, Harley. I know how important that is to you, and thanks to Dakota, I understand enough about the sport to know you're going to be real busy training for the next few weeks. The last thing I want is to get in your way."

"You think I'd let you?"

That took her back, and she shrugged. "You won't let me counsel you, and I won't sleep with you, so there's no point in me hanging around any longer, is there?"

The alarm escalated. He crowded closer to her. "I can think of a good reason for you to stay."

A glimmer of hope lit her brown eyes. "What is it?"

Another flash went off, closer this time. Harley turned to tell the photographer to back off, and found Gloria standing beside him, chatting him up.

Well hell.

Would she tell everyone about his sexual preferences? Probably.

He shook his head. "You see that?"

"One of your many admirers? They're everywhere, in case you haven't noticed." Stasia nodded toward the brunette, Crystal, that he'd been dancing with the night that she'd first shown up. "You probably have trouble keeping track of them all, don't you?"

"Jealous?"

She snorted.

Smiling at her, Harley said, "Mostly I meant the damned photographer. The press is going to hound me until the fight. My uncle expects me to play along, but I don't want to have to hassle with every photo-hungry babe around who hopes to get her face in a magazine or on the Net."

"Without running interference for you—which I won't do—I don't see how I can help with any of that."

"You can be a more permanent babe." Before she could object to the endearment, he put a quick, soft kiss on her mouth. "If you're with me when I'm out in public, I can appease my uncle, feed the press what they want, and fend off other women who probably would interfere with my concentration on the fight."

"But I wouldn't be a distraction for you, huh? Gee, Harley, I'm so flattered."

Damn, but she amused him. "You know how much I want you, Anastasia Bradley. Never doubt it. But you're easy to be around, more so than most women I've known."

"Really?" She lifted a brow. "I guess that's a compliment of sorts."

"There's something else, too." He flattened both hands on the wall on either side of her head. "If you leave now, I'll spend a lot of time worrying about you. Until we hear back from the cops on your crazy stalker, it'll be easier for me to have you close at hand, where I can see that you're okay."

She touched his chest. "I appreciate the concern, Harley. But the thing is, I'm not sure I can be around you and *not* try to help. My advice is free, but it can be a bother."

"I know how to tune out the noise when I'm in training.

"Noise?" She playfully swatted him.

That she wasn't insulted and instead chose to laugh with him proved his point. Harley captured her hand, then caught the other hand, too. Keeping her bright gaze locked in his, he pinned both of her wrists behind her back and leaned down until his mouth just barely touched hers. "The way you're dressed tonight, it's a wonder I can think straight. So do me a favor and tone down the sexy."

"I'll do my best."

Harley couldn't help himself. He kissed her, and even knowing the photographer was right there, snapping one photo after another, he got carried away.

Her mouth opened under his, she arched her back to press her breasts into his chest, and he knew that if a room was available, he'd have her flat on her back in a heartbeat.

Separating a mere inch from her, he said, "I think you're right. Let's get out of here."

She kept her eyes closed, her head back. Harley counted his heartbeats, two, three, and she said, "No."

God, she was torturing him. "Change of heart?"

"It's my brain that makes the rules, Harley. Not my heart." She opened her eyes and while they held sadness, they also showed stark determination. "My head tells me that sleeping with you would be the wrong thing to do— regardless of how badly I want to."

"This could be your last chance, honey." Their hot breaths mingled; he could feel her thundering heartbeat against his chest. "After tonight, it's going to be all prep work. What free time I have will be for promo."

She shook her head; Harley felt her soft sigh.

"You are one amazing temptation, Harley Handleman.

But . . ." She smiled up at him, then shrugged. "I'm going to have to pass."

He groaned. "Suit yourself then."

At that moment, Barber and Jasmine launched into another rousing rock song. Looping his arm around Stasia's shoulders, Harley turned to watch. Thinking of Barber's present dilemma helped him to forget his own throbbing need.

In her present funky getup, Jasmine really did look great, very much a part of the band. And the other guys seemed to have accepted her, not that Barber gave that part of it much thought. He ran the band, and the rest of the guys followed. They were an easy group, but they knew the real talent was Barber.

Their success hinged on him.

Anyone with eyes could see that Barber had the hots for the new redhead, in a big way. But that played into their presentation. They fed off each other, and the chemistry vibrated in the music, in the depth of their lyrics.

When the song ended and the audience roared its approval, Stasia said, "They're breathtaking together, aren't they?"

Harley nodded. "Now Barber has to make some tough decisions."

"Like?"

"The girl, or the gig?"

Without looking at him, Stasia said, "If he actually cares about her, he should take the girl."

"It's his career." Touching Stasia's chin, Harley brought her face around to his. "He has to choose the gig—at least for now."

Whether or not she understood him, Harley couldn't say. But after he won the title belt, he'd have more time to devote to Stasia—and more time to explore his growing feelings for her.

Six weeks. Surely he could hold it all together for that long.

Chapter 18

IGNORING his feelings for Stasia proved harder than Harley had ever imagined. Three weeks had passed since she'd agreed to stick around and be his cover for the press.

He spent a lot of hours at the gym, and a few nights with promotion. Overall, he was in the best shape of his life. Stronger, faster, more fine-tuned. He was injury-free and his body felt great.

He'd just finished going five six-minute rounds with Simon, and he wasn't winded. He could run three miles in under twenty minutes, and did so every other day without fail. He had great cardio. His body was shredded, without an ounce of fat to be found.

With the fight only a few weeks away, he had more than enough to occupy his thoughts, but still, he spent what little spare time he had wanting Anastasia.

In the middle of his preparations to take the title belt, he'd stupidly become obsessed with her. He didn't let it interfere with his training, and he wasn't sure if anyone else had noticed. Uncle Satch had no idea, because if he did, he'd be bitching.

For that matter, Dean and Simon would be giving him hell, too.

Did Anastasia realize, or was she as duped as everyone else?

Harley heard her voice and at the same time, he felt her presence. Damn. It didn't help his situation that she now felt free to frequent the gym. On any given day she showed up with a notepad and pen, jotting down observations, studying equipment, watching old tapes.

Harley knew she wanted to learn as much about the sport as she could, so he didn't discourage her. And as long as he kept her close at hand, he knew nothing could happen to her.

Although there'd been no more incidents, the police had been unable to confirm her ex-client's whereabouts. Far as they were concerned, Larry Grimes could be on vacation, so his lack of appearance didn't implicate him in any way. Without some evidence to go on, they weren't willing to pursue him. They took a report and told Harley and Stasia to contact them if anything else happened, but that was the extent of their investigation.

Stasia's laugh reached him, and Harley turned to look at her. As he'd requested, she'd toned down the sex appeal by wearing trim jeans with bulky sweaters and oversize sweat-shirts.

It didn't help.

In fact, the casual clothing only made him more curious to see her naked, to touch her body all over. He remem-bered the feel of her that night at the station, how her legs and hips had looked in that body-hugging skirt, and it was enough to make his heart race.

"Shit." Standing at the back of Dean's gym, covered in sweat, Harley stared toward the far corner where Dakota explained training techniques to Stasia and Jasmine. He was done for the day, but instead of daydreaming about Stasia's body, he should be concentrating on his upcoming fight.

"Yeah," Simon said. "Sorry about that." As one of Harley's sparring partners, Simon was equally sweaty. He lifted a water bottle, tipped his head back, and let a stream of water pour into his mouth.

He passed the bottle to Harley.

"For what?" Harley took a drink, then capped the bottle and tossed it toward Barber.

One leg bent and his back against the wall, Barber caught it. "Thanks."

Simon nodded toward the women. "Dakota is so at home here now, she sees no reason not to march other women through." He swiped a forearm over his face. "If it bothers you—"

"It's fine." Harley picked up a towel. Far as he was concerned, the damned fight couldn't come soon enough. Once he annihilated Kinkaid, he planned to get Anastasia in his bed—whatever it took to convince her.

"What I'd like to know," Barber said, "is why the hell Jasmine is tagging along. She's not even interested in fighting."

"She's interested in you," Harley pointed out.

"And she doesn't have that many friends in town yet." Simon grinned. "Unless you want her to hang out with the rest of the band?"

"No." Barber pushed to his feet. "I already told those bozos what'd happen if they even look at her funny."

Dean came up with a chart in his hand. He took one look at Barber and Harley and he shook his head. "They're pathetic, aren't they?"

Simon just grinned.

"It's bullshit," Barber complained as he threw the towel to the floor and glared at the women. "Here we are doing without and being miserable because of it, and they go about their day, smiling and chatting as if they don't miss sex at all."

"Speak for yourself," Simon said. "We married men go to bed happy."

"*Every* night," Dean added.

"So that's why your mood is so mellow." Harley grinned. "I did wonder."

"Damn straight. Married life is sweet."

"It has its rewards," Simon agreed.

Harley gave Barber a shove. "Maybe Jasmine doesn't know what she's missing yet. You should try telling her."

"Already have," Barber said. "But she's stubborn."

"Or smart," Dean said.

"Or maybe she just has high standards," Simon added.

Trying not to laugh, Harley said, "You know, it could be Barber's idiotic rule about not sleeping with band members." He looked toward Jasmine and saw her watching Barber. "She's hooked, man. All you have to do is reel her in."

Barber gave him an evil look. "I'm done." He headed for the showers.

Simon watched him go. "I do believe he's lovesick." Then he grinned. "I like it."

When he finished laughing, Dean asked Harley, "How's the elbow?"

"Perfect. No problems. I feel great all over."

"Here on out, I only want you to go seventy, maybe eighty percent. We'll concentrate on situational drills. Light sparring, specific kicks. Your takedown defense is good, but we'll continue with that. I have some new guys coming in to work with you. We'll mix it up a lot."

"Sounds good." Harley watched some of the other fighters as they watched Stasia. Surprisingly, it didn't bother him much because he knew she wasn't the type to play off them. Stasia wouldn't lead them on, was never more than polite to them, and most times, she barely noticed their efforts to get her attention.

Uncle Satch came in the front door and made a beeline to the back of the gym. He went around the full-size ring, the cage, and past a lot of fighters in various acts of exercise and practice.

He paid no attention to the women.

Before he'd quite reached Harley, he called out, "You have another interview. Tonight. I set it up at Roger's for nine o'clock."

Dean slapped Harley's shoulder in commiseration and

walked away. They all knew how badly he hated the press stuff, and for a few weeks it had lightened up. But Satch pushed hard, more so than other managers.

Simon stayed beside him and listened as Satch reached them and gave the details.

"Kinkaid says he challenged you and you hid behind Simon."

"So?"

Bristling on his behalf, Satch said, "You have to give the right details, set that bastard straight."

"I already did. There was a reporter there that night. He caught it all."

"You should have told me! I need to do damage control."

"I don't know," Simon said. "Kinkaid is a loose cannon. The more crap he talks, the dumber he's going to look when he gets beat. There's no reason for Harley to get into a bunch of back-and-forth bullshit."

Conceding to Simon's experience, Satch said, "Maybe. But if an interviewer asks him, he has to explain."

Harley felt Stasia looking at him. He glanced her way, and saw her concern. Over Satch? Or had something happened? To his uncle, he said, "I'll handle it, Uncle Satch, but no more interviews. I've had enough."

"But—"

"Don't worry. It'll be fine."

When he stepped around him to go to Stasia, Satch bristled. "Wait a damn minute."

"We can talk at home." Harley lifted a hand in farewell and went to Stasia.

She greeted him with a small smile. "Hey there. You done for the day?"

"I still need to shower—obviously."

She wrinkled her nose. "I never quite understood the appeal of sweat."

Harley shrugged. "It comes with the sport." He smoothed a hand over her glossy dark hair. "You look worried about something. Is everything okay?"

"It's nothing."

"Tell me anyway."

She rolled her lips in, considered it, and shook her head. "You don't want to hear it and I don't want to pester you."

He let out an exasperated breath. "I've been working my ass off for hours. I'm ready to call it a day, but you're over here scowling and now you don't want to say why?" He shook his head. "Why can't women ever give a straight answer?"

"You want it straight? Fine. I don't like the way you let your uncle coerce you into things you don't want to do."

Harley hadn't expected that. "You're fretting about Uncle Satch?" From his perspective, Satch was just a fact of life, a relative he loved, and one he had to deal with. "Why?"

"You're a smart man, Harley. You have great instincts, and you know how to manage your own career. Yet you constantly let your uncle badger you into stuff. Talk about a distraction. That can't be helpful to you."

"He's my uncle, Stasia. Family. The only family I have left." Far as Harley was concerned, that said it all.

"I'm not suggesting you boot him out of your life. Just reclaim the reins, that's all. Set some boundaries for him. Much as you love him, he loves you, so I know he'd understand."

Done with the ridiculous topic, Harley said, "I'll think about it."

"I hope you do."

"What do you have planned? I can be done showering in ten minutes. Want to grab something to eat?"

"I could eat."

"Why is that always your answer?"

"Because I'm always hungry?" She grinned. "Where would you like to go?"

"Roger's is fine. I have an interview there later anyway."

"I'll need to change. You can pick me up on your way to the bar if you want. I'll be ready."

Harley looked out the door. "It's dark already. Be careful, okay?"

"Jasmine is riding with me. We'll be fine."

Harley hesitated. They'd kept things pretty platonic since her final decision weeks ago. But now . . . He bent and pressed a kiss to her forehead. "See you in a bit."

Stasia stood there, unmoving, even as Harley turned away. Damn, but they both were bad off. If only she'd admit it . . . not that it'd be wise for him to get sexually involved right now. Hell, he didn't have that long before the fight. He'd be better to save it . . .

Harley laughed at himself. If she said yes right now, he'd be all over her, and they both knew it.

It bugged him that she called all the shots. A lot. Maybe, just for the hell of it, he'd work on her a little.

STASIA watched Harley walk away, knowing he had no idea how he affected her with his nearness. Even hot from his workout, his blond hair slicked back, his chest hair dark with sweat, he had the most incredible body she'd ever seen on a man. In his low shorts and nothing more, he was devastatingly sexy.

Jasmine nudged her. "Seeing these guys mostly naked, all hot and sweaty, is downright torturous, isn't it?"

She glanced at her new friend and laughed. "Barber getting to you?"

"I don't know how much longer I'll last. Did you see him sparring? He's good. Even Dakota said so." She frowned. "Do you think he's still in love with her?"

"No." Stasia didn't have to think about it. She'd heard all the rumors, and for weeks now she'd watched Barber and Dakota together. Simon didn't seem worried, and that said a lot. Dakota treated Barber like a best friend, and he reacted to her as he would a little sister. He was protective and sweet, and affectionate. Nothing more.

But with Jasmine . . . "He's got his eye set on you, and you know it."

Jasmine nodded. "He wants to sleep with me. He's said so." She sighed. "Multiple times."

"Sounds like Barber. He's pretty up front about stuff."

Jasmine flattened her expression. "If it was just up to me, I'd say yes in a heartbeat. I'm not crazy or a masochist."

"So what's the problem?"

"I love singing." Jasmine looked at Stasia with pangs of regret. "And if we get intimate, I can't be in the band."

"Barber actually said that?" Stasia shook her head. Harley had hinted at Barber's boundaries, but Stasia couldn't believe he'd actually abide by such a lame rule, especially when everyone was aware of the chemistry between them.

"I don't know what to do, Stasia. I'm damned if I do, and damned if I don't."

"Well, I don't buy it."

Filled with hope, Jasmine stared at her wide-eyed. "You don't?"

"No." She wasn't sure if she should get involved or not, but seeing Jasmine's desperation, Stasia couldn't hold herself back. "Let me ask you this. Do you think Barber cares for you, or just wants you?"

"Hard to say." Jasmine stepped back to lean on the wall and stared unseeing at the fighters currently sparring. "He's nice. Courteous. But I've known guys who'd do that just to get in my graces."

"Men are men." Stasia laughed. "But . . . have you seen him with any other woman recently?"

After she thought about it, Jasmine brightened. "No." She straightened from the wall. "In fact, he told me he wasn't cut out for celibacy and that I should take pity on him."

Huh. "If he just wanted sex, he could have sex. Right?"

Nodding, Jasmine said, "Groupies are always hanging around, coming on to him. He flirts, but I haven't seen him actually show interest in any of them."

"Not since you came along."

She grinned.

"Maybe Barber would find out that he wants you in bed *and* in the band."

"You really think so?"

"What I think doesn't matter so much. It's what you think. Is it worth the risk to you? What if you sleep with him and he fires you from the band?" When Jasmine winced, Stasia hurried to say, "I can't imagine him doing that. In the three weeks you've been performing with him, everyone has raved. You two are incredible together. Barber's a good businessman, so he's surely recognized that."

Suddenly Jasmine's shoulders went back. "You're right. This is ridiculous. I'm tired of sleepless nights and feeling tense all the time."

"Think it through, though, Jasmine. There's always the possibility that things won't work out between the two of you. Barber's been a bachelor for a long time, and he's set in his ways. He's outrageous and used to doing what he wants, when he wants. If you two fall apart, it would be awkward to perform together. You might not even want to be in the band."

"You're right." She scrunched up her brows and paced a short distance away, then came right back. "I'm going to talk to Barber, feel him out about it."

From behind them, Barber said, "I'm all for you feeling me out, or feeling me up, but about what in particular?"

Both women froze. Stasia cleared her throat. "Dang, Barber. For a big guy, you're awfully sneaky."

He blinked at Stasia, then turned his attention to Jasmine. "Or maybe it's just that you two babes were so busy plotting no good that you didn't notice a two-hundred-pound man approaching."

"That's possible," Jasmine said.

Barber's gaze went all over her. "God above, girl, I do love the way you pull an outfit together."

Stasia smiled. Today Jasmine wore tight black boot-cut jeans and a white thermal shirt with red and black trim. She had her hair pulled up in a ponytail at the very top of her head so it hung down around her face like a fountain. Exaggerated makeup gave her an edgy rocker look that Barber all but drooled over.

Deciding to leave the lovebirds alone, Stasia told Jasmine, "I'll wait up front."

She was standing by the door, watching the street lights come on as night fell, when Uncle Satch caught up to her.

"Got a minute, Anastasia?"

She greeted him with a hug. "How are you, Satch?"

"Well, now, that's the thing." He rubbed his chin. "I'd be doing better if you'd be doing your job."

"My job?"

"Harley dodges more press than he accepts."

Her mouth fell open. Irritation set in. "How can you say that? You have him running from one interview to another. For weeks now he's spent over half his waking day preparing for the fight, and then hours more appeasing your idea of good press."

Her verbal attack had Satch backing up a step. "Bring it down already, will you?"

Stasia looked around and noticed that a few people glanced their way. Her and her big mouth. "Sorry. But you're pushing him too hard," she said lower, determined to make her point. "Harley is a big boy who can make his own decisions, *good* decisions, if you'd just give him a chance."

Satch bunched up on her. "I thought we were on the same side."

"I'm on Harley's side," she assured him. "I've been studying the sport, and Dakota agrees, he doesn't need to seek out promotion. The promoters that come to him would be more than enough."

"Women." Satch threw up his hands. "You know how long I've been involved in the SBC? Since Harley first started, which is a lot longer than Ms. Dakota and you combined. You honestly think I don't know what's best for him?"

Gently, Stasia said, "No, I don't."

His face went red.

"I'm sorry, Satch, but I think you're more ambitious than Harley is. All he wants is the belt. Not the fame or the attention. It's something personal and private to him. Something he's proving to himself, not to anyone else. When he gets the belt, the rest will come naturally. He'd enjoy the journey more if you backed off a little."

Out of the corner of her eye, Stasia saw a tall, strong form coming toward them, and she glanced over to see Harley staring at her as he approached.

She gave Satch notice by turning to greet Harley. "All done?"

He stopped in front of them, his blue eyes narrow with suspicion. "Yeah." He looked at his uncle. "What are you two so chatty about?"

"I was asking Stasia if she'd accompany you to a pre-fight party here in town. Plans are in the works right now."

The suspicion lingered. "Now you want to wrangle my dates for me?"

"It wouldn't be a date. I suggested Stasia because you need a smart woman with you, not some . . ." He glanced at Stasia, and amended the slur against women. "Someone more than just arm candy."

"And I qualify? Why, Satch, I can certainly see where Harley gets his charm."

Harley smiled at her.

Satch wasn't amused. "This is serious." He glared a warning at Stasia. "Instead of just photographers, they'll have a television crew. They plan to piece together bits of conversation and run them with the live interviews in Vegas the night of the fight."

"Where's the party taking place?"

"That's the exciting part. Dean's gym has gotten so much good press, Drew Black wants it here, in Harmony. After shooting some clips of the town, the different fighters, and the gym, we'll have the party at Roger's, and the whole town will get in on it."

"That's fine, Uncle Satch." Harley took Stasia's hand. "Is it a date?"

"Can I at least try to look like arm candy?"

"Sounds like a plan." Harley looked around, spotted Jasmine and Barber stationed in a corner, their foreheads almost touching as they talked. After a roll of his eyes, he yelled, "You driving her home, Barber, or should Stasia wait?"

Barber waved him off.

Laughing, Harley said, "There you go." He put a hand on his uncle's nape. "Uncle Satch, you want to come along with us to grab a bite to eat?"

"I'll get a burger on the fly. Thanks anyway."

"You sure? You haven't had dinner yet, have you?"

"I don't want to be a third wheel. Besides, I have some other stuff to do yet. You'll be at the bar at nine?"

"I'll be there."

He looked at Stasia. "You going to be there, too?"

"Unless it's a problem."

"No. Of course not." He gave Stasia a calculated look. "Keep the distractions at bay." He stalked off toward Dean and Simon.

"That was interesting." Harley started them out the door. "Anything going on between you two that I should know about?"

She didn't want to lie to him. Holding her coat closed against a brisk wind, she said, "Just a mild disagreement, that's all."

"About what?"

Trying not to offend, Stasia measured her words. "I like your uncle, but I think he's too invested in your success. He's young enough and smart enough that he should have a life all his own, not one tied so closely to you."

"I know. It gets tedious. But don't worry about it. Satch is pretty damn good at what he does, he just goes overboard on occasion. I trust him, and that's what's most important."

Rather than be a hypocrite, Stasia decided to let Harley handle his life how he saw best. "Sounds like you have it all in hand."

He took her keys from her and unlocked her truck. "Now if I could just get you in hand, I'd be doing okay."

She looked up at him. "Meaning?"

"I need you." He curled a big, warm hand around her nape. "I'm starving for you."

The words, combined with his low voice, weakened her resolve. "Are all fighters as persistent as you?"

"What do you think?"

"I think you're sexier than most."

His breath frosted between them. He lifted his other hand and held her face up to his. "Maybe I'm just more desperate than the others." He put a quick, teasing kiss on the bridge of her nose and stepped back. "I'll be right behind you, Stasia. Drive careful." And with that, he left for his Charger.

Stasia slumped against her truck. Holy cow, much more of his sexual teasing and she'd be the desperate one.

Who was she kidding? More than once, she'd considered taking the same advice she'd given to Jasmine. It was fear that held her back.

Fear of having her heart broken.

Fear of getting in the way of Harley's dream.

Fear of losing because she never even tried.

For one of the few times in her life, she wasn't sure what to do. She told herself to wait until after he'd fought. It was only another three weeks away. Not that long.

Roger now rented the room to her at a weekly rate. She was used to hotel rooms and temporary situations. It was her life.

But this time, with each day that passed, she found herself liking the town of Harmony and the people there more and more.

With all decisions well out of reach, Stasia got behind the wheel, fired up the truck, and kicked on the heater. Until she knew for sure what to do, she'd simply continue to be with him, encouraging him, listening . . . falling in love.

CHAPTER 19

BARBER held her hand tight and charged through the foyer of the hotel. A few people tried to talk to him, but he ignored them.

Breathless, rushing to keep up, Jasmine whispered, "Barber, you're embarrassing me."

"I'll embarrass myself if I don't get you alone. Trust me. You don't want this playing out in the hotel lobby."

Her hand tightened in his, then she said, "Okay. Hurry."

Damn, but she turned him on. He reached his door, fumbled with the damn key card, and finally fell into the room with her. In a heartbeat he had her on the bed, kissing her long and hard and relishing the taste of her.

"Coats," she managed to say.

"Clothes," he agreed, and sat up long enough to jerk off his outerwear, then his long-sleeved tee. "Well?" She lay there, watching him, her green eyes bright and filled with excitement.

"You are so gorgeous."

"Oh hell, woman, don't do that. Trust me, I don't need any more encouragement." He stood, hopped on one foot while he jerked off a boot, then the other boot. Hands on his belt, his gaze glued to her, he said, "Jasmine. Get some clothes off. Fast."

"Okay." She stood without his burning haste and removed her coat. Next she opened her snug-fitting jeans, smiled at him, and pulled down the zipper.

A striptease? Hell yeah.

"Wait." Barber shucked off his jeans and stretched out in the bed. He was already hard, drawing her attention to his dick. "Go on now. Let me enjoy the show."

She giggled.

And even that ridiculous sound turned him on.

"How awesome it is," she said as she removed her boots, "to have a musician be so buff and sexy."

"As long as it gets you in bed, I'm glad."

"You blow me away, Barber." She pulled her top off over her head and folded the shirt, then set it aside on the dresser.

"That's a hell of a look for you, babe. Tight jeans and a bra. If you came onstage like that, the audience would riot."

"I'm not much for showing off my body."

"Just for me, then. I like that idea even better."

She must've liked it too, because she smiled as she pushed away her jeans.

Barber soaked in the sight of her, the lushly rounded curves, the way her pubic hair showed through her sheer pink panties. Breathing hard, unable to look away from her, he put a hand to his dick. "Now the bra."

She watched his hand as he wrapped it around himself. She breathed hard too, and reached behind herself to release the catch. The bra dropped to the floor.

Barber growled. "Great rack, baby. Really great."

Hooking her thumbs in the waistband of her panties, she bent and down they went, all the way to her ankles. She stepped out, and when she straightened, she was completely naked.

"Your hair," Barber rasped, so turned on he felt on fire.

"Okay." Reaching up, Jasmine pulled out the band that held her hair constrained atop her head. The long curls tumbled down around her shoulders, wound around her breasts, her nipples.

He groaned.

Suddenly a little shy, she held up her hands, posed, and said, "Well?"

With complete honesty, he said, "I could come just looking at you."

Her breath shuddered out. "You are so overly sexual."

"No, just honest." Turning to reach the nightstand, Barber got out a box of condoms and quickly rolled on one. "Come here, Jasmine."

After stepping over to the side of the bed, she touched the blankets and hesitated. "I've dreamed about this so many times, I can't quite believe I'm actually doing it."

She was so cute—and young. Barber thought of her age, only twenty-two, and the fact that she couldn't have as much experience as him. He shouldn't rush her, but damn, his patience had ended about two seconds after getting into the room.

"Come here, woman. Let's make out." He caught her hand and tumbled her into the bed. Praying he'd be able to hold out until she was ready, Barber pinned her under him and kissed her silly.

To his surprise, he lost himself in the taste of her, her soft curves, her warmth. She was young and tender, receptive to his every touch, and when he slipped a finger into her, she was already wet and hot and more than ready.

He couldn't get enough of kissing her everywhere, but she was just as busy touching and tasting him.

Before long, it was Jasmine panting and pushing him back to say, "Stop teasing, Barber, and get on with it. I can't take much more."

"I love a demanding woman." He settled between her thighs, looked into her glittering eyes, and said, "Hold on tight, baby. I have a feeling this is going to be a hard ride."

"Oh goody. I hope so." She put her arms around his neck, locked her ankles at the small of his back.

With her every word prodding him, Barber positioned himself, pushed into her and captured her gasp with a searing kiss.

As he'd predicted, his control slipped and he rode her hard.

But she loved it, matching him with every thrust, digging her nails into his buttocks, biting his shoulder and then crying out just when he thought he wouldn't last another second.

Barber felt her inner muscles squeezing him, felt her nipples stiff against his chest, and he let himself go.

A minute or two later, Barber felt her squirming. He smiled and said, "You okay?"

"You weigh a ton and I can't breathe."

He laughed and rolled to the side, but put a hand on her thigh. "You are so damn hot."

Knowing he should get up, and actually getting up, were two different things. Barber faded out, and probably dozed for ten or fifteen minutes—until he heard her sniffle.

His eyes shot open. He looked over at her, and she was still flat on her back, her beautiful hair spread out over her pillow, spilling onto his pillow. Her mouth quivered.

Ah hell. "Really, Jassy, I'd prefer that you not cry."

The sound of his voice seemed to set her off.

"My name is *not* Jassy." She launched herself from the bed and stormed around the room, upset and pissed and looking ready to flay him.

Eyeing the spent condom, Barber considered a quick trip to the john, but he preferred watching Jasmine and her antics. He grabbed a tissue and disposed of it in the waste can, then scooted up in the bed.

Watching as Jasmine moved around his room naked, her hair like a wild red cape, he asked, "What's the problem now?"

She slanted him a look so mean, Barber drew back. "Good God, woman. Did I leave you wanting?"

"What? No!"

Barber knew he hadn't, but it was nice that she'd admit it. "So then why all the theatrics?"

"Don't you even think of replacing me."

Ah. He hid his grin and asked, "In my bed, or in the band?"

She went blank for one second, then said, "Either!"

"Hmmm." Barber watched as she struggled into her panties and wrestled with her bra. "Where exactly are you going?"

"Away from here to think."

Not likely. He wasn't done with her, not by a long shot. Patting the bed, he told her, "Come here and let me help."

She paused with her bra unhooked. "Help how?"

"I'll give you a rubdown. You look tense."

"Barber . . ."

He could see her weakening already, and he loved it that she was as physically attracted to him as he was to her. He also loved her amazing talent. And her girly ways. And her body.

Definitely her body.

He patted the bed again.

Dashing away the tears, Jasmine glared at him, then flounced over to the bed. Instead of sitting beside him, she sat with her back against the footboard and stretched out her legs. "My feet are killing me. You can start there."

He loved her temper too, and the way she always tried to get one up on him. "Yes, ma'am." Hell, he even loved her feet. They were small and cute. Knowing it'd throw her, he announced, "I'd like to introduce you to Drew Black."

Her brows came down. "Who is he?"

"President of the SBC. Nice guy. Incredible business-man. I'm contracted to perform live for some of the fights, and to have my music play at others. I think he'll like what you add to the mix."

Worry clouded her eyes. Watching him, she swallowed, hesitated. "What if he doesn't?"

Barber shrugged. "Then to hell with him."

She breathed slow and deep. "Barber?"

"Hmmm?"

"My feet are fine now."

He rubbed his thumbs into her arches. "Good."

"I think I'd like for you to work on something else now." She crawled up the bed toward him. "Something else that's . . . aching."

"Yeah?" Damn, but he was getting hard again already.

She crawled right up and over his body until she straddled his lap. "Yes."

That was one hell of a turnaround on her part, and Barber wondered at it. Did she want him again because he was willing to make her a priority in the band?

Because she saw him as a way to promote her own singing career?

Disliking that idea a lot, Barber put his hands on her thighs, looked into her eyes, and asked, "Why the quick change of heart, doll?"

She cupped his face and kissed him. "Because you're a man who does what he wants to do, without coercion." She wiggled, getting more comfortable and making him nuts in the process. "And that must mean that you want me, Jasmine Petri, or we wouldn't be here, right?"

Women were so damned confounding. "My wanting you was ever in doubt?"

"Of course it was."

"And here I thought I was pretty obvious."

"Well, I thought you wanted every woman."

"No." Barber shook his head, then rethought that. "Okay, maybe most, but not all." He laughed when she tried to hit him. "And not anymore." Then with total gravity, "Not since you."

Her eyes warmed. "Seriously?"

"You bowl me over, woman. I haven't been able to see straight. And I haven't been with anyone since I met you."

She sucked in her breath, grinned hugely. "Barber?"

"Yeah, doll?"

Toying with his chest hair and not quite meeting his

gaze, she said, "If it'll really make you more comfortable, I'll quit the band."

Ah hell. Now how could he not love that? "If you do, then I'll have to quit, too."

On a deep inhalation, she locked eyes with him. Her breath came out in a whoosh. "You mean that?"

Barber pulled her down to him and gave her a smacking kiss. "I mean to keep you very close at hand, Jassy." He settled his hands on her plump behind. "Whatever it takes."

SIMON followed Harley's line of vision to where the ladies had just entered. "They've all become pretty friendly."

"Yeah." Harley sipped his ice water with a twist of lime. He was nearly on weight, but saw no reason to risk added calories.

"Dakota likes her."

Sensing that Simon had something on his mind, Harley said, "You've probably got less than one minute before they join us. Might as well spit it out."

Crossing both arms on the table, Simon nodded. "The fight is only a few weeks away."

"I'm ready."

Frowning in intense thought, Simon hedged, then made a decision. "I want to give you some advice that I had trouble following when Dakota had me running in circles."

Harley gave up his perusal of Stasia and the way she looked in fashionably worn jeans and a V-neck black sweater. "Hell, Sublime. From what I can tell, she's still running you in circles."

"True." Simon grinned. "I imagine she always will. But the difference is that I stopped trying to fight it."

"Meaning?"

"You've got more innate talent than just about any other fighter I've worked with. I have complete faith in your ability to defeat Kinkaid in any scenario. If the fight stays standing, you can outbox him, outkick him, and outthink him. If it goes to ground, your grappling is heads and tails better than his. You're faster, and stronger."

"Is this a pep talk, or is the flattery going somewhere?"

"The point is, I can see this fight ending with a knockout or a submission. If I was a betting man, I'd say it'll end in the first round."

Harley waited.

"But I can also see you making a mistake and giving Kinkaid the edge he needs."

"Fuck that."

To make his point, Simon crowded closer. "Sometimes a small edge is all a lesser fighter needs. One lucky punch, a bad cut—and the fight is over."

"Not going to happen." Come hell or high water, Harley intended to claim the belt.

Simon snorted. "It happens to the best and you know it. So when you face off with Kinkaid, I want you one hundred percent there."

"I will be." From the corner of his eye, Harley saw Stasia coming their way, but with the conversation so serious, he paid her little mind.

"Bullshit." Simon sat forward and scowled. "Whatever game you're playing with Anastasia, it's time to end it."

"Meaning?"

"Go get laid. Get it out of your system before we fly out to Vegas."

Harley laughed. He couldn't help it.

Stasia stood right behind Simon, shocked, horrified, her face hot. He looked up at her. "Simon was just about to go. You can have his seat."

She looked like she might take flight. "I'm sorry to interrupt. I'll just, uh . . ."

Groaning, Simon twisted around to see her, scowled again, and said, "I give up." He rose from the table, but leaned back in to say, "You two need to work it out, now, tonight if possible." Then he walked away with both hands locked behind his head.

Harley kept grinning even as Stasia dropped into a chair. "You have impeccable timing."

After a fast glance at Simon's retreating back, she whispered, "Was he actually—"

Enjoying her flustered embarrassment, Harley said, "Telling me to get you in bed, yeah."

Eyes wide, she shook her head. "Talk about personalized coaching."

Harley laughed again. Everything Stasia said amused him. Everything about her excited him. Maybe Simon was right. What did it matter who won their little game? As long as it ended in bed, he'd be happy. "What do you say, honey? Seems Simon thinks my fate depends on you."

Very real concern replaced her embarrassment. "Is it a problem, seriously?"

Feeling lazy and strangely content, Harley rolled one shoulder. "Ever heard of blue balls?"

Flashing him an annoyed frown, she said, "As a myth to coerce innocent high school girls out of their panties, yes." She sniffed his drink, helped herself to a swallow, and sat it back in front of him. "But that wouldn't apply to you, so be honest with me, Harley."

"Okay." He watched her, and appreciated her concern. "Simon is worried that I've got too much pent-up frustration. Sexual frustration, that is. He wants me focused solely on the fight, not on what I'm missing."

"Sex?"

"Is that so hard to believe?"

"I thought fighters abstained anyway."

"That's a bigger myth than blue balls, believe me."

"Oh." She closed her arms around herself, thinking it through and fretting over it.

"Since that night with you in the garage, which was fun but hardly satisfying for me, I haven't been with anyone."

She chewed her bottom lip. "I assumed . . . but I wasn't sure . . ."

"I haven't wanted anyone else." Harley reached for her hand. "But if you want honesty, then no, it's not going to affect my performance in the fight. If I blow it, it won't be because of anything you did."

"Or didn't do?"

"No guilt, Stasia. I'm a big boy." He lifted her hand to kiss her fingers. "That said, just give me the word, and we'll be in bed within minutes."

Harley felt the trembling in her hand, saw the way the pulse in her throat began tripping.

"Hell, honey, you need it as much as I do. I see it every time you look at me."

"It's that obvious?"

"Yeah." His heart picked up pace. "It's only going to get worse and we both know it."

Nodding slowly, she said, "I have an idea. Something that can work for us both." She laced her fingers with his. "Instead of you tying mc down, why don't you let me do the honors?"

Every male part of Harley went on high alert. "Come again?"

"Think about it, Harley. You're so into bondage and control, and I'm convinced you need to give up some of that iron will of yours. Well, how would it feel for you to be helpless to my whims?"

Hot enough to breathe fire, Harley leaned closer to her. "Tell me about these whims."

She sat back in surprise. "You mean you'll do it?"

Before meeting Stasia, he would have replied with an unequivocal no. But now . . . the idea more than intrigued him.

The problem from Harley's perspective was that from the beginning, she'd had him jumping through hoops. It had to end. "I'd love to hear what you have planned. Spell it out for me."

She stared at him, then looked around to ensure no one could listen in. "To be honest, I've thought about it so many times that I know exactly what I'd want to do."

It was Harley's turn to be surprised. "Tell me."

"I think I'd just want to look at you for a while first. Seeing you in your boxer shorts is pretty exciting. You show so much skin, and every part of you is gorgeous. But I've been wondering how you'll look without them, too."

Damn. "I've got nothing to hide, honey. I'd be happy to show you."

Warming to her subject, Stasia propped an elbow on the table. "I'd like to touch you a lot, too. You've got all those big muscles, but there are other things about you that turn me on, too."

"Like?"

She reached out and trailed her fingertips down his arm. Her voice lowered to a husky whisper. "How smooth your skin is here, on the underside of your biceps and inside your elbow. How tight your stomach is, and how the skin is drawn over your hipbones." Her lips parted and her eyes went heavy. "And I love that sexy trail of hair that goes from your navel down into your shorts."

Her breathing deepened.

So did his.

She looked up into his eyes. "I even like your feet, Harley. And your knees. And the strength in your thighs—"

He shoved back his chair and caught her arm. "Let's go."

She pulled him to a stop. "We're really going to do this?"

"Hell yes."

"No bondage?"

Catching the back of her neck, Harley kissed her hard and quick. "Honest to God, honey, I'm not sure I'd last long enough to bother."

Her mouth lifted in a smile. "Good." She took his hand. "Let's go."

CHAPTER 20

C AM nudged Roger and said, "Another one bites the dust."

He looked up from his conversation with the bartender to see Harley in a heated, and possessive, lip-lock with Anastasia. A second later, Anastasia took Harley's hand and rushed him for the door.

Roger grinned. "Those two have been almost as entertaining as Simon and Dakota."

"I want everyone to be as happy as us."

"Impossible." He tipped up her chin. "No one else has you, so how can they be as happy as me?"

"You're getting mushy, Roger."

He laughed—until he noticed the blonde following on Harley's heels. Her expression bordered on mean. Roger had heard the woman bragging about her time with Harley, and her detailed descriptions on what they'd done. It disgusted him, but it was Harley's problem to deal with.

"That's Gloria," Cam told him, and she too looked displeased with the woman. "I don't like her. She has a big mouth."

To hear Cam speak so unkindly of someone surprised Roger. "Has she bothered you?"

"No. But she's obnoxious, and she has no idea what should be kept private. What Harley ever saw in her, I can't imagine."

Watching as the stacked blonde exited the bar, Roger raised a brow. "I'd say he was looking at the wrapping, not what's inside."

"Men."

He hugged her close. "Some women aren't much different, and you know it."

"I hope Harley realizes what a catch Anastasia is."

"He's no dummy. In case you haven't realized, he hasn't played the field much since Anastasia's been around."

"I noticed." Cam turned sheepish. "We're terrible gossips, aren't we?"

"I prefer to think of it as being concerned friends." And, Roger thought, as a friend, he'd keep an extra eye on the blonde. He couldn't abide troublemakers, especially in his place. In fact, it might be a good idea to tell Harley's uncle about her. Satch liked to run interference whenever possible, and with Harley's fight right around the corner, it wouldn't hurt to make his life a little easier.

"THIS is your house?" Stasia looked around as Harley pulled the Charger into the garage.

"Yeah." With a press of a button, Harley closed the garage door.

Stasia released her seat belt. "Won't your uncle be here?"

"No." Harley turned to face her, and Stasia noticed that though he looked drawn, filled with anticipation, he sounded calm enough. "Satch is out of town doing a background check on Kinkaid. He's like that. The man can find out anything."

"Okay then." Lacking his control, she licked her lips and said, "Race you inside."

Harley grinned, nodded. "You're on."

Because the passenger side of the car faced the door into the house, Stasia was the first one in, but she'd only taken two steps into the interior when he scooped her up from behind.

"Wrong way." He turned a corner, went down a hall and up a few stairs and into a large room.

Stasia barely had time to draw breath before Harley had them both out of their coats and had pinned her against the wall. His big hands opened on her derrière and his mouth crushed down on hers. His hands contracted, drawing her closer, and she felt his erection.

Her breath caught. She freed her mouth and said urgently, "Lights, Harley."

He took her mouth again in a voracious, hungry kiss that made her coherent thought scatter. At the same time he lifted one hand, groped on the wall and found a switch.

Light filled the room.

Breathing hard, Anastasia held his face and said, "Clothes off, buster. I've been dying to see you, all of you."

He looked at her with such heat, she felt scorched. Then he stepped away, reached back and knotted a hand in the back of his sweatshirt. It came off with one tug to be tossed aside.

Humming with excitement, Stasia flattened both hands on his chest. "From that first day in my cabin, I've wanted to touch you."

"Feel free." In between heated kisses to her cheek, her ear and throat, he toed off his shoes, then unsnapped his jeans and eased down the zipper.

Stasia looked at him, and wavered on her feet. Oh Lord. Definitely as big as she'd imagined. The idea of him pressing inside her left her so hot she couldn't pull together a coherent thought.

"Harley?" She was so turned on, she shook all over.

"Better yet," he whispered, and he captured her wrist in a strong grip.

Their gazes locked.

Slowly, letting her anticipation build in a deliberate bit of foreplay, Harley carried her small hand to his erection. As she touched him, wrapped her fingers around him, his eyes closed and his nostrils flared.

Marveling that her fingertips didn't quite touch, Stasia measured him. She could feel him pulsing in her palm, heard his low groan as she stroked to the base, then up to the head.

He took her mouth, thrusting his tongue deep, mimicking what she knew he wanted to do with her body. She held him tight, squeezing, teasing—

"Enough of that or I won't last." He pulled her hand loose and stepped back. While watching her, he shucked off his jeans, taking his boxers and socks off at the same time. Without an ounce of modesty, he stepped back for her to look at him. "Take your time, but it'd be nice if you shed a few clothes, too."

Never had she had a qualm about her body. But she wasn't in his league and she knew it. "I'm a little more shy than you."

"Then I'll help." He pulled her close and tangled his hand in her hair, kissing her until she thought her legs would give out. With him now naked, her hands were able to feel a lot of solid muscle, sleek skin, and warm flesh.

She put both hands on his backside and squeezed. There wasn't any give to him at all, and it thrilled her.

Then she realized that he had her jeans opened.

He lifted his mouth from hers, but only long enough to catch the hem of her sweater and draw it up and over her head.

Wearing only a bra and opened jeans, she leaned back on the wall.

Harley looked her over without haste. When he stepped close again, she expected him to kiss her, and he did, but not where she expected it.

Putting one arm behind her back, he arched her body upward and closed his mouth over her nipple through her bra.

The sensation was so hot, so shocking that Stasia knotted both hands in his hair and held him tight. Her bra went loose and she realized that he'd unhooked the front closer. He put just enough space between them to let the cups separate, baring her but leaving the straps to twist around her arms.

When she tried to free herself, he used his other hand to knot the bra tighter, pinning her arms back.

Even knowing what he did and why, Stasia could not find it in herself to protest. She liked being held captive by Harley. She liked the hungry way he sucked at her nipples, the heat that poured off him and his low groans of pleasure.

Suddenly he lifted her and put her on the bed. He pulled away her ankle boots and socks, then he caught his hands in the waistband of her jeans and tugged them away.

Stripped naked, Stasia stared up at him. He just stood there, unmoving, as he looked her over with that awesome intensity that intimidated so many people.

Knotting her hands in the coverlet, she bent one knee— and let her legs fall open.

Harley cursed low, touched her inner thigh with a featherlight caress. He stared between her legs as he said, "Put your arms above your head, Stasia."

Stasia's heart hammered. She licked her lips in indecision, but there really was no fear on her part. Only excitement. Trembling, she forced her fingers to release her desperate grip on the coverlet. She watched Harley's face as she brought her arms up high and relaxed them again.

His brows came together in concentration. He looked at her breasts, then straddled her thighs and cupped both breasts in his hot hands. He ran his thumbs over her nipples, teased her, lightly pressed. "You're beautiful."

Stasia wanted to speak as casually, as controlled as he did, but she couldn't manage it. Turning her head to the side, she closed her eyes. But when Harley did nothing else but play with her nipples, she couldn't take it and looked up at him again.

He'd been waiting for her to do just that.

"You want me to rush?" he asked with a small, very satisfied smile.

She dropped her gaze to his pulsing erection. "You don't want to?"

"I want to so much it scares me." With an edge of emotion that she couldn't decipher, he said, "I'm not a man who scares easily."

"Then—"

He lowered a hand and pressed it between her legs. "Shhh." He stroked, opened her, and pressed two fingers in.

Startled by the sudden intrusion, Stasia arched her hips. Harley had big hands, and she felt filled by him. But the knowledge was there, that two fingers were nowhere as big as what would soon be inside her.

He watched her, almost detached as he brought his thumb up to her clitoris and teased.

"Harley," she said, on a moan.

"Tell me."

The tension built so quickly, it astounded her. But this wasn't what she wanted, and she had to remember that it wasn't what Harley needed.

Stasia dropped her arms and caught his wrist. "Wait, please."

"You're close, Stasia," he predicted. "I can feel it."

She shook her head. "Harley, please. I want you. Not games. Not control. *You.*"

"You're wet," he told her. "You're excited. Admit it."

She couldn't very well deny it when even now, he felt her small spasms around his fingers, pressed so deep inside her. "You're an incredible man and I've been thinking about being with you for years."

His gaze shot up to hers.

"I'm not so different from other women, Harley. I see you the same way they do."

He smiled and cupped her breast.

Desperate, Stasia said, "But not like this." His fingers shifted, and she caught her breath. "I want . . ." She had to stop, to swallow and gather her thoughts. "I want what you haven't given other women, damn it."

For the first time, Stasia noticed the rigid tension in his breathtaking body, how tightly he'd locked his jaw.

"You, Harley. Without the control." She released his wrist and held her arms out to him. "You don't need it with me, I swear."

For what felt like a lifetime, he hesitated, watching her, primed but holding back. He breathed harder, his eyes flinched, and suddenly he broke.

"Fuck it." He was on her in a heartbeat, his hands everywhere, his mouth hot and hungry. He fit himself between her thighs, but didn't enter her.

Stasia hugged him tight. "Protection."

"Yeah." Between deep, wet kisses, he said, "In a second." He licked her throat, her shoulder, moved down and sucked hard at one taut nipple.

She wrapped her legs around him, for the first time that she could ever recall almost uncaring about the use of a condom.

Harley put his hand between her legs again, but now it was an unconscious need to touch her. She knew the difference, and she reveled in it. As he stroked her, she clamped down on him and cried out.

"Jesus." He levered away, fumbled in his nightstand drawer and found a rubber. Hot color slashed his cheekbones and his hands shook as he rolled it on. He was back over in seconds. "Stasia, look at me."

She saw him through a daze of need.

"You're tight."

She felt the head of his hardened penis penetrating, and he was big enough that it alarmed her. She couldn't help but tense.

"Shh. Relax." He caught one of her knees in the crook of an elbow and lifted, opening her.

"Harley . . . !"

Staring down at her, he pressed in. "Easy, honey. That's

it." He kissed her open mouth, nuzzled her throat. "I'll go slow. And you'll love it. I swear."

"It's . . . it's been a while."

"Hush." He flexed his hips, working into her, and without meaning to, she dug her nails into his shoulders. "Yeah. Hold on to me."

He kissed her, softer this time, but deep, his tongue in her mouth—and he drove in the rest of the way.

Stasia stiffened, but Harley didn't let her hold back. He buried himself in her, then withdrew and drove in again.

The sensations were so much, both physically and emotionally, that it felt like he turned her inside out. She wanted to moan, to cry out, but his mouth swallowed every sound she made. He kept her locked to him, too tightly for her to do more than accept him.

And she loved it.

On his third stroke, she exploded, shaking all over, sweating, holding on to him with near desperation.

He groaned and rode her harder, faster. With the arm he had hooked in her knee, he levered up more and tangled a hand in her hair, keeping her mouth right where he wanted it. His other hand he used to lift her hips more. Stasia felt him so deep inside her, filling her, setting sparks off every nerve ending, and another climax rippled through her.

She jerked her mouth free to gasp for air, but Harley didn't allow that. He was right there, reclaiming her mouth, taking everything in every way, and giving her so much pleasure that as the sensations finally began to fade, Stasia felt light-headed.

He stiffened over her, let her mouth go so he could press his face into her shoulder, and she heard his ragged groans as his big body shuddered and convulsed.

Tears burned her eyes. She wrapped both arms as tightly around him as she could. When he settled against her, going limp but still gasping for air, she had to bite her lip to keep from speaking.

She loved him, had known it for a long time.

But now that she'd had him, all of him, how would she ever get by without him?

HARLEY rolled to his back and stared at the ceiling. He had no words. His brain felt more at ease than he could ever recall.

There was no discontent. No lack of satisfaction.

Smiling, he turned his head and saw Stasia watching him through sleepy eyes. Damn. Could a woman look more beautiful?

He turned to his side, but didn't touch her. "You okay?"

Still on her back, she gave a slow, lazy blink of her eyes and let out a slow breath. "I am remarkably sated."

She was remarkably sexy. "Yeah? Me, too."

Closing her eyes, she waited, and Harley felt her growing tension until she finally asked, "Now what?"

He couldn't blame her for the uncertainty. He'd been so damned insistent on things.

Harley put a hand on her stomach. Her skin was soft and pale. So pretty. "I'll be right back. Do me a favor, and don't move."

"I'm not sure I can."

He left for the bathroom, disposed of the condom, and came back with a cool washcloth. In an unconsciously provocative pose, she had one arm behind her head, the other folded over her middle. Her hair spread out on the mattress like a silky fan. Her long legs were parted, her left leg slightly bent at the knee.

Very at ease, with her and the situation, Harley stretched out beside her and pressed the damp cloth between her legs.

Her arm came down and her eyes shot open. "Harley—"

"Relax."

She caught his wrist with both hands. "Stop that! I can—"

"I want to." Feeling devilish and playful, Harley moved the cloth over her. "Don't make me tie you up now."

She rolled to her side toward him. "This is ridiculous. I'm more than able—"

"So much bitching. Can't a man just enjoy himself a little after sex?" Grinning, he tossed aside the cloth and turned her to her back again, pinning her in place with a heavy thigh over hers.

"Bitching!" Stasia swatted at him, half-laughing, half-embarrassed.

Wrestling with her was fun, so Harley let the play go on just long enough to get her winded before catching both her wrists in his. "Now."

"Don't even think it, Harley."

"Think what? This?" He pressed her arms high, stretching her out and turning himself on at the same time. As he coasted a hand over her ribs, she squirmed, ticklish and uncertain of his motives.

"Stop struggling, woman."

"No!"

He bent to her breast. "Give in." He licked her, and murmured low, "Let me enjoy you."

She said, "Damn it, Harley, I don't want—" Then he sucked a now soft nipple into his mouth.

Stasia froze. But not for long.

On a groan, her body still sensitive from her recent pleasure, she tried to flinch away. Holding her tightly, Harley circled her nipple with his tongue, teased, and then, using just the edge of his teeth, lightly tugged.

She stopped fighting to arch into him. Her legs shifted and she tried to open them, but he kept them still with one of his own. "Not yet, honey."

"Harley . . ."

"I know. I told you so."

That irked her, as he intended. She started struggling anew. He lifted up to watch her face as he played with her nipples, rolling them, tugging.

"Do you know all the ways I can make you come, Stasia?"

Her eyes half-closed. "No."

"Why don't we find out?"

"Why don't you stop being a jerk?"

He laughed and put a hand to her heart. It beat hard and fast. "You love it."

"I want you."

"Which part of me?" Before she could answer, Harley said, "Tell me what you want, honey. My cock, my fingers, or . . . my mouth?"

Her body flushed with excitement. Her chest rose with each deepening breath.

"Unsure?" Harley teased. "How about I decide for you?"

She licked her lips, then nodded.

Already anticipating the taste of her and her reaction to the stroke of his tongue in the most responsive of places, Harley released her wrists and bent to put a kiss to her stomach. He breathed in the heated scent of her skin, and the muskier scent of sex.

Stasia put a hand in his hair. "But know this, Harley Handleman. Everything you do to me, I plan to repay in kind."

Those words nearly dropped him. Well hell. He was already hard again, and now he felt on the volatile edge of detonating.

"In that case . . ." He caught her hips and with one firm tug, readjusted her at an angle on the mattress. He parted her legs and settled between them. "Bend your knees."

When she hesitated, he helped her. With a hand on the inside of each thigh, he held her open wide so that he could see every inch of her.

Tracing one fingertip along her still swollen lips, he avoided her clitoris while testing her readiness. She shifted in growing need, and he pushed his finger into her in one long, firm stroke.

She pressed her head back, her mouth open, her eyes closed.

Adding a second finger to the first, Harley worked her until every breath was a moan and moisture bathed his hand. He couldn't wait any longer. He leaned in closer and licked over her, around his fingers buried deep, up and over her turgid clitoris.

Her knees bent more and she lifted her hips up to him, pressing closer, begging for more with her body movements and soft cries.

He drew her into his mouth and sucked very softly, using his tongue to stroke her at the same time that he twisted his fingers, pushing them deeper, stretching her.

As she came, her cries were loud and raw and real, just as Harley liked it. Her climax lasted, lingering, until finally her muscles went lax and she sank boneless against the mattress.

He wanted her, no doubt about that, but other, softer emotions held him. Harley kissed her thighs, hugged himself to her, tasted her sweat-damp skin and the tangier taste of her excitement.

Simply put, he wanted to wallow in her, to somehow make it last when in the past, he'd only wanted fast relief followed by a faster good-bye.

Coming up alongside her, Harley kissed her open mouth and then her palm, before carrying her hand down to his erection. He curled her fingers around him—and saw her smile.

"Oh God, Harley. I need a minute."

Feeling heady with need, he whispered, "Take all the time you need." She could take a lifetime, and he wasn't sure it'd be enough.

He cuddled her breast, not to incite her, but just because her body was a part of her and somehow all of her had become so precious to him.

"That was enough to knock me out."

He nuzzled her throat. "Sleep if you want." He wasn't going anywhere, and neither was she. He could wait if he had to.

As a reply, her fingers tightened on his shaft. "You won't get off that easy." She rolled toward him, then half onto his chest. She stroked him, smiled at his clenching jaw, and kissed his chin.

Like a curtain, her shoulder-length hair fell around her flushed face. "You are such a devastating man."

"I'm a horny man."

"Good." She bit his earlobe, then his shoulder. "I could just eat you up."

God, he hoped so. "Feel free."

She licked his collarbone, bit a pectoral muscle, and teased her lips over his left nipple. "You know just how far to take things, don't you, Harley?"

"Meaning?"

"When you bit me."

She put her teeth to him, and Harley froze. "Uh, Stasia . . ."

Kissing him, she said, "Don't worry. I won't hurt you."

He tangled both hands in her hair. In contrast to her hot skin, it felt remarkably cool. "I'm better at teasing than being teased."

"Tough." She nibbled her way along his ribs. "How is it that you know when to stop? My heart was pumping so hard, and I was half-afraid of what you'd do, but loving it anyway."

"I take my cues from you, honey."

"A learned talent, no doubt gained from lots of experience."

He did not want to talk about other women with her. "We're the only two here."

She held his cock in her hand, tight, still. "I haven't had as much practice as you, so I hope I don't . . ." She nipped his hip with her sharp little teeth. "Hurt you."

Ah hell. His every muscle drew tight, especially given he could feel her breath on his dick. "Stasia—"

"Relax, Harley." Stroking slowly from the base to the head, she smiled up at him. "Let me learn."

She was much better at teasing than she wanted to admit. "I don't know if I like this, babe."

"Let's find out." She licked her smiling lips, wetting them, then pressed a soft kiss to the underside of his shaft. When he automatically flexed, she did it again, then followed up with a hot lick.

"Damn."

"You are so big, Harley." She ran her tongue around him, below her fist, above it—up and over the sensitive head of his dick.

He jerked hard, he couldn't help it. "Enough, Stasia."

"I don't think so." She licked him again, then drew him into her mouth, sucking him while stroking with her hand.

He knew he wouldn't last. He closed his eyes and tried to hold on. Her hot little mouth felt so good that he wanted to enjoy it more.

With any other woman, he might have succeeded.

But this was Stasia, and he couldn't obliterate that thought, couldn't separate the reality of it, of who she was and what she'd come to mean to him.

Eyes burning, Harley looked down at her. Resting on her belly, her adorable ass was there for him to see, her small hand held him, her hair teased his abdomen.

Her cheeks hollowed out—

"Enough. I give." Against her protests, Harley caught her shoulders and pulled her up alongside him. "Get a condom," he managed to growl. "There in the nightstand."

Smiling in satisfaction, looking sexier than any woman should, Stasia turned and in record time came back with a condom. She went up to her knees and opened the little packet with her teeth.

"Hold still."

"Yeah, right." Harley fisted his hands and tried to concentrate on something, anything other than the fact that Stasia had him in her hands and was preparing to fuck him.

As soon as she had the condom in place, he said, "Ride me."

Puzzled, she looked at him, and Harley caught her waist. "Ride me, Stasia." He lifted her up and over him so that she straddled him. "Come on, sugar. Put me inside you. I want to see you sitting on me, taking me deep." He was killing himself now, but he couldn't stop. "All of me."

Her nipples went tight. A pulse fluttered in her throat. "All right."

She held him steady and slowly lowered herself onto him.

Harley watched as the head of his cock pushed inside her. Hell yes. The muscles in her slim thighs flexed. Her belly sucked in.

Eyes closed, her bottom lip caught in her teeth, she took about half of him and stopped.

He held her waist. "All of me, Stasia."

"I don't know . . ."

"Sit down."

She squeezed her eyes shut. "You're awfully big—"

"I know. And you're small and tight and it feels so fucking good, I could die happy right now." It took all Harley's concentration not to thrust up into her. He swallowed, and said again, "Sit down."

Leaning forward to brace her hands on his thighs, Stasia looked at him. Their gazes locked.

"Do it."

Taking deep breaths, she eased down. Her eyelids went heavy. Her lips opened. She panted.

Harley gripped her hips tighter and said through his teeth, "You're killing me, baby."

She closed her eyes, braced herself—and pushed down. Oh God.

Harley struggled with himself, but damn, it felt so good being deep inside her, so deep . . . He couldn't hold back any longer.

It didn't matter.

Giving up all control, Stasia dropped her head back and groaned. Harley drove up into her, guiding her hips, metering the pace, harder and faster. He brought his knees up and said urgently, "Lean back."

She did, and the position lifted her breasts.

Harley growled. Seeing her, feeling her, watching her pleasure build was a big mind blow. She cried out in a sudden orgasm, and that was all it took. He joined her on a rush, and as she lay down over his chest, he cradled her close . . . and cherished her.

CHAPTER 21

HARLEY took his time regaining his wits this time. He felt it when he slipped from Stasia's body, but she didn't budge. She was a limp weight against him, their skin melded with sweat, the scent in the air heady and rich, filled with pleasure.

He could have slept like that, Harley realized, with Stasia as his blanket, comfortable atop him. But he had to dispose of the condom. Moving carefully, he turned her to his side. She mumbled something and curled up as if, having lost his body heat, she felt chilled.

A lump the size of a cantaloupe caught in his throat. He smoothed her hair, touched her soft mouth with his thumb. In the past few months, she'd given him hell, taken him on a damn chase, and numbed his mind with incredible sex.

She wanted to shove her idea of guidance down his throat, but maybe that wasn't such a bad thing. Stasia was an intelligent, intuitive, honest woman. And she seemed to know him, better than most in fact.

The least he could do was consider her comments.

Harley left the bed and looked at her again. He realized

she was dead center in the middle of the mattress. He smiled.

Not since Sandy had left him years ago for another man had he slept with a woman. *Slept.* Well, there was that night at the garage with Stasia, but he'd remained awake all night, listening for trouble, thinking—resisting.

He was so tired, he swayed on his feet.

Fuck it. He couldn't very well wake her and tell her to leave, and he'd feel like an ass camping out on the couch.

Besides, there was a terrible yearning inside him. He wanted to be beside her, to hold her and protect her. It would only mean what he wanted it to mean. Nothing more.

He controlled himself and his life. He could control this, whatever it was, too.

Harley pulled the displaced blankets up and over Stasia and went into the bathroom. After quietly cleaning up, he went out to make sure the house was locked up. Everything was quiet and still, peaceful in a way he'd never considered or noticed before.

Thoughts churning, he returned to the bedroom. Stasia still hogged the middle; that lump remained in his throat.

He turned off the lights, squeezed in beside her, and pulled her against his body. As if she'd slept with him for years, she adjusted herself to his body, got comfortable, and sighed back to deep sleep.

Harley wondered if he'd get any rest at all.

It was his last thought until morning sun came through a small opening in the curtains.

STASIA woke with her nose against a hairy chest. Instinctively, she knew it was Harley, and before she'd even gotten her eyes open she was smiling.

Blond hair disheveled, light beard shadow covering his jaws, he looked incredible.

And peaceful.

She didn't have the heart to awaken him. And because

she had no idea how he'd react to finding her still in his bed, she didn't have the nerve.

Feeling like a coward, she eased away from him and slid to the edge of the mattress. Harley stirred, turned to his back, and settled back to sleep.

He worked so hard, pushed his body to the limits, and let his uncle run him ragged. He divided his concentration between training, promotion, family duty, and friends. He had to be exhausted.

The sheet barely covered his lap, leaving his torso bare for her perusal. One big foot stuck out at the bottom. He raised an arm, and she looked at the paler underside of his heavily muscled arm, the softer armpit hair, the gentle way his lax hand rested with his fingers open.

She drew a shuddering breath.

Even after last night, seeing him again sent her heart into a tailspin. She knew she was head over heels in love with him, but she didn't really know what to do about it. Harley had never misled her, and she wasn't about to kick up a fuss.

But . . . God, it hurt.

Cool air sent a chill over her skin and she picked up his discarded sweatshirt from the night before, slipped out of his room, and eased the door closed again.

Had anything really changed between them? To her, it felt like a whole new dynamic had been added to their relationship. But she couldn't trust in her own perspective, and she knew it. For her, sex was a commitment.

For Harley, it was . . . sex.

To clear her head and get her bearings, Stasia needed caffeine in a very bad way. After pulling on the sweatshirt, which hung to her knees and helped to ward off the chill, she crept to the kitchen.

Everything about Harley's home screamed male domain. It was obvious men had decorated the house, and that men lived in it. The furnishings were masculine and heavy and dark. Everything was functional, but tasteful, and it suited Harley.

She found a jar of coffee in the cabinet above the sink, a coffee machine on the countertop, mugs, and sugar. Within minutes the scent of brewing coffee filled the air, rejuvenating her. Crossing her arms around herself, Stasia went to the kitchen window to watch the bright red sun rising over the snowy landscape.

What would happen today? How would Harley act? How should she act?

She honestly had no idea if he'd be pleased to find her still there, or wish her long gone. Either way, she had to be prepared. When he woke up, she hoped to already be dressed just in case her pride demanded a hasty exit.

The coffee machine hissed to a finish and Stasia hastily prepared a cup of morale-boosting caffeine.

She was just about to take her first drink when she heard a squeak behind her. Prepared to greet Harley, to bear his mood whatever it might be, she pasted on a firm, if uncertain, smile, and turned. "Good morning."

At the sound of her voice, Harley's uncle drew back, let his gaze flash over her, head to toes, and glared daggers. "What are you doing here?"

The mug of steaming coffee slipped right out of Stasia's numb fingers. Glass shattered, and burning hot coffee splashed against her legs.

JARRED from a sound sleep by the sound of breaking glass, Harley turned and looked at the other side of the bed.

Empty.

Sunlight poured into the room and a quick glance at the clock showed that morning had arrived. He'd slept through the night.

With Stasia.

Where the hell was she? He threw back the sheet and left the bed. Then he heard his uncle hiss, "Damn it, girl, look what you've done to yourself."

Harley stalled. Oh hell.

What was his uncle doing home? Had Stasia left the bed naked? He glanced at the floor and saw all her clothes still piled there.

Harley charged down the hall, down the short flight of stairs and around the corner to the kitchen.

He came to a sudden stop.

His uncle held Stasia in his arms. She wore only Harley's sweatshirt, which in no way preserved her modesty. Crunching over broken glass while Stasia screeched and tried to free herself, Satch said, "Move, boy. She's burned herself."

Slack-jawed, Harley stepped back while his uncle strode into the living room and put Stasia on a couch.

She scrambled fast to readjust the sweatshirt. "Harley!"

His uncle raced back into the kitchen.

"What the hell happened?"

Face pale, Stasia said, "I dropped my coffee and—"

Satch returned, dropped to one knee, and slapped wet rags against Stasia's bare legs even as he unleashed his temper on her. "You slept with him!"

Her gaze scuttled from Satch to Harley and back again. "Satch . . ."

"That wasn't our agreement, damn it." He patted the wet towels into place over her thighs. "I didn't hire you for that."

"*Hire* her?"

Stasia and Satch both jerked around to stare at him. Tears gathered in Stasia's eyes. Satch looked furious.

Harley glanced back into the kitchen at the shattered mug on the tile floor, the spilled coffee. He looked at his uncle, crouched in front of Stasia.

Icy control came to the fore.

Buck naked and uncaring, Harley strode to her. "First things first. How bad are you burned?"

"I'm okay."

Satch snorted. "She dropped her mug and spilled steaming coffee all over her legs."

Satch moved out of the way as Harley knelt in front of her. "Let me see."

"Harley," she implored, "you're naked."

He lifted one cloth to look at her skin. It was bright red, raised, making him wince. "My uncle has seen me before."

"Not in front of me!"

"Oh for God's sake." Satch marched out of the room but returned moments later with Harley's jeans. "Put them on before she expires."

Harley stood. He felt curiously detached, from himself and from the situation. As he pulled on the jeans, he eyed Stasia's overly composed posture. "Do you need to go to the hospital?"

"No." She smoothed out the towels on her legs. "I'm sorry, but the glass went everywhere."

He glanced at his uncle. "Satch?"

"I'll clean it up." He didn't move. "But first, why don't you tell me what she's doing here?"

Harley didn't look at him. "I don't have to explain myself to you."

"You don't want to explain to anyone, do you? Not the press and not your own uncle."

Harley's jaw clenched. "My private life is no one's business."

"It becomes my business when I get confronted with a mostly naked girl making herself at home in our kitchen!"

"You weren't supposed to be here." Harley took the cloths from her legs and went into the kitchen to soak them again in icy water. He avoided the glass that had scattered everywhere.

"So now I need to give you an itinerary? I got done early. That's all."

"Give me a minute, damn it."

Grumbling, Satch went in search of a broom and dustpan.

Harley came back to Stasia. As he gently placed the icy towels over her, he said, "It looks like you might get blisters."

She swallowed. "Usually I take creamer, but you didn't have any, otherwise the coffee wouldn't have been so hot."

His face felt frozen. Inside, acid burned in his guts. He

stepped away from her and waited while his uncle cleaned up the bulk of the mess.

"The floor will have to be mopped."

"I can do it," Stasia offered, and Harley noticed that she watched him, waiting for an outburst.

Crossing his arms over his chest, fighting the urge to check her burns more carefully, Harley eyed his uncle. "So you hired Stasia? Mind if I ask what for?"

"She's a life coach." Satch dumped broken glass into the trash with unnecessary flair.

"So?"

"I wanted her to work on you. I thought she could talk some sense into you." His gaze zeroed in on Stasia. "I didn't expect her to be like all the rest."

Offering no denials, saying nothing at all, Stasia stared at Harley. When he stayed quiet too, she slumped a little, then stiffened her shoulders with new resolve.

"I'm not working for Satch."

"When you first got here, you told me you wanted to make me your newest job." He walked a slow circle around her, wanting to touch her but not trusting himself. He didn't know what he wanted to do. "You've gone to the trouble of learning a lot about the sport."

"Yes."

Damn it, she was too calm, too collected to suit him. "A dedicated worker like you wouldn't take a job without knowing what she was getting into."

Lifting the wet cloths off her thighs, Stasia stood and carried them to the sink. She avoided the remnants of spilled coffee. The boxy sweatshirt curved beneath her derriere, showcasing her long—and now burned—legs.

Still without a word, she left the kitchen and walked around Harley for the hallway.

He wanted to follow her so badly, resisting the urge cut into him. He turned on his uncle. "You overstepped yourself too far this time, Satch."

His uncle responded in a fury, "You told me she wasn't your type!"

"Who is or isn't my type is none of your damn business."

"I'm your manager."

"Maybe that was a mistake, too."

Falling back a step, Satch went pale. "What the hell are you saying?"

He felt like he'd just ripped the life from his uncle. But damn it, he hurt too much to temper his rage. Pushing off the wall, Harley walked over to Satch. "If you want to stay my manager, you will never again involve yourself in my personal life."

"But—"

"Never. Is that understood?"

Suppressing his own fury, Satch nodded. "Fine. Suit yourself."

Harley turned and almost ran into Stasia. In record time, she had dressed and now wore her coat. There was no color in her face or lips.

She didn't quite look at him. "I called a cab. I'm going to wait outside."

Harley thought his head would hit the roof. He worked his jaw, trying to find words while Stasia just stood there, her makeup smudged from the night before, her hair tangled, her expression . . . wounded.

"God damn it."

She flinched.

He wanted to put his fist through the wall, and he wanted to take her back to bed and pretend the morning hadn't happened. "How much did he pay you?"

She shook her head. "Nothing."

"What?" He forced a laugh that sounded sick even to his own ears. "You enjoyed tormenting me so much, you did it for free?"

Now she looked at him. Her eyes narrowed. "You're angry, Harley. And I can understand that. But if you'd stop to think—"

"Then what? I'll realize you had only my best interests at heart?"

Her mouth firmed. "I refuse to get into a big blowup with you this close to your title fight." She turned her back on him and went out the front door.

Harley couldn't believe it. He rounded on Satch, but his uncle held up both hands. "I haven't paid her a dime."

"So you still owe her?"

Looking confounded, Satch crossed his arms. "I don't really know. We never set a price, and she's never asked me about it." He looked down at the floor. "In fact, she told me she wouldn't be your life coach unless you accepted her."

"In bed?"

"No!" Infuriated, Satch said, "Damn, boy, get your brain out of the bedroom, will you?"

Harley ran a hand over the back of his neck. "Fine. Explain yourself, damn it."

Glaring at Harley with every other step, Satch paced across the kitchen floor. "I meant as a life coach. She was real clear on that. She said it wouldn't work unless you accepted her and wanted to work with her."

"And I didn't."

Brows furrowing down, Satch said, "So maybe she wasn't working for me."

Harley considered howling. "Then *why* the hell did you think she was?"

"She showed up." He lifted his shoulders. "Back at Echo Lake, when I told her I wanted to hire her, she said no because you never wanted to see her again and she didn't want to bug you. I told her to think about it. She said if you contacted her, proving that you weren't opposed to talking with her, she'd maybe come here and try to convince you to work with her."

"Jesus."

"I know you called her, Harley. So when she showed up, I just assumed . . ." He jutted out his chin. "Well, what else was I supposed to think? You told me she wasn't your type."

"She's not." God knew, Anastasia Bradley was nothing like any other woman he'd been with.

"If she wasn't here for that, then why was she?"

"Hell if I know." Harley strode to the front door and got it opened just in time to see Stasia get into a cab. "Son-of-a-bitch."

He stood there in the cold, but she never once looked back.

HARLEY called the hotel a half hour later, but didn't get an answer. Throwing on the rest of his clothes, he rode over there and beat on Stasia's door.

She didn't answer.

He didn't know what to think, but damn it, he hated that she had him tied into knots. He was pacing in the foyer when Barber emerged from his room and spotted him.

He was practically strutting, and when he got alongside Harley, he said, "My night went well. Yours?"

"I'm not in the mood, so don't start."

Barber did a double take. "What's your problem?"

"I'm sick to death of everyone nosing into my damned business."

Giving him a long look, Barber muttered, "Well, fuck you, too." And he headed for the coffeepot set up near the front desk.

Feeling like an ass, Harley stomped up next to him. "I'm sorry. Anastasia is . . . missing."

"Again, huh? You should really keep better track of her."

"Barber . . ."

His friend grinned. "Relax. She's pulling into the lot right now." He nodded at the front window.

Harley watched her emerge from her truck, pick her way slowly across the lot, and all but creep inside.

"What's wrong with her?" Barber asked.

Harley walked away without answering. Until he opened the door for her, Stasia hadn't noticed him. When she did, she blanched, tucked in her chin, and forged past him in a stiff-legged walk.

"Where were you?"

"I went to get my truck."

"You need to see a doctor for those burns."

"No," she said, glancing back at him. "I don't." She dismissed him again and continued on.

"We're going to talk, Stasia."

"Your uncle didn't hire me."

Well, hallelujah. "I've already figured that one out for myself. So why don't you tell me why you're here?"

She got to her door, unlocked it, and stepped inside. "My burns aren't bad, I promise, but I really need to get out of my jeans."

"Hell of an idea." He pushed inside against her protests and shut the door. "Do you think a cool bath would help?"

"I'm not changing in front of you, Harley."

"Why not? I've seen every inch of you." Hands on his hips, Harley faced her. "I can keep my hands to myself." Maybe.

She shook her head. "I'd like you to leave, please."

"I'd like to talk to you." Hating himself, Harley sat on her bed. "Don't you think you could give me that much?"

Her neck stiffened. "Fine." She turned her back on him, rummaged in a drawer, and took out a nightshirt. "I'm changing in the bathroom first."

"Need any help?"

"No." Face hot, Stasia went around the bed and into the bathroom.

Harley forced himself to lounge back on her bed. He wanted to see her thighs, to ensure she wasn't hurt worse than she'd said. But he owed it to her to respect her privacy.

When she came back out fifteen minutes later, she had her makeup washed off, her hair brushed and pulled into a ponytail, and her legs were bare.

She perched on the edge of the bed beside him.

Fighting the urge to touch her, Harley sat up on one hip. "How are the burns?"

"Superficial at most. They sting, but no blisters. I'll be fine in a few hours, I'm sure."

With her head bent forward, Harley could see the baby-fine hairs on her nape. His heart beat too hard. "Will it offend you too much if I look for myself?"

One shoulder lifted, and she turned her face toward him. "As you said, I have nothing left to hide from you."

Why did it sound like she was talking about more than the details of her body? Torturing himself with the nearness, Harley braced one arm behind her back, leaned over her shoulder, and reached around to lift her shirt.

The sight of her burned thighs hurt him. "Damn. Still pretty red."

"I put some ointment on that's supposed to help."

"I hope it does." Her thighs were smooth, too pink, and shiny with the medicine. He wanted to kiss her.

"Your uncle startled me so badly." Their faces were near enough, he could feel her breaths. "I thought it was you, and I was shoring up my courage to face you."

"Courage?"

"The night had ended, and I was still there. I didn't know how you'd feel about that. But I can read you pretty good."

"You think so?"

She nodded. "If you were dreading the proverbial morning after, I knew I'd see it on your face." She half-laughed. "Instead, it was your uncle, and he was furious, and all hell broke loose."

"And you burned yourself."

She hesitated, then pushed up off the bed and moved away from him. Wrapping her arms around herself, she accused, "You actually thought I'd work for your uncle."

No way was Harley going to be pulled into a verbal trap. "You said it yourself—all hell broke loose. I didn't have much time to think either way." Some facts remained. "He did ask you to work for him, though."

Restless, she strode to the dresser and straightened a few items there. "He wanted me to encourage you to do those things that he felt would advance your profile in the organization."

"The photo shoots, the exposé, the interviews?"

"Yes."

Memories intruded. "That little conflict you two had at the gym. You told me that you thought my uncle was too intrusive."

"Yes. Satch approached me there and told me I should be working harder to get you to do the promo spots. We . . . disagreed on that."

Not once could Harley recall her urging him to make a decision one way or the other. "Instead, you just accompanied me for most of them."

"You're the one who said you didn't want to have to deal with other women."

"Mostly," Harley told her, disliking her defensive stance, "I wanted to keep you around until I knew the police had caught whoever it was hassling you."

"Very noble of you." Her sarcasm came back in spades. "So it wasn't that you wanted me in your bed?"

Why did she have to try to nail him down? He shrugged. "That, too."

"Well, as enjoyable as you are, I came here to try to help you." She flashed him an antagonistic look. "Not that you'd appreciate it. But I realized in a very short time that your uncle intruded too much into your life."

"Anyone with eyes can see that, honey. Doesn't take a psychic. Or a life coach." He tipped his head, studying her. "Family does that sometimes. But you put up with more from a relative than you would anyone else."

Her lips compressed. "I understand that."

"Do you?"

"Of course. I was hoping to help you work out a way to break free of him without injuring his pride. I know he means well, but he's got you so distanced from emotion, from the real you, that he's causing you more unhappiness than helping."

"And you called me noble? Hell, woman, you should be sainted." She made him sound so dependent, so pathetic, that Harley couldn't take it. Distanced from emotion? Is that what she really thought? "You gave up everything, including paying jobs, just to come save me?"

"Harley—"

He laughed. "And look at your reward for all that sacrifice."

She squared off with him. "Looks like we were both misguided."

"Speak for yourself. I've always known exactly what I was doing."

"No. You've let what happened with Sandy color your life. You blame your current attitude on missing the title shot, but if you're honest, you'll admit that isn't true."

"I think you see what you want to see."

Sadness slumped her shoulders. "Well, there haven't been any attacks or mishaps for a while, so I can leave without you having a single reason to worry." Lips trembling, she went to the closet and dragged out a suitcase. "In fact, since you're flying out tomorrow for Vegas, I may as well get out of here today."

The hell she would. "You agreed to accompany me to the party, and it's tomorrow night."

Keeping her back to him, she said, "Ain't happening, Harley."

One way or another, Harley knew he had to convince her. Until he sorted out his thoughts and decided exactly what he wanted, he couldn't bear the thought of letting her go.

"You want me to look like a fool?" Taking the suitcase from her, he shoved it back in the closet. "Is that it?"

Stasia glared up at him. "What are you talking about now?"

"Every damn bit of exposure lately has included you. Everyone has jumped to the assumption that we're a hot couple. So now, days before I fight, you want to fall out of the public eye?" He shook his head. "What will people think?"

"You don't care what anyone thinks!"

Harley looked her in the eyes and told a laudable

untruth. "That doesn't mean I want people thinking I got dumped again. Like you said, it was bad enough being dissected when Sandy switched alliances. I don't relish going through that again."

A hand to her forehead, Stasia paced away. "But . . . now it *will* be awkward."

"Not for me."

That earned him a searing glare. "Bully for you, but I'm not as cold-hearted as you are."

Harley eased closer to her. "Meaning what, exactly?" Was she in love with him? He held his breath and waited.

She put her chin up. "I'm insulted."

One corner of his mouth lifted. "Because I had two seconds of doubt? I think you'll get over that, don't you?"

"You never wanted me here in the first place. You were crystal clear on that. You've ridiculed my attempts to help. And now your uncle hates me."

"He does not."

Stasia shook her head. "I don't know, Harley. A party . . . I'm not in much of a partying mood."

Harley studied her. Stasia thought she knew him, but that went both ways. He knew her too, knew her compassion, her kindness. "All right, fine. I guess you have to do what you think is best."

"Thank you."

He headed for the door. "But if you change your mind, I'll be at the party, no doubt answering difficult questions and fending off gossip-mongers." And just to lock in the guilt and ensure her participation, he added under his breath, "Don't worry. No matter what the exposé says about it, I won't let any of this affect how I fight for the belt."

Harley was just out the door when Stasia gave in to an aberrant fit of temper and slammed it hard. He smiled.

She'd be there. And somehow, he'd get this all figured out.

CHAPTER 22

STASIA saw Harley standing within a circle of people, men and women alike. She recognized the men as the reporter and photographer who'd become familiar to him lately. The woman plastered up to his side was one he'd danced with before. On his left, hanging on his every word, was the blonde, Gloria somebody.

Sick uneasiness stirred. He certainly didn't look like he needed her assistance in any way.

Jasmine touched her shoulder. "You're sure you're okay?"

Drawn from her ridiculous jealousy, Stasia summoned a smile for her friend. "I'm fine." She waved her away. "Don't worry about me. Go have fun."

Barber studied Stasia. "Before we get onstage, you want me to get you a drink? Might take the edge off."

Did she really look that tense? "Honestly, Barber, I've been enough of a bother. You got me here, and that was plenty."

He slung a heavy arm around Jasmine's shoulders. "You know, sugar, Harley would have picked you up."

They shared a new intimacy, Stasia realized. They both looked so happy, it left her feeling bereft. Why couldn't Harley accept emotion so easily? "I know he would have. But I didn't want to ask him."

She couldn't believe her stupid truck wouldn't start. Thank God she had Barber's cell phone number, and that he'd answered between shifts on stage.

Barber nudged her chin with a gentle fist. "You need to lighten up on him, hon. He's running in so many circles, he'll be too dizzy to fight."

"Oh God." Stasia closed her eyes on a brief pang. "The last thing I want is to interfere with his concentration for the bout."

"Then hustle your cute little self on over there and save him from those barracudas. He'll appreciate that."

She eyed the cozy group, saw Harley grin, and had her doubts. "Are you sure he needs saving?"

"Positive. Trust me, love, I know the man well."

Swallowing down her discomfort, Stasia nodded. "All right then." With a final nod at Barber and Jasmine, she headed across the floor.

The soft, loose skirt that she wore tonight was long enough that ankle boots kept any skin from showing, and allowed her to skip hosiery that might have aggravated her still tender thighs. She'd dressed it up with a soft leather belt, cinched at her waist and worn over a tucked-in cream-colored sweater with a ruffled neckline.

It wasn't exactly a party outfit, but with her hair up in a twist and long, dangling earrings, she figured she looked appropriate enough.

Because of the horrible weather, the toes of her black boots were still wet. Most of the snow had dissolved under a freezing rain that left everything clean and shiny and slick. She stepped carefully to keep from slipping on the polished floor.

Harley saw her long before she reached him. Blue eyes burning, he stepped away from the women to reach for her.

Smiling, Stasia accepted his hand.

"There you are." He tugged her into his side and put a warm arm around her, letting his hand rest familiarly on her hip. "Everyone was just asking about you."

The reporter looked confused, assuring Stasia that no one had noted her late arrival.

"My truck wouldn't start. I had to find a ride."

Harley's smile stiffened. "You should have called me."

"And deny your fans your presence?" Stasia put a hand to his chest and kept her smile firmly in place. "I wouldn't think of it."

Being sly, one woman asked, "So who did give you a ride?"

"Barber."

"The musician?" She hung on Harley's arm. "My, my, my. That must've been an interesting . . . ride."

The insinuation was so rude, Stasia's smile hurt. "He's Harley's very good friend. And Jasmine came with him." She looked the woman in the eyes. "They're a couple now, you know."

Harley said, "They are?"

Standing a little off to Harley's other side, Gloria smiled. "Well, it's nice that you made it."

"Thank you," Stasia said, but Gloria had already turned to walk away. Apparently, with competition around, she lost interest.

Unfortunately that didn't work with all women. It seemed to be an especially clinging group tonight, and for his part, Harley didn't exactly discourage them. He posed with fans, laughed at idiotic jokes, accepted drinks, and politely refused dances.

The photographer loved it.

Stasia began to fume. Not since they'd started this farce of a relationship had he been so detached. That he'd be this way now told her all she needed to know.

Just when she thought she couldn't take it anymore, Harley excused himself from the group. "We're going to go shoot some pool. I'll see you all later."

The women pouted, the men grinned, and Stasia allowed

herself to be tugged along to a more private room of
twenty or so people. Barber was there on a break, staking a
very public claim on Jasmine by keeping her pinned to his
side and constantly nibbling on her—her ear, her shoulder,
her fingers.

"I think you're right, Anastasia. Barber has it bad." As if
in pity, Harley shook his head.

Frustrated with him, Stasia changed the subject. "You
leave early tomorrow morning?"

"Yeah." He grabbed a beer off a tray. "Want one?"

"No." She eyed him as he slugged back half. "Should
you be doing that?"

"Drinking half a beer? Why not?"

"Well . . . I don't know." Fed up, she crossed her arms.
"Harley, is everything okay?"

"Great." He plunked the glass back down on a table.
"Why didn't you call me instead of Barber? And don't give
me that bullshit about stealing me from my fans."

He was strangely antagonistic. "Fine. The truth is, I
didn't want to be dependent on you to get home."

"Dependent?" His left eye twitched.

"You'll probably have to stay here late." Stasia shrugged.
"I had planned to leave early tomorrow morning too, but
now I'll have to find out what's wrong with my truck first."
She muttered, "I think it's a dead battery."

Zeroed in on her, he said, "This is our last night together."

Her heart felt flattened, but she was determined not to
show it. "I know. I'm sorry I didn't get here earlier. I tried
calling a cab, but they were all busy. I couldn't imagine
changing a battery in this weather." She cleared her throat.
"Is the interview over?"

"Finally, yeah. I'm done till Vegas." His gaze took a
slow path over her. "You look nice."

"Thank you."

"The burns are okay?"

Given how he watched her, she could barely feel her
legs. "They're fine. Almost gone."

Harley stepped closer. "Let me see." He caught a fistful of her skirt.

Stasia gasped, then clamped a hand around his wrist and leaned in close to whisper, "Honest to God, Harley, I'll kill you if you even think it."

Grinning, satisfied that he'd gotten a rise out of her, Harley released her and propped himself against the edge of a table. "So Barber left the stage to go back to the hotel to get you?"

His mood was starting to annoy her. "He said it wasn't a problem."

Harley rubbed his chin. "You want to know what I think?"

"Um . . . no, not really." In his strange mood, Harley looked more than capable of causing a scene.

She'd rather avoid that if she could.

"What's this? From jump, you've shoved your opinions down my throat. Now I want to share a thought or two of my own and you start retreating?" He pushed away from the table and loomed over her. "Do I make you uneasy, Anastasia?"

"I'm not afraid of you, Harley, if that's what you mean."

"Bullshit. I know you too well."

But that was the problem. "I think you probably don't really know me at all."

"Because I don't have your insights, huh? I don't have your level of empathy. What was it you called me? Oh yeah, a cold-hearted bastard."

Appalled that he'd make such an accusation, Stasia protested. "I *never* called you that."

"Yeah, I tacked on the bastard part for flair." He grinned. "But you know what, honey? I don't think you're the altruistic angel you play at being either."

Stasia's temper sparked. "I never claimed to be an angel."

"No, you're just the benevolent life coach, putting your own life on hold so you can fix mine."

"Harley." She looked around and realized people were

starting to pay attention to them. Barber frowned at them, and Dean and Simon and their wives watched with curiosity. Stasia didn't think anyone could hear the details of their conversation, but Harley's hostile posture gave them away.

How did they always end up in these situations? "I never said you needed to be fixed." Had she? She hoped not.

"Adjusted. Amended." Harley slashed a hand through the air. "Whatever you call it, you think I need your help." He leaned down toward her. "That's why you came here, right?"

Because it was a partial truth, she nodded. "I had hoped to offer some insights, yes."

He laughed. "I think the truth is just that you wanted to get laid, but you won't admit it."

Her lips felt stiff. "Your ego is inflated."

"I don't think so, Anastasia. Hell, you've admitted, repeatedly that you lust for me as much as I do you." He leaned closer, and whispered, "The other night proved how sexually compatible we are."

Her heart ached. "God knows you're so overcharged, you'd be sexually compatible with a goat."

His eyes sparked. "Let's don't get any more nasty rumors going, okay? It's women only for me, babe. Willing women."

"Don't you mean any willing woman?"

He caught her chin. "What is it, Stasia?" His fingers caressed her jaw. "Do you want to be special to me?"

Because she wasn't, and she knew it, she shook her head. "No!"

He withdrew. "You sure about that? Maybe you want me to let go of my control so that you can get a toehold. You figure if you fix what's broken, I'll fall in love with you. Admit it."

Time stood still.

"At the moment," Stasia finally said, her voice shaking so badly she could barely get the words out, "I don't want you for a single second, much less a lifetime commitment."

Harley froze, but recovered quickly. He laughed and picked up another beer.

Stasia wanted to cry. She wanted to be alone to curl up and choke on her own misery.

Not just yet, though.

"You win, Harley."

"Yeah?" He set the beer aside. "What's the prize?"

She held his gaze. "You don't want or need my help. I admit defeat. I'll even admit I was an idiot to come here in the first place."

"No one would ever call you an idiot."

Her forced smile wavered. "You're partially right about things. I do care for you. Far too much. It's a bad combo. Me caring, and you . . . not. So I'll butt out of your life and let you get on with your social preferences."

She turned, more than ready to escape.

"You still don't have a ride, Stasia, or have you forgotten?"

"I'll manage."

Satch came up to Harley then and said, "I need to talk to you about Gloria."

Rolling her eyes, Stasia said, "I'm out of here."

Harley called her name, but she fixed her gaze on the door and headed for it, tuning out everything else. Satch called her too, but she wasn't going to stop for him either.

Barber intercepted her. "Rushing off, doll face?"

"Yes." She kept walking. "The sooner, the better."

She'd just reached the door when Harley and Satch both caught up with her.

Barber told Harley, "I'll run her home and be right back."

"*Forget it.*"

Stasia winced. Everyone in the near vicinity had to have heard Harley's snarling voice. It rattled her so much that she could barely draw air into her constricted lungs.

Satch threw up his hands. "If you two would quit this childish bickering, I'd like to tell you something."

"About *Gloria*?" Stasia asked.

"Yes, damn it."

Harley said, "She's not riding with you, Barber."

Stasia ignored Satch and said to Harley in a quieter voice, "What do you care who I ride with?"

A foreign emotion turned his blue eyes burning hot. "It's a damn ice storm out there. More cars are off the road than on it." He leaned down nose to nose with her, and smiled. "We both know how you react to being stranded with a man."

Stasia went hot, then cold with rage.

After a long whistle, Barber pulled Stasia close to his side and said, "Let's get out of here, girl, before anyone commits murder." With a look of disgust to Harley, Barber muttered, "Idiot."

Wishing she was already out of there, that she had never come in the first place, Stasia stayed close to Barber as he forged a path to the door.

How had she fallen in love with Harley? She knew better, damn it. As a life coach, she knew to stay detached while helping people with their problems. Not that she'd helped Harley at all.

She had to accept failure, because she'd had zero influence on him.

When they stopped by the front door to reclaim their coats, Stasia glanced back and saw Harley standing there, arms crossed, watching her with burning intensity. At his side, Satch talked fast and gestured repeatedly.

"You okay?" Barber held her coat for her as she slipped in her arms.

"Other than being a fool, yes."

"You're not. Harley's just . . . guarded."

"No, it's more than that." She buttoned up and pulled the lapels tight to her throat. "He's right."

"About?"

"Me. Why I cared so much." Stasia shook her head. "If you tell him, I'll come back and hurt you, but . . . I am in love with him. I just hadn't really realized it—or admitted it to myself—until recently. And by then, it was too damn late to stop myself."

With one arm around her as he led her through the door, Barber glanced back at Harley. "Don't you think you should tell him?"

"God no. That's the last thing he'd want to hear."

"Wrong. It's exactly what he wants to hear."

"No."

Barber sighed long and loud. "Come on, Stasia. Why not just admit you're too chickenshit to go first?" They stepped into the frozen lot, and Barber started to say more, no doubt to try to convince her.

Headlights blinded them.

In an instant, it all came back to Stasia. She remembered this scenario only too well.

As an engine roared, Barber said, "What the hell?" With little time to react, he started to push Stasia back, but the truck hit the gas and came barreling toward them with a splatter of ice from under the tires.

Stasia strangled on a scream, and a second later, a body hit her and Barber both, knocking them sideways onto the frozen parking lot.

Harley!

The truck roared past, up and onto the curb, and then into a lamppost.

In the midst of Barber cursing a blue streak, Harley levered up to see her. He was more furious than she'd ever seen him. "You okay?"

Her entire body hurt, but . . . "Yes."

Barber jerked around and stared toward where the truck spun its tires, trying to find traction. "They were going to hit us!"

"I know." With a slow smile and narrowed eyes, Harley got to his feet. "Enough already."

Two men left the truck and took off running on foot.

Before Harley could take chase, Barber shouted, "Harley, do *not* be an idiot!"

Harley kept going.

Oh God, oh God. Stasia's heart pounded. If he got hurt and couldn't fight, she knew she'd never forgive herself.

"Go inside," Barber ordered. "Call 911, and get the others. Fast." And he went after Harley.

But Stasia didn't have to fetch anyone. The word spread so quickly that almost before she'd regained her wits, a group of fighters came out and began searching the lot. Off in the distance, sirens sounded, proof that the police had already been called.

When Barber reached him, Harley shook him off and pointed in the direction one of the men had gone. Friends headed in that direction. Showing he had more sense than she'd given him credit for, Harley returned to the truck with Barber and turned it off.

He emerged from the cab with a wallet, and a registration.

Hand to her throat, Stasia stood back and watched the events unfolding. She didn't realize she was crying until Jasmine sniffed beside her.

"I'm sorry," Jasmine said when Stasia looked at her. She dug a tissue out of her pocket. "If you cry, I cry. I can't help it."

Stasia swiped her cheeks and felt the track of icy tears.

Not what Harley needed, she knew, so she wiped them away and drew several deep breaths to calm herself.

The police pulled up.

Harley spoke to them very briefly before turning them over to Barber. He took three steps toward Stasia. She was so emotionally overwrought she almost couldn't swallow. Too much had happened tonight, far too much.

Harley said, "Stasia." He held out a hand.

"Go," Jasmine prompted her. "He probably needs it as much as you do."

On a watery laugh, Stasia agreed. She picked up her long skirt and rushed to him. Harley caught her close, one hand at the back of her head, the other arm around her waist.

"Jesus, honey, are you sure you're okay?"

"Yes."

"No bruises? I didn't hurt you when I pushed you out of the way?"

She leaned back and stared him in the eyes. "You broke my heart earlier, but my body is fine."

He didn't smile. "Your body is better than fine." He smoothed her now ruined hair. "So your heart is involved?"

She punched him in the shoulder. "I'm in love with you, Harley."

"Yeah?"

He looked so skeptical that Stasia laughed. Maybe Barber was right and she was too emotionally involved to see what Harley really felt. Well, she was done being chickenshit, as Barber had accused.

Stasia touched his face. "I've told you many times now, you're the most incredible man I've ever met. How could I not be in love with you?"

He looked over her shoulder, then back at her face. "Do you think you can put up with my uncle, too? Because, Stasia, it's sort of a package deal. Yes, he sometimes intrudes, but always with good intentions. And yes, I don't always like his plans. But I had so many regrets when I lost my mother. So many things I hadn't done, hadn't shown her, hadn't told her. Satch is the only family I have left."

"And you're all he has left?"

"That's about it."

Satch stood behind them, breathing hard and scowling fiercely. "What's this?" He put his hands on his knees, sucked in some deep breaths, and finally straightened. "You don't always like my plans?"

Harley shook his head. "No, Satch, but I love you, so it evens out."

The emotional confession threw Satch, but only for a moment. "Well, damn it, boy. That goes both ways, you know. I only want what's best for you. But you're smart. Real smart. So you know what's worth doing, and what isn't. Always tell me. I can take it."

Harley held out a hand. "Deal."

Satch laughed. "Well hell, maybe the little life coach had a point all along."

"She has something, all right," Harley said, and he bent

to kiss her forehead. "Now Satch, why did you come charging up here?"

Satch threw up his hands. "You two almost made me forget!" He looked between them with anticipation. "They got her."

"Her who?" Stasia asked.

"Gloria." He gave a hard nod. "It's what I was trying to tell you, if you two hadn't been having such a conniption. Roger had some doubts about her, and I checked her out."

"Your talents know no bounds, Uncle Satch."

"True, true. Anyway, she's a wealthy socialite, and she's been known to get fixated on people. She settled out of court with another guy who claimed she was a stalker. I had my eye on her, but I told Roger to keep a watch out, too."

"I'm not sure I'm following you," Stasia said.

Harley gave her a brief hug. "Gloria planned it all, hon. Not so much trying to get you, but to get me."

"Said she was going to teach him a lesson." Satch nodded. "I guess death would be a lesson all right."

Pained, Harley said, "I met her at Echo Lake."

"But . . ." Stasia had a hard time absorbing all that. "She's the one who cut my brake lines?"

"To hurt me, she said."

"She's admitted all this?"

Harley nodded. "Roger caught her making the call to the truck drivers." They all looked toward the two men now held captive. They were busy spilling their guts.

Screeching echoed over the parking lot as police emerged from the bar with Gloria in tow. She wasn't going to go peacefully. "It's *her* fault," she yelled toward Stasia, and then in the next breath screamed, "Harley! I did it for you, Harley. I swear."

"Good God." Stasia couldn't believe the woman's demented state. "So it was never my old client."

"No." Harley kept touching her, cuddling her, hugging

her. "Poor old Larry is back with his wife. They were actually on vacation when the cops went to check on them."

"Wow." Stasia gave herself a moment, then said politely to Satch, "Could you excuse us, please?"

"What? Oh." He flushed. "Yeah, sure. But Harley, don't do anything stupid. You're fighting in just a few days."

"I know."

Satch glanced at Stasia, then nodded. "I already got another ticket." And with that, he strolled over to Barber and Jasmine.

"Another ticket?" Stasia asked.

Laughing, Harley said, "My uncle truly is amazing. I swear he knows stuff even before I do."

"I don't understand."

"The other ticket is for you. For Vegas." Harley held her jaw. "You're coming with us."

He said it not as a request, but as a fact.

Stasia tried to sort it all out in her mind. "Uncle Satch is a little overenthusiastic, but he's still a great guy."

"I agree."

No more chickenshit. "Do you love me, Harley?"

"Yes."

Joy expanded, but Stasia kept it banked. "Are you sure? I don't mind giving you time to think about it. I know you have the fight coming up and—"

He kissed her.

She expected it to be a quick kiss, but it wasn't. He held her tight and kept on kissing her, even after she started to giggle and struggle against him.

Barber cleared his throat. "Pull back a little there, buddy. The cops are starting to eyeball you."

Harley let her come up for air. "I love you."

Stasia's knees went weak. "Just me?"

"Good God, woman, I know I'm good, but do you really think I could handle more than you?"

Barber chuckled.

"If I'm going to Vegas," Stasia said on a grin, "I need to get home to pack."

NOW that the fuss had ended, Barber looked around for Jasmine and found her in a close conversation with Roger. He scowled—until he saw that Cam was nearby, too.

Walking up, trying to look cavalier, Barber asked, "What's going on?"

Jasmine turned with a huge grin. "Roger offered me a job."

That took him aback. "A job doing what?"

"Singing. What else?"

It took a lot to get him riled, but that about did it. Staring at Roger, Barber asked, "You did what?"

"Jasmine and I have come to an agreement. Six performances a year at the times of her choice."

Barber heard Jasmine chuckle, saw Cam smiling, but all he wanted to do was take Roger apart.

He was trying to steal Jasmine right out from under him!

Pointing a finger at Roger, Barber said, "I never did trust you, you—"

"He was hoping," Jasmine said in a rush, "that it'd encourage you to sign on, too."

Barber pulled back. "You were?"

Roger shrugged. "You're getting to be one hell of a commodity. I told Jasmine I'd be happy to have her as her own act, but that if she could convince you to sign an agreement too, that'd be even better."

"Well hell, man, why didn't you just ask? I love this place, you know that." Barber drew Jasmine into his side. "But since we're now a couple—" He looked down at Jasmine. "You will marry me, right?"

Her mouth fell open. Her eyes watered. Then she squealed loud enough to split eardrums.

To Roger, Barber asked, "Is that a yes, do you think?"

Roger grinned. "I'd say so."

"Then where Jassy goes, I go. We're a package deal. If she likes your offer, I have no quarrel with it." Barber tried to shake on it, but Jasmine started bouncing around, and he couldn't get steady enough.

Cam said, "Time for you to go, Barber."

"I was thinking the same thing." He kissed Jasmine to silence her excitement. "Better. Now let's go find some-place private where you can demonstrate how much you adore me."

EPILOGUE

HARLEY paid no attention to anyone in the audience. The cheers of the crowd faded from his mind. He didn't feel the sweat on his body, or the heat from the lights.

Barefoot, wearing only boxers' shorts and fingerless gloves, he stared across the mat at Kinkaid and thought of how many opportunities he'd missed.

He wouldn't miss another one.

The ref asked Kinkaid if he was ready. Shaking with pent-up anticipation and fueled fury, Kinkaid nodded.

He asked Harley, and Harley gave a very small nod.

A bell rang.

Like an enraged bull, Kinkaid shot toward Harley. He roared his intent, his eyes glazed, his chest heaving.

Harley dodged one wild haymaker, turned, blocked a vicious kick, and planted one crushing blow to Kinkaid's chin.

Kinkaid staggered back, tripped on his own feet and went down.

Wasting no time, Harley dropped onto him and followed with another punishing blow. One more.

He pulled back his fist, but seeing Kinkaid's face, he hesitated, giving the ref a chance—and the fight was stopped.

Harley stood.

Confused, his eyes unseeing, Kinkaid tried to get to his knees. He couldn't quite make it. His corner came in, along with the doctor.

A second later Simon was there with Satch, the two of them lifting up Harley as they shouted out in triumph. Dean joined them, cheering and laughing, pounding on Harley as he draped a shirt over him that announced a valuable sponsorship.

It finally hit him, and Harley threw a fist into the air, then grabbed his uncle up close for a sweaty bear hug.

The audience was on their feet, screaming and shouting in approval, when Drew Black sauntered up with a huge grin that Harley returned.

Harley lifted his arms and Drew fastened the belt around his waist. Damn, it felt good. Real good.

A microphone was stuck in his face. For the next few minutes, Harley talked through the fight, what his strategy had been, what mistakes Kinkaid had made, and whether or not he and Kinkaid still held any animosity for each other.

Harley didn't really care about any of that.

When the camera finally moved away and everyone started to go about closing out the show, Harley left the center mat, hopped down to the lower level, and walked into the audience.

He saw Stasia's wide-eyed confusion as he headed her way. The camera crew caught on, and Harley knew he was on television. With every step, fans congratulated him, slapped his back, took pictures galore.

None of it mattered.

Stasia stood up before he reached her.

Gloved hands on his hips, Harley grinned down at her. "I have the belt."

She laughed. "Yeah, I noticed."

Damn, he loved her. "Now that that's over with, will you marry me?"

Her eyes rounded. Her mouth followed suit. She blinked hard. "Harley!"

He could barely hear her over the cheering audience. He shouted, "Marry me, Anastasia Bradley."

The crowd went nuts again. The camera zeroed in.

Laughing, crying a little, Stasia nodded. "Yes."